PRAISE FOR HELEN C. ESCOTT

Operation Wormwood

"Brilliant! Absolutely brilliant! With skilled, detective-like precision, Escott kept me at the edge of my seat throughout this well-told story of hurt and faith. Filled with a ton of well-researched facts and figures regarding Newfoundland and Labrador's history, criminal investigative processes, and relevant political complications, this novel fills the reader's need for action, suspense, and emotion. This book will make every Newfoundlander and Labradorian reflect on their complicated history and fully intrigue those who come from away. *Operation Wormwood* is wicked . . . simply wicked . . . in every definition of the word." — E. B. MERRILL, S/SGT. (RTD.), ROYAL CANADIAN MOUNTED POLICE

"At the heart of this gut-wrenching, savagely realistic novel is a deep theological struggle: why does evil against the most vulnerable go unpunished by a loving, all-powerful God? Escott combines first-hand police experience, superb storytelling, and deep faith in this Dan Brown–style epic." — REV. ROBERT COOKE

"*Operation Wormwood* . . . gives us a sense of what first responders deal with in their daily lives. A well-written book. Great job, Mrs. Escott." — EDWARDS BOOK CLUB

"*Operation Wormwood* is one heck of a thriller."
— THE TELEGRAM

PRAISE FOR HELEN C. ESCOTT

Operation Wormwood: The Reckoning

"*Operation Wormwood: The Reckoning* is the sequel that readers will love to hate! Its raw emotion is palpable and shocking yet will leave you hopeful in knowing that there are good people in the world fighting for humanity and justice. Hats off to Helen C. Escott on the conclusion to this crime thriller!" — FIRESIDE COLLECTIONS

"Fans will be pleased . . ." — THE TELEGRAM

"I don't think it is too much of a stretch to say that Helen C. Escott is Newfoundland's premier crime-thriller author. Her novels such as *Operation Vanished* (2019, Flanker Press) and now the two *Operation Wormwood* books will cement her career as such. I highly recommend the reading of the two books in order, so if you haven't read *Operation Wormwood* already, then you should do so before reading *The Reckoning*. Both books are well-written and contain enough plot lines to keep the reader thoroughly engaged. I know I was! Well done, Ms. Escott!" — THE MIRAMICHI READER

PRAISE FOR HELEN C. ESCOTT

Operation Vanished

"*Operation Vanished* is a powerful page-turner that will resonate with any reader who enjoys a good murder mystery. Helen C. Escott doesn't just seek justice and remembrance for female victims of crime but makes a brilliant attempt to emancipate them from the bonds of yesteryear." — FIRESIDE COLLECTIONS

"*Operation Vanished* is a must-read Newfoundland mystery-thriller!" — THE MIRAMICHI READER

Operation Vanished was awarded a Silver Medal for Best Regional Fiction at the 24th annual Independent Publisher Book Awards

PRAISE FOR HELEN C. ESCOTT

Operation Trafficked

"Helen C. Escott crafts a story that is both shocking and gut-wrenching. Though the subject matter is heavy, there is relief! Readers will have a hard time putting this book down. *Operation Trafficked* by Helen C. Escott shines a very bright light on the heinous crimes that exist when a marginalized group are exploited for pleasure and gain. Kudos to this award-winning author for giving a voice to the voiceless!" — FIRESIDE COLLECTIONS

"You will not be able to put this down because you absolutely need to know what the resolution will be. Escott does an unbelievably fantastic job stirring emotion in her readers. There was a lump in my throat and a ball of anxiety in my stomach as I read, knowing that this is so very true to life: fiction out of fact. Relentless in its pursuit of the truth, it is impossible to read this and not have it make a huge impact on how you view the world around you. With *Operation Trafficked*, Escott continues to dominate the crime thriller genre."
— NICOLE LITTLE, NO SHELF CONTROL BOOK REVIEWS

"With her fourth novel, Helen Escott takes us into a seamy underworld most of us are either unaware of or decline to think too much about. The story twists and turns to an ending that offers satisfaction but reminds us that victories are small and incomplete in this dark environment." — NORTHEAST AVALON TIMES

OPERATION MASONIC

Helen Escott

OPERATION MASONIC

HELEN C. ESCOTT

FLANKER PRESS LIMITED
ST. JOHN'S

Library and Archives Canada Cataloguing in Publication

Title: Operation Masonic / Helen C. Escott.
Names: Escott, Helen C., author.
Identifiers: Canadiana (print) 20220260052 | Canadiana (ebook) 20220260060 | ISBN
   9781774570999 (softcover) | ISBN 9781774571002 (EPUB) | ISBN 9781774571019 (PDF)
Classification: LCC PS8609.S36 O62 2022 | DDC C813/.6—dc23

© 2022 by Helen C. Escott

PRINTED IN CANADA

MIX
Paper from
responsible sources
FSC® C016245

This paper has been certified to meet the environ-
mental and social standards of the Forest Stewardship
Council® (FSC®) and comes from responsibly managed forests, and verified recycled sources.

Edited by Donna Morrissey   Illustrated by Albert Taylor

Cover Design by Graham Blair

FLANKER PRESS LTD.
1243 KENMOUNT ROAD, UNIT 1
PARADISE, NL
CANADA

TELEPHONE: (709) 739-4477   FAX: (709) 739-4420   TOLL-FREE: 1-866-739-4420

WWW.FLANKERPRESS.COM

9 8 7 6 5 4 3 2 1

We acknowledge the financial support of the Government of Canada through the Canada Book Fund (CBF) and the Government of Newfoundland and Labrador, Department of Tourism, Culture, Industry and Innovation for our publishing activities.
We acknowledge the support of the Canada Council for the Arts, which last year invested $157 million to bring the arts to
Canadians throughout the country. Nous remercions le Conseil des arts du Canada de son soutien. L'an dernier, le Conseil a
investi 157 millions de dollars pour mettre de l'art dans la vie des Canadiennes et des Canadiens de tout le pays.

This book is dedicated to my husband, Robert, our children, and grandchildren. Every day you inspire me with your achievements, drive, and love of life. Remember always:

I shall be telling this with a sigh
Somewhere ages and ages hence:
Two roads diverged in a wood, and I—
I took the one less travelled by,
And that has made all the difference.

— "The Road Not Taken," Robert Frost

For love is as strong as death,
jealousy is fierce as the grave.

Song of Solomon 8:6–7
English standard version

Ecclesiastic Circle

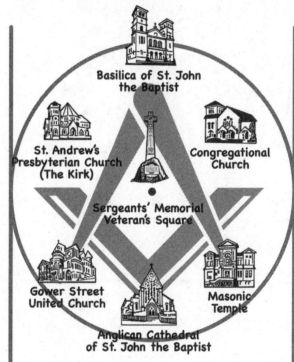

Basilica of St. John
the Baptist

St. Andrew's
Presbyterian Church
(The Kirk)

Congregational
Church

Sergeants' Memorial
Veteran's Square

George
Street
United
Church

St. Thomas'
Anglican
Church

Gower Street
United Church

Masonic
Temple

Anglican Cathedral
of St. John the Baptist

1

A late November winter blizzard engulfed the city of St. John's. It ripped down, buried, and destroyed whatever could not withstand its brutal assault. The city transitioned from its orange and red fall glory to a white frozen tundra overnight. Centuries-old trees fell to its slaughter. Roads were buried in knee-deep snow as roofs groaned under its heavy mass.

Wicked squalls of northerly winds refused to give up and kept their strength throughout the long night. Residents peered out of their windows at the strange weather phenomena that lit up the sky. Streaks of lightning and claps of thunder led an aggressive air campaign over the city. An unusual full moon hung brightly in the sky, watching it all happen.

Blasts of frozen winds gave raw, primal screams as they ambushed houses, buildings, and highways in an armed insurgency that brought the city to its knees.

Shortly after midnight, a Royal Newfoundland Constabulary patrol car struggled to get down Cathedral Street, leaving long streaks of tire skids behind it in the snow. The constable behind the wheel kept pumping the brake as the Impala fishtailed down to the centre of the hill.

A slight acceleration allowed the driver to gain traction, and she plunged into the snow-covered parking space.

"Put the handbrake on," her partner warned, "or else the car will be in the harbour by the time we come back out."

Cst. Ryan pushed the emergency brake to the floor. She looked up at the ominous tall, red brick building that loomed over them. "I don't think this car is going to move until spring. This place gives me the creeps." She zipped up her thick, black storm coat and pulled her cap tight around her ears. "Of all the times for a break and enter at this place, it had to happen tonight."

"Could be worse." Cst. Stuckless pulled on his black leather gloves and followed her out of the car. "We could be at that ten-car pileup on Topsail Road," he added, looking around at the snow-buffeted street.

As if on cue, a bolt of lightning hit a transformer at the top of the hill, sending sparks into the night sky.

The city went black.

Cst. Stuckless reached under his coat and took the flashlight off his duty belt. He turned it on and pointed it under his chin. It lit up his face, casting shadows over his pale skin and the bags under his eyes.

He dragged out a loud, evil laugh. "Now it's even scarier. *Mmwahahaha.*"

"Oh, shut up." Ryan took out her flashlight and headed toward the historic building. "What is this place, anyway? Looks like a church."

Stuckless followed Ryan. "It's the Masonic Temple. They sacrifice virgins in here."

"Very funny." Ryan looked down at the knee-deep snow on the stairs and pointed to several depressions. "Looks like someone has been here, but judging by these prints, they left long ago." Clinging onto the metal handrail, Ryan pulled herself up the snow-blocked staircase, taking care not to disturb the footprints. "What's it used for now?"

"It's a theatre." Stuckless navigated around the indented snow on the steps as he struggled to get up to the entrance. "There's a new Masonic Lodge off Kenmount Road. I think this was the original one."

Cst. Ryan waited at the top of the landing while her partner negotiated the last steps. "I've never heard of a Masonic Temple before."

"You've never heard of Freemasons?" Stuckless pulled himself up beside her, brushing the snow off his woollen uniform pants. "I don't know what they do. It's some kind of secret society."

"Really." She looked up at the two pillars framing the front door.

"Oh . . . and they don't allow women in." Stuckless chuckled.

"Well, if they want to catch whoever broke in, someone had better get here with a key and let this woman in, or I'm heading back to my warm patrol car." She tilted her head, gave it a little shake, sheltering her face from the snow falling from her hat.

The heavy snow was up past their ankles on the small concrete landing. The smell of wood stoves and an earthy freshness hung in the air. Snowplows droned in the distance, working hard to clear the main thoroughfares.

"Check the door," said Stuckless. Without waiting, he leaned ahead and pulled on the thick brass door handle. The door swung open. "The alarm must have stopped. I don't hear anything."

He looked to Ryan with a raised brow. A seriousness fell over the officers as they looked in at the moonlit foyer. Ryan put her index finger to her lips as she slid inside. She quietly closed the door behind them and stayed on her heels.

Moonlight reflected off the snow, sending shadows across the black and white tiled floor in the foyer. Ryan pointed up at the emergency light and whispered. "Why is it not on?"

"I don't think any of the emergency lights are working." Stuckless pointed at Ryan, then toward the room straight ahead. He pointed at himself and toward the room to the right.

Cst. Ryan eased open her door. It led into a large banquet room full of tables and chairs arranged around a small, empty stage. The long, narrow windows on its far side emitted no light. She stayed close to the wall, shining her flashlight around the room until she spotted a door at the far end.

Her wet boots squeaked on the hardwood floor as she negotiated the table and chairs on her way toward the door. A draft of cold air crept down her neck. She shivered. Someone was there. In one quick motion she flipped the safety clasp on her holster, put her hand on her gun, and turned around.

There was no one.

Her eyes struggled to adjust to the darkness. Chilled, she gave herself a shake and continued toward the door, where she waited and listened.

There was movement on the inside, a clanging of metal, and shuffling of feet.

She held the grip of her gun tightly and slowly pushed the door open. Her flashlight lit up Stuckless, who was rubbing his head.

"Don't shoot, for God's sake," he quickly said.

A trace of moonlight shone through a side window. Ryan quickly scanned the room.

"Holy crap." She took her hand off her gun and closed the safety clasp. "This place is haunted."

"I banged into a goddamned pot hanging from that contraption." Stuckless pointed up at a selection of cooking pots hanging from a rack attached to the ceiling. "Did you see anything?"

Ryan felt the cold air against her neck again. She glanced around, then shook it off. "I tell you, this place is bloody haunted."

Stuckless pointed toward the room behind him. "Must be

teens breaking in to steal liquor. There's a load of it there. But I didn't see any damage. There's a coat lying on the bar. It looks expensive, but that could belong to the owners."

"Why would anyone leave without their coat on a night like this?" Ryan shone the flashlight at the floor. "I haven't seen any snow tracked in. Maybe they left before the storm started." She looked at her watch. "The snow didn't get bad until about ten. It's twelve thirty now."

"Didn't the Communication Centre say the alarm call came in at nine?" Stuckless replied uneasily. "I guess everyone was tied up at the accident on Topsail Road."

"They have to prioritize calls. I suppose we got the call because we finally got clear of that accident. If it came in at nine, chances are there won't be any tracks."

A loud thud reverberated through the building. The two officers reacted quickly and headed toward the staircase.

Stuckless pointed his flashlight up to the next landing. "They're still here."

The ancient stairs groaned and creaked under their weight.

A mouse scurried across the top stairs, and Stuckless jerked backward. "Goddamn mice are everywhere."

Ryan pointed her light at the floor only to catch one scurrying through a small hole in the wall. The officers entered a room at the top of the stairs, where Ryan's light caught the shadows of a strange room full of odd pieces of furniture and objects. "What the hell is this place?" she whispered.

"I think it's theatre props or something." Stuckless struck against something with his leg and fell back, his light flashing on a white hand. He swiftly reacted as he swung around and grabbed the wrist below him.

Ryan let out a muffled laugh. "It's a mannequin." She put a hand over her mouth to suppress her amusement. "You should have seen your face."

Stuckless looked down at the headless, naked mannequin lying on the floor and put his hand on his heart. "Jesus H. Christ! What a fright. I thought it was a demon."

Ryan gestured toward the room next door. "Come on." A cold breeze blew across her face. "I keep feeling this draft. It feels like a window is open."

"I think the building is just drafty," Stuckless said. He looked around the dark hallway. "There must be a fire escape outside one of these windows."

They pushed open double doors that led to an inside chamber. The large room was lit only by the full moon and the snow-filled sky reflecting light in through the tall, narrow windows. They carefully manoeuvred around more theatre props and old furniture until they stood staring up at a massive wall organ.

"Jesus, it looks like something from *Phantom of the Opera*." Ryan lifted the keyboard cover and touched the yellowed keys. They made no sound.

A squeaking sound came from the stairs. They both turned quickly and ran. The old banister made a creaking noise as they leaned against it, flashlights scanning the steps.

"Must have been those damn mice." Stuckless went back to the main room while Ryan lingered, watching the shadows for movement, before following her partner.

Stuckless shone his flashlight down onto the burgundy carpet with a gold symbol woven in a pattern throughout it. He studied the rectangular, black-and-white tessellated pattern framed by a blue-and-black tiled border in the centre of the room. He headed toward it. In the centre was a five-point red star. He gestured to Ryan to come over.

"Take a look at this."

Ryan headed to the middle of the room, chuckling. "This must be where they sacrifice the virgins."

"Look up." Stuckless pointed toward the ceiling. "What the hell is that?"

Centred on the ceiling, in plaster and paint, was an eyeball surrounded by a gold sunburst in a white plaster circle.

"It's the All-Seeing Eye," Ryan informed him.

"What's that?"

"I watched a financial documentary about investing." She shone the flashlight beam on it. "The All-Seeing Eye is on the US dollar bill, above a pyramid, and underneath it is the Latin translation for 'New World Order.' It's symbolic of the Eye of God."

"Interesting. And extremely creepy at the same time. Why is the Eye of God in the Masonic Temple?"

The sound of breaking glass and a loud thud sent them running back into the hallway. This time the cold draft felt like a gust of wind. They followed it to a small room at the end of the hallway.

Ryan pointed her flashlight at an open window. A large broken glass vase lay shattered across the floor, on top of music paper that blew around the small room. She kicked the broken pieces with the toe of her boot.

Looking through the window, she saw a black metal fire escape. Its landing was capped with newly fallen snow about a foot deep. "No footprints. It's untouched." She picked up a piece of thick board on the floor in front of the window. The board had duct tape on each of its corners and was the size of the window. "This may have been taped over the broken window," she said. "A good gust of wind would've blown this in. Perhaps that's the thudding sound we heard." She laid it next to a small overturned table.

"Do you smell candles?" Stuckless put his nose in the air and sniffed. "I can smell a candle burning."

"So can I."

They looked around the small room. It had an ochre-painted plank floor that differed from those in the other rooms. Stuckless pushed the toe of his boot into a hole in the floor about five inches by five inches in diameter.

The officers circled the room on separate sides, assessing where they were.

"There's a trap door in the floor." Stuckless moved in closer. The toe of his boot tapped a wooden object. He bent, picked it up, and held it against the beam of his flashlight. "It looks like a plug that fits into that hole."

Ryan crouched down and poked at a small brass ring on the floor. "It's a hatch. I'm going to lift it. You get ready."

Stuckless drew his gun. "Ready."

The wood creaked as Ryan struggled to open the heavy door. She slid it to the side with a grunt. "What's in there?" She stood, staring down into a small, dark concrete room, waiting for her eyes to adjust.

Stuckless shone his light in the hole. "It's a hidden room under the floor and another mannequin." He put his weapon back in its holster. "This one is dressed in some weird costume. There are candles, but they're out. That's where the smell is coming from."

"Looks like someone was having a seance. How could there be a hidden room under the floor on the second floor?" Ryan let out a sigh of relief as she looked down into the room. She moved to the left of the opening and shone her flashlight down in the room. "Look, there's a ladder. I'll go down."

"I'm not going to fight you on that one. I can't handle small spaces." Stuckless kept his flashlight fixed on her as she descended the rungs.

She stopped at the bottom and shone her flashlight around the damp room. A mouldy odour mixed with candle smoke choked her and led to a coughing fit.

"Are you okay?" Stuckless knelt to get a better look.

Ryan cleared her throat. "It's just the smell down here." She took her time turning around the room and examining it. "It's a concrete room, no window at all, and it's about eight by ten. It looks like a dungeon. There's lots of dust down here, and footprints." She took off a glove and felt the top of a candle. "These candles are not out that long. There's lots of soft wax around them, so they were burning for a while."

"This is the weirdest thing I've ever seen." Stuckless squinted in the darkness. "Why would they put a dungeon in the middle of a building?"

"I don't know." Ryan looked down at what appeared to be an elaborately dressed mannequin laid out on the floor. "It's wearing a weird-looking apron and some kind of a big chain around its neck. Its face certainly looks real."

She bent down for a closer look. "There's a note next to it. *Iota Pulchra.* I think it's Latin. But there's an English phrase below it: *For love is as strong as death, jealousy is fierce as the grave.* It looks like it was written by two different pens."

"Must be something from one of the plays they do here." Stuckless reached down for it.

Ryan passed it up. "It's written on music note paper. Maybe it's a song."

"There's music paper all over the floor up here." Stuckless looked at the note and passed it back. "Put it back where it was."

Ryan laid the paper back on the floor. The flashlight flickered. She noticed the colour of the lips of the figure lying on the floor. "I don't think this is a mannequin."

She leaned down and put her fingers on the figure's wrist. She looked up at her partner.

"This is no mannequin. It's a man, and he's dead."

2

Insp. Nicholas Myra stared through the snow clogging his windshield as he fought a losing battle against the northerly wind. His wipers groaned as they tried to lift and clear the snow. He held tightly to the steering wheel as he manoeuvred through the heavy snowdrifts. Soon, he pulled into a parking spot on Gower Street, behind the Anglican Cathedral standing sentry over the crime scene, and parked behind the medical examiner's van.

Myra nodded at a snow-covered constable who shivered while guarding the barricaded intersection.

"Inspector." The constable wiped the back of his glove over the icicles that hung from the beak of his fur cap. "The city's plow just got here. They say the road should be cleared in about an hour."

"Thanks." Myra continued to the Masonic Temple, past a small army of police officers working on the scene. He spotted Cst. Ryan on the sidewalk in front of the building. He slid down the walkway and locked up just feet from her.

"Whoa!" Ryan moved aside from his tall, heavy frame. "You all right?" she asked as Myra skidded to a stop.

Myra steadied himself. "Nothing like a murder and a bloody snowstorm to wake you up."

He shook the snow from his short brown hair that had just recently begun to turn grey. Brushing the snow off the shoulders of his black wool peacoat, he looked up at the historical building.

Ryan stomped her feet to keep warm. "I've lost the feeling in my toes. When is this snow going to stop?"

"I don't miss the street, that's for sure." Myra looked around at the officers guarding the premises. "What do we have?"

"The call came in at nine p.m. The caller reported a break and enter but wouldn't leave his name. We didn't get dispatched until midnight. Everyone was tied up at the fatality on Topsail Road." Ryan rubbed her gloved hands together and rocked back and forth. "But every alarm went off at some point last night. We got here at twelve twenty. The front door was unlocked, so Stuckless and I went in and started to search the building."

Myra and Ryan scaled the half-cleared staircase. Identification officers were photographing the footprint indents on the stairs and dusting the door handle for fingerprints.

Sgt. Bill Morgan looked up when he recognized Myra. "Inspector, we're just about finished with the outside and most of upstairs. We had a good look around the basement, too. Nothing down there but locked offices."

"Great." Myra pointed at Morgan. "Ryan, have you met Bill? He's in charge of the Identification Section."

"Yes, we've worked together before."

Myra followed the officers inside the building.

Morgan said, "Once you're finished with the scene, we'll let the medical examiner take the body, and we'll remove the items around it."

Myra quirked a brow. "Items around the body?"

"Yeah." Morgan nodded. "It looks like some kind of weird ritual killing. Haven't seen anything like it before."

"Thanks." Myra glanced at the winding staircase that led to his next case. He followed Ryan, listening intently as she recalled the details leading up to finding the victim.

"Thank God the lights came back on." Ryan stopped outside a small room where the medical examiner was waiting. "You wouldn't believe how creepy this place is in the pitch dark.

"It's creepy enough with the lights on." Myra looked around at the theatrical mannequins on the floor. "Thanks, Ryan. Don't let anyone else in this area until I say so."

"Yes, sir." The constable took the hint and left the room.

Myra grinned with recognition at the medical examiner and extended his hand. "Simon, always a pleasure."

The tall, thin man shook Myra's hand and answered with a hint of a British accent. "Pleasure is mine."

Simon looked down the short ladder to where the victim's body lay undisturbed. "It's called the Chamber of Reflection. I've already been down for a look, and I'll warn you, you're going to have a hard time getting down there. I don't think they made this for people over six feet."

"Chamber of Reflection?" Myra crouched down to investigate the concrete room. "What is this place?" As he lowered his face to the opening, the strong odour of feces mixed with mildew and candle wax hit him. He pulled back. "Smells awful down there."

He picked up a floodlight left by the Identification Section and shone it into the opening and down into the strange room. "It's like a basement in the middle of the second floor."

"I believe it's some kind of ritual chamber." Simon leaned in for another look. "This was the Masonic Temple. Now it's owned by a theatre company. Seems they left this intact. I don't know how they could have moved the chamber out without destroying the building."

"Any idea who the victim is?" Myra tried to calculate the strength of the wooden ladder under the weight of his six-foot-four bulk.

"No. I had a look. He's dressed in Masonic regalia. I'm going to guess and say he is a Freemason."

"Any idea how he died?"

"Nothing obvious. I don't see any blood spatter. I'll have to wait to get him on my table to say for sure."

Myra stomped the melting snow off his boots and called out to an Identification officer working nearby. "Pass me in some boot covers, please." He took blue rubber gloves out of his coat pocket and pulled them on.

The officer stopped what he was doing and pulled two blue cotton booties out of his bag and passed them to Myra. Myra's knees cracked as he bent to pull them on over his size twelve boots.

"Ah," Simon said. "I hear signs of old age in those knees, Nick. Could retirement be far off?"

"I wish." Myra grabbed the sides of the ladder and placed one foot on the top rung, testing its strength. "My girls are two and three. I'll be working until I'm a hundred."

He gripped the wooden slats and descended into the concrete room. Reaching the bottom, he picked up the hanging floodlight and shone it around the room.

"Lots of dust and someone's footprints," he yelled up to Simon. "The candles were lit for a while, according to the wax. There are no lights or wiring down here."

"Ident took photos of the room before I went down. I can't wait to hear what you have to say about it."

Myra crouched to accommodate his height. He pulled the light closer to the area around the body. Three tools lay on the floor nearby.

"What were these tools used for?" He looked around the room. "I don't see any construction down here."

"I didn't, either," Simon called back.

"I wonder if the responding officers interrupted the killer's plans." Myra moved the light closer to the body. "He's dressed up for something in a black suit and tie and his Masonic regalia. You wouldn't happen to be a Mason, would you?"

Simon chuckled. "Wouldn't tell you if I was. It's against the rules."

Myra rolled his eyes as he looked up through the opening. He spotted the note next to the corpse. "What's this?" He leaned in for a closer look. "It's music paper that someone wrote *Iota Pulchra* on." He struggled with the pronunciation. "What does that mean?

"I don't know, mate. Latin wasn't my best subject."

"Latin?" Myra looked up at Simon, who was now standing over the opening. "How do you know it's Latin?"

"It may not have been my best subject, but I did go to Brit school."

"There's an English sentence below it. '*For love is as strong as death, jealousy is fierce as the grave.*' But the lines are written in two different ink colours and different handwriting." Myra stood, forgetting the room's confines, and smacked his head off the ceiling. "Goddamn! Even the ceiling is concrete."

"Very cryptic, if you ask me." Simon laughed at Myra's predicament in the small room. "Maybe two people killed him. Or it could be a line from some old musical in the theatre downstairs."

Myra rubbed the top of his skull. "Ask Ident to pass me down a few evidence bags, please."

He could hear Simon talking to someone and coming back into the room.

"Here." Simon handed down a handful of clear plastic bags with white tabs at the top. "Move over. I'm coming down, too."

Myra took the bags and moved back to allow room for the medical examiner.

"You can't stand up here," Myra warned.

"Don't worry, mate, I do yoga. You should try it. It's good for the joints." Simon covered his nose and mouth with his hand as he crouched next to Myra. "You never get used to that smell. What do you make of it?"

"I don't know. It's bizarre, really. It looks like a sacrificial rite." Myra bent over the body, his knees cracking and echoing in the chamber to Simon's great amusement.

"Mate, you need physio or something for those knees. I'm taking you to yoga with me."

"Over my dead body." Myra carefully picked up the note, placed it in a bag, and sealed it. He took a pen out of the pocket of his coat, dated and signed the label, and laid it near the ladder.

Simon dug his hands into the pocket of his worn brown tweed blazer. "I'll leave the Masonic garb on him until he gets to the morgue so we don't disturb any DNA."

Myra lifted one of the tools and placed it in a bag. "I'm no carpenter, but I know this is a square ruler."

He sealed the bag and laid it next to the first one.

"This one is a level." He dropped it into the bag and sealed it.

Myra picked up the third tool and examined it.

"It's a plumb rule," Simon offered.

"Weird." Myra tugged at a coarse hair in his thick, greying moustache.

Simon pushed his glasses up off his nose and nodded his agreement.

"Interesting." Myra placed it in the evidence bag. "Were they going to build something?" He looked up at the opening. "I wonder, were they going to close in that hole?"

"May I suggest you talk to the Mason's Most Worshipful Grand Master about those tools? He may be able to enlighten you."

"Most Worshipful Grand Master? You're kidding, right?" Myra tried to straighten his long legs to ward off the numbness in his ankles. "You are a Mason?"

"Nice try."

"All right, then, let's see who our victim is." Myra examined the man's face. "I don't see any obvious signs of trauma. There's some slight bruising around his eyes and cheeks."

The medical examiner crouched next to him and tilted the victim's head back. "The bruising around his eyes indicates to me that he has a severe head injury, but I don't see any blood. I'll get a better look in my office."

"Who is he?" Myra rolled the body slightly and felt his back pockets. He pulled out a tattered black leather wallet. "Let's have a look."

He flipped through the plastic cards until he found a driver's licence.

"Meet Mortimer Williams, sixty years old, and lives in the east end." Myra flipped through the photos tucked in the back and picked out one showing the victim with a woman. "Looks like he's married, but there are no pictures of kids in here."

Simon snickered. "Wise choice, I'd say."

Myra dropped the wallet in an evidence bag and sealed it. "I'll get Ident to bag whatever else they find down here." He stood up a little too quickly and banged his head again. "Crap."

"Watch that ceiling, mate, it's tricky one."

Myra collected the evidence bags. He caught something out of the corner of his eye and bent over the body for another look.

"What is it, mate?" Simon asked.

"There are two footprints, one on either side of his chest. Did you make them?" Myra asked.

Simon lifted one foot, showing his blue coverings. "Not me. I'm covered."

"You didn't stand over the body like that?"

"No."

"Could have been the responding officers. I'll get Ident to check their boots against these prints."

"Good call."

Myra bellowed out to Sgt. Morgan. "Bill, can you come here?"

Morgan appeared over the opening. "What is it?"

"Take these, please." Myra passed the evidence bags up to him. "Can you make sure you get photos and moulds of the footprints on either side of his chest? Then check them against the responding officers' boots."

"Sure." Morgan took the bags and reached out to help Myra up while filling him in on the latest information. "The coat on the bar belongs to a Mortimer Williams, and we found his car parked around the corner on Gower Street. I guess he didn't want to take a chance on getting stuck on this hill."

"That means he was planning to leave. But he's our guy. I just checked his wallet. Have the car towed to the lot." Myra climbed the rickety ladder back into the room above. Morgan was already placing the bagged evidence in a larger clear plastic bag and sealing it. A constable was dusting for prints around the room.

"Why did he leave his coat downstairs?" Myra wondered out loud.

"Don't know yet," Morgan answered.

The young constable spoke up. "Sir, I found something."

Myra moved closer to him. "What is it?"

"Blood and hair, sir, on the corner of this table." He pointed a blue-gloved finger at the corner of a small, heavy wooden table in the corner.

"Seize the table as evidence," Morgan ordered.

"Jolly good luck," Simon said with mock cheer.

Myra scratched his moustache as he looked down into the Chamber of Reflection.

"What do you make of it?" Morgan asked.

"I don't know yet." Myra put his hands in his coat pocket. "The scene is yours now. After you remove everything, give Simon's people a hand to remove the body."

17

"Will do." Morgan walked into the hallway and called his team together.

Myra tore off his rubber gloves and stuffed them in his coat pocket while extending his hand to the medical examiner. "I guess you'll be in touch shortly."

Simon shook his hand and looked at his watch. "The body won't be in the morgue until after noon, at this rate. Gives me time for a cuppa tea and a biscuit." He stretched his long arms and yawned. "I should be able to get to the autopsy this week. It will take a couple of weeks to get all the results. I'll send them to you, of course."

Myra nodded. "Okay. I'll see if this guy has been reported missing by anyone. Someone will need to know he's dead."

Simon stood tall in a theatrical pose and spoke with a pronounced British accent. "Death must be so beautiful. To lie in the soft brown earth, with the grasses waving above one's head, and listen to silence. To have no yesterday, and no tomorrow. To forget time, to forget life, to be at peace." He took note of the curious look on Myra's face. "Oscar Wilde, my dear friend."

"Every man's life ends the same way," Myra added. "It is only the details of how he lived and how he died that distinguish one man from another."

He buttoned up his wool coat as he left. Looking back at the medical examiner, he said, "Ernest Hemingway."

3

Insp. Nicholas Myra waved his key card to unlock the door to the Major Crime Unit at Royal Newfoundland Constabulary Headquarters. The main room, divided up into cubicles, was dark and empty this morning.

A gust of stale, uncirculated air greeted him as he made his way to his inside office, leaving the main room dark. The door opening sent a whirl of more stale air and dull mid-morning sunlight around the room. His desk and chair were perfectly aligned and exemplified tidiness, adjusted to hold his large frame and long limbs.

The top of his desk was carefully organized, not only alphabetically but colour-coded as well. Seven sharpened wooden pencils stood in a black plastic cup next to seven black ink pens. A simple silver frame aligned next to it held the picture of everything he held dear: his wife, Maria, and their two daughters, Clara and Doris.

He flicked on the fluorescent lights, bringing the room to life. His coat was heavy from the wet snow. He shook it off and hung it on the hook behind the door, then brushed the last of the melted snow out of his damp hair. The overhead bulbs highlighted the wariness in his deep-lidded eyes and the stress etched across his rugged face.

"What a morning." Sgt. Bill Morgan tapped on the main office door and turned on the lights. "Anyone in?" He followed the light into Myra's office, laid down a tray with two coffees, and took a seat. He took a coffee and pushed the tray toward Myra. "My treat."

"Thanks," said Myra, turning on his computer.

"Nick, my team is still processing the scene. They'll be there most of the day." Morgan had the tall, regal posture of a military man. His uniform sleeve proudly displayed eight chevrons: one for every five years of service. The last twenty were in the Forensics Identification Unit. Even with his sought-after expertise, he remained a soft-spoken, by-the-book police officer. "I was listening to the news on the drive in, and they're calling it murder at the Masonic Temple."

"Sounds like a dinner theatre," Myra joked.

"Either way, everything has been tagged and the body is on the way to the morgue. Officers are going through the outside of the building now and canvassing the neighbourhood. The snow is making it difficult."

Myra stretched his long arms above his head. Several cracking sounds from his spine echoed in the room. "Simon says he'll get to the autopsy this week."

"I'm short a few officers this week. I'll need one of yours to sit in on the autopsy and collect evidence." Morgan sipped his coffee. "Any idea what this is about?"

"I have a new officer starting this morning. I'll send her to the autopsy. I don't know what to make of it yet." Myra pulled at his thick moustache. "I don't think it's going to be an easy case."

"They never are."

"I need to find out why Mortimer Williams was at the Masonic Temple, during a snowstorm, dressed up in his Masonic gear."

"Mortimer Williams?" Morgan twisted his lips as he looked up at the ceiling. "Mortimer Williams? That sounds so familiar."

"You think you know him?"

"I don't know. But I've heard that name before."

"I was thinking the same thing." Myra typed the name into Google. "Let's see what comes up."

Morgan leaned across the desk to get a look at the screen. Myra turned it toward him.

"Mortimer Williams is a local businessman. Owns a chain of coffee shops and is a Shriner."

A page of pictures featuring Williams wearing a burgundy Shriners fez hat at several different functions filled the screen.

"That's where I know him from," Morgan recalled. "He organized a Shriners keystone cops fundraiser in our jurisdiction one year for a family who had a child burnt badly in a house fire."

"Interesting." Myra leaned back in his chair.

"Why?"

"Well, why was he wearing a Masonic apron and chain, not a Shriners?"

Morgan's eyes widened. "That is interesting."

Myra printed off some of the photos. Their conversation was interrupted by the door to the main office opening. Holding a handful of photos, Myra headed out with Morgan in tow.

"Good morning, Donna."

Cst. Donna Whiffen stood in the doorway holding a worn, burgundy leather briefcase, an overstuffed purse, and a Thermos full of coffee. Her dark brown hair was pulled back in a short ponytail. Melted snow had turned the strands around her face into a curly mess. She had a sporty edge that exuded strength and power and stood almost the same height as Morgan. A long, black puffer coat was draped across her arm. Her face was round and lit with what seemed like a permanent smile.

"Morning, sir." She looked around. "Which one is mine?"

"Take the one by the window."

"Thanks." She laid everything down on top of the desk and opened the Thermos, taking a long swig. "This is nice. Great view." She looked out the window at the snow-covered streets.

"Donna, this is Sgt. Bill Morgan from Ident." Myra turned to Morgan. "Bill, this is Donna Whiffen. She just transferred in from Commercial Crime."

"Nice to meet you." The constable extended her hand, and they shook.

Myra stood in front of a whiteboard at the front of the room and began taping photos to it.

"Nothing like a murder on a Monday morning to get your first day in Major Crime started." He grinned under his thick-set moustache and stood back from the board.

Whiffen hung her coat on a rack near her new desk. She adjusted her black blazer and the collar of her white blouse, then quietly began to unpack her briefcase as she listened intently.

"Our victim is most likely Mr. Mortimer Williams, according to the ID found in the wallet on the body." Myra pointed to the smiling man in the fez hat. "My Internet search says he's a sixty-year-old businessman and is a Shriner. Now he is dead."

"Do we know how he died?" Cst. Whiffen asked.

"Not yet. I suspect there's going to be a large volume of information for you to take care of." As an afterthought, Myra looked around the room and added, "I am incredibly happy that you chose the Major Crime Unit."

He looked at Morgan. "I was lucky enough to lure Donna away from her old unit. I've been asking for a criminal strategic analyst for over a year now. I had to fight Drug Section to get her."

Whiffen lowered her head with a humble nod. "I'm happy to be here."

"I've heard nothing but good things about your work." Morgan gave her a grandfatherly smile.

"Unfortunately," Myra continued, "we are short-staffed and stretched thin. Everyone else in the unit is tied up on other files, and I have one off sick and another on maternity leave. We'll have the team for backup when needed, but for the most part, it's going to be you and me on this file."

"I'm the same in Ident," Morgan added. "Short-staffed and stretched thin should be the motto of the Royal Newfoundland Constabulary." He turned toward Whiffen. "We'll be working closely on this one, too."

Whiffen logged onto her laptop. "Yes, sir."

Myra tugged at his moustache. "All right. What do we know?" He picked up a black marker and began making notes on the whiteboard. "We know our victim most likely is sixty-year-old Mortimer Williams. The medical examiner will officially confirm that and the cause of death."

He wrote the name across the top of the board. "We don't know who killed him. What he was doing beforehand. When he was murdered. Where he was murdered. Was he killed at the Masonic Temple, or somewhere else and brought there? Why he was murdered. Or how he died."

He stood back from the board and let out a sigh as he scanned the picture of the victim in his Shriners fez. "We don't know anything about his family, friends, or business."

"We do know he's a Shriner, which means he's involved in his community." Whiffen searched Williams's name on her laptop. "There are dozens of pictures of him at charity events. There's a bio online that says he's married to wife, Doreen, and they have no children."

Myra wrote the information on the whiteboard. "I don't want the details of how our victim was found getting out to the media.

Let's keep the Masonic apron and chain under wraps for now." He tapped a marker on the board. "Morgan, when will Ident have the evidence and pictures sent to us?"

"By tomorrow." Morgan headed toward the door.

"Masonic apron and chain?" questioned Whiffen. "I thought he was a Shriner."

"Maybe he's both," offered Morgan.

"Busy guy," Whiffen said with a nod.

"Something else." Myra turned to face them. "I found three tools laid out by the side of his body. I don't know if they are the murder weapons or not. Bill, I'll wait for your word on that. There was also a note, but I don't know if it's related to the death or not."

"Ten-four." Morgan winked.

"He was laid out with care like he was in a coffin." Myra wrote on the board as he spoke. "He was also laid out in some weird secret concrete room called the Chamber of Reflection on the second floor of the Masonic Temple. The only way to get into the room is through a trap door in the floor."

"A trap door?" Whiffen chuckled at the improbability. "I'm going to need to see that."

"I think it's a good idea for us to do a tour of the crime scene as soon as possible." Myra nodded at Whiffen. "Can you find me an expert on Masons and set up a tour?"

"Sure thing." Whiffen tapped on her keyboard.

"The photos will give you a better idea of what he's talking about," Morgan advised her.

"Hey, something here." Whiffen turned her laptop screen toward them. "Patrol officers took a missing person's complaint last night from Doreen Williams. She told officers that her husband met a friend for supper and didn't come home, which was unusual for him. She was concerned that he was stranded in the snowstorm."

"So, what do we know?" Myra asked again. "By all accounts Mortimer Williams is just an ordinary guy, with an ordinary family, an ordinary job, ordinary friends, and an ordinary life. Then why is his death so extraordinary?" He squinted at the board. "Basically, we know nothing. So, let's get to work."

"Has there been a name assigned to the investigation yet?" Whiffen asked as she typed. "I need one to create the file for the system."

"Not yet. How about Operation Masonic?" The corners of Myra's mouth curled up. He laid the marker back on the edge of the board and headed to his office. "I'll go talk to the victim's wife."

"I'll get everything processed as quickly as I can and send it to you," Morgan said, then closed the door behind him as he left.

Myra headed to his office and pulled on his damp peacoat. Whiffen tapped on the open door.

"Sir, can I have a private word with you?"

"Sure, come in."

Whiffen lowered her voice. A slight quiver ran through her voice. "Sir, did you get my email about me not being able to work after five?"

"Yes, I understand you have childcare issues. That's fine. I have two girls under four, so I get it."

"Thank you, sir. I just wanted to make sure you understood my situation."

"Not a problem."

Whiffen smiled awkwardly and headed back to her desk.

Myra let out another sigh as he left the office. "There's nothing worse than having to tell someone their loved one is dead. I hate Mondays."

4

A snowy Christmas wreath swayed in the wind on the front door of Doreen Williams's blue heritage home. A heavy knock shook the late-morning silence, and she immediately sensed it was a police officer.

She opened the door wide and felt the strength drain from her limbs. Propping herself up against the cold wooden frame, she looked up into the grim face of the tall man on her doorstep. A layer of icy rain covered his short hair and wool coat. A gust of freezing rain pushed her back, making her unstable on her feet. She folded her arms around her body to ward off the chill.

"Yes?"

"Mrs. Doreen Williams?"

"Dear Jesus, how did he die?" Her voice had a husky quality that trembled when she spoke. Her pale hand flew over her mouth.

"Mrs. Williams, I'm Insp. Nicholas Myra with the Royal Newfoundland Constabulary Major Crime Unit. May I come in to speak with you?"

Her eyes blinked rapidly. It took her a second to react. "Yes, yes, of course. Come in." She moved back to allow the officer room to enter.

"Was it a car accident? He doesn't drink. Not really. Christmastime, if we're at a party or a toast or something, but he doesn't drink at supper. He doesn't like the taste of alcohol, so it couldn't have been his fault."

"Do you mind if I keep my boots on?" Myra wiped them on a rug by the front door.

"Yes, no problem. Come in."

She led Myra into the front room. Plastic tubs of Christmas decorations were piled around the room. It had been carefully remodelled to maintain its architectural history. A 1980s-era French provincial couch and chair had been reupholstered with sleek white leather. They fit perfectly into the Wedgewood blue room. A white mantelpiece, full of photos, framed a wood-burning fireplace that looked like it had never been lit. Two large crystal lamps stood on end tables flanking both ends of the couch. It was the room reserved for important company. Or police officers who were about to deliver bad news.

"I was going to start decorating last night. I'm always the first in the city to put up my Christmas decorations. Morty teases me." She broke off. "I won't be doing that now, I suppose."

Mrs. Williams sat on the edge of the couch looking at Myra with dread. He sat on the matching chair across from her.

"Mrs. Williams, you reported your husband missing last night?"

"Yes. Morty met a business associate for supper. I told him he should reschedule due to the snowstorm. The evening news said the snow was going to get worse around 9:00 p.m. He said he'd be home by eight to watch TV with me. He's never late."

Her hands shook in her lap. She ran them through her short, grey spiky hair. She absently straightened the collar on her navy blue polo shirt, then brushed away the wrinkles on her army-green cargo pants. Doreen Williams was a woman who didn't care about self-presentation to appease the male gaze.

"Tell me, was it a car accident?" Tears danced in the corners of her eyes.

"It wasn't an accident."

"What was it?" She brushed away a tear from her cheek.

"Mrs. Williams, a man's body was found last night at the Masonic Temple on Cathedral Street. We believe it's your husband, Mortimer."

"The Masonic Temple?" Doreen froze. Her lips moved slightly, and her head swayed slowly back and forth. "No, that's not possible."

"The medical examiner will be the one to confirm his cause of death. You or another family member will need to go to the morgue today for final confirmation."

A shiver ran through her. She rubbed her forearms and stared at him but said nothing. Myra recognized the glazed-over look of shock.

"Mrs. Williams, I need to ask you a few questions."

"Doreen." She spoke as if she had just woken up. "Call me Doreen."

"Thank you, Doreen." Myra reached into the pocket of his coat and took out a small, tattered, black leather notebook. "You said your husband met someone for supper last night. Can you give me the details of who he met, when, and where?"

Doreen glanced toward the ceiling as though looking for answers. "I don't know. I think they were meeting at six thirty. I don't think he mentioned the name of the restaurant or who he was meeting. Let me think." She took in a deep, ragged breath. "It was something about a charity event he was involved with. I wasn't paying attention to what he was saying. I was taking these Christmas decorations out."

"That's okay." Myra looked around and studied the photos on the mantelpiece. "Take your time."

"I don't know." Doreen rocked herself gently and occasionally choked back tears. "I can't remember. I don't think he said who he was meeting."

"Was it common for him to have supper meetings like that?"

"Yes, of course. He owns several businesses. He is always meeting someone or other for lunch or supper."

"Okay, think about it and maybe it will come back to you." Myra took out his business card and laid it on the white marble coffee table. "Here's my number in case you need to reach me."

She drew the card toward her. "Thank you." Her face was covered in red splotches that indicated a long cry before she had opened the door. Now, the colour was retreating from her face as the grief and realization of her situation came over her.

"Just a couple more things." Myra tapped his pen on his notepad. "Can you tell me what he was wearing when he left last night?"

"What was he wearing?" Doreen thought for a moment and stammered when she spoke. "He had on a white shirt, his black suit, and tie. I had picked it up from the dry cleaners a few days ago and hung it on the bedroom door for him so he wouldn't miss it. I remember seeing him yesterday taking it out of the plastic bag and commenting on how they got a stain out of the lapel."

Myra jotted this down. "Okay, that's great. Mrs. Williams, was your husband a Shriner?"

"Yes, yes, he was. He loved being a Shriner. Over the years he has raised thousands of dollars for the burn camp. Just recently he raised money for a child badly burnt in a car accident. It was a cause near and dear to his heart."

"Why was that?"

"His parents died in a car accident when he was nineteen. He always felt he wanted to do something to keep their memory alive."

"Was your husband also a Mason?"

"Yes, of course." She looked to him. "You can't be a Shriner without being a Mason."

Myra looked up from his notebook. "I didn't know that."

"I'm sorry. You would have to be a Mason to know that. I didn't mean to belittle you. Forgive me. I don't know much about it myself, but it was very important to Morty."

"No problem. I guess you learn something new every day. Was he wearing his Mason apron when he left last night?"

"No, I don't think so. Why?"

"Can you describe his Mason uniform?"

Doreen thought for a moment, then stood and walked toward the fireplace, where she picked up a photo. She gave an involuntary sob and wiped her eyes. "Here," she said tearfully. "Please excuse me. This feels like a dream. I'm sure I'll wake up soon."

"I'm sorry, Doreen, to be questioning you at such a time, but we have to learn what we can as soon as we can."

"Of course, I understand." She fought for control and passed Myra the picture of her husband. "This is Morty at his installation as Masonic Grand Master."

Myra took the photo. It confirmed the victim was Mortimer Williams. In the frame he stood proudly in an expensive black tux with tails, white shirt, and grey-and-black striped tie. He wore a white glove on his right hand and held a wooden gavel. He held another white glove in his left hand. A heavily gold-fringed white apron, decorated with gold-embroidered symbols, was tied around his waist. A wide chain collar was draped around his neck, the golden Masonic symbol of the Square and Compass dangling in the centre. The wrists of his tux were covered by large royal blue and gold cuffs. A golden "G" and two pillars were carved into the wall behind him.

"Masonic Grand Master? What is that?" Myra took out his phone and photographed the picture.

"It means he presides over the Grand Lodge. It's a big deal to the Masons, and like I said, it was extremely important to Morty."

"You mean the Masonic Temple?"

"No, they sold the Temple years ago and moved to the Grand Lodge in Mount Pearl."

"How long has he been a Mason?"

Doreen thought for a few seconds. "He joined around 2002, I believe. So, that would make it almost twenty years."

"That's a long time. Does he go to the Temple?"

"No, not since it was sold." She gave him a questioning look. "It's not used by the Masons anymore. Why would he be at the Temple?" She looked out her front window at the mounds of snow on her lawn. "Especially during the storm last night. It doesn't make sense."

"Doreen, you mentioned your husband owned several businesses. Had he been having any trouble from anyone lately? Maybe a colleague at work, a supplier, or employee?"

She shook her head. "No. Everyone loved Morty." Her voice quavered. "He was the most understanding, empathetic boss a person could have. To a fault, really."

"How's that?"

"Morty would give you the shirt off his back. To me it seemed like he looked for people to help. Every one of his employees will tell you that Morty helped them out in some way. He treated them like his children. He loved helping people."

"Did he have any financial issues?"

"No, not at all. We're very well off. Morty was generous, but he was also a penny-pincher and wise investor."

"Do you have children?"

"No."

"Was anyone with you last night?"

"No, I was home alone."

"Do you know where he was meeting this person for supper?"

Doreen adjusted herself in the chair. "I didn't pay attention to what he was saying." She gulped in a sob. "My God, why didn't I listen to him? I never dreamt he wouldn't come home."

"Is there anything you can think of that would help me out with this investigation?"

She shook her head, biting into her fist. "My mind is in such a tizzy right now. I don't know what to think."

"That's okay. If anything comes to you, just call me. I will need you to come into headquarters at some point to give a statement. It's standard procedure in a sudden death investigation." Myra stood up and walked over to the mantelpiece. "Do you mind if I look at your pictures?"

"No, of course not." Doreen stood and joined him.

Myra looked at the pictures with great interest. He focused on one that had the matte glaze of an early 1990s photo. Two women dressed in hiking gear were laughing, their arms entwined around one another. He immediately recognized Doreen Williams, and the other had a familiarity to her. "Who's this?"

Mrs. Williams took the photo from his hand. "It was taken on a camping trip in Ontario. That's me and Barbara, Morty's sister."

"He has a sister?"

"Yes." Doreen laid the photo back down.

"The medical examiner may want to talk to her about providing DNA, considering he doesn't have children."

"She died in 1997."

"I'm sorry. May I ask how?"

"Breast cancer."

"I'm so sorry." Myra moved along the row of photos and pointed to a more recent one. "This was last Christmas?"

"Yes, the Masonic Lodge has a Christmas dinner and dance every year."

"When was Morty sworn in as Grand Master?"

"About four months ago."

"Was everyone in his lodge okay with that?"

"Yes, I believe so. Morty didn't mention anyone having a problem." She picked up an older photo in a silver frame. "This is our wedding photo."

They were both younger, thinner, laughing arm in arm. He wore a black suit and she a white casual pantsuit.

Myra tucked his notebook back into his pocket. "Do you mind if I take a few pictures of these for the file?"

"Of course not. Go ahead." Doreen walked over to her large front window and pulled back the lace curtains. "Our street hasn't been properly cleared from the storm. I'm surprised you found a place to park. My neighbour was good enough to come over this morning and clear my driveway. The snow was up to your waist."

"Good to have neighbours." Myra clicked away on his phone, documenting every photo and secretly capturing a photo of Doreen in the process.

"Do you have someone you can call?"

"For what?" Doreen turned to face him.

"To help you. You're going through a traumatic experience, and I suspect you're in shock right now." Myra noticed how her hands had stopped shaking and her demeanour seemed calmer. "The next few days and weeks will be hard as you process what happened. You'll need support. Do you or Morty have family close by?"

"My family is in Nova Scotia, but we're not close. Morty has a brother, but they didn't get along. I guess I'll have to call him."

"I would recommend you have someone go with you to the morgue when the medical examiner calls. Or send someone in your place," Myra advised. "It's not something you'll want to do alone. It would be a good idea to have a driver." He walked to the front door.

"I'll call my friend to go with me," Doreen said as she followed him to the foyer. "I'm sorry, I forget why the medical examiner would want to talk to me."

"He'll need you to identify the body and sign some papers."

"Yes. Of course. He'll send Morty to the funeral home, will he? I guess I'm going to have to start thinking about the burial."

"Not right away. The medical examiner has to do an autopsy first, and that may take a few days."

"Autopsy?" Doreen's jaw dropped, and her eyes widened. "No!" she squealed.

"It's how he will determine the cause of death. It's standard in a case like this."

"I don't want an autopsy." Her voice rose in anger. "I won't consent to that."

Insp. Myra turned around, trying to digest what she had just said. "Mrs. Williams, it's out of your hands. Morty may have been murdered, and we have a duty to investigate that."

Doreen's whole body trembled and a sheen of sweat broke out on her face. She paced in circles in the small foyer, running both of her hands through her short hair. "No. No. No. I don't want an autopsy. Please don't do this."

Myra regarded her closely. "We have no choice, Doreen. It's the only way we can find out how he died. Don't you want justice for him?"

"You don't understand." She backed herself into a wall, closed her eyes, and emitted a wail that sent chills down Myra's spine. A small puddle of water seeped onto the hardwood. She had wetted herself.

"Doreen, I'm going to call for medical assistance. I think you've gone into shock."

"Don't touch me!" she screamed, her arms flinging over her head for protection. "Don't touch me. Get out. Get out. I'm fine." She pounced at the front door and opened it, banging it off the foyer wall. "Get out." She grabbed Myra by the coat sleeve and dragged him with a strength that seemed unnatural for a woman her size. "Get out," she repeated.

Myra allowed her to move him. Within seconds he was on the snow-covered doorstep, facing her. "Doreen, I'm truly sorry. The medical examiner will explain more when you speak to him."

The woman pointed a shaking finger at him. "I won't allow this. You won't do this to him. Hasn't he suffered enough?"

She slammed the door in Myra's face, leaving him staring at a swinging Christmas wreath.

And wondering what had just happened.

5

Insp. Myra leaned back in his black leather office chair, which groaned and squeaked under his weight as he rocked. He tapped his pen on the top of his cherrywood desk.

"Why doesn't she want an autopsy?" He directed his question at Cst. Whiffen, who was sitting across from the desk.

"Could be a religious thing?" Whiffen suggested.

"I thought about that." Myra laid the pen down, sensing his colleague's annoyance at the clicking. "I explained to her that autopsies are required by law when a death is the result of a crime or suspicious circumstances. It may be the only way to determine as precisely as possible what caused his death. It's a no-brainer in this case. The medical examiner doesn't need the family's permission."

"Why wouldn't she want to know how her husband died?" Whiffen questioned. "It doesn't make sense, does it?"

Myra leaned forward in his chair, picked up his pen again, and pointed it at Whiffen. "I need to know who he met for supper and where they went. I got the sense that she was holding back information."

Whiffen added to her growing list. "His phone is in evidence. I'll get a warrant to search it."

"Also, search any social media profiles he has and charities he's involved with. Doreen said he was meeting someone about a charity event."

"Will do." Whiffen typed into her phone.

"She said Morty had a sister who died of breast cancer twenty-five years ago and a brother he didn't speak to. Can you check into that, too?"

"Yes, sir."

"Another interesting thing she mentioned was that his parents died in a car accident."

"Jesus." Whiffen looked up from her phone. "The guy is a bag of bad luck. You sure he didn't kill himself?"

The corners of Myra's moustache turned up in a rare smile. "A lot going on there, isn't it? But according to the wife, he was a happy-go-lucky guy who helped everyone. Loved everyone. Was a rich penny-pincher but was good to his employees."

"Then why didn't the brother like him?" asked Whiffen.

"Good question. That's what I need to find out."

"He raised money for sick kids. Donated to charity. You couldn't ask for a nicer guy," offered Whiffen. "Who would want to kill a guy like that? Is he worth more dead than alive?"

Myra raised an eyebrow. "He was well off, according to his wife. Owned a chain of coffee shops. Lives in a big old mansion. I wonder what his insurance policy payout is."

"You think it's the wife?"

Myra chuckled. "Oh, it's the tale as old as time, isn't it? Follow the money. It's the first step in any investigation."

"Oh, come on," Whiffen playfully teased. "Why do you always suspect the wife first?"

"Because the wife always has means, motive, and usually a good reason. I may not agree with murder, but I perfectly understand it."

Cst. Whiffen nodded.

Myra twirled the hairs at the end of his moustache. "He was laid out with care, though. It's as if whoever killed him wanted him to be found while maintaining his dignity. I wonder if it was the killer who called in the break and enter."

"That would make sense. If it wasn't the wife, could it be a lover?"

"I spoke to Bill Morgan about the physical evidence collected at the scene." Myra turned on his laptop as he spoke. "They found fingerprints on some items, but whose are they? We don't know yet. They may not even be good enough to ID anyone."

"Any idea what killed him?" Whiffen asked.

"No. I haven't heard from the medical examiner yet. I was hoping he'd call by now." Myra looked at his watch. "Morgan says they found some partial prints on the three tools collected at the scene. He's going to send them to the lab for analysis."

Whiffen rolled her eyes. "The tools don't exactly look like murder weapons. I mean, a level, a plumb rule, and a Mason's square? Surely he could have defended himself against those."

"Not if he was drugged." Myra raised an eyebrow. "That's why we need to find out who he had supper with and where."

"I'll get on that right away." Whiffen headed back to her desk.

"We'll need to find out why he was at the Masonic Temple if it's not used by the Masons anymore. Oh, and Whiffen," Myra called, "did you find me an expert on Masons?"

The constable returned to his office before he had finished asking the question. "This is the expert on Masons," she said, laying a yellow Post-it Note on his desk. "He's going to meet us at the Masonic Temple tomorrow morning at ten. And see below," she added, "a number for the Latin expert. He'll decipher the note for us."

"Remember when murders weren't complicated? Now we have to know Latin. Anything on the second sentence in the note?" Myra asked.

"Yes. It's from a poem in the Bible by Solomon. There are several versions of it. I'll email you the whole thing."

"Thanks."

Their conversation was interrupted by the vibration of Insp. Myra's cellphone. **Medical Examiner's Office** flashed across his screen. Whiffen left the office, closing the door behind her.

"Hi, Simon," Nick answered.

"Nick, old boy." The familiar posh accent was unmistakable.

"What's the news? How did our guy die?"

"Don't know yet." Simon's answer was followed by a pause. "And it may be weeks before I do."

"Jesus, not cutbacks again."

"Not this time. I was just served with a temporary injunction by the victim's wife."

"What?"

"It was just hand-delivered by a chap from her lawyer's office. She is refusing to give her permission for an autopsy and is demanding the body be handed over for immediate burial."

"But we don't need her consent. He's a possible murder victim."

"I haven't determined that yet."

"Come on, Simon, he didn't lie there and die."

"Could be suicide."

"Is it?"

"I don't think so, but I've seen stranger things. I had one gentleman who fed his dog wine. He watched the poor drunken beast try to walk, and he found it so hilarious, he literally laughed himself to death."

"That's not a real thing."

"Oh, yes it is. It's called fatal hilarity," Simon said with a chuckle. "Look it up. Death is usually brought about by asphyxiation or heart failure."

"Sometimes I think you enjoy your job too much," Myra grumbled. "You can legally have it done without the consent of the victim's family."

Simon was still chuckling. "Of course, I know that, Nick. But to appease the wife I'm going to play along and keep him in the freezer for a few days. There's no rush. He's not going anywhere."

"It slows me down, though."

"I'll call this lawyer chap and tell him I'll put it off until next week to give the wife time to deal with her grief. It will give you time to sort through your evidence."

"Do you have any idea how he died?" Myra picked up his pen and began tapping it on his desk again.

"I haven't undressed him yet. I was waiting for you to send an officer to observe. I was able to draw some blood and send it for analysis. I'll have that back within a week."

"Well, at least that's something. Can you also check the blood for any type of sedative? Something that could have knocked him out. Then I guess the conclusion to this case comes back to good old-fashioned police work."

"Doesn't it always, Inspector? I'll call you when I'm ready to do the autopsy. You can join me if you like. Just like the old days."

An image flashed in Myra's mind of his days as a constable when it was required that a police officer be present during autopsies. The image of Simon opening a rib cage with his elbows, while balancing his glasses on the tip of his nose, then taking a bite of a sandwich moments later, would never leave him.

"Yeah, let me think about it," Myra answered snidely. "I have a new constable in the unit, and I think that's a good job for her."

"Have it your way. It's fascinating stuff. It really is." Simon's voice went up an octave, as it always did when he was intrigued by something. "I have no interest in why people kill, but how they do it can be really fascinating."

Myra shook his head at the phone. "Give me a call when you're ready, and I'll send her over."

"Will do. Cheers, mate."

"Cheers." Myra hung up the phone.

Whiffen stopped what she was doing, anticipating Myra's news. Myra picked up the black marker from the whiteboard and underlined Doreen Williams's name.

"The wife just moved up on our list of who wanted him dead."

6

The Masonic Temple stood dark, perched on top of the steep hill. City council trucks and plows rumbled in the distance, removing snow from the narrow streets as morning traffic moved around them. The snow had been removed from Cathedral Street, and parking spots were quickly filling up. Six-foot drifts of snow had been pushed up against the black metal fence belonging to the Anglican Cathedral across the street from the Temple. A grey, foggy, mid-morning mist settled over the city, turning the thick slush underfoot into sheets of ice with jagged edges. The smell of curry drifted up from the East Indian restaurant at the bottom of the street and mixed with the aroma of fried cod and chips from the restaurant next door.

Insp. Myra held on tight to the black metal rail leading up the stairs to the Masonic Temple. He nodded to the police officer sitting in a patrol car guarding the crime scene.

"Be careful," Myra called behind him. "The stairs are salted, but they're still slippery."

Cst. Whiffen followed at a safe distance. "I should have gone first," she called back.

"Why?" Myra looked behind at her.

"Because I don't want a big galoot like you falling on me." She grinned as she tried to keep her balance on the last step.

The two officers steadied themselves on a wide concrete landing at the top of the stairs. Myra looked up and down the street.

"Where is he?"

"There he is." Whiffen pointed at a black pickup truck backing up to park across from the Temple.

Tom Miller held on to the driver's door as he carefully got out. He checked his footing on the icy road before committing to letting go and shutting the door. He looked up at the two officers watching him and gave a wave before carefully crossing the street and attempting the stairs. At the top, he extended a hand toward Whiffen.

"My goodness. That was treacherous. I believe you're the one I spoke to on the phone."

"Yes, I am." Whiffen turned toward her colleague. "This is Insp. Nick Myra."

The men exchanged handshakes and greetings. Miller sized up the giant of a man in front of him. Myra was a full head taller with shoulders twice the size of his own. He moved closer to Whiffen, who was more his height. Miller's gloved hand scratched his three-day-old stubble. His bald head dripped with melted snow, and he continuously brushed it away as he spoke. He was a heavy man who moved with a slow gait. His glasses fogged up, hiding his pale blue eyes. Everything about Miller was ordinary, yet there was an air of something extraordinary about him.

"Hard stuff, this is." Miller shook his head. "We're all very shook up about Morty's murder."

"It hasn't been declared a murder," Myra reminded him. "Why would you call it that?"

Miller looked at him abruptly. "That's what everyone is saying."

"Don't listen to gossip."

"Yes, of course, how foolish of me," Miller answered in a matter-of-fact tone.

"What we would like you to do," said Myra, little grey puffs accompanying his words in the cold air, "is to give us a tour of the building and explain a few things."

"Sure." Tom Miller reached into his coat pocket and pulled out a set of keys. "The theatre manager wants to know when you're going to release it back to him. Apparently he had to cancel all his shows, and the Christmas season is a big money-maker for the Spirit of Newfoundland Theatre."

"As soon as it's no longer a crime scene," Whiffen offered.

"Before we go in, I guess the tour could start right here." Miller stood back and pointed at the concrete pillars that flanked the front door. "These two pillars are constructed at the entrance of all Masonic lodges and temples. In the Bible, the two pillars are known as Boaz and Jachin. They stood at the porch of Solomon's Temple."

"Solomon's Temple?" asked Myra. "As in the Song of Solomon?"

"Same one."

Whiffen took out a miniature digital recorder.

"I hope you don't mind if I record your tour. My hands are too cold to take notes."

"No, not at all. But at times I may have to ask you to turn it off."

"Why's that?"

"There's only so much I'm permitted to tell you."

"That's right." Myra watched him closely. "You're a secret society."

Miller winked at the officers. "We're not a secret society. We're a society with secrets. There's a difference. We don't hide who we are. I wear a ring that advertises it." He took off his glove and showed Myra a gold ring on his left ring finger emblazoned with the Masonic symbol.

Miller stood back, running his hand over one of the pillars before the entrance of the building. "Boaz is the left pillar, which means 'In Him is Strength,' and the right pillar is Jachin, meaning 'He Establishes.'"

Myra stood back, trying to see the ball at the top of each pillar. "What do the pillars symbolize?"

"They symbolize opposite pairs. Such as good and evil, light and darkness, active and passive, positive and negative, yes and no, outside and inside, man and woman."

"Interesting." Myra took out his phone and took pictures.

"They also represent life and death, which are total opposites. Masons believe that death is a necessity to extinguish that which is old and withering. This creates room for germinating young ideas and principles." Miller unlocked the front door and opened it. "Masons are taught how to create a balance between our own thoughts and external actions."

A cold chill ran down the spine of each officer. They gave each other uneasy glances.

"The two balls on the top of each pillar have faded, but they were once two globes. One is the celestial globe atop Boaz, and the other one is a terrestrial globe atop Jachin." Miller looked up at the concrete spheres. "The celestial globe symbolized the spiritual part of human nature, and the terrestrial globe symbolized the material side."

Myra pointed to a symbol, higher up, centred above three windows. "That's the Masonic symbol, isn't it?"

"Yes. The Square and Compass, one of the most recognized Freemasonry symbols. Its origin is traceable back to the Middle Ages through the stonemasons guild."

Whiffen could barely make it out. "What does it mean?"

"The square in Masonry symbolizes morality. To deal with someone squarely refers to treating a person the way we want to be treated. It indicates the Masons' ability to apply the teachings of conscience and morality in testing the rightness of their actions. The compass stands for the ability to mark a clear boundary around our desires and passion. It represents self-restraint and control, which is the basis of morality and wisdom. Together, the Square and Compass, combined, serve as a reminder to Freemasons to explore personal desires and passions while maintaining morality."

"We should all do that," Myra agreed.

"Just above that," Miller continued, "are three emblems." He pointed to the top of the building. "You have a square, a plumb rule, and a level, representing the three main officers of the lodge: the Master, the Senior Warden, and the Junior Warden."

Myra walked back as far as he could on the landing to get a better look. "A square, plumb rule, and a level?" He looked at Whiffen but said nothing.

Miller added, "At the very top near the roof is the All-Seeing Eye, which represents the grand geometrician of the universe."

"The grand what?" Whiffen's eyebrows lifted.

"You see," Miller explained, "Masons don't have one God. Anyone from any religion can join. Inside the square and compass is a letter 'G'. Some say it stands for God, while others say it stands for geometry."

The cold mist was seeping into their bones. The smell of wet wool and exhaust from the downtown traffic wafted around them. "Let's go inside before we freeze." Miller led them into the ornate foyer.

Myra looked up at the ornamental staircase. "Why is it still called the Masonic Temple?"

"When the building was sold, the name was sold with it. Our new building in Mount Pearl is called a Freemasons Hall, not a temple." He turned on the lights in the hallway. "I can tell you it was a stressful and tough decision to make."

"Why is that?"

"Well, a lot of Masons felt this is our home and we should have stayed here, but others felt the upkeep was too much and we should sell." Tom Miller led them into the bar at the right of the foyer.

"How did you feel about it?" Myra asked.

"I wanted to stay. I love this building."

"What about Mortimer Williams?"

Miller paused before answering. "Morty wanted to leave. He was very practical when it came to money. He felt our mission was to help charities, not spend thousands of dollars on upkeep here every month."

"What's the difference between a temple and a lodge?" Whiffen asked.

"The word 'lodge' refers to a local chapter of Freemasons meeting as a body. However, the term is often misused to refer to the buildings or rooms that Masons meet in. Masonic premises are also sometimes referred to as temples of philosophy and the arts. That's what this is, a temple of philosophy and art." He stopped and looked around as if he were home. "I love photographing this building. Each time I do, I get a different perspective of it."

"You're a photographer?" Whiffen asked.

"Part-time. I'm an accountant full-time." Miller ran his fingers over the woodwork on the wall. "You know, this is the first Masonic Temple built in North America."

He cleared his throat as a professor might do before giving a lecture.

"Actually, the first formal Masonic building was built on Long's Hill in 1885, where the Kirk is now, but it burnt down in the Great Fire of 1892. The $28,000 the Masons received in insurance money was used to help finance this Temple. The cornerstone was laid on August 23, 1894, by Freemason and former Newfoundland Prime Minister Sir William Whiteway."

"Really?" Myra looked around, admiring the architecture. "Is that significant?"

"Is it significant?" Miller looked up at him. "Do you realize how many US presidents were Masons?" He didn't wait for an answer before listing them off. "George Washington, James Monroe, Andrew Jackson, James Polk, James Buchanan, Andrew Johnson, James Garfield, William McKinley, Theodore Roosevelt, William Howard Taft, Warren Harding, Franklin Roosevelt, Harry Truman, Lyndon Johnson, and Gerald Ford."

"I had no idea." Myra looked around the bar as he listened.

"Not to mention Benjamin Franklin," Miller continued. "And Ludwig van Beethoven, Harry Houdini, Mark Twain, and Oscar Wilde, just to name a few."

"That's quite the list." Myra stopped to examine some of the historic photos hung around the room. "So, does that make this building important?"

"Important?" Miller repeated the word like he didn't understand the question. "It's probably the most significant and historic building in all of North America. Did you know that Premier Joey Smallwood's entire first Cabinet after Confederation were all Masons?"

"I had no idea. I remember my father saying there was a lot of controversy around the vote on whether or not Newfoundland should join Canada. Many believe the vote was rigged."

"There's even a rumour that there's treasure buried under this Temple," Miller offered enthusiastically. "Some believe that

Freemasons predicted the First World War and moved some very important objects from their hiding place in Europe to a British colony."

"Like what?" Myra asked. "And what colony?"

"Newfoundland was a colony of Britain before 1949." Miller leaned against a tall radiator next to him as though preparing for a lively debate. He lowered his voice and looked around. "Freemasons had control of a very important object: the Ark of the Covenant. They needed to move it to a place where no one would look."

Myra let out a laugh. "Ah, come on. You can't believe that. If that were true, someone would have torn down this building long ago."

"Or decommissioned it so it could be torn down," Miller offered.

Myra shook his head. "I have enough to deal with besides trying to find the Ark of the Covenant."

Miller's lips moved as if he was going to argue with Myra. The two officers exchanged glances. Miller thought better of it. "Let's move on."

"What's the significance of this floor?" Myra looked around the room as he spoke.

"The black-and-white tiled floor is standard in any Masonic building. Down here is just the reception area. It was used for parties, weddings, other events, and was open to the public. We used to rent it out. The basement was where the caretaker lived at one time. I believe the theatre turned it into offices. There's nothing significant down there." Miller walked back to the foyer and looked up at the grand staircase.

"Do you notice anything off about this staircase?" He didn't wait for an answer. "Take note of the vertical spindles in the longest flight of the steps—there is a code in the way they are spaced. If you look at all the vertical spindles, you'll find they are not consistent. Normally, a carpenter would space them evenly. These are not spaced that way. We believe there is a Masonic code in the way they are spaced, but we can't break it. Maybe you detectives can figure it out." He pointed at the elaborate plaster ceiling. "Upstairs is where the Temple is."

Myra waved a hand. "Lead the way."

The officers followed Miller up the stairs to a hallway outside a darkened room. "Let me find the lights," said their host. He fumbled around until he found the switch that lit up the whole floor. "Come in here."

He led them into a large room full of theatre props. The floor was covered with faded burgundy carpet; the walls were bare.

"A windowless room," Myra remarked.

"There are windows," Miller corrected him. "They're just covered up. I'm willing to say ninety per cent of temples on this planet have no windows. That's also why lodge rooms are generally found above the ground floor of a building. This room is the Chapter Room."

"But you're not a secret society," Myra noted.

"That's right. I was the last Grand Master for my lodge at this Temple. I held the last meeting here."

"What's this room all about?" Myra stepped over boxes piled up in the hallway and opened a door leading into a bigger room.

Miller followed him into the room. "This is the temple of arts and philosophy. It's where the lodge meets."

The two officers and Miller stood in the centre of the dismantled Masonic room filled with stage props and junk. Myra turned toward the left wall, which was almost entirely taken up by an elaborate pipe organ.

"That's some piano." He walked over to it.

"It's a pipe organ that was given to us in 1916 by Sir John C. Crosbie. He was a prominent St. John's merchant and the grandfather of former federal Cabinet minister John Crosbie."

"More politicians." Myra glanced at him.

To the officers' surprise, Miller touched a key and began to play the instrument. It filled the room with its tremulous tones. "I love the sound of this one, although it really needs some love and care." He played the chords to "Amazing Grace" and stopped before the chorus.

"What's this all about?" Myra pointed at a section of floor in the centre of the room. The floor was covered with black-and-white tiles. In the centre was a red star surrounded by a blue circle.

"The mosaic pavement represents the ground floor of King Solomon's Temple." Miller bent down and ran his fingers over the cracked and damaged tiles. "It's the ritualistic floor of all Masonic lodges. It's the pavement on which initiations occur and is emblematic of human life—checkered with good and evil."

"What about the red star?"

"The star means so many things," said Miller. "Look at the stars around the seal of the President of the USA, or the US flag. The medal of bravery is a star. It is one of the most important symbols of Freemasonry. The Masonic Blazing Star represents God, the Creator and Supreme Being who purifies us and makes us better and wiser men."

Myra pointed at the ceiling. "What's with the eye up there?"

On the ceiling, a blue eye surrounded by a golden sunburst looked down upon them.

"That is the All-Seeing Eye of the Supreme Being," Miller informed them. "It is a symbol recognized by Freemasons everywhere as a beautiful representation of the watchful care of the Supreme Architect."

Miller stood with his hands in his pockets, silently admiring the faded glory of this past temple. A smell of mould and dampness lingered in the air until brushed away by strong drafts breezing through the old windows, touching cold upon their faces.

"Do you have any more questions?"

"Yes, I do," Myra answered. "Can you explain what the concrete room was used for?"

"Concrete room?" Miller turned to face him. "Where?"

"It's outside the Chapter Room."

"Oh. You mean the Chamber of Reflection."

Miller led the officers to a small room with a planked floor painted red. In the middle was a square hatch with a wooden plug in the centre. "This is the Chamber of Reflection. It's a place of meditation and . . . of course, reflection. It's used for initiation into Freemasonry."

Myra reached down and pulled up the heavy hatch to reveal the dark concrete room beneath and the small wooden ladder leading down into it. A dank, musty smell, mixed with the odour of candles and death, floated up.

"It looks like a dungeon to me." Cst. Whiffen bent down for a better look. "Like a cell or torture room."

Miller let out a chuckle. "It's used for rituals. It's where we go to tell our secrets and confess our sins."

"Was it used for punishment?" Whiffen shone her phone's light into the darkened hole.

"It's simply part of a ritual," Miller answered, "and our rituals are something we don't discuss." He looked at the recorder in the constable's hand.

Myra grinned. "But you're not a secret society," he repeated.

"Your police force has techniques and procedures it doesn't reveal to the public," said Miller, grinning back. "We're no different."

Miller took out his phone and shone its light down into the chamber and spotted a discarded blue rubber glove. "What was down here? This room shouldn't be used. Why is that glove there?"

Myra watched his reaction carefully. "It must have been left behind by one of the Identification officers."

Their host adjusted the ladder as if to go down into the chamber. "The room should be empty."

"Don't go down there." Myra grabbed him by the arm and pulled him back. "It's still a crime scene."

"The chamber is a crime scene?" Miller looked at the two officers. His mouth hung open.

"The investigation is ongoing, and we can't discuss the details right now. Like I said, we haven't called it a murder yet." Myra tried to redirect the conversation. "So, you're saying this room would normally be empty?"

"Yes, it would." Miller's eyes were frozen on the dark hole in the floor. "I don't even know why Morty would be here. We don't have anything to do with this building anymore. Everything is done at our building in Mount Pearl. This is a theatre now."

"So, you don't know why Morty would be at this Temple?" Myra watched Miller's facial reactions closely.

"No." Miller shook his head, his eyes still locked on the floor.

"Do you know why Morty would have been dressed in his Masonic uniform?"

"No. I don't know of any event. As a matter of fact, I can tell you nothing was happening because of the storm. Everything was cancelled that night."

"Do you know why he would have had some Masonic tools with him? Like the square, level, and plumb rule?"

Miller scratched the top of his head. "They're all Masonic symbols we use for formal events like photos or ceremonies, but we don't carry them around. I doubt if any Masons really own them."

Whiffen stood back attentively, holding her recorder and watching the exchange between Insp. Myra and Tom Miller. The first interview, she determined, had started.

"Tom?" Myra's voice lowered to a calming tone. "Do you know any reason why someone would want to kill Mortimer Williams?"

Miller shook his head and shuffled his feet. "No, I don't."

"So, you're a past Grand Master, and he is the current one? Is that right?"

"Yes."

"How's that?"

"Morty is the Grand Master of the lodge. I'm a past Grand Master."

"You mentioned you wanted to stay in this Temple and Morty wanted to leave?"

"That's right. Morty loved this building, but he said financially we couldn't justify keeping it."

"Morty was supposed to meet someone for supper the night he was killed. Do you know who that could be?"

"I don't know."

"When did you last speak to him and where?"

"It was at our lodge meeting last Tuesday night."

"How did he seem to you?" Myra asked. "Was he out of sorts? Maybe preoccupied, frightened?"

"I'd say preoccupied, but then again, he always was. He ran several businesses and gave a lot of time to the Masons. There was a rumour his marriage was on the rocks, but I don't know anything about that. It could just be gossip."

"His marriage was on the rocks? Do you know why?"

"No, I don't. That was the rumour going around. I probably shouldn't have said anything."

"Could Morty have been having supper with another woman?"

Miller laughed at the suggestion. "Morty? He wasn't like that. I mean, I didn't hang around with him outside of the Masons. He and Doreen were very private people. She seemed rather standoffish. Kind of odd, really."

"In what way was she odd?"

"Hard to describe." Miller took a long breath as he tried to find the right words. "She's very domineering."

"Okay." Myra reached down and closed the lid to the Chamber of Reflection. "Thank you for giving us this tour. We really appreciate it. I don't think we need to keep you here any longer." He led them into the hallway. "Did you know Morty before he joined the Masons?"

Miller took another deep breath before answering and let it out slowly. "No, I met him through the Masons."

"Who joined first?"

"Morty joined before me."

"When did you join?"

"In 2005. I think Morty had a few years on me."

"But you were Grand Master first?"

"Yes, it's all about achieving different degrees, and I did it quicker, that's all."

"Thanks for answering our questions."

"I hope I was of some help."

"You were a great help to me," Myra answered. "You've given me an education on the Masons, that's for sure."

"Mr. Miller?" Cst. Whiffen asked as they followed him down the winding staircase, "can women be Masons?"

Miller stopped in the foyer and considered his answer before speaking. "The simple answer is no. It's a fraternal organization. There are lodges for women, but they were never recognized by any Grand Lodges. I recently found out some are now being recognized, but that's very new."

Whiffen nodded. "I see. Thanks for that."

Myra reached in his coat pocket and pulled out a business card. "Mr. Miller, if you think of anything else or hear anything, call me. No matter how small or insignificant you think it may be."

"I will." Tom Miller took the card and put it in his coat pocket. "It's a shame that our Temple should be smeared with this horrible crime. Twice, now, a murder has been committed in our Temple. Maybe it's cursed."

On the front steps, Myra and Whiffen turned around to face him.

"What are you talking about?" Myra held the door. "There was another murder?"

"Not here," Miller said as he buttoned up his coat. "The first was the architect of King Solomon's Temple."

"He was murdered?" Myra questioned.

"Oh, yes." Miller's eyes widened as he spoke. "I can't give you the details because of my Masonic oath, but you should research the murder of Hiram Abiff."

7

Bucky Williams leaned over the engine of a late-model SUV, trying to manoeuvre a wrench through a small opening next to the engine. An assortment of spare auto parts and discarded oil tins littered the garage around him. A greasy, black slick covered every inch of the faded grey concrete floor. A thin layer of sand had been thrown around for safety. The fumes of hundreds of previous vehicles polluted the air.

The clang of Bucky's wrench hitting the engine echoed outside the small, weather-worn garage. The two large garage doors were closed, their small windows blocked by years of grime. If it wasn't for the neon OPEN sign flashing in the dirty front window, the building on the main road in the Goulds could easily be mistaken for being abandoned.

A light snow began to fall, turning the pavement outside white. Insp. Myra parked his unmarked police car in the pothole-riddled lot. He pulled on his black leather gloves before touching the dirty brass door handle to the main door.

Bucky bobbed his head up at the sound of the bell. "I'll be right there."

Myra looked around the waiting room of the "Fix It All

Auto Repair Shop." The red-and-white tiled floor was thick with grime. Two black chairs were positioned across from the main counter. The vinyl seat of each was split. The stained wood wainscotting nailed to the front counter was warped from the bottom up to the midpoint from years of neglect. The counter was a yellowed white laminate. A blazing red heater sat at one end, the cash register at the other. A girly calendar nailed to the wall featured a scantily clad Miss November draped across a motorcycle. A framed business licence hung next to Bucky Williams's mechanic certificate.

"What can I do you for?" Bucky wiped his grease-stained hands on a dirty rag. He quickly assessed his customer as he slid in behind the counter and threw the rag down. "You're a cop."

"Is it that obvious?" Myra took out a business card and laid it on the counter. "Insp. Nicholas Myra, RNC."

Bucky picked up the card and squinted at it. His thinning brown hair was slicked back and flat against his head. His knobby hands testified to years of hard labour under the hoods of cars and trucks. He only glanced at the card.

"What do ya want with me?"

"Are you Bartholomew Williams?"

"Bucky." He tucked his hands inside the pockets of his old blue coveralls.

"Are you Mortimer Williams's brother?"

Bucky snorted a chuckle. "Yeah."

Myra was taken aback. "What's funny about that?"

Bucky cleared his throat. "Nothing. I always laugh at his name. It certainly would have got him shit-kicked on playgrounds."

"Would have?" Myra took note of the way Bucky's eyes blinked toward the floor.

"What do you want with me?"

"You know your brother died two nights ago?"

Bucky nodded, his eyes cast down.

"Do you know why anyone would want to kill him?"

"No. I certainly had no reason."

"His wife told me you and your brother didn't speak to each other."

"That's right."

"Why is that?"

"It's the past, and I don't live in the past anymore." Bucky looked toward his garage bay. "I've got work to do if there's nothing else."

"What about Barbara?"

Bucky's eyes widened. "Barbara?"

"Your sister."

"Barbara." Bucky nodded his head and sniffed. "She died years ago."

"I'm sorry for your loss." Myra moved closer to the heater to stay warm. "I'm also sorry for the loss of your brother. I'm just trying to find out what happened to him."

"You'll have ask Doreen about Morty." Bucky hunched over the counter. "His wife." He lingered a little too long on the word for Myra's liking.

"You don't like her?"

"I don't like her. She doesn't like me. Let's just say there's no love lost between us."

"Why is that?"

Bucky shrugged. "I don't know. Does anyone get along with their sister-in-law?"

"When was the last time you spoke to Morty?"

"Weeks ago."

"Do you remember the date?"

"I don't know. Around mid-October." Bucky's voice rose a few octaves with each answer.

"But you just told me you don't talk. Now you're telling me you spoke a few weeks ago." Myra watched as Bucky moved away from the counter and kept his back to the wall.

"We hadn't spoken in a while, then a couple of weeks ago he called me."

"What for?"

"Christmas is coming. I guess he wanted to talk."

"And did you?"

"No. I was busy."

"Where did you see him?"

"Where? It was on the phone. All of our contact was by phone."

"Why is that?"

"Look, we're not close, okay? It's not like he comes over for Sunday supper." Bucky moved closer to the counter and held up his hands as though showing they held nothing. "We're just not close."

"Were you at one time?"

Sweat formed on the top of Bucky's lip. "When we were younger." He looked toward the vehicle in his garage. "Look, is there anything else? I got work to do. The lady who owns that SUV is on the way to get it."

"Why did you and Morty have a falling-out?"

Bucky ran his grimy fingers through his hair. "I didn't say we had a falling-out. Sometimes siblings don't get along, that's all."

"Did you get along with Barbara?"

Bucky blinked and swallowed hard. He drew in a deep breath. "I loved Barb. We were twins. Did you know that?"

"No, I didn't."

Red blotches covered Bucky's wrinkled face and neck. "I loved my sister."

"She died of breast cancer, didn't she?"

"Breast cancer?" Bucky huffed. "I suppose that's what that bitch Doreen told ya. Always lookin' for pity, that one is."

Myra stood silently, waiting for Bucky to continue, but he just stared back. "Did she die from breast cancer?" he repeated.

Bucky's lips moved, but nothing came out. He took short, quick breaths while he formed his thoughts. "Yeah, it was breast cancer."

"You don't sound sure."

"I don't want to talk about it." The man's eyes glossed over, and he turned his focus to the snow falling outside.

Myra looked out the window at the snow accumulating on top of his car. "Bucky, you haven't asked me how Morty died."

The man put his hand over his mouth, wiped the sweat off his lip, and looked straight at Insp. Myra. "I don't know Morty. I buried my sister years ago. Morty became a stranger to me then."

"Do you blame Morty for Barbara's death?"

A taxi pulled into the parking lot and let a passenger out at the front door.

"That's the owner of that SUV." Bucky gestured toward the garage bay door. "I'm not finished with it yet. Is there anything else?"

"Your parents, they died in a car accident?" Myra asked.

Bucky's eyes glistened, and he looked away. His voice was barely audible. "Yes. Since Doreen came into our lives, it's been one tragedy after another."

"Why do you say that?"

"A lot of bad luck follows her."

The door opened, and a woman walked in, shaking the snow out of her long blonde hair. "It's getting bad out there now." She looked up at the two men watching her. "Is my car ready? You said it would be ready by five."

"It won't be long," Bucky said, heading toward the garage. "I'm almost done."

Insp. Myra grabbed the door before it closed. "Thank you for your help, Bucky."

"Any time, Officer." Bucky winked. "Any time."

8

A large, full moon peeked in through a break in the curtains hanging in Myra's bedroom window. It was just enough for Maria to see her husband sitting on the side of the bed, where the blue glow of his phone lit up his face. She looked over at the clock: 3:00 a.m.

"Can't sleep again?" She pulled the comforter around her shoulders and crawled toward him.

Myra finished sending an email to Cst. Whiffen and laid the phone back down on the nightstand. "I start to doze off, and then I'm wide awake again."

Maria wrapped herself around her husband's back, her arms tight across his shoulders. "You should try taking those sleeping pills the doctor gave you."

"No. They leave a weird taste in my mouth and make me feel stupid the next day."

"Let me get you some of my melatonin. There are no side effects, and you're not going to feel groggy the next day. It just takes the edge off."

"No, thanks."

"Nick, give it a try. You can't keep doing this to yourself. You're going to collapse."

Maria tightened her grip around him. The silk of her night-dress pressed against his bare back. "You want me to rub your back?"

He looked at the clock. "No, that's okay. Go back to sleep. You have to get up with the kids in a few hours."

"Where are you tonight, Nick? I mean in your head." Maria had been with him in this dark place many times.

"I'm just having trouble falling asleep."

"You're having the night terrors again. I can tell by the sweat stains on your side of the bed." She ran her hands over the cotton sheet. "Your pillow is soaking, too."

"It's nothing."

"Maybe you should go back to that psychologist again. You know, just for a tune-up."

Nick thought about it. "I don't think I need to do that again."

"I don't think you need to go back full-time. You seem to have your daytime PTSD symptoms under control, but your insomnia is back."

"I can't seem to relax lately, that's all."

She held him a little tighter. "What are the dreams about? And don't say you're not having them, because you talk in your sleep. At times it's like you're wrestling a ghost."

"Maybe I am." He reached up and held her hands. "The dreams are so vivid sometimes. Most times I can't remember them by the time my feet hit the floor."

"It's all part of the past trauma of your career."

"I know."

"Do you want to go back to the sleep apnea clinic? I know you didn't like the last device, but they may have one that fits you better."

"No way. It's too claustrophobic. I feel like I'm being strangled when I wear it."

"Do you remember anything about the dreams? Maybe there's something there that we can talk about."

"There's no dream at all, really. It's just this gripping feeling of fear. I don't know why."

"Nick, you have yourself convinced that you're this invincible RoboCop capable of handling everything. However, the truth is that policing comes with a tremendous amount of occupational stress."

"Maybe I need to start running again. I found that helped."

"That's a good idea. I think you also need to realize that you are called out to a new incident before you have mentally processed the impact of the last file. You need to give yourself time in between cases."

"Easier said than done. You know my unit is down staff, and I can't leave the new constable on her own. That's not fair."

"But what's fair to you? To us?"

His phone lit up, and he glanced at the screen to see that Whiffen had answered his email.

"Is there something about this case that's really affecting you?"

"I don't know. Lately all the cases have been intertwining themselves in my head. I see this victim in so many scenarios that I've investigated. Sometimes I have to go back to the file and look at the pictures to see which one he is."

Maria rubbed her hands up and down his arms. "Do you want me to make coffee?"

Nick looked at the clock. "No, thanks. You need to get your rest. Go back to sleep."

"Only if you're going to get back in bed with me. I don't want you downstairs sitting in the dark, mulling over your night terrors."

"I'll try to get another hour's sleep." Nick crawled back into bed. He reached his arm over Maria and spooned her tightly.

Maria reached up and rubbed the back of his neck. "All right. Let's do this. Name three things that you know for sure."

"Do we need to do this now?" he groaned.

"Yes." She tried to look over her shoulder at him. "The psychologist said when you're stressed, we need to do this. Now, name three things that you know for sure."

He nuzzled her neck. "Number three, I'm happy and safe at home. Number two, I'm good at my job and I will win this battle with PTSD. Number one, I love you and the girls more than anything in this world, and you love me back."

"If you know these things for sure, then you have to keep playing those in your mind instead of your dark thoughts. Every time a memory comes back to you, you have to replace it with the laughter of our children, how they need you, and how much I love you."

"I do."

"But it worries me, because I know it's hard to remember that when you're in the throes of a battle in your mind."

The pitter-patter of tiny feet running down the hall caused Maria to sit up and listen. "I think one of them is up."

The bedroom door squeaked open, and two tiny girls in matching onesies came running into the room.

"We want to sleep with you, Mommy." Clara dragged Doris behind her and helped pull her up on the bed. They tucked their tiny bodies in between their parents under the comforter.

"Okay, but you have to go to sleep. Daddy has to work in the morning."

"Night, Daddy." Doris grabbed Myra's face with her tiny hands and kissed his cheek.

Maria reached over and ran her fingers gently over his forehead. "Remember, everything that's important in life is here in this bed with us right now. Nothing else matters."

9

Cst. Donna Whiffen was laying out pages of information across her desk when Sgt. Bill Morgan knocked on the office door and let himself in. "Early bird gets the worm?" He balanced a tray of three coffees in one hand and his briefcase in the other.

"Here, let me help you." Whiffen took the tray and laid it on a desk.

"Thanks." He put his briefcase down on top of a vacant desk and shook off his overcoat. "Two sweeteners, two cream, right?"

Whiffen pointed to herself, surprised. "Is one of them for me?"

"Yes, I get coffee once a week, and Nick gets it once a week. It's a tradition we started back in our constable days. No matter what unit we're in, we keep the tradition alive. It's our way of staying in touch."

"I really appreciate you including me." Whiffen pulled a paper cup out of the tray. "I didn't have time to stop this morning." She wiped the sleep from her eyes.

Morgan opened his coffee and sat on the edge of her desk. "You look tired. Is this case keeping you up at night?"

"No. Jack was up till four last night, and now I'm exhausted."

Morgan picked up a black-framed five-by-seven photo from her desk. "Is this Jack?"

"Yes." She continued organizing her stacks of paper.

"I guess we'll get to meet him at our annual Christmas lunch."

"Christmas lunch?" Whiffen dropped the file she was holding. It landed on the floor, and she hurried to put it back together.

"Didn't Nick tell you about our Christmas lunch yet? It's an annual tradition. Nothing fancy. Just our two units, spouses, and kids at a local restaurant."

"I don't think I can take Jack to that. He doesn't do well in restaurants."

"Why was he up all night?" Morgan laid the photo down. "I don't understand teens these days, up all night playing video games. I'd pull the plug right out of the wall."

Whiffen looked up and smiled slightly.

"Does he play sports?

"No." She nervously glanced at the office door.

"Big strapping boy like him would make a great hockey player."

"He can't play hockey."

"Well, it doesn't have to be hockey. It could be soccer or basketball. Anything to keep him away from video games."

"He actually doesn't play video games."

"My youngest was as lazy as a cut cat." Morgan sipped his coffee while he spoke. "Too lazy to get out of his own way. Well, one Saturday morning I went in his room at nine o'clock and pulled the mattress right onto the floor and said, 'Get up and do something with your life.'" He laughed at the memory. "Well, he was madder than a puffed toad. But he got up. Eventually he found his way in life. He's in university now."

Whiffen turned her back to him as she fixed her files.

"How old is your boy?"

"He just turned eighteen."

"Eighteen? My son is twenty-one." Morgan looked at the photo again. "Is he going to university?"

"No."

"Trade school?"

"No."

"What does he do all day?"

Whiffen sighed. "Jack has non-verbal autism with high service needs."

The office door opened, and Insp. Myra came in. He sensed tension in the air.

"Morning."

"Morning." Morgan's face was red. He turned toward his briefcase on top of the desk and opened it.

Myra watched both of them out of the corner of his eye while unlocking his office door near Whiffen's desk. "What's on the go?" He threw his coat on the hook behind his door and came back to the main office.

Morgan handed him a legal-sized white folder. "I have the photos from the scene for you. And I had a chat with the theatre manager at the Masonic Temple."

"Good work." Myra reached for the folder.

"There's two hundred and fifteen there—fifty of areas around the outside of the building. The rest are of the victim and inside the building."

Myra flipped through them. "Did you find anything of interest?"

"The snow was not disturbed at any entrance besides the front door. The ledges outside every window were not touched, including the fire escape. The snow on the window ledges measured anywhere from five to seven inches. So, if they had been disturbed, we would know it. It looks like there could have been several people who used the front door. Hard to tell because of the amount of snow that fell."

"The two constables first on the scene said the piece of wood that was duct-taped over the window by the fire escape was on the floor," Myra reminded him. "The glass vase fell and broke when they were there."

"Yes," Morgan agreed. "The theatre manager confirmed the window was broken months ago. He had fitted the plywood over it and duct-taped it."

"Real handyman. What time did they close that night?" Myra continued to look through the photos.

"They weren't open at all that day. The show had been can-celled because of the weather, according to the manager, but I found a set of keys in the victim's coat pocket that unlocked the front door, and a black bag under the coat."

Myra looked up. "He had his own keys?"

"I asked the manager how our victim had keys to the front door, and he didn't know, but he did confirm that the locks were not changed after they bought the building, to his knowledge. He didn't recognize the bag, so I'm wondering if the victim brought his Masonic gear in it."

"That would make sense. I'll show it to his wife to confirm that. He is a Grand Master, but would he still have keys to the building? What about the note we found?"

"The manager said he didn't hear those lines before. It's not from any production they performed."

"So, it could be from the killer." Myra handed the photos to Whiffen. "Did you check the footprints next to the body against the responding officer's boots?"

"Yes. There were footprints from Constable Ryan's boots around the bottom of the ladder, but they didn't match the footprints on either side of the body. The Ident officers wore protective booties, but they didn't match any of theirs, either."

"Did you find anything of interest in his car?"

"No. It was clean as a whistle, even the trunk." Morgan looked down at the cup still sitting in the tray. "Here's your coffee. If you're finished with me, I have a meeting to go to."

"Thanks, Bill. Appreciate it."

Myra waited until the office door closed before turning to Whiffen. "You were up late last night."

"Yeah, couldn't sleep."

"That makes two of us, but don't feel obligated to answer my emails late at night." He looked over at the neatly piled folders on her desk. "What did you find?"

Cst. Whiffen straightened up her separated piles of notes. "Miller was right. It's not the first murder at a Masonic Temple."

"There really was another one?" Myra sat on the edge of a desk. "When?"

"In 957 BC. Hiram Abiff was the chief architect of King Solomon's Temple, which all Masonic Temples resemble. He was murdered inside the Temple by three ruffians after they failed to force him into giving them the Master Masons' secret passwords."

"Really? So much for not being a secret society. Why did they need it?"

"Rumours of treasure." Whiffen took a sip of her coffee. "He was ambushed as he was leaving work. Hiram was challenged by each, and at each refusal to divulge the information, his assailant struck him with a mason's tool. He was injured by the first two assailants and struck dead by the last."

"The tools?" Myra tugged at his moustache. "The square, level, and plumb rule, like those we found at our crime scene."

"His murderers hid his body under a pile of rubble, returning at night to move the body outside the city."

"So, are we looking for one killer or three?"

"I don't know, but I think someone is trying to re-enact the murder of Hiram Abiff."

"But why?" Myra wondered. "For what purpose?"

"I don't know, but I've been doing some digging, and the Williams family has a very interesting past, too."

Myra leaned against the window frame and tapped his fingers on the sill. "How so?"

"Let's start with Morty's parents." Whiffen held up some newspaper clippings and a police report from the first pile.

"They died in 1992, but it wasn't exactly a car accident. They were parked by a lake and fell asleep with the motor running and the windows up. The report says two empty wine bottles were found in a paper bag in the back seat along with the remains of a picnic lunch. The mechanic's report said their vehicle had a defective exhaust system. The cause of death was ruled as carbon monoxide poisoning.

"If they were sitting there after drinking two bottles of wine with the car running, they would be a bit drowsy. The heater system would pull the fumes into the vehicle and put them into a deep sleep. Then death."

Whiffen walked up to the whiteboard at the front of the room and taped the newspaper clipping to it. "The medical examiner's final report stated the cause of death was accidental."

Myra looked closely at the clipping. "Who got the insurance money?"

"That's the thing." Whiffen picked up another newspaper clipping from her desk. "Bartholomew Williams was outraged by the final report and told the media it was wrong because neither of his parents drank or ever went on a picnic. He said they would never fall asleep in their car at a lake or anywhere else. He also said *he* had replaced the exhaust system on his parents' car himself and there's no way there was a hole in it."

She handed the clipping to Myra.

"He goes by Bucky."

Whiffen nodded and picked up a report from her desk. "According to the investigator's report, the insurance money went to their daughter, Barbara. Bucky got nothing. There's no mention of Morty. But in the media coverage, Bucky claimed his parents were murdered and his sister cheated him out of his inheritance. He hired a lawyer and tied up the insurance payout for years." She handed the report to Myra. "I've searched in several sources, but I couldn't find a follow-up to the story."

"Why did the parents leave Bucky and Morty out of the will, I wonder?" Myra asked.

Cst. Whiffen shook her head. "I don't know."

"Was the money paid out?"

"I called the insurance company and told them I was following up on the file. The agent told me they paid out in 1997. Barbara got half a million dollars." Whiffen sorted through her mountain of paperwork and pulled out the insurance documents. "Was it enough to kill for?" she wondered aloud.

"Well, that's what we need to find out." Myra picked up a black marker and wrote *Insurance payout* under Morty and Bucky's names. "Did you say 1997?"

"Yes."

"Barbara died of breast cancer in 1997."

"Really?"

"Really. So, where did the money go?"

"One more thing." Whiffen went back to her desk and picked up a police file. "Bucky has a police record." She opened the file and began to read down through a laundry list of charges. "Mostly drunk and disorderly. His record started around 1992, after his parents' death." She handed it to Myra.

"One thing of interest in there," she went on. "Doreen called

911 about Bucky in 1997. She claimed he threatened to kill her and burn the house down. Doreen dropped the charges shortly after, claiming it was just a family squabble. It was Bucky's parents' house."

Myra studied the file. "So, Bucky threatened to kill Doreen. Why? And why was she living in his parents' house? It's the house she still lives in."

"There's not much information on the file. Once the investigating officer showed up, she changed her mind and wouldn't give any information, claiming it was a family fight that was resolved."

"Okay." Myra closed the file. "We need to track down the original investigator and interview him. I need to know more about their deaths. Does it say who the investigator was?"

"Yes. As a matter of fact, it was Sgt. Morgan."

"Bill?" Myra looked toward the closed door, then back to Whiffen. "He probably doesn't realize Mortimer Williams is the child of the couple who died in that incident. Funny, because Bill's mind is like a steel trap." He folded his arms. "When I told Bucky that Doreen said his sister died of breast cancer, he seemed shocked to hear it. Donna, can you find out if she did die of breast cancer or something else?"

"Yes, sir."

Myra was deep in thought as he headed back to his office. "Oh." He stopped in the doorway and turned back toward Whiffen. "My wife, Maria, is booking a restaurant for our annual Christmas brunch on December 15. My unit and Bill's always get together for Christmas. Can you and your family make it? Maria likes to book early."

Whiffen looked troubled. "I don't think so. But thanks for asking." She tucked her head down behind her computer screen and went to work.

"Okay. That's too bad. If that changes, let me know."

Myra walked back into his office with an inkling that something was happening in his unit that he was not aware of. He slipped his arms into the sleeve of his coat as he left the office.

"I'm going to interview your Latin expert his morning." As an afterthought, he said to Whiffen, "I have trouble sleeping. Don't feel obligated to answer my emails late at night. I don't expect that."

"Don't worry about it," Whiffen said. "I was up anyway."

10

Upon this rock I will build my church. That statement ran through Insp. Myra's mind every time he entered the Basilica of St. John the Baptist. He had been there so many times throughout his life that it felt like home. He breathed in that familiar and distinct church smell of burnt incense, hymn books, and candles. The morning sun gave life to the ancient church. Sunbeams pierced the stained glass windows, sending a kaleidoscope of colours throughout the church.

"Beautiful, isn't it?" James Fitzgerald, the executive director of the Basilica Heritage Foundation, spoke with an effortless smile. His eyes had a gentle expression, and his voice a musical quality to it. He extended his hand.

"You must be Insp. Myra."

"Yes." Myra shook his hand. "Thank you for agreeing to meet with me. Sorry I couldn't give you more information on the phone."

"No problem at all." Fitzgerald ran his fingers through his neatly combed white hair, which perfectly framed his round face. "There's nothing I like more than talking about this church. I was truly excited when you called."

"It's not actually the church that I want to talk about. I'm conducting an investigation, and I need someone who understands Latin. I'm told you're an expert."

Fitzgerald gave the officer a quizzical look. "I studied in Rome, but I'm not an expert on Latin. I can have a look."

"Have you ever heard of the Latin term *iota pulchra*? I googled the term, but nothing came up. Instead, I got the term *tota pulchra*. Can you explain it?"

Fitzgerald winced. "That's a very interesting question, Inspector."

"Why is that?"

"Because very few people know about it."

"I don't understand."

"Come with me." Fitzgerald led him to the centre of the nave and looked up at the magical light around them. "The Basilica has an exceptional collection of stained glass windows. It's the largest single collection in Newfoundland and Labrador. They were donated entirely by parishioners."

He pointed up at the large windows above them.

"These were the work of only three stained glass artists: the celebrated William Warrington of London, and Charles Lévêque and Louis Lichtenheldt-Koch of Beauvais, France. They were installed between 1857 and 1905. During the Great Fire of St. John's in 1892, the Basilica did not burn. The church and most of its large windows are one of the few remaining intact pre-1892 collections of nineteenth-century stained glass in St. John's."

Fitzgerald picked up a brochure titled *Stained Glass Windows of the Basilica* from a stand near the foyer and handed it to Myra.

"This church is not oriented on an east-west axis, nor does it face toward the Narrows, as people often say. It was constructed on an orientation with its facade facing the line of the rising sun on the winter solstice, and the setting sun at the summer solstice, just as the medieval Chartres Cathedral in France is. That's when these windows put on an incredible show."

Myra turned around, admiring the craftsmanship. "Whether you're Catholic or not, this is still one of the most beautiful museums in the country," he admitted. "But what does it have to do with *iota pulchra*?"

"Because it's a spelling mistake on one of the windows." A deep groove between Fitzgerald's eyebrows gave away his frustration.

"A spelling mistake?" Myra' looked at him with incredulity. "How could that be?"

"Follow me."

Fitzgerald led him into the marble foyer and unlocked a blond wooden door that led them up a flight of stairs in the east tower. The wooden treads were worn from the feet of countless choirs. They entered the three-walled organ loft that overlooked the whole of the Basilica. In the centre of the loft sat the organ, which was surrounded by the choir stage and chairs. On the walls to the left and right were the organ's floor-to-ceiling pipes. Behind the organ was a balcony that looked down over the church. The back wall was graced with three large stained glass windows that looked out over the parking lot in front of the church. Each window had three smaller stained glass windows at the bottom. Fitzgerald pointed to the window in the middle.

"This is the only window in the Basilica created from a photograph. The photo was taken at a ceremony in 1905 when Bishop Howley became *Archbishop* Howley, and the diocese became the archdiocese and was set up as a distinct province of the Roman Catholic Church. At the bottom of the window are three smaller windows. The first represents the Immaculate Conception diocese in Harbour Grace, the middle represents the archbishop, and the one on the right represents the diocese of St. George's on the west coast."

He went back to the Immaculate Conception window.

"This window was removed about ten years ago because we were restoring the outside and it had to be re-leaded. It had to be fixed because it was starting to fall apart."

Myra examined the lead lines around the coloured glass. "How did it get damaged?"

"Just time. The church is a hundred and sixty years old."

Fitzgerald pointed to the small window on the left. The masterfully designed glass was a whirl of coloured leaves. In the centre of the window was a royal blue shield that featured twelve white stars forming a circle floating above a white crescent moon on its side. A white banner stretched just below it read: *Iota Pulchra.*

"That's it." Myra could barely contain his enthusiasm.

"Wait. Let me explain what you're looking at." Fitzgerald pointed to the top of the window. "Look here. There's a broad-brimmed green hat called a galero with tasselled strings, which is worn by the bishop. Below it is the blue shield with the twelve stars and crescent moon, which represents the Virgin Mary."

His finger slid down the glass to the white banner below the crest.

"We used a local glassworks company to fix this window." Fitzgerald shook his head, the sting of disappointment on his face. "It should say *Tota Pulchra*, but the artist couldn't make out the 'T' and thought it was an 'I,' so he misspelled it during the restoration."

"Couldn't you fix it?" Myra used his phone to take a picture of the window.

"It's not that easy. It's not like we could use whiteout on it. The damage was done. It was expensive enough to fix this window. They would have had to remove it and start over. They claimed it was our fault, we claimed it was their fault. In the end we had to leave it until we could pay to have it fixed."

"What's the difference?" Myra looked closer at the window. "What does it mean?"

"Well, *Tota Pulchra* is an old Catholic prayer written in the fourth century. It is one of the five antiphons for the psalms of Second Vespers for the Feast of the Immaculate Conception. The title means *You are completely beautiful*. Meaning the Virgin Mary is completely beautiful."

"Then what does *Iota Pulchra* mean?"

"*Iota Pulchra* means you are only a little bit beautiful, or . . ." Fitzgerald hesitated. "It means you're ugly."

Myra pictured the note next to the body of Mortimer Williams.

Fitzgerald took a tissue out of the pocket of his black blazer and wiped his fingerprints off the window. "I know it's an insult to the Virgin Mary, but we're going to fix it eventually. It just comes down to money. Why do you ask, anyway?"

"Just interested in Latin, I guess. You said earlier that very few people knew about this window. Who are they?"

Fitzgerald crossed his arms over his chest. "I don't know, really. Me, the archbishop, the glass-maker. He died a few years ago. A few people here at the church. Not many. We certainly don't advertise it."

Myra's eye caught a reflection of light hitting the gold on James Fitzgerald's wedding finger. It was a symbol he knew all too well. "Are you a Mason?"

Fitzgerald looked down at his ring. "Yes, I am. Why?"

"I've done some research, and I read that Roman Catholics couldn't be Masons."

"The Catholic Church has difficulties with Freemasonry because it is indeed a kind of religion unto itself." Fitzgerald twisted the ring on his finger. He spoke with a tone of academic crispness. "Freemasonry includes temples, altars, a moral code, worship services, vestments, feast days, a hierarchy of leadership, initiation and burial rites, and promises of eternal reward and punishment."

He moved toward the organ in the centre of the loft and sat behind its yellowed keys. "Most Masons are Christian and display a Bible on their altar. In the same lodges, Jews, Muslims, Hindus, or other non-Christian religions can be admitted and may use their own sacred scriptures."

"So, they can be Masons?"

"The church believes that the Masonic rituals involve the corruption of Christianity. For example, for Masons the Cross is merely a symbol of nature and eternal life, devoid of Christ's sacrifice for sin."

Fitzgerald leaned across the organ and pulled out a small white knob. A hiss of air seeped out through the wall of pipes. "Do you remember seeing a small sign at the feet of Jesus on any crucifix that says INRI? For Christians, *Iesus Nazarenus Rex Iudaeorum* means Jesus of Nazareth, King of the Jews. For Masons, it means *Igne Natura Renovatur Integra*—the fire of nature rejuvenates all— referring to the sacred fire's regeneration of mankind, just as the sun regenerates nature in the spring."

Fitzgerald pumped the organ with his foot as he pulled at the white buttons on the side of the instrument. His fingers floated across the keys, filling the Basilica with angelic musical notes.

"You didn't answer my question." Myra looked down over the waist-high rail, at the long drop to the bottom, and slowly moved backward toward the wall.

"The two traditional enemies of Freemasonry are royalty and the papacy. Masons even believe that Christ, dying on Calvary, was the greatest among the apostles of humanity, braving Roman despotism and the fanaticism and bigotry of the priesthood."

He suddenly stopped playing and looked up at Myra.

"When one reaches the thirtieth degree in the Masonic hierarchy, called the Kadosh, the person crushes the papal tiara and the royal crown with his foot and swears to free mankind from the bondage of despotism and the thralldom of spiritual tyranny."

"You still didn't answer the question."

"The Church's negative position on Masonic association remains unaltered, since their principles have always been regarded as irreconcilable with the Church's doctrine. Hence, joining the Masons remains prohibited. The way the Church sees it, Catholics enrolled in Masonic associations are involved in serious sin and can't take Holy Communion."

"How do you balance your Masonic and Catholic beliefs?"

"I don't take communion."

"Have you ever heard of the Song of Solomon?" Myra asked.

"Of course. I have a master's in theology." Fitzgerald gave him what seemed like a condescending glance. "Why?"

"Nothing. Did you know Mortimer Williams?" Myra's baritone reverberated off the limestone walls.

"Yes, I did." Fitzgerald gently closed his eyes and, with the excellence of a master, played a few notes of a hymn on the organ.

"How did you know him?"

"I met him through the Masons," said Fitzgerald, reluctantly pulling away from the organ. "He was very active. I'm more of a background guy. I do a lot of research for them. We weren't friends."

"I see. What did you think of him?"

"I hated him," Fitzgerald said simply. "I don't think he liked me, either. You seem surprised to hear me say that."

"I am, and I also think you're the only one telling me the truth." Myra shook his head. "Everybody says he was such a great guy. Gave to the poor. Helped the needy. Why didn't you like him?"

"We didn't see eye to eye on some things. I thought he was a phony."

Myra found Fitzgerald's answer a little humorous and let out a chuckle. "You do know he's dead?"

"I do." Fitzgerald pulled the wooden cover down over the keys of the organ. "It doesn't make him any less phony."

"Tell me about your relationship."

"Not much to tell, really." Fitzgerald's voice dropped to a whisper. "I joined the Masons five years ago. We disagreed on a lot of things. I'm a scholar, but he wouldn't acknowledge my research on Masonic history in this province."

"Did you argue about it?"

"All the time. It was like talking to that wall there. Something about him seemed off. Fake, almost."

"Was it because he was rich?"

An exaggerated grimace overtook Fitzgerald's face. "No, it had nothing to do with money. As a matter of fact, I didn't know he was rich until almost a year after I met him."

"Have you ever met his wife, Doreen?"

This time Fitzgerald let out a laugh. "Doreen. Oh my God, don't get me started."

Myra stared at him blankly. Fitzgerald took this as a cue to continue.

"That woman is a complete and utter bitch." He lowered his voice further as he looked around the organ loft. "Horrible person."

"Why would you say that?"

"There's only one person who hated Morty more than me, and that's Doreen."

Myra listened intently but stayed stone-faced.

"I'm probably implicating myself in his murder, but believe me, if anyone killed him, it would be that witch. She treated him like dirt."

"Have you heard any rumours about their marriage?"

"Everybody knew they were splitting up. Morty made no secret of it. For God's sakes, he even told me, and he disliked me!"

"Why did Morty dislike you?"

"That's the funny thing." Fitzgerald tilted his head toward the stained windows. The morning sun caught the questioning look in his eyes. "It was weird. I sensed he didn't like me. But last year I was raising money to fix one of these windows, and Morty wrote a cheque for the whole amount."

"Was it this one?" Myra pointed up at the centre window.

"No." Fitzgerald pointed to the left side of the nave below. "It was one of the windows up front." He paused for a few seconds. "One time I called him a fake to his face, and all he said was, 'I know.' Then walked away." The man's shoulders slumped. "I feel awful about it now."

"What exactly was fake about him?"

"I think he was hiding a secret. What it was I guess we'll never know."

Fitzgerald patted the organ as he might a departing friend and headed toward the small wooden door that led out of the loft. Myra followed as they descended the stairs. He held the rickety railing while carefully treading on the ancient wooden steps. At the bottom, Fitzgerald locked the door behind them and led Myra to the large, dark wooden doors at the front of the Basilica. He pushed the centre one open and walked out onto the snow-covered terrazzo. The door closed silently behind them. Traffic hummed up and down Harvey Road. A drunk from the nearby soup kitchen staggered across the parking lot, stopped in front of the statue of the Virgin Mary for a break, then continued stumbling toward the road. Myra put on his sunglasses and noticed the top of the Masonic Temple sticking out behind a crop of trees.

"Have you ever been to the Masonic Temple on Cathedral Street?"

"Many times."

Myra turned to face him. "Why?"

"It's part of the Ecclesiastic Circle." The scholarly tone returned to Fitzgerald's voice.

"What is that?"

"This area is an Ecclesiastical District National Historic Site of Canada." Fitzgerald's words formed a cloud around his face when his breath hit the cold air. "The official Ecclesiastic Circle includes this Basilica," he said, pointing down the hill toward the spires reaching up to the sky, "St. Andrew's Presbyterian Church, also known as the Kirk, Gower Street United Church, and the Anglican Cathedral of St. John the Baptist."

Myra tried to map out the churches in his mind. "Where does the Masonic Temple fall into the circle?"

"It's the lost cathedral. It's in the circle but not officially part of it. So is the old Congregational Church on Gower Street, which is now an apartment building."

"Why were all these churches built in a circle?" A cold wind cut through Myra's coat. He pulled it tighter. "Religions go to war with each other. Why would they build so closely together?"

"Maybe they're guarding something important." Fitzgerald opened the large wooden door to the Basilica to go inside.

"Like what?"

"Ark of the Covenant, the Holy Grail, the Spear of Destiny." James Fitzgerald smirked as the heavy door began closing behind him. "It's your job to find out."

The rawness of the winter wind forced Myra to run to his car. Before getting in, he took another look around. He had gone to school a block from here. He grew up a twenty-minute run south of here. He worked five minutes from here. But not once had he ever noticed the churches that formed a circle in front of him.

"What are they protecting?" he asked out loud. "And would they kill for it?"

11

Cst. Donna Whiffen sat across from her lawyer's desk, nervously glancing at her husband, Steve, sitting beside her. Brad Wicks's expensive downtown office was afforded by his thirty-year legal career and reputation for fighting the good fight and, when necessary, fighting the dogfights. Wicks sat behind his large oak desk, continuously pushing his thick glasses up the bridge of his nose.

"You're going to have to apply for legal guardianship."

"Legal guardianship?" Donna looked at Steve. "He's our son."

"Once Jack turned eighteen, he became an adult, and you have to apply to the court to get legal guardianship." Wicks nodded in appreciation of their frustration. "I understand how you feel, but this law is in place to protect those who can't protect themselves."

The worry lines around Whiffen's face grew deeper. "It's just one more damn thing. I feel like I'm drowning in autism."

The lawyer gave a dull smile. "I can't tell you I know what you're going through, but I can tell you that I have helped other families like yours go through this process."

Steve looked at his watch. "Donna, let's just do what he says. I'm exhausted, and Mom can only stay with Jack until five thirty."

"I'm just so frustrated." A deep sadness etched its way into

Donna's face. "We're his parents. Why do we have to ask the court if we can continue taking care of him? They certainly didn't care about him before."

"Donna, I've had two hours sleep. Come on. He has to eat at five thirty. We have to get through this."

"So, why do we need legal guardianship? Wouldn't power of attorney be easier?" she asked the lawyer.

"No." Wicks pushed his glasses up the bridge of his nose again. "To get power of attorney, Jack would have to have the capacity to give it to you, which he doesn't. Legal guardianship gives you the ability to make all decisions for him."

She sniffed back her anger. "Okay. What do we have to do?"

"I'll fill out the forms and apply by proxy. We have to prove that he has a lifelong disability, and he is unable to speak, read, or write."

Steve took an envelope out of his coat pocket and slid it across Wicks's desk. "Here are the letters from Jack's pediatrician and neurologist detailing his condition."

"Couldn't we just bring him before the judge?" Donna gestured helplessly with her hands. "All he has to do is spend five minutes with Jack to know how unnecessary this is."

"We won't need to do that." Wicks opened the envelope and pulled out the letters. "It would take months to get a court date. We can do this by proxy."

"Why would we take him into a courtroom?" Steve turned toward his wife, the muscles tense in his face. "He has sensory issues. He can't go into a place like that without having a meltdown. Is that what you want? You want him to have a meltdown so the judge can have pity on us?"

"That's not what I'm saying," Donna replied cryptically. "Every day, dirtbags go before judges. But I have to wait months to get my own son a court date."

"So, you want to treat him like a criminal?" Steve rose from his chair and paced irritably in front of the large window overlooking downtown St. John's.

"Stop twisting my words." Donna crossed her legs and turned away from him. "You know what I mean, Steve. Do I have to quit my job to raise my child?"

He turned around. "No. I did that, remember? You get to go to work every day and drink hot coffee and eat doughnuts."

"Is that what you think I do all day?" Donna slapped the arms of the chair. "I spend my days investigating murders to get away from the stress at home."

"Steve." The lawyer's voice was calm. "Please sit back down." He turned to Donna. "This is not helpful. I know this is stressful, but I'll make it as easy as I can."

Steve reluctantly returned to his chair. "I'm sorry." He rubbed his temples. "Jack suffers from insomnia. He stays up all night crying and having meltdowns. I'm sleep-deprived. I shouldn't have had an outburst like that."

Wicks waved his hands at him. "Don't worry about it. Let's just focus on the paperwork." He pulled a long form out of a folder. "Can he talk at all?"

"No." Donna Whiffen's voice was shaking. "He can't speak. He does have some non-verbal ways of communicating, but unless you know him very well, it's hard to pick up on it. It's very subtle."

"Okay." Wicks scribbled something on the form. "Do you have any support?"

"No." Whiffen looked at her husband, the colour drained from her face. "Just me and Steve. It's not like we can get the kid next door to come babysit. We need someone who is trained to deal with a person with autism. Jack is almost six feet tall and a hundred and fifty pounds. When he has a meltdown, you have to know how to restrain him properly without hurting him."

"The one good thing his eighteenth birthday brings," Steve offered, "is respite workers through Community Health Services and a little funding through social assistance."

"Will that help?" Wicks laid his pen down.

"The extra money will help. I had to quit my job years ago to take care of Jack. Donna had medical benefits and a pension that I didn't, so it made more sense for me to stay home. A respite worker will give me a break from the physical and emotional demands of taking care of Jack. Right now, I can't even go for a walk." Steve looked at Donna, his eyes filled with sadness. "We can't go out for supper. We haven't gone away for a night alone in eighteen years."

Donna leaned on the arm of her chair, rubbing her temples. "It's the little things, you know. My boss's wife is organizing a Christmas lunch for our unit, and everyone's bringing their kids. They don't realize that Jack can't sit down in a restaurant. He has no understanding of how to act in public. To be honest, I can't wait for Christmas to be over."

She covered her face with her hands. Steve reached across and took her hands in his.

"It's hard." The corners of his eyes glistened with tears. "Christmas is hard. We try to tune everything out. Parties, social media. We don't begrudge other families their joy, but watching everybody else's kids opening gifts and doing activities kills us, because we know Jack has never had that and never will."

Donna wiped the back of her hand across her eyes and sat up straight. "Let's get on with it. What do we have to do?"

Wicks picked up his pen again. He glimpsed the gold-framed picture of his son's university graduation on the corner of his desk. He could feel the pain of his client's life. It reminded him of why he became a lawyer. "I'll fill out the rest of this form and send it by proxy to the judge. It should only take a couple of weeks to get it back. The legal guardianship will allow you to speak for Jack in terms of his care. The next thing is a trust fund and to make sure your will is updated."

"Our will?" Donna asked.

"In the event that anything happened to either of you or both of you. Who would take over the care of Jack? Who would handle his money and your estate?" Wicks pulled out another form from the file and handed it to Steve.

"That's our biggest fear." Donna's face fell as she looked at Steve. "My brother says he'll do it, and Steve has a niece who offered."

"Are they capable and trustworthy? I only ask because I've seen this so many times where a family member is put in charge of an incapacitated person's life. Then they drain their account and leave them penniless." Wicks hated having to say that. "I suggest we be very specific with the trust fund rules and make sure it's only used for his care."

Donna blew out a slow breath. "I mean, we're both in good health. I don't think we have to worry about that."

"Donna?" Wicks looked at her over the top of his glasses. "You're a police officer. I don't need to remind you of the dangers of your job."

"I don't work on the street anymore. I'm in an office. I don't have to worry about being injured on the job." She gave an involuntarily shiver. "Just show us where to sign."

"I'll have the paperwork done up, and you can sign everything at the same time." Wicks took his glasses off and laid them on the desk. "I have your last will here. It's pretty much going to be the same with a few slight word changes to reflect Jack's care as an adult, and I'll add in a paragraph about the trust fund."

Steve looked at his watch. "Donna, it's four thirty. It's going to take a half-hour to pick up supper at the drive-through and get home." He turned toward Wicks with the nervous anticipation of knowing what would happen if Jack was taken off his schedule. "He has to eat his hamburger at exactly five thirty."

"I understand." Wicks opened their file and pushed all the forms back in. "I'll finish this, and my secretary will call you when we need your signatures."

"Thank you." Donna stood up and reached for his hand. "Sorry, Brad, about the outburst. I feel bad about that."

He shook her hand with a grin. "You should hear me and my wife go at it. I'm surprised my neighbours haven't called the police on us."

Steve zipped up his winter parka and extended his hand. "We'll pay your bill when we come in to sign, if that's okay."

Wicks shook his hand, the picture of his smiling son in his cap and gown judging him from his expensive oak desk. "There's no charge for updating forms."

12

The sound of a bullet hitting the front window of Doreen and Mortimer Williams's historic home could be heard blocks away. The flash of the bullet leaving the rifle lit up the frozen midnight sky like a streak of lighting. The air took on a thick odour of sulphur with a hint of metal. A plume of blue smoke hid the shooter from view. The sound of breaking glass woke the neighbour's dog. He scrambled to his feet and bolted to the front door, howling. Porch lights quickly came on while curtains were pulled back, and peeking neighbours wiped the sleep from their eyes, all trying to make sense of what they heard.

Doreen Williams and her guest flew to their feet. Thousands of shards of glass glittered as they showered down over the couch in her front room. The white linen drapes flew off their rods in different directions, exposing the room to a flood of cold air. A second shot sent an explosion of ceiling plaster around the room. The vintage chandelier fell to the floor.

The two women bolted out of the living room into the hallway. Their hearts pounded as they crouched down, pressing their backs against the wall. Droplets of blood appeared on their bared arms from the assault of glass fragments. The glass had seemed to fall in slow motion, blanketing the room. Police sirens wailed in the distance, getting closer by the second.

"What the heck was that?" Doreen asked, her voice verging on hysteria.

"I don't know." Flora Pardy hid behind Doreen's broad shoulders as Doreen moved to peer back inside the room. "It sounded like a gunshot."

Within seconds the sound of the crashing glass stopped, and a dull silence hung in the air. The dog next door stopped barking, as if waiting to see what was to happen next. Doreen sat back down.

"Don't move till the police get here." A cold drop trickled down the side of her face. As she wiped it away, she saw little blood streaks on her hands. She looked back at her next-door neighbour, whose skin was clammy and white. Flora was wheezing out prayers, her eyes tightly closed.

A calm came over Doreen as she collected herself. Her pale lips formed a grim line. She grabbed the top of the hall table and pulled herself up. Glass fell from her clothes onto the shiny hardwood. She reached for the door frame and fell against it, grabbing the ornate moulding for support. Her eyes flickered as they tried to adjust. The front window was gone. A frosty wind blew around the curtain, which was hanging on by a string. The room was covered in shards of glass. A gaping hole in the ceiling exposed the beams and insulation. The chandelier had impaled the wooden coffee table. She looked out at the empty street through the hole that used to be her big bay window.

"He's gone."

"Thank God," Flora mumbled.

Flora struggled to stand. Weakness overtook her, and she slipped, sprawling out on the floor. She squealed as glass cut into her knees and the palms of her hands.

"It was him. I told you he's dangerous," Flora whimpered, getting to her feet.

"Shut up." Doreen looked back at her. Flora seemed much weaker to her now. "Shut up," she repeated.

"I told you he'd kill us, but you wouldn't listen." Flora's voice faded as she slumped against a wall.

"I said shut up."

"He's not afraid of you." Flora covered her head as if expecting a blow. "He won't back down."

Doreen spun around and clamped her meaty hand over Flora's face, squeezing it. "I said shut up!"

A heavy knock came at the front door, followed by the voice of a police officer.

"Police, open up."

"What if they caught him? What are we going to say?"

"Shut it." Doreen pushed Flora up against the wall with a warning glance before limping to the front door and opening it. "Officer, thank God you're here."

The two policeman blinked wildly as they observed the two women covered in blood. "Are you okay?" asked one of them.

"Shaken up for sure," Doreen answered, smiling weakly.

"Has anyone been hurt?"

"No, the bullets hit the ceiling."

"Are you the only ones in the house?"

"Yes."

The officer turned to his partner. "We need two ambulances."

Doreen moved back to allow the officer to come in.

"Are you okay?" He shone a small penlight into her eyes.

"I think so." Doreen caught a glimpse of herself in the hall mirror. "I don't think anything is broken."

He looked at the shaking woman leaning up against the wall. She was holding her bleeding palm. "Ma'am, are you okay?"

Flora nodded but said nothing.

The police officer rushed over to her, shining the light in her eyes. "Can you speak?"

Flora nodded again, but no words came out.

"You're in shock." He reached out, grabbed a coat from a hook behind the door, and wrapped it around her shoulders. "You're trembling. The ambulance is on the way."

Flora only nodded and kept her eyes cast down.

The officer turned around to investigate the front room. His patrol boots crunched the glass underfoot as he shone the flashlight at the ceiling and stopped at a bullet lodged in a thick beam.

Doreen tried to follow him in for a look. "Thank God it missed us."

"You can't come in here. It's a crime scene now." The officer led her back to the hallway. "You're going to the hospital now for observation, and you'll be interviewed there."

"Did you catch the shooter?"

"Not yet. Officers are searching the area now."

"I can't believe this happened." She ran her fingers though her short grey hair and brushed out the remaining shards of glass.

"Do you know who could have done this?"

Doreen looked back at Flora. "No. I can't think of anyone."

Two ambulances arrived at the same time, their red lights bouncing off every house. A group of neighbours stood on the lawn, trying to look in through the front window. A news van and reporter were setting up across the street.

"Can you walk?" The officer looked out the door at the reporter interviewing a neighbour. "It will be quicker to get you to the ambulance."

"I don't need to go to the hospital." Doreen wiped the blood from her face with the sleeve of her sweatshirt.

"Yes, you do. You have quite a gash on your forehead. You're going to need stitches."

She looked into the hall mirror and realized he was right. "I didn't know I was cut that bad."

The officer held Flora by the elbow and led her to the front door. "Let me help you." She silently allowed him to lead her out of the house.

Ambulance attendants met them on the walkway and escorted the two women to the waiting ambulances.

"Can you tell me what happened, Mrs. Williams?" the reporter shouted, the light from her camera blinding Doreen. Doreen raised her hand to block the light from her face.

The police officer moved in front of the camera. "We can't comment right now. The RNC's investigation is in its preliminary stages. Please respect the police line and leave the victims alone."

Another officer dragged a yellow caution tape roll around the perimeter of the property and tied it to fence posts and trees as other officers moved into position to guard the scene.

Doreen and Flora sat on the back steps of their ambulances as they were assessed.

"Flora," Doreen said, pointing to a man standing on the lawn next door.

Flora looked up. "Art." Her voice faded. "Art. I'm okay." She waved frantically as she tried to stand, then fell backward. The ambulance attendant caught her and helped her back down. "That's my husband. Can you tell him I'm okay?"

"Yes, ma'am. You stay there now. I'll ask one of the officers to talk to him."

The attendant wrapped a blanket around Flora's shoulders before asking a nearby constable to bring her husband over. Flora watched the uniformed officer approach her husband and have a brief conversation. The officer turned and went back to his post. Art sauntered toward the ambulance.

"Ya all right?" Art pushed his hands into the front pockets of his old khaki pants. The stubble of an unkempt beard framed his ashen face.

Flora's eyes darted about, then flitted back to her husband. She reached up and grabbed the lapel of his red checked flannel shirt.

"Was it you?"

Art pulled away from her. "Seriously? You're asking me that?"

"Art, this has to stop."

"I'm not stupid enough to go to jail for you or that bitch." He nodded toward Doreen. "Call me if you need a ride from the hospital."

Art pushed his way through the crowd toward their house. Flora watched him close the front door without looking back.

"Mrs. Pardy?" The ambulance attendant brought her back to the present. "We're going to help you lie down on the stretcher now to transport you to the hospital. Are you ready to move?"

Flora pulled the blanket around her shoulders. "Yes."

"Flora. I'll see you at the hospital, Flora," Doreen called.

Flora's face was blank, and her hands shook as they grasped the safety bars on the ambulance. Two attendants helped hoist her inside and onto the stretcher. She could still hear Doreen yelling her name. "Please close the doors. I'm cold."

"Of course," the attendant agreed. "You're still in shock. I'll put more blankets over you." He cocooned her in white woolly blankets, then strapped her in.

"Does that feel better?"

A tear escaped Flora's right eye and slid down to her ear. "I don't think anything will ever feel better again."

13

The Basilica of St. John the Baptist is perched on a high point overlooking the downtown section of St. John's at the head of the Ecclesiastical District. The snowbanks surrounding it reflected a brilliant light on its grey limestone, obtained from Kelly's Island, Conception Bay, and white granite quarried in Galway and Dublin, Ireland. Each rock had been hauled to its final resting place on the backs of Irish Catholic immigrants and the people of Newfoundland between 1838 and 1855. Built in the shape of a Latin Cross, the building was once the largest of its kind in North America. Today it is the mother church and symbol of Roman Catholicism in Newfoundland.

James Fitzgerald spread the large map of downtown St. John's across the wooden table in his office, keeping the rolled corners down with empty coffee cups. He stood back to admire his work. His large office was tucked away inside the Basilica above the Marian Chapel overlooking the Presentation Mother House. Three walls were covered by floor-to-ceiling bookshelves filled with antique books, small religious statues, historical documents, and any number of collectible knick-knacks that only a church historian would understand.

The aroma of freshly brewed coffee floated around the room, temporarily overpowering the damp, musty church smell. The sound of footsteps coming up the stairs informed him that his guest had arrived.

"Good Jesus, you couldn't find an office deeper inside this place?" Tom Miller huffed and puffed, leaning against the doorway.

"It's a historical building." Fitzgerald spoke with a natural enthusiasm. "Come in. Sit down. I have coffee on, but I can boil the kettle if you want tea."

"Not yet. I need to catch my breath." Miller held on to the back of a chair and sat down. He spread his knees and dropped his arm on the table across the map, much to Fitzgerald's dismay.

"Supposed to be another heavy snowfall tonight?" Fitzgerald ran his hands over the map, smoothing out invisible wrinkles.

"I can feel it in my knees." Miller rubbed his hands over his kneecaps.

Fitzgerald drew a deep breath. "Before we discuss the map, as Masons we should discuss Morty."

Miller finally noticed the map across the table. "Why?"

"Because he was the staunchest opponent to this project, and that Insp. Myra is going to find it out soon enough."

"How's he going to find it out?" Miller grumbled. "It's just a game. A bit of fun."

"He may not see it that way."

"It's a treasure hunt, for God's sake," Miller said gruffly.

"Morty was dead set against us seeing that map and the contents of the cornerstone from the Temple. Everyone knew that." Fitzgerald watched him closely. "As a past Master, you should have access to that map."

"They didn't show it to me. According to all the information I could find, it only contains some newspapers from 1894, some coins, and a gold watch. There's no mention of a map."

Fitzgerald grinned sheepishly. "Tom, you and I both know we haven't spent months doing this research to find some old newspapers, coins, and a watch. If our research is right, what we find could change the world. That map is there. I know it."

Miller cocked one eyebrow. "Will this make us rich?"

"And famous," Fitzgerald added. "You have no idea what this will do for my career."

Miller scratched his bald head. "What about me?"

"Well, of course you. But I'm the historian. I'm the one with the knowledge."

"Yeah, and I'm the one with the Masonic knowledge. As a past Grand Master, I should be the spokesperson."

"Of course. Now, can we just get on with it?"

"Did you talk to Myra yet?" Miller pried.

"Yes. Of course I did. I know you did, too."

"I had to give him a tour of the Temple. What did he want with you?"

Fitzgerald shrugged. "He had some questions about the Basilica's windows, that's all. Did you bring him to the basement?"

Miller shifted in his seat. "No, I only showed him around the main floor and the old Temple upstairs. I told him downstairs was just offices, but I'm sure they already searched it. Apparently Morty died upstairs in the Chamber of Reflection."

Fitzgerald's jaw dropped. "He died in the Chamber of Reflection? Are you sure?"

"Pretty sure." Miller looked at him curiously.

"You didn't mention anything about the hidden staircase, did you?"

Miller looked chagrined. "No, I didn't. And you still haven't answered my question. What did he want with you?"

"I told you." Fitzgerald looked toward the stained glass window in his office. "He wanted to know about our stained windows."

"Window?" Miller asked. "Why would Myra want to know about a window?"

"Not window, Tom. Stained glass windows. We have an exceptional collection."

Miller rolled his eyes. "Why did the cop want to see them?"

"Strange, really." Fitzgerald folded his arms. "He wanted to see the Immaculate Conception window. Remember? I showed you that one when I took the Masons on a tour of the Basilica a few weeks ago."

Miller only nodded.

"Morty was on that tour, too." Fitzgerald tapped his index finger on his lips. "That's right. You two were arguing about something. What was it?"

"I'm his accountant. We're always arguing. But that day we were discussing when he wanted me to take his picture as the Grand Master."

"There was something going on between you and Morty." Fitzgerald pointed an accusatory finger at him. "Is that why he wouldn't show us the map?"

"You're one to talk. You hated him."

"But I didn't pretend I liked him." Fitzgerald gave his friend a slow once-over. "He was a bit of a mentor for you, wasn't he? Then something went wrong. What was it?"

"I don't know what you're talking about." Miller jumped out of the chair. "Are we going to look at this map or not? You said you had some exciting news. What is it?"

Fitzgerald kept his eyes on Miller for a few seconds longer before turning them to the map. "I guess we should get on with it. I do have exciting news." He leaned over the map. "What I found is that we're looking in the wrong place."

"What do you mean?"

"We thought the treasure was buried inside the Masonic Temple." Fitzgerald pointed at the downtown section. "But I believe we were wrong."

"Then where is it?"

Fitzgerald ran his fingers over the map. "This is the Ecclesiastic Circle. This Basilica is at the head. Then it goes to the Congregational Church here."

"Wait." Miller leaned in and squinted at the map. "There's no church there."

"Now it's an apartment building. But in 1895, it was the Congregational Church. Years ago, it was turned into an apartment building."

"Okay."

"Then, over here, it's the Masonic Temple, the Anglican Cathedral, Gower Street United, and then St. Andrew's, also known as the Kirk. Then back to the Basilica. It's a full circle. Every one of these buildings has Masonic and Knights Templar symbolism in it."

"So, that's the Ecclesiastic Circle, is it?" Miller traced the circle with his index finger.

"Yes, but what I discovered is that if we take the Masonic Symbol of the dot within the circle, we get a very different map."

Fitzgerald lifted the corner of the map and pulled out a piece of tracing paper with the symbol on it. He laid it over the map.

"Look at this. The lines on either side of the circle represent St. John the Evangelist and St. John the Baptist, the two Masonic patron saints. The point in the middle represents an individual Brother. The circle represents the boundary line of a man's duty to God and his fellow man. A man should not stray beyond this circle. He should not let his selfish interests, passions, and other things make him stray."

"I know this," Miller retorted. "I was a Grand Master."

"What I am saying is we strayed outside the circle."

"No, we didn't. How?"

"According to this symbol, the Temple is part of the circle and not where the treasure is buried. The dot in the middle is where the Sergeants' Memorial is, in Veteran's Square. Don't forget, the circle with a dot in the middle is also the ancient symbol for gold."

Miller studied the tracing paper covering the map. "Was there a church there?"

"No." Fitzgerald tapped his finger on the map. "Back in the 1700s, it was the site of a whipping post. That ground is soaked with the blood of hundreds of Irish immigrants."

"Why would they bury it there?"

"Because it was a field in the centre of the circle. They could have easily buried it there." Fitzgerald took out a picture of the memorial. "Someone else knows it's there, too. I believe that's why they built a memorial on top of it."

"You're crazy."

"Look. The Sergeants' Memorial was unveiled on July 1, 1921." Fitzgerald pointed to the Cross at the centre of the memorial. "It's made up of two pieces. A large Cross that was sourced from Edinburgh, Scotland, at the end of the First World War."

Tom Miller's mouth fell open. "It was the Scottish Lodge."

"That's what I think," Fitzgerald answered eagerly. "The stone on the bottom is Newfoundland granite. They bought the Cross sometime around 1919, but it wasn't installed until 1921."

Miller examined the carvings on the monument. "You think it's under that stone?"

"I do." Fitzgerald stood up straight. "It's the safest place in the world. You can't dig there. It's a sacred place. It's constantly surrounded by military and police. And it's guarded by the Ecclesiastic Circle. If we can find the entrance to a tunnel, we can get to it."

"The tunnels are an urban legend."

"They're not. I think the entrance is through the hidden staircase in the Temple."

Miller stared at the map a long time. "I don't know."

"Tell me, where else in the world will you find that many churches of different religions happily co-existing in a circle?" Fitzgerald tapped the centre of the circle. "It's got to be there. It's the only place that makes sense."

"I don't know." Miller picked up the picture. "What about the lines on either side of the circle?"

"The St. John the Evangelist line on the left runs through George Street United on Buchanan Street, and the St. John the Baptist line on the right runs through St. Thomas' Church on Military Road."

"That's stretching it."

"Not really." Fitzgerald turned the tracing paper around. "They're outside the circle but perfectly in line with this diagram."

"What do we do now?" Miller asked. "We can't dig there."

"We can't now that there's a cop car parked outside the Masonic Temple." Fitzgerald paced in front of a huge stained glass window. "I have a plan."

"What is it?"

"We may be able to get permission to go over the land with ground-penetrating radar. I've researched it. I can create some historical reason why we need it done."

"You'll never get permission. There are Masons in all levels of government. They'll block it."

"No, not if we're just looking for the ancient footprint of an old church."

"What church?"

"I don't know yet." Fitzgerald turned to face him. "Morty's death is throwing a wrench into this."

"Do you know who killed him?" Miller asked softly.

Fitzgerald was caught off guard. "I have my suspicions."

"Was it you?" Miller stared blankly at him.

"No," Fitzgerald answered in disgust. "Was it you?"

"No." Miller rubbed the stubble around his chin. "You know what that means?"

"What?" Fitzgerald's eyebrows were knitted in thought.

Miller looked down at the symbol laid over the Ecclesiastic Circle.

"It means that someone else is on to us."

14

A search of Mortimer Williams's bank account told Cst. Whiffen where he ate his last meal but not with whom. A hum of happy lunchtime chatter filled the fish-and-chip shop on Freshwater Road. The air swirled with the smell of deep-fried fish and crispy fries. A short, chubby-cheeked woman wearing an aged, white cook's uniform and a paper wedge hat greeted Cst. Whiffen at the counter with a smile.

"What can I get ya?"

"I'm looking for Rosie Walsh."

"Oh, that's me." The woman wiped her hands in the apron that hung around her neck. "You're the constable who called, are ya?"

"Yes." Whiffen extended her hand. "Is there a place where we can talk?"

"Sure." Rosie called back to another employee. "Ann, take the cash, please."

Rosie led Whiffen to a tiny back office that was covered in a permanent sheen of grease. Stacks of restaurant supplies were poked in any available space around the room.

"Sorry about the mess." Rosie moved a bag of plastic forks so Whiffen could sit. "We're always so busy."

Whiffen looked down at the grimy seat. "That's okay. I'll stand."

"All right." Rosie clapped her hands together. "What's this all about? Is it one of the employees?"

"No." Whiffen closed the office door. "I see you have a video surveillance system around the outside of the store."

"Oh, yes. Ya gotta have that these days. They'd rob us blind if we didn't." Rosie didn't have an issue with giving out too much information. "We have a robbery here once a month. We call you guys almost every day. I mean, you're basically across the street."

"Do you have a video inside?" Whiffen interrupted. "Around the tables?"

"Yes, ya got to these days." Rosie moved a box of plates off her desk and revealed a laptop hooked up to a security system showing a view of the cameras pointed randomly around the business.

"Rosie, I am doing an investigation that doesn't really involve your restaurant." Whiffen glanced toward the security system. "But you may have video that could help me solve this case. Would you mind if I go through your backup video? I can get a warrant if you'd prefer."

Rosie's mouth drooped like a sad child. "My God. Yes, girl. Go ahead. Here." She pulled up a chair that looked slightly cleaner than the other. "Take a seat and do your job. Do you need me to show you how it works?"

"No, I can do it." Whiffen sat down and picked up the mouse. "Thanks for doing this. It's a real help to me. If I find what I'm looking for, is it okay if I copy it and email it to myself?"

"Yes, of course, girl. Do what you got to do. There's no sound on the cameras."

"Thanks." Whiffen locked eyes with her, then glanced at the door.

Rosie took the hint. "I must get goin' now. You don't need me over your shoulder."

When she was alone, Whiffen turned to the video history on the laptop. She scrolled back to the night Mortimer Williams was murdered. She toggled down to 6:00 p.m. and carefully watched each screen. Leaning her elbow on the grimy desk, she cupped her chin in her hand as she watched.

People entered and exited the restaurant every minute. She slowed down the camera and zoomed in each time a male walked onscreen. She scanned each for any signs of Williams. The 6:30 p.m. mark hit, and a slight man in a dressy black overcoat pulled at the handle on the front door. He stood inside looking around, turning a small gold ring on his right hand. Whiffen stopped the video for a closer look.

The man was tall and slender with greying hair. He took off his overcoat to reveal a white shirt, black tie, and suit. He typed something into his phone. Cst. Whiffen zoomed in on his face. It was without a doubt Mortimer Williams.

Mortimer went to the counter and placed an order. He paid with a credit card, then took a seat in a dark corner. Moments later, another man entered the restaurant wearing grubby blue coveralls. He ran a hand over his sparse hair and looked around. Spotting Williams, he gave a slight wave and headed toward the table in the back. Williams rose from his chair and hugged the man.

Shortly after they sat down, a waitress brought two orders of fish and chips. The two men spoke excessively with their heads close together. Each kept glancing around the room to ensure privacy.

At 7:20 p.m., they rose, hugged again, and walked slowly toward the front door. Outside, Williams and the man in coveralls walked to their respective vehicle. Mortimer took out his phone and appeared to respond to a text. He turned and headed out of view.

The man with the coveralls opened the door of a black pickup truck parked just down from the restaurant. Whiffen froze the screen and zoomed in on the logo on the truck's door. She grabbed a pen and notepad from the desk and wrote down *Fix It All Repair Shop*.

Whiffen cut and pasted several sections of the video and emailed them to herself and Myra. She followed the email with a text: Can you meet me at the coffee shop ASAP?

It only took a second for the response: Just pulling into the parking lot of Headquarters. Will meet you there in 5 mins.

15

Cst. Whiffen flipped open the lid of her cup and slid into a seat facing the dining area of the coffee shop. She could see Myra's dark SUV pulling into a parking spot. Two homeless-looking young men smoking outside the door stopped what they were doing and mock-saluted him as he entered the store. He smiled and nodded back. Myra acknowledged Whiffen with a wave, ordered coffee, and sat in the chair across from her. He took the lid off his paper cup and took a long sip of the rich black liquid.

"Ah, I needed that." He picked up a napkin and dabbed at the droplets of coffee under his moustache. "What a day. What a day."

"Did you get my email?" Whiffen bit the corner of her lip and tried to suppress the smile that ran across her face.

"I did, but I haven't opened it yet. Why?" Myra took his phone out of his inside coat pocket and opened his email.

"Play the video." She looked around the coffee shop. "There's no sound."

Myra hit the play button and watched the footage with great interest. His eyes followed Mortimer Williams into the shop. He watched him order and then sit down. He grinned when the second man entered the restaurant.

"That's Bucky Williams."

"I know. Keep watching."

Myra scrolled through fifty minutes of Bucky and Mortimer eating their meal, then leaving the restaurant.

"What do you make of it?" Whiffen asked.

"Well." Myra closed his email and put his phone back in his pocket. "I think Doreen lied to me about not knowing who Morty was having supper with. I know Bucky lied to me about his contact with his brother. Now I'm wondering if they are in cahoots with each other for the insurance money."

"Doreen made out like a bandit when Bucky's parents died. She's still living in their house. You said Bucky fixed the exhaust on the car days before their deaths. Could he be in on it? Maybe he did those media stories to throw off the investigators."

"A lot to unpack there, isn't it?"

"What were they meeting about, I wonder?" Whiffen sipped her coffee. "They hugged each other several times. But I think Morty seemed stressed."

"I was thinking the same thing. He was looking around a lot." Myra finished his coffee. "Why did Bucky keep hugging him? It was like he was offering him support in some way."

Whiffen nodded. "I think so, too. They certainly didn't seem like they didn't like each other."

"Maybe they reconciled behind Doreen's back."

"But why would they have to hide it from Doreen?"

"I got a call from patrol. Someone shot out the window of Doreen's house last night. She was sitting on the couch with her next-door neighbour when it happened. I was going to head over and have a chat with them next."

Whiffen's phone vibrated. She picked it up and frowned at it. "That's Morgan. Simon is going to do the autopsy this afternoon."

"You don't mind going, do you?" The colour that had drained from Whiffen's face concerned him. "Everybody has to get that first one under their belt."

She regretted drinking the large coffee. "I'm good."

"Are you sure?"

"Yes. I'm good."

"Bill will walk you through it. He's done this a thousand times. You'll be okay."

"I know. I'll be fine." Cst. Whiffen picked up her paper cup and threw it in the garbage. Myra did the same with his and followed her out into the cold air. The two homeless men, still smoking, stood at attention as they walked by.

Myra reached out and shook the hand of the one closest to him, slyly placing a twenty-dollar bill in his palm. "Good to see you boys."

"God bless ya, Inspector." The man held up the money to his friend and flashed a toothless smile. "God bless ya."

The two men happily went inside the restaurant. Whiffen got in her car and drove away.

Insp. Myra sat in his SUV, rewatching the video. Something about it bothered him, but he couldn't put his finger on it. On the fourth viewing, it struck him. He opened an earlier email from Sgt. Morgan listing the items found on Morty's body. The only jewellery listed was a wedding ring.

He looked at the video again. Mortimer Williams was not wearing the Masonic apron, but he was wearing his Masonic ring.

16

Sgt. Bill Morgan plunked his large, black camera bag down on the sterile floor of the autopsy room in the Health Sciences Complex. Cst. Whiffen arrived shortly after, carrying a box of evidence bags and her briefcase. He had anticipated the look of dread on her face.

"It's freezing in here." She shook off a chill.

"They have to keep it cold because it significantly reduces composition. Keep your coat on."

She swallowed hard.

"First time attending an autopsy?"

"Yes."

"Here." Morgan pulled a jar of Vicks VapoRub out of his camera bag and pulled off the lid. "Wipe this under your nose."

"No, thanks." Whiffen pulled back at the strong stench of menthol. "I'm not that cold."

"It's an order." He took a generous dollop and wiped it through his grey moustache. "The menthol is so overpowering that it tricks your brain into thinking that you're breathing better. That way you won't smell whatever is coming out of the corpse."

Whiffen apprehensively dug her finger in and rubbed the

thick, clear cream under her nose. She flinched at the strong smell. "Does this really work?"

"You tell me once Simon takes Mortimer's large intestine out and weighs it." Morgan picked up his bag and pushed open the door. Whiffen dragged her feet behind him.

A petite woman wearing a white medical coat over green scrubs wheeled a stretcher into the room. On top of it lay Mortimer Williams's body inside a zipped-up black body bag. She parked it next to the autopsy table. The aluminum table was tilted slightly, with raised edges and several faucets.

"Hi, Bill, good to see you again." The woman held up a blue rubber-gloved hand and gave a small wave to Whiffen. "I'm Karen, Simon's assistant."

"Nice to meet you. I'm Donna."

"Simon is finishing his lunch. He'll be along shortly." Karen went about getting ready for the autopsy.

"What are they for?" Whiffen asked, pointing to the drains.

Morgan crouched down over his camera bag and began to unload his equipment. "To drain away any fluid or blood that comes out during the internal investigation."

Whiffen could feel the coffee coming back up her throat.

The doors swung open, and Simon entered, eating the remains of a ham sandwich. "Bill, good to see you again." He wiped his hands in a napkin and extended one to Morgan. "And who do we have here?"

Morgan turned to Whiffen. "This is Cst. Donna Whiffen. She's new in Myra's unit. This is her first autopsy, so I'll be giving her some instructions as we go. If you want to jump in at any point, feel free."

"Jolly good." Simon readily shook her hand. "Quite interesting work we do in here. It's the side of investigations that very few people get to see up close. You'll learn so much. I guarantee it."

Whiffen could feel the blood draining from her face. "I'm looking forward to it."

"Just a few rules," Simon said as he scrubbed his hands in the sink. "Everyone gets a little woozy the first time. No shame in that. If you feel like you're going to hit the floor, sit down and put your head between your knees."

He pointed to a grey plastic chair. "Karen, can you move that behind the constable, please?"

His assistant moved the chair closer to Whiffen.

"Have you met Karen?" Simon's glasses swung on a cord around his neck, and he perched them on the tip of his nose. "Yes? Good. She will undo the body bag and get ready to move Mr. Williams to the table."

Morgan moved to the foot of the table and glanced at Whiffen. "My job is to photograph the body as it was brought here, untouched, and then every step along the way. I get one chance and one chance only to document the evidence collected at each autopsy. These photos may be used in court. As the investigator, you will take control of the exhibits. You have to make sure each item of clothes is bagged separately and tagged."

Whiffen's throat dried as she breathed in the smell of Vicks and disinfectant.

Karen unzipped the bag and pulled it open. Mortimer Williams's cold body lay lifeless on the stretcher, still dressed in his expensive suit and Masonic uniform. His grey hands were covered in paper bags. A foul odour escaped into the room.

Simon took out a small, black voice recorder and laid it at the top of the table. "We are now recording. Go ahead."

Karen began her analysis.

"I confirm that the body bag was new when the victim was put in it. There is no chance of cross-contamination."

She picked up his arm.

"Both hands are wrapped in paper bags to preserve any evidence that may be collected from them."

The click of Morgan's camera echoed in the sterile room.

She peeled back the body bag from Mortimer. "The body is ready to move."

Simon snapped on blue rubber gloves and tied a protective paper robe around himself. He laid two paper robes on the chair. "Put this on," he instructed the officers. "This could be messy."

Morgan and Whiffen quickly tied their robes around themselves. Whiffen pulled out the evidence bags and stood ready to document the crime.

"All right." Simon stood at the head of Mortimer. "Let's get this bloke on the table."

With expert precision, Simon and Karen lifted the body from the stretcher to the autopsy table in one swift move. Karen slipped the bag off the table and handed it to Whiffen. "Constable Whiffen has taken control of the body bag," she said near the tape recorder.

Whiffen carefully folded the body bag and sealed it inside an evidence bag.

Simon lifted the Masonic collar off Mortimer's shoulders, speaking loudly for the recorder. As he documented each item, he handed it to Whiffen. "Let's do the contents of his pockets."

Next, he handed Whiffen a set of keys, some change, and a small ornate pillbox. Morgan photographed each item. He stared at the pillbox for a moment and carried on.

Simon smirked as his eyes darted between Morgan and Whiffen. "Is that Vicks I smell? Works like a charm."

Morgan kept his eye on the camera lens as he snapped away, knowing Simon liked to have a little too much fun with new constables who ventured into his autopsy room.

"I have always believed that the first time a constable attends one of my autopsies they should experience the bloody well full extent of it." He untied Mortimer's Mason apron and passed it to Whiffen. "You need to smell it so you don't forget what it smells like."

Whiffen only grinned as she bagged the apron.

"He's been locked in the freezer for two weeks, so you won't smell much until I open his chest cavity." He casually looked toward Whiffen. "Constable, are you okay?"

Whiffen felt herself swaying. She forced herself to focus on a spot on the wall behind Simon's head. "I'm good. Don't worry about me."

"Remember the days when you used film, Bill?" Simon continued to undress the corpse. "My goodness, the rolls you used to go through."

"Everything's digital now." Morgan continued to focus on his work. "Makes it a lot easier. I remember having to mark every roll and hope that I got the best pictures."

They continued their banter as if a dead man weren't on the table in front of them.

"Remember that one punter who went arse over tits down Kenna's Hill during a winter's night?" Simon let out a loud chuckle. "Rolled right into the graveyard and into an open grave. The caretaker thought he had kicked his way out of a coffin."

Morgan took the camera away from his eye to laugh. "Yes. He was there for three days, wasn't he?"

"He wasn't even frozen when I got him. His blood alcohol level was five times the legal limit." The crow's feet around Simon's eyes creased into deep lines each time he smiled.

"I always wondered if they cremated him." Morgan's tone was as casual as if he were in the office. "It would have taken a week to get the fire out with the amount of alcohol in him."

The two men continued their chatter, to Whiffen's great relief. She forced herself to swallow repeatedly to prevent herself from throwing up and was happy to be left out of the conversation. Half an hour passed before Mortimer Williams lay on the cold autopsy table wearing only his underwear and an undershirt.

"There's no reason to expose his willy," Simon explained to Whiffen. "I would only expose the genitals in the case of a sexual assault. Let's allow the man to keep his dignity."

Simon continued to work with Karen to weigh and measure the corpse. As Whiffen concentrated on her notetaking, she forgot about her initial apprehension and focused on her work. Karen wheeled over a small steel table containing an arrangement of needles. Simon drew several vials of blood, explaining each one as he went. Whiffen moved in closer to the body and realized she was becoming incredibly interested in what they were doing.

"So, what will you be checking for in his blood?"

"I'm checking for any irregularities in his system such as over-the-counter prescription and illicit drugs, as well as alcohol and other toxicants, such as metals, inhalants, environmentals like pesticides, insecticides, carbon monoxide, cyanide, and other possible toxins and poisons. I'll run the full gamut on him because we suspect he is a victim of homicide. I took some blood when he first came in, too."

The medical examiner moved to the top of the table. Karen handed him a clipboard with a sheet of paper attached to it. It had the outline of a male's body drawn on it.

"I'm going to check him over for things like bruises, scratches, blunt force trauma, wounds of any nature that may have led to his death. Then I mark it on this diagram for the file, and Bill here will photograph it while you write it down. Let me look at his hands before you fingerprint him."

Karen took the paper bags off Mortimer's hands and handed them to Whiffen to bag.

Simon closely examined Mortimer's hands. "No defensive wounds at all. Not even a hangnail." He looked at his assistant. "Scrape him."

Karen dutifully scraped the underside of his fingernails with a pick-like tool and spread the contents on a cardboard handprint for Whiffen to bag. Morgan photographed the front and back of each hand, then set up the fingerprint kit.

"You still fingerprint him even though he's the victim?" Whiffen asked.

Morgan carefully rolled each finger on the card. "It's done for a number of reasons. It could be how we identify a victim. Or if they had a criminal record, we would send the prints to Ottawa to have the person removed from the national system."

"Interesting, isn't it?" she asked.

"Yes, it is," Morgan agreed. "Very interesting."

"Okay, let's start the examination." Simon stood over the corpse and examined his head. "There is a large bump on the back of his head, big as an egg. There's a very small cut on it, but I don't think it would have bled much. He is clean-shaven, and there's no noticeable trauma to his face. He has dark circles under his eyes consistent with a concussion. Let's continue."

Simon lifted the white undershirt up over Mortimer's chest and looked at his torso. "No stab or gunshot wounds. Looks like he had a bit of surgery on his chest."

The medical examiner adjusted his stance to look closer. "Pass me the scissors please?" he asked his assistant.

Karen obliged, and he cut the undershirt up the middle, exposing the victim's full chest.

"Is something wrong?" Morgan asked.

"I don't know if something is wrong, but something is definitely not right," Simon answered.

He looked closer at the two lollypop-shaped scars around

Mortimer Williams's nipples. Tilting the victim's head back, he ran his fingers down over the dead man's throat.

Simon stood back from the table and crossed his arms. He looked from Morgan to Whiffen to Karen.

"What is it?" Morgan took his camera away from his face and watched Simon.

"Well, this is a first." The medical examiner moved back to the autopsy table and lifted the waistband on Mortimer Williams's underwear. He took off his glasses and let them dangle from the cord.

The two police officers stood with their mouths hanging open in stunned silence. Simon placed his hands on his hips and looked at them.

"Your *he* started out life as a *she*."

17

Insp. Myra's phone vibrated with an incoming text. He looked down to see Whiffen's name just as Flora opened the front door. He stuffed the phone back into his pocket.

"Yes?" Flora opened the door just a crack, her voice low and weak. Her bandaged hands pulled her white cardigan tighter around her chest. "Can I help you?"

"Mrs. Pardy, I'm Insp. Nick Myra with the RNC Major Crime Section. I would like to talk to you about the shooting."

She looked over her shoulder, then back at Myra. "It's not a good time right now. Can you call me, and we'll set up an appointment?"

Myra placed his hand on the door. "Mrs. Pardy, you're a witness in a shooting. You're required to provide a statement."

The woman looked over her shoulder again, her lips pursed. "I guess you'll have to come in, then." She opened the door wider and stepped back. The sound of daytime TV murmured in the background. "Wipe your boots on the rug."

Flora led him down the hallway to a generously large kitchen with grey cabinets and white marble counters. She pulled out a white leather chair at a long country table that sat twelve. "Do you take tea or coffee? I'll put on both."

"Thank you. I'm fine."

"No, you must have something. I don't want you to think me a bad host."

"I don't need anything," Myra voiced his objection firmly.

Flora busied herself at the counter. "Excuse me while I boil the kettle and make the coffee." She stood on her tiptoes to reach the coffee container. She was a small, thin, shrewish woman with bobbed white hair in a style that had not changed since the 1980s.

Myra made himself comfortable at the kitchen table. He looked around at the woodwork and the large window that overlooked a landscaped backyard. It was the kind of house he wanted for Maria and his daughters, but he knew it would never be in his price range. Flora placed a tray on the table just as her husband entered from the back door, shaking snow from his red-and-black Scotch plaid flannel jacket. Art Pardy was about to say something to his wife but stopped short when he noticed the big man in the black peacoat sitting at his kitchen table.

"Art." Doreen hurried around the kitchen. "This is that detective who's looking into Morty's death. He wants to talk to us about the shooting." She took three cups out of the cupboard and laid them next to the coffee maker. Her breath quickened with each word. "I can't think of your name right now. What did you say it was?"

Myra stood as he spoke and extended his hand to Art. "Insp. Nick Myra."

Art hesitated before taking off a black leather glove and weakly shaking the officer's hand. Myra took out a business card and gave it to him. Art looked at it and tucked it in his pocket, then proceeded to kick off his boots.

"Lay them on the mat, Art," Flora warned. "I don't want water all over the floor. It stains the marble."

Art obeyed and pulled off his black stocking cap to reveal a shock of grey hair with a bald spot on his crown. Doreen gave him a handful of paper towels to wipe the water off his white moustache and long beard. In his stocking feet and suspendered pants, he looked like a gnarled old gnome.

"I want to talk to you about the shooting, but maybe it's a good time to talk about Morty's death, also."

Art darted a worried glance toward Flora before answering. "Not much to say about either."

"The smallest detail sometimes breaks open the biggest cases." Myra tried his best to smile as he sat back down.

Doreen delivered a wooden tray holding three cups of coffee with sugar and cream in fancy crystal containers. She pulled out a chair and curled her feet tightly around the legs.

Art leaned up against a cupboard with his arms crossed, standing in Myra's peripheral vision.

"Do you mind sitting at the table?" Myra pulled out a chair next to him. "It's easier for me to take notes."

Reluctantly, Art sat down with the broody look of a cantankerous old man. He held tight to his wet cap and continuously twirled it in his hands. His gold ring caught Myra's attention.

"You're a Mason?" Myra pointed at the ring.

"Yes."

"When did you join?"

"Years ago."

"Is that where you met Morty?"

"Yes."

Myra took note of Flora's shaking hands as she pushed coffee cups toward him and Art.

"Do you take it black? This is cream." She tilted the crystal jug toward him. "Do you want tin milk? Some people prefer tin milk to fresh or cream. I don't. I like cream. Art says I drink too much coffee, but I love it. Especially when it's so cold outside. This is real crystal."

Art slapped his hat down on the table, sending a jolt into Flora.

"Sorry. I tend to ramble sometimes," she said with a nervous look at her husband.

"That's okay." Myra pulled the cup toward him. "I like it black."

Art tucked his hands under his armpits and leaned back in his chair.

Flora smiled tensely. "So, what can we help you with?"

Myra took out his notebook and clicked his pen. "Flora, you were at Doreen's the night the house was shot at, is that right?"

"Yes. Yes, I was." She picked up a napkin and wiped her forehead. "We were sitting on the sofa in the front room when the window exploded over our heads. Glass went everywhere. Even the next day when I got showered, glass fell out of my hair."

Art cleared his throat, staring at her. She stopped talking.

"You must have been very traumatized." Myra relaxed his shoulders and sat back. "My God, what a fright."

"Honest to God," she said, leaning in toward him, "I thought I was going to die. I mean, getting shot at wasn't something I could ever predict. What a thing to have happen to you. The doctor at the hospital said I was lucky to be alive. He was such a nice doctor, too. He checked on me all night. He was so worried."

Arts voice was gruff and quick. "That's the doctor's job."

Flora stopped talking.

"Well, you're safe now. Just to be clear, I want to explain that I'm with the Major Crime Unit, and we investigate serious crime. That includes events like the death of Mr. Williams and shootings. That's why I'm here today."

"Very good." She continued to dot her cleavage with the napkin. "Morty was a nice man. I mean, not my kind, but he was sweet. You're quite handsome, too. You look like a cop. I suppose you get that all the time with your moustache and height. Are you married?"

Art kept his eyes cast down on the tabletop and loudly cleared his throat.

Myra looked at Flora's bandaged palms. "Are you okay? You were pretty cut up."

"The cuts on my head and neck weren't big enough for stitches. I do have a few stitches in both palms and one knee. I knew I would need them. I'm a nurse. Retired now. But I understood my own injuries." She turned her leg and tried to lift her pants leg. "Let me show you."

"That's okay, you don't need to show me." Myra gave her a sympathetic look. "I know you're in pain."

"You have no idea." Flora batted her eyes and dramatically waved a hand in front of her face. "The doctor gave me some pain medication and something for my nerves to settle me down. When I take them, I just sleep all day. Which is probably best, anyway. I keep hearing the sound of the bullet hitting the glass."

Art let out a laboured sigh with a look that said *Get on with it.*

"Can you tell me exactly what happened?" Myra reached out and patted her hand.

She released a long, shaky breath through her pursed lips. "Where to start. Where to start." She looked around the room.

"Take your time. If you need to stop, just let me know."

"It's just all a jumble in my mind right now." She ran her fingers through the back of her hair.

"Let's start with why you were at Doreen's house."

Flora gave Art a quick look and inhaled sharply. "Doreen called me. She was upset about losing Morty, so I went over to sit with her."

"Are you and Doreen friends?"

She glanced at Art before answering. "Yes. We've lived next to

each other for two years now. They were here when we moved in."
She picked up a silver spoon and stirred sugar in her cup.

"Flora, my research says that Doreen and Mortimer Williams own this house and you're renting. Is that right?"

The spoon clinked as it hit the table. She looked toward Art again and said nothing.

Art spoke up. "Yes. We're renting. Is that a crime?"

Myra shook his head. "No."

Art went back to staring at the table.

"Flora, let's go back to that night." Myra worked to keep eye contact with her. "What were you talking about while you were sitting on the couch?"

"I can't remember right now. I . . . I think we spoke about Morty's funeral. Yes!" she said decisively. "That's it. We were talking about Morty's funeral."

"Art, were you friends with Doreen and Morty Williams?"

Art blinked as if surprised by the question. "I'd see them from time to time, but I wouldn't say we were good friends. They kept to themselves, and so did we. Ya know, we didn't hang out in the same circles. We were tenants to them."

"Where were you both on the night that Mortimer Williams died?"

Art and Flora looked at each other as if wondering who should speak first.

"We were home," Art answered. "We were watching TV."

Flora nodded in agreement. "That's right, we were home. I wasn't feeling well."

"You weren't?" Myra prodded her.

"No. Woman trouble, if you know what I mean." She rubbed her stomach.

"Very well, then. So, you didn't know the Williamses that well?"

"I wouldn't say that. They invited us to things," Flora said, contradicting what her husband had said.

"Like what?"

"Morty was involved in lots of charity events. Always raising money for something or other. I wanted to go, but Art's not much into being social. Sometimes I'd go by myself." Her face grew sombre. "He was a nice man."

"What kind of events did you go to?"

"I went to a silent auction this past September and bought a lovely purse. Got it at a real deal. There was a gala at the hotel last summer to support something or other. Some choir, I think. One of their friends couldn't go, so they invited us. Art was busy, but I went. Had a ball, too. They were a lot of fun."

She fell silent beneath her husband's stare.

"Flora, did you see who shot through the window?"

"No, my God, no." She raised her bandaged hands to her mouth. "We were sitting with our backs to the window. As soon as it happened, we flew off the couch and ran to the front hall. To tell you the truth, I don't even remember how I got to the hall. The doctor at the hospital said I was in shock. He was such a lovely doctor."

"Yes, of course you were in shock." Myra's tone was calm and sympathetic. "Do you know who did it?"

She looked toward Art as if to ask for permission to speak. "No, of course not. I can't imagine who would do such a thing. A crazy man, I suppose."

"Here's the thing. We have a witness who told us the shooter may have been looking for your house, not Doreen's."

"Who told you that?" Flora asked, her eyes wide.

"A neighbour turned in some video surveillance footage from his doorbell camera. It showed a man watching your house earlier that night. He was also spotted outside after you walked over to Doreen's." Myra sat back and let the information sink in.

Art's stare lingered on Flora. She kept her eyes on the table but said nothing.

"He had other footage that showed the same man pounding on your door earlier in the week," Myra continued.

"I don't remember any man coming around," said Flora, shaking her head.

"I have a picture." Myra opened his phone and noticed several texts from Whiffen. He held up a still frame from the video. It showed a blurry image of a man wearing a winter coat with a stocking cap pulled down around his ears. "Does he look familiar?"

Flora gave the photo a quick look. "No."

Art leaned over to see it. "No. Don't know him."

Myra put his phone in his pocket and felt it vibrate again. "Do you know anything about Morty's death? Remember, the smallest detail could have a huge value to me as the investigator."

"No." Flora's eyes widened. "I don't know anything about that. Truly, I don't."

"What about you, Art?"

Art's shoulders tensed. His voice was a low growl. "No."

"I'm still having nightmares about the whole thing," Flora blurted. "I mean Morty's death. Being shot at. It's all too much for me. The doctor was so lovely. Did I tell you that? You're quite lovely, too. Are you married?"

"You've been through a very traumatic event." Myra looked between the two. "What you're feeling is completely normal. This was a terrible crime. I'm sorry it happened to you."

"You have no idea." Flora tutted toward her husband. "Art says I should get over it, but he wasn't there. He doesn't know how frightened I was. I think about it all the time. Would you like some cookies? I can't believe I didn't offer you a bite to eat. That's so unlike me. Are you hungry? You remind me of that doctor." A glazed look came over her face. "That doctor reminded me of our son,

Michael. You remind me of him, too. He'll be home from school soon. Do you want a cookie?"

Myra gave her a friendly smile. "No. I'm good. But thank you so much for offering. You're very kind."

"And you are so nice. Are you sure you don't want something to eat? It's no bother."

"No, thank you." He patted her hand again before taking another business card out of his pocket and laying it on the table. "Flora, if you or Art think of anything, don't hesitate to call me. Remember, the smallest detail could be of the utmost importance. I suspect, as you think back over this terrible event, you may recall more details."

"Do you think so?" She picked up the business card and ran her finger over the raised phone number.

"Yes, of course, it happens all the time."

The phone in Myra's pocket vibrated several times, indicating a phone call was coming in. He looked down, annoyed, but didn't answer.

"I've kept you long enough." He stood and reached across the table to Art. "Thank you. I'll let you get back to your snow clearing."

Art barely touched Myra's hand and let out a gruff goodbye, then tucked his hands back under his armpits.

Flora led Myra out to the front door. She looked up at his broad shoulders and tall stance. "Mind your head." She laughed as he walked through the doorway.

The woman leaned against the open door frame, fanning herself with his business card. "I'll call you if I think of anything."

"Please do."

He looked toward Doreen's house next door. The front window was boarded up, and police tape was still tied around the trees in front. He caught someone peeking out from behind the curtain in the dining room window. Just as quickly, the person was gone.

Myra headed toward Doreen's house with the intention of interviewing her next. His phone vibrated again. This time he fished it out of his pocket and looked at the screen.

Donna Whiffen flashed across his screen.

"Hello."

"Why didn't you answer me? I've been texting and calling for an hour."

"Because I'm in an interview," he said sternly. "If I don't answer, it's because I *can't* answer."

"Did you at least read my text?"

"No." He scrolled down through her messages and stopped on the last one. "What does that mean?"

"He used to be a she," Whiffen blurted out.

"I don't understand. Who? What *he*? What *she*?"

"Mortimer Williams," Whiffen explained. "Morty was born a female."

18

Doreen Williams waited until Insp. Myra's car was out of view before she tiptoed across the joined backyards to Art and Flora Pardy's back door.

"Come in," Flora whispered, looking around the backyard before closing the door behind Doreen. "Insp. Myra just left. He could still be watching us. You shouldn't have come over."

"I just watched him drive away." Doreen shook off the cold. "He's gone."

"Where's your coat? It's freezing out."

Doreen looked down at her jeans and black T-shirt. "I was too distracted to put one on, I guess."

"There's fresh coffee on." Flora headed to the counter and poured up two cups. "Do you want coffee? I could make tea. Is that top new? It looks nice on you."

Doreen looked down the hallway toward the front door before sitting down. "Where's Art?"

"I don't know." Flora gave her a withered look. "He's here somewhere. He's always around. Art never leaves me for too long."

"I need him here, too. He's part of this." Doreen jumped up

and stuck her head out into the hallway and bellowed, "Art. Art, it's Doreen. I need you here."

The sound of the first-floor toilet flushing announced Art's location. Moments later he walked into the kitchen, his face twisted in anger.

"What the fuck are you doing here?" Art jabbed his finger toward Doreen. "Get out of my house."

Flora positioned herself between the two of them. "Stop. Stop. Listen to me. We have to work together."

"I'm having no part in this." The dark circles around Art's eyes emphasized his tiredness. "Our dealings were with Morty, not you."

"Morty's gone, and now I'm in charge." Doreen jabbed her finger back at him. "So, shut up and sit down." She dragged a chair out from the table and pushed it at him.

Flora laid a tray of raisin buns and a crock of jam as if she were hosting a tea party. "Let's all sit down and be civil, at least. Come on, now." She sat, patted the seat next to her, and looked at Art. "Arthur, sit down, please."

He reluctantly agreed and plopped himself down in a chair with his arms wrapped around his body. "We should never have gotten involved with you two shysters."

Doreen sat at the head of the table. "Too late now."

Art punched the table with his fist. "This is your fault. You set us up."

"You had no problem spending the money, though, did you?" Doreen shot back.

"Please. Stop." Flora's shrill voice interrupted them. "We need to get our story straight. This Insp. Myra is not stupid. He'll see through us."

"What did he want?" Doreen demanded.

"He asked me about the shooting," Flora answered.

"What did you tell him?"

"The truth." Flora picked up a raisin bun and pinched a piece off. "I told him we were sitting on the couch and someone shot at the window."

"Did you tell him who it was?"

"Doreen, I don't know who it was. I didn't see anyone." Flora rolled her eyes as she spoke.

Doreen slammed her hand on the table, spilling her untouched coffee. "Don't play games, Flora. I'm not stupid. Did you tell him who we suspected?"

"No, of course I didn't." Flora tutted and looked toward Art for support. "But he had pictures and video from a security camera across the street.

"Did he know who it was?"

"You couldn't tell who it was."

Art chewed the inside of his lip, kept his eyes focused out the kitchen window, and made no sound.

"Art, was it you?" asked Doreen.

His head slowly pivoted toward Doreen. "Why would I shoot at the window when I have a clear shot of you on any given day? If I wanted you dead, you'd be dead, and they certainly wouldn't find your body."

Doreen sat back in her chair. "I had to ask."

"My God, Doreen." Flora's face was flushed. "You know it wasn't Art. Why would Art do a thing like that? He never would. Art is a lovely man if you'd just get to know him."

"But you suspected him," Doreen spat. "I heard you ask him that night when you were sitting outside the ambulance."

"I was frightened, that's all." Flora busied herself by wiping crumbs off the table.

"But you still asked."

Art's eyes went back to the kitchen window. Flora kept hers on the raisin bun.

"He'll find out," said Doreen. "He's not stupid."

"I'm sure the list of people who want to kill you is long," Art answered without looking at her.

"But they didn't want to kill me. They wanted to scare me. If they wanted to kill me, they could have shot me on my doorstep. And what makes you think it wasn't you they wanted to scare?"

"I think it was Bucky," Flora stated.

"He's top on my list." Doreen drummed her fingers on the table. "I know he would love to see me dead. But why would he want to scare me? What would the purpose be? I think this has more to do with you than me."

Flora pursed her lips. "Me? Why would anyone want to kill me?"

"Drop the bullshit, Flora, you know why. You owe a lot of money."

Flora shook her head. "We're going to pay that back very soon. I told the guy that. It must be someone else."

"There's one other person." Doreen leaned forward, her elbows on the table. "Morty had a stalker years ago who recently came into his life."

Doreen's eyes widened. "Do you know who it is?"

"I had my suspicions, but Morty would never say."

"Why would she want to frighten you?"

"To blackmail me, maybe?"

"Like you're doing to us." Art banged his two fists on the table, spilling coffee. He stood up, towering over Doreen. "You've been nothing but trouble ever since we met you. Moving here was the biggest mistake of our lives."

"Art, honey, please stop," Flora pleaded.

"And you." He pointed his finger at Flora. "You caused all this. Why did I let you talk me into this? I am sick and tired of you constantly burning down everything we build."

"Art, you don't mean that." Flora's bottom lip quivered in fear.

"Like fuck I don't," he said angrily. "Every time we get one step ahead, you got to take us two steps back. I warned you to get help."

Flora tried to answer but dissolved into a flood of tears.

Doreen threw her hands up in the air. "Oh, fuck, here we go again." She pushed herself away from the table and stood up. "You're a victim, are you, Art? Poor you."

Art gave a snort. "You didn't deserve Morty. He wanted to leave you, and everyone knew it."

"But you had no problem taking the money, did you?"

"You always have to bring that up, don't you? My wife is sick, and you took advantage of us."

"Sick my ass." Doreen laughed. "Anyone can see she's faking it. You think that cop fell for that act? I bet he played you like a fiddle."

Art pointed to the back door. "Get out of my house and don't come back," he said slowly.

"It's not your house, Art. It's mine. You rent from me, and I do believe you're behind on your rent."

Art stomped toward the door and flung it open. "Get out. Get out!"

Doreen looked at Flora, who was trembling in her seat. "I guess we'll meet for coffee some other time." She snarled at Art on her way out, "Let me tell you something, Arthur."

"What's that?"

"The only thing between you and prison is me."

19

Insp. Myra stared off into space. He absentmindedly twirled the edges of his moustache and tried to make sense of the new information regarding Mortimer's gender.

"Did you hear me?" Cst. Whiffen waved her hand in front of his face. "There's no death certificate for Barbara Williams, but there are death certificates for her parents."

"I heard you. I'm still trying to process that Mortimer Williams was a transgender male and not one person has mentioned that to us."

"Does it change anything?"

"None of the facts, for sure. He's still dead and we don't know why or who did it."

"Does it change why you think he was murdered?"

"I have no idea why he was murdered, but it does explain why Doreen Williams fought to have the autopsy stopped. She didn't want anyone to know." Myra focused his stare on the whiteboard at the front of the office. "Who is Mortimer Williams?"

"As a female, Mortimer certainly couldn't be a Mason. No women are allowed," Whiffen reminded him. "And what a crisis it would cause if word got out that the Grand Master was born a female. Old dead guys would be rolling in their graves all over the world."

"Did someone figure it out and kill him because of it?" Myra wondered out loud. "Morty probably joined the Masons to prove he was a man. It was the ultimate test . . . getting to the top of the oldest fraternal organization in the history of the world."

"Would it be worth killing for?" Whiffen took a closer look at the newspaper clippings on the whiteboard. "I mean, sure they'd be pissed about it, but it's not exactly the Crusades. They're just a bunch of guys doing charity work. Why kill over it? Why not just ask him to step down and keep his mouth shut?"

"I'm pissed at Bucky." Myra tugged at a loose, wiry strand in his moustache and flinched. "Not once did he give it away. He just played along. But if he was so angry at Morty, why did he keep his secret when he was talking to me? Why not just come out and tell me who Mortimer was? He had to know I was going to figure it out."

"Not if they got to bury him and stop the autopsy."

Myra bit the inside of his lip and stared at the board. "Follow the money. We need to stay on that track."

"Bucky had to benefit from it. But how? Why did he protect Morty's secret? He supposedly hates Doreen." Whiffen walked back to her desk and sat down. "Or is he lying about that, too?"

A tap on the office door stopped their conversation. Sgt. Bill Morgan poked his head around the door. "Is this a good time?"

"Sure. Come in," Myra invited.

Morgan closed the door behind him. He carried a thick legal-sized file folder that held three inches of paperwork.

"I brought the file with me." He laid it on the nearest desk. "It's best if I take you through it." He stood straight and rubbed his hands together. "I did not make the connection between Mortimer Williams and Kate and Joseph Williams."

"I appreciate that." Myra sat in the nearest chair. "When you investigated their deaths, you didn't know about any other children besides Barbara and Bucky?"

"No. I went through the file again today, and the Williamses only had two children. Twins, Barbara and Bartholomew. Who we know as Bucky. There was no Mortimer mentioned."

"Interesting." Myra slowly rocked as he thought. "Could Mortimer be a child from another relationship? Maybe one Kate gave up for adoption. Did Joseph have an affair? Maybe he's not related at all. Doreen is living in the Williams family home, but she could have inherited that from Barbara. She could have met Mortimer after Barbara died."

"You could ask Bucky to provide a DNA sample, and we can test it against Mortimer's," Morgan offered.

"Good idea." Myra sat up and looked at the thick file. "What do you have for us?"

Morgan opened the file. "Remember, when these deaths happened, policing looked a lot different than it does now. Our patrol officers had a radio in the car, no vests, no handgun, and we had two-person patrols. When you were out of your car, you were on your own. If you were in a really remote area and it went sideways, it could get ugly fast. It was up to you and the person in the next area to cover each other's butt. So, I don't want you judging a file from 1992 with 2022 hindsight."

Myra nodded. "Understood."

"The communications centre received the call at 1900 hours on April 1, 1992," Morgan began. "A couple had been out for an evening walk and found the Williams car. By that time the car had run out of gas and the doors were locked. The walkers could see two people asleep in the car. They knocked on the windows but couldn't get any response. They ran to a nearby corner store and called the police."

"Did the couple know them?" Whiffen asked.

"No. No connection at all."

Morgan shifted the stack of paper and pulled out an eight-by-ten photo. He passed it to Whiffen first.

"The first patrol officer arrived at 1930 and requested Ident." Morgan pointed to the photo. "I got there about forty minutes later, and this is exactly how we found them. Kate was in the driver's seat, and Joseph was in the passenger's seat."

"What did the medical examiner rule?" Myra took the photo from Whiffen and examined it.

"The M.E. ruled it death by carbon monoxide because of a hole found in the exhaust system and the amount that was found in their bodies. There weren't any traces of alcohol in their systems, and the contents of their stomachs showed sandwiches and soda. No soda tins were found in the car or around it. But both had traces of sleeping pills."

"Sleeping pills?" Whiffen asked.

"I interviewed their family doctor, who said Mrs. Williams was having trouble sleeping and he prescribed the pills to her. The prescription was filled, but the pills were never found. There was a small, empty, decorative metal pillbox found on the dashboard. Barbara identified it as her mother's. It was later returned to her." Morgan took a medical report out and handed it to Myra.

"Do you have a photo of that pillbox?" Whiffen asked.

"I believe I do." Morgan sorted through the file as he spoke. He handed a photo to Myra. "This is the back seat, which showed the two empty wine bottles in a paper bag and a wicker basket with plastic wrap containing crumbs from two sandwiches."

Myra screwed up his face. "Odd. Weird time of year for a picnic."

"Bucky said his parents never had a picnic in their lives." Morgan continued searching through the file.

"Could it have been a suicide?" Whiffen asked.

"That's what it looked like. But when I looked a little further into their lives, it didn't work out. They had planned a trip to Corner Brook the next weekend to attend a wedding. The gift was wrapped on their dining room table. Mr. Williams was supposed to go moose hunting with his brother. They had no debt and no illness. There was no reason for them to kill themselves. It just didn't fit."

Myra looked up from the report. "No trace of alcohol was found in their blood. But they found two empty wine bottles in the back seat."

"Yes," Morgan answered. "But when did they drink them? We had no way of knowing. They could have drunk them the night before. They could have been there since Christmas. We had no way of knowing."

"Or they could have been put there to look like they drank them," Myra suggested. "Too bad they didn't find the soda tins."

"We searched the whole perimeter, and they weren't found. The wine bottles being planted was a possibility and one that I considered very carefully." Morgan took more photos from the file and passed them around. "But we couldn't find any evidence to back that up."

"You interviewed Bucky and Barbara." Myra took another photo from Whiffen. "What did you think of them?"

Morgan rocked on his heels and dug his hands into his front pockets. "Barbara was in shock. She could barely answer questions. Bucky was very angry. He started making accusations right away."

"Like what?" Whiffen asked.

"Bucky had just opened his garage and was building his business. He argued that there was no way the exhaust system was faulty because he had replaced it himself the week before. He provided the work order and bill." Morgan pulled a yellowed five-by-seven-inch bill from the file and handed it to Myra. "I personally checked the product number on the invoice to the one on the Williams car, and it matched. I had a mechanic look at it, who confirmed the exhaust system was new, but there was a puncture hole in it."

"How did it get there?" Myra asked.

"Bucky told me Barbara's friend had borrowed the car two days before this happened. He said his parents hardly used the car. So, it had been parked since she brought it back."

"Did you check the friend out?" Myra examined the bill.

"Yes. She gave a statement, and she had an alibi. Bucky made a lot of allegations at the time." Morgan considered the question further. "He said his mother didn't know how to drive. So, there was no way she should have been in the driver's seat and his father in the passenger's."

"Maybe the father couldn't drive for some medical reason," Whiffen suggested.

"There was nothing that suggested he couldn't drive," Morgan replied. "The medical examiner checked for heart attack and stroke but found nothing."

Whiffen examined the photo again. "Someone took the soda tins but left wine bottles on the back seat."

Myra sorted through the photos in his hands. "They were being set up."

"Bucky said his parents were devout Christians and never touched alcohol. I remember distinctly that he said, 'They don't even drink the wine at Holy Communion,'" Morgan recalled.

"Was there a check done on their bank account to see if they went to a liquor store?" Myra asked as he carefully examined the back seat photo.

"I did get their bank statement. It's in the file. No alcohol was charged to their credit card or bank account, and no money was taken from their account in the week leading up to their deaths.

The last transaction was to Bucky's garage for the work he did on their car."

"In all the media interviews Bucky did, he always stated that it was ridiculous that his parents were on a picnic and fell asleep in the car," Whiffen offered.

"That's right," Morgan agreed. "He was very vocal about the whole thing."

"The sleeping pills could have been ground up and put in the soda tins, explaining why they are missing," Whiffen suggested. "Bill, did you find that picture of the pillbox yet?"

"Still looking." He went back to searching the file. "In the end, we had to go with the medical examiner's cause of death. I didn't like it, but I was a young constable and was outranked." Morgan handed Whiffen the photo she had asked for.

Myra looked at his watch. "Bucky's garage is closed now. I'll be there when he opens tomorrow morning." He steepled his hands over his chest. "So, what do we know?"

"We know the Williamses didn't drink and didn't go on pic-nics," said Whiffen.

Morgan nodded. "We know there was no reason to suspect suicide."

"Bill?" Myra asked. "What is the name of Barbara's friend who borrowed the car?"

"Doreen Power." He handed Myra a handwritten statement. "There's a photo of her on the page."

Myra took both and carefully looked at the black-and-white photo. "Doreen Power is Doreen Williams."

Whiffen held up the photo of the pillbox and pulled another photo out of her evidence file. "I knew it!" She turned the photos toward Myra and Morgan. "The pillbox that was found on Mor-timer Williams the night he died is the same pillbox that belonged to Kate Williams."

"Really?" Morgan leaned in closer. "How did our victim get Kate Williams's pillbox?"

Myra tapped his steepled fingers together and twisted his mouth to the side. "Because he didn't exist."

Morgan and Whiffen watched him hurry toward the whiteboard.

"What are you doing?" Whiffen asked.

Myra picked up a marker and pointed it at Mortimer's picture. "You didn't know about Mortimer Williams because in 1992 Mortimer was Barbara."

20

The early morning light flooded in through the kitchen windows of Insp. Nick Myra's home. Maria spread maple syrup over fluffy pancakes and arranged fresh blueberries into a happy face as she hummed along to a song on the radio.

"You spoil them rotten." Nick gently kissed her neck on his way to the coffee machine.

He stopped again to bend down and kiss his daughters on top of their heads. When he filled his cup, he watched his two little girls bouncing in their chairs, waiting for breakfast. Maria was happily absorbed in preparing their breakfast. The smell of pancakes and coffee filled Myra with comfort, sprinkled with the only hint of sanity in his life. This was his safe place.

"Mommy?" Clara whined. "Why does Doris get more blueberries than me?" Her bottom lip curled out.

"You both have the same number of blueberries," Maria reassured her.

"I got more." Doris popped a handful in her mouth and smiled broadly at her father. "Daddy gave them to me."

"Oh, no I didn't."

"Daddy gave me blueberries," Doris insisted defiantly.

"Nick, did you give her blueberries?" Maria scolded.

"I didn't." He tried to hide his smile behind his cup. "You just watched me come into the kitchen."

Maria opened the tub of blueberries and plopped a handful on each child's plate. "There, you both have lots now. Eat your breakfast."

The girls dug into their warm pancakes and blueberries, allowing their parents a rare moment of conversation in peace.

"You slept well last night." Maria filled up her own coffee cup. "You didn't talk in your sleep at all."

Myra smiled. "You're watching me sleep now?"

"You know what I mean. Have you thought about going back to the psychologist?"

"No, I don't have time."

"Nick." She stomped her foot.

"I feel better, that's all. This is the best pill there is." He looked at his daughters happily eating their pancakes.

"What do you want for supper tonight?" she asked. "I was thinking of taking out that roast we bought last week."

"That sounds good to me." Nick poured a second coffee and refilled Maria's.

"Did you ask Bill and Donna about the Christmas luncheon?" Maria put a sweetener and milk in her coffee.

"Yes, Bill and Sharon will be there. They are waiting to see if their son can make it, and he'll let me know this week. Sharon is already baking for it."

"I hope she makes those Christmas cookies she made last year. I hope their son can make it, too. I know he's getting to the age where it's not cool to hang out with your parents, but it's Christmas." Maria looked back at their two daughters forking pancakes into their mouths. "I hope the girls never leave us."

Nick laughed. "With the way you spoil them, they'll be here until they're sixty."

Maria smiled. "Like you're any better. What about Donna? The luncheon would be a great way to make her feel at home in your unit."

"I asked her, and she said her husband and son can't make it, but she'll think about it."

"Oh? Why is that?"

"She didn't say." Nick suspected Maria would keep asking until she got the answer she wanted, so he continued. "I know she has a son with non-verbal autism. I was told when she transferred in my unit, but I didn't want to pry. From the picture on her desk, he looks to be in his late teens. She'll tell me when I need to know."

"Oh, no. That's too bad."

"I don't think they can take him to a restaurant. I called her last supervisor. He told me Donna's husband gave up his career and stays home with him."

"Well, I guess that's the only way to make sure he gets the right care."

Nick watched Doris sneak a blueberry off Clara's plate. "We're so lucky."

Maria caught the theft from the corner of her eye. "Doris, put it back."

The little girl giggled as she threw the berry back on her sister's plate.

"I wonder, should I call her in privately and tell her not to worry about coming?" asked Myra.

"What do you mean?"

"I just don't want her to feel pressured to come to the luncheon."

"You mean you're not comfortable with her taking her autistic son to a restaurant where he could make a scene?"

Nick's eyes widened. He laid down his empty cup. "That's not true."

"I'm not saying you're a bad person, Nick, but you're not good with things like that."

"I deal with all kinds of people all day long. That's not fair."

"You're uncomfortable with her situation."

"I'm just trying to create a work environment where she feels comfortable. I don't care if she brings her son. We could get the private room instead of being in the restaurant if it would make him more comfortable."

"That's not a bad idea. Mention it to her."

"I don't want to badger her."

"Nick." Maria laid her empty cup on the counter. "She was more than likely happy that you included her."

"You think so? I just don't want to put pressure on her."

Maria pushed her long, messy hair out of her face and tightened the belt on her bathrobe. "Nick, you get up. Get showered. Have coffee and go to work all day. Do you realize that I'm in this bathrobe until noon because I don't get a chance to get dressed?"

"No, I had no idea. You always look great to me."

"Makeup is now just a swipe of an old moisturizer and a lip balm. I wash my hair every second or third day. People in prison get more hot meals than I do."

Nick smiled at this petite yet powerful women in front of him. "But you don't need makeup. You're beautiful."

"You're missing the point." Maria poured the last of the coffee into her cup. "Parents who stay home work. It's a lot of work taking care of these two."

"I know that."

"But I don't think you appreciate the amount of work that goes into staying home and taking care of a child. Especially a child with special needs."

"Are we still talking about Donna, or have we moved on to us?"

She took a long sip of her coffee while watching him. "Maybe a little of both."

"Do you need me to take a day off to help? I could possibly take this Friday off and make it a long weekend."

"No. That's not what I mean, but yes, that would be great."

Clara reached for the last of the blueberries on Doris's plate. Doris pushed her hand away and, in the process, knocked over a glass of milk, sending both Clara and Doris into crying fits.

"Oh, for the love of God." Maria laid her cup down on the table. "Two of you, upstairs and brush your teeth. I'll be up in a minute to deal with you."

"Here, let me help." Nick pulled off sheets of paper towel and blotted the streaming milk.

"I got it." Maria took the paper towel and spread it around the table. "You're going to be late. Go on, and don't forget your lunch. It's in the fridge."

Nick glanced at the clock. "Sorry. I really do have to go." He opened the fridge and took out his lunch. "Do you want me to come home early?"

"No. Go on. I got this."

Nick kissed her cheek before heading toward the front door.

"Nick," Maria called out.

"What?"

"My point was," she said, brushing the hair out of her face, "Donna may say no a hundred times before she finally says yes. But I know she appreciates being asked, being included."

Milk dripped from the soaking paper towels in her hand. "I know that for sure. Because I do."

21

The gas fumes coming from the old garage smelled like the whole place could blow if someone lit a match. A small window allowed a breath of cold air to occasionally drift in, giving Bucky Williams a chance to clean out his lungs. He lay on his back on top of a tattered, padded back support on wheels, trying to fix a late-model minivan that was up on a jack. A small fortune in hard-to-find spare parts lay within easy reach around his legs.

Bucky stopped what he was doing at the sound of the bell over his front door. He tried to turn on his side to see who was walking toward him. The size twelve black jackboots, wet from snow, told him exactly who was standing in the bay. He held on to the bottom of the minivan and pushed himself out from under.

"Why are you here again?" Bucky rolled himself off the back support and stood up.

"Because you're lying to me, Bucky." Insp. Myra spotted two well-worn black vinyl office chairs discarded near the workbench. "And you knew I would find out and come back. So don't act like you weren't expecting me, because you and I both know it's what you wanted."

Myra pulled the chairs out and pushed one toward Bucky. "Sit down and let's have a chat."

Bucky pulled a dirty handkerchief out from the pocket of his overalls and made an attempt at wiping his hands. He slumped down in the chair but said nothing.

"Now, why don't you start telling me the truth?"

Bucky shook his head. "I don't know where to start. You won't believe me. Nobody does."

"Try me. You lied about the last time you saw Mortimer. You're the one who met him for supper the night he died. We have you on surveillance camera at the restaurant." Myra leaned toward him. "Why didn't you tell me the truth about Mortimer being Barbara?"

Bucky leaned forward, putting his elbows on his knees, his head in his hands. "I loved my sister."

"But did you love her when she became your brother?"

Bucky looked up at Myra with tormented eyes. "That didn't matter to me. I didn't understand it at first. I needed time to grieve the loss of my sister, but we were close. We did everything together. That's not why we fell out."

"Why did you fall out?"

"Foolishness, really." He sat up. "We shared a baseball card collection. We had been collecting since we were youngsters. There were some expensive and rare cards in the collection."

Myra cocked his head. "You fell out over baseball cards?"

"When Barb told me the truth about her relationship with Doreen, I freaked out." Bucky looked up at Myra. "I'm not proud of that, but it was the 1990s. I said some things I'm ashamed of, and she took the baseball card collection and burnt them all. We hardly spoke after that. But in the end, I know it had nothing to do with stupid old baseball cards."

"But the divide really happened when you argued again about your parents?"

Bucky took a gulp of air. "Yes. That was the nail in the coffin for us."

"You believed they were murdered."

"I *know* they were murdered." Bucky slapped his rough hands together. "Morty finally agreed and said he had proof."

"Was Morty involved in their murder?"

"For years I believed he was, but I don't think that now." Bucky put his head back in his hands.

"Why didn't you tell me Morty was Barbara?"

Bucky shook his head trying to find an answer. "I had lost my twin twice. I had sworn on my life that I would never tell anyone Morty's secret. After what we've been through, I wasn't going to betray him."

"Where did Morty go after he left the restaurant?"

"I don't know. He didn't say."

"Come on, Bucky." Myra raised his voice. "You're the last person to see him alive. If you want my help, you better start talking."

"I don't know." Bucky's voice rose, too. "He didn't say where he was going. He gets really bad indigestion, and the grease from supper was upsetting his stomach, so I assumed he went straight home."

"Did you ask why he was dressed up in an expensive suit?"

"Morty was always dressed in an expensive suit. That night was no different."

Myra took a moment to size Bucky up. "Did he say he had any stops to make on the way home? Or did he mention having to meet anyone?"

"No. He didn't say. Look, I've been over this a thousand times in my head. If I knew, I would have told you."

"Did he take any calls or texts while you were at supper?"

Bucky shook his head. "No. No, he didn't take his phone out at all."

"Did anyone know you were meeting for supper?"

"Not that I know of." Bucky's face contracted suddenly with fear. "I don't suppose Doreen found out?"

"She didn't know you had made up?"

"No, Morty didn't want her to know."

Myra suddenly felt claustrophobic in the small garage and unbuttoned his coat. "Tell me about what happened to your parents."

"We had a normal family." Bucky gazed at the oil-covered floor. "Mom volunteered at school in the library. Dad was an accountant. Barbara and I were twins. Instant family, Mom used to say."

Myra said nothing. He sat and listened.

"I guess I knew before anyone that Barbara was different. She . . . before she changed . . . was better at sports than I was. She wasn't girly. She would get teased about it all the time. She only had one boyfriend, and it turned out badly."

Bucky wiped his old handkerchief over his forehead, leaving a faded black streak.

"Twins just know, ya know? We always knew when the other was hurt or upset. Even after we stopped talking, I could feel in the pit of my stomach when he was upset. We still had that connection. The night he died, I had the worst migraine of my life. The next morning, I knew something was wrong."

He swallowed hard to stop his voice from quivering.

"I think Mom knew Barb was different, too. She didn't say anything, but back in the 1990s, families didn't speak about it. I don't think it would've made a difference, though. We were a tight family. We did everything together. My parents wouldn't have stopped loving Barb for that. They would have protected her."

"When did Doreen come into the picture?" Myra asked.

"When Barb went to university. They met at a party or something."

"How did you feel about her?"

"I was at trade school doing my mechanic's diploma. I was always good with my hands, but Barb, she was smart like Dad. She was doing business. At that time, we weren't spending a lot of time together. I had a girlfriend and school. Barb was busy with her life, and she had a lot of friends there. Doreen was just another friend. Or so we thought."

"When did you know it was something more?"

"Mom suspected there was something more happening. She and Barb started arguing about Doreen. Mom felt Doreen was too controlling. Then, after one big blow-up, Barb moved out and moved in with Doreen."

"How did your mother feel about that?"

"Both of my parents were very upset about it. They wanted Barb to stay home until she finished her degree. They felt Doreen was isolating her, keeping her away from her family and friends."

"Did you think the same thing?"

Bucky paused before answering. "I only knew what Mom told me, but when I met Doreen, I instantly didn't like her. She didn't want Barb and me to spend time together. She knew we could communicate without speaking. That twin thing, right?"

"How did Barb feel about it?"

"I could tell she didn't like it. One evening she showed up at Mom's, bawling. She could barely talk. She said she was afraid of Doreen and didn't want to go back there."

"Did she move home?"

"No. She stayed the night, but the next morning she went back to Doreen. By this time the jig was up. We knew they were a couple. That part didn't bother us. We were prepared for that. But we also suspected Barb was being abused. This was only her second relationship, and like I told you, the first one didn't end well. She had a boyfriend in high school who wouldn't leave her alone after they broke up. I don't know what happened. She kept him a secret, really. They only dated for a few weeks. I think he still pestered her at university, too." Bucky began to choke up and cleared his throat. "Barb thought of him as just a friend, but he thought they were more than that."

"Had you ever seen any signs of abuse on her?" Myra recalled the photo on Doreen's mantelpiece of the two laughing women.

"Not really. I believe it was mostly mental abuse. I mean, no black eyes or anything. By this time Barb had been living with Doreen for about six months. One day, Barb called me and asked me to pick her up for a drive. It was then she told me that she wanted to leave Doreen and asked for my help."

"Did Barb leave her?"

"She tried." Bucky blinked constantly to hold back the tears. "Doreen begged her to come back, and eventually Barb gave in. At that point we hated Doreen. But once Doreen realized we wanted Barb to end their relationship, she hated us, too.

"We decided then as a family that we needed a plan. We knew that banning Doreen from the house meant we couldn't keep an eye on Barb, that having them closer would be better. I started to do some checking and found out Doreen was from Nova Scotia and came from a bad background."

"What do you mean?"

"Her family threw her out when they found out she was a lesbian. I guess that's just the way families acted back then. We found out her father used to beat her senseless, trying to straighten her out, so she ran away. And see, that was right up Barb's alley, because she loved a sob story. Barb constantly helped people. We used to call them stray cats. If she knew someone didn't have a friend, she would be their friend. If she thought someone at school didn't have lunch, she would give them hers."

Myra thought back to Doreen's description of Morty constantly helping people. "Do you think that's what attracted Barb to Doreen?"

"Absolutely." Bucky knotted the handkerchief through his fingers. "Barb loved to fix people like I love to fix cars. She was good at it."

"You said your family had a plan. Tell me more about that."

"Barb had just finished her business degree. Like I said, we needed to keep an eye on her, so we did everything we could to befriend Doreen. I had just started this garage and got married, so I was busy. Dad told me Doreen asked to borrow the car, but he wasn't fussy about giving it to her because the muffler was loud. I told him to bring it in and I would fix it."

"I read the report on your parents' death. You replaced the muffler a few days before they died of carbon monoxide poisoning."

The man's lips trembled as he answered. "I didn't put a faulty exhaust on that car. I wouldn't do that to my parents. I loved them. We were a good family."

"I believe you, Bucky."

"You do?" He looked up at Myra. A tear escaped, leaving a streak down the side of his face. "Thank you. Thank you. I can't even begin to tell you what a burden that has been on my life. Their deaths destroyed me. I lost my wife. My kids." He looked around at his two-bay garage. "My business. But I know Barb knew the difference."

"Tell me what happened."

"After the car was fixed, Dad lent it to Doreen. She used it for a day and brought it back." Bucky rubbed his hands across his eyes, leaving a dirty streak. "Mom and Dad went for a drive every Saturday. The car didn't move until that Saturday."

"Did you talk to them that day?" Myra asked.

"No. Uncle Gary stopped in the garage that morning. He

needed help with his alternator. Dad was supposed to come by later because they were going hunting and needed to get their gear together." Bucky folded his arms. His head tilted down toward the floor. "Dad didn't show up, and Uncle Gary figured he had forgot. A police officer showed up on my doorstep that evening. I couldn't believe it.

"I couldn't breathe. I told the officer that it was a lie. It had to be a mistake. My mother couldn't drive. They didn't drink. They were not the type of people who drank two bottles of wine and slept in their car."

"How did Barb take it?"

"She went into shock. She didn't speak for days." Bucky wiped his cheek with the handkerchief. "All through the funeral, she barely spoke. I had to make all the arrangements. After they were buried, she didn't get out of bed for weeks."

"How did Doreen take it?"

"She went around telling anyone who would listen that I put a faulty exhaust system on the car to save money. The police questioned me, and I showed them the receipt. I would never do that to my parents. I loved them. I lived under that suspicion ever since. After the funeral, Barb and Doreen moved into Mom and Dad's house."

"When did Barb become Mortimer?" Myra spotted a box of tissues on the desk, grabbed a handful, and passed them to Bucky.

"I think the process had begun at that point, because I could see she was changing the way she looked and dressed. About a year later, they moved to Vancouver and she cut contact with me. That was the hardest part. It was bad enough that everyone thought I had killed our parents, but having Barb think it—that was too much for me."

"When did you see Barb next?"

"She moved back in 1997. I tied up the will and insurance payout. I knew our parents had left everything equally to the two of us. When the lawyer told me the will had been changed a week before their deaths, I knew it was murder. There's no way our parents would leave the house and insurance money only to Barb. Then I suspected Barb and Doreen were in on it together. I was an angry drunk by then, and I went to confront Barb. That's when I learned she was transgendered and was living as a man."

"How did you feel about that?" Myra leaned forward in the chair.

"To tell you the truth, I almost expected it. It was the first time Barb—or Morty, sorry—seemed whole to me. It was the twin thing, I think." Bucky discarded the tissues in an empty oil tin and wiped his face in the sleeve of his overalls. "We had some angry words at first. I mean, I didn't get to mourn the loss of my sister, did I?"

"Did you ask Morty if he killed your parents?"

"Of course I did. He denied it, and I kind of believed him. Then I asked him if Doreen killed them. Morty refused to answer and cut off contact again after that."

"Bucky, what do you think happened to your parents?"

Bucky looked toward the ceiling, then back at Myra. "Doreen killed them."

"Do you have proof?"

"Morty said he had proof. He told me after their deaths he was going through Doreen's credit card statements. She had made a purchase at a liquor store the day before the murder, and he kept the statement.

"Morty told me that, a few months ago, someone in the family reached out to him, saying that Doreen asked our parents to meet her at the lake that day. He wouldn't tell me who it was because he felt he had to protect them. Morty also said that, during an argument, Doreen admitted that she impersonated Mom and changed the will over the phone. Doreen tried to convince Morty it was for his own good. Doreen told him she knew I was planning to murder our parents and frame her for it."

"Do you know who the person was who reached out to him?"

"No idea, but I'm asking around the family to find out who it was."

"Call me if you figure it out," said Myra. "When did Morty make contact with you again?"

"About three months before he died. He begged me to forgive him." Bucky tucked his hands into the pockets of his coveralls. "He told me that he was leaving Doreen and wanted my help."

"What did you tell him?"

"I told him yes. I loved Morty. I just wanted my twin back. All these years I felt like half of me was missing."

"Did Doreen know?"

"No, we kept it quiet. Morty knew it wasn't going to be easy. On the night he died, he gave me a cheque that covered our parents' insurance policy plus lots more. I didn't want to take it, but he said he needed to hide the money from Doreen and asked for my help."

"So, you took it?"

"Yes. Morty told me to deposit it right away. He said he needed to protect his assets. Doreen doesn't know this, but Morty sold the coffee shops three months ago. He was liquidating his assets so Doreen couldn't get them."

"Morty was planning his escape for a while, then?" Myra stretched his long legs and leaned back in the chair. "And you were helping him."

Bucky nodded. "Yes, and the last time Morty tried to get away from Doreen, she killed our parents to stop it."

Myra stood up and walked over to the grimy garage window. He watched the snow gently falling on the parking lot for a few seconds, then turned around.

"Bucky, did you kill Morty?"

He bolted upright. "No. I was finally getting my brother back in my life. I would have died for Morty. I would never kill him."

Myra carefully studied the mechanic's face. Years of grime had embedded themselves into his skin, aging him well beyond his years. "I know, Bucky. I know. I'm going to need you to come in to the station and write out a full statement. By the way, are you a Mason?"

"No. I have no interest in the Masons."

"Do you really think Doreen killed Morty?"

Bucky drew in a ragged breath and thought for a moment. "If she knew Morty was leaving, I think she would have killed him. But there's one other person I think you should look into."

"Oh? Who's that?"

"I told you about the boyfriend Barb had in high school who wouldn't leave her alone."

"Okay." Myra waved his hand for Bucky to continue.

"Well, Morty told me he ran into this guy years ago. The guy didn't know Morty was Barb at the time, but he soon figured it out. I think Morty helped him out financially. After Morty became the head of the Masons, the guy threatened to out him."

Myra blinked. "Morty was being blackmailed?"

"Yes, but not just for money."

"What did he want?" Myra massaged his temples to ease a pain in his head that had come on suddenly.

"Power . . . it was something that would give him power. I don't understand it, exactly. Morty didn't elaborate, but whatever it was, he wouldn't do it. The guy got pretty threatening after that."

"Who was the guy?"

"I don't know." Bucky ran his dirty fingers through his hair. "Morty wouldn't tell me the guy's name. He blew it off as just idle threats. He was always so secretive."

"Bucky, think. Are you sure he didn't give you a name?"

"No, he wouldn't tell me. Some kind of Mason thing."

"The guy was a Mason?"

Bucky walked over to his desk and pulled out a drawer. He searched around for a few seconds, then pulled out a blue hard-covered book with a white crest on the front. He handed it to Myra.

"I pulled out our old high school yearbook to see if I could figure it out. Barb had everyone sign the inside cover. Here, our class page is folded down."

Myra flipped through the pages. He ran his finger over the folded page until he spotted the small square black-and-white photos of Barbara Williams and Bartholomew Williams.

The line of pictures below theirs caught his attention. He looked up at Bucky, then back at the page.

"You can't be serious."

22

Cst. Donna Whiffen lifted a slat of the blinds covering the living room window. "A car just parked in front of the house. I think it's her." She looked over her shoulder at Steve, who was busy keeping Jack entertained.

"She looks okay." Donna hurried toward the front door to catch the woman before she rang the bell. "God, I hope she's better than the last three. I can't keep doing this."

Steve let out a mournful sigh. "Me neither." He turned to see Jack wandering off to the kitchen. "Jack, can you stay in the living room, please?" Steve took him gently by the arm and led him to the couch.

"Hi, you must be Erin." Donna extended her hand toward the middle-aged woman. "Come in."

Erin took her hand and gave it a weak shake. "Yes, I am." She looked around the foyer. "You have a lovely home. I brought my resumé with me." She handed Donna a manila envelope.

"Thank you. The agency sent it to me, but I'll take this, anyway." She showed the care worker into the living room. "I'm Donna Whiffen, and this is my husband, Steve, and our son, Jack."

"Hi." Erin gave a shy wave. Her freckled face lit up into a broad smile. She nervously pushed a stray strand of her short, dark-blonde hair from her face.

"Hi." Steve waved back. Jack rocked in short, repetitive motions, clutching a small stuffed giraffe, gazing off at nothing.

"Come in." Donna gestured toward the black leather recliner. "Sit down. It's going to take Jack a few minutes to get used to having someone new in the house."

"I don't mind." Erin sat in the recliner, and it gave out a loud *pffft* sound, causing her face to glow red. She let out an embarrassed laugh.

"I forgot to warn you about that chair." Donna's face shared her embarrassment. "Would you like coffee or tea?"

"No, thank you. I'm fine." Erin pulled her long floral blouse down over her black elastic waist pants.

Steve pulled a tissue from a box on the coffee table and wiped Jack's mouth. "Okay, then, we should get on with the interview. Sorry to rush this, but I have to keep Jack on his schedule."

"I understand. I've worked with other autistic children and adults." Erin smiled as she sized Jack up.

"We're very impressed with your resumé." Donna opened the envelope and pulled out several sheets of stapled paper. "You have a lot of experience working with autistic people."

"I was with my last client for twelve years," Erin explained. "I would still be there, but the family moved to Corner Brook, and I couldn't go. I have my own family here."

"That's understandable." Steve glanced at the resumé over Donna's shoulder. "Twelve years? You must have been happy there."

"Yes, I started when George was ten and stayed on until he was twenty-two." Erin nodded at her resumé. "His parents gave me a reference and said you're welcome to call them."

"That's a long time." Donna flipped the page to look at the family's name.

"He was like my own child by the end of it. It broke my heart when they moved, but his father got transferred, and that's all you can do." A sadness crept across her face. "I stay in touch with them."

"He was verbal, was he?" Donna asked.

"A little bit, yes. He could tell me what he wanted."

"Jack is non-verbal. Will that be a problem?" Steve asked.

"No, not at all. I'm sure over time I'll figure out what he wants."

"We get thirty-five hours of home care a week. Are you good with that?" Donna asked.

"Yes, that's great, and I'm pretty flexible, too. It doesn't have to be Monday to Friday, nine to five. I can come Saturdays or stay overnight if you need to go out of town. As long as it adds up to thirty-five hours, who cares how it's distributed?"

Donna and Steve looked at each other, each running a list of possibilities in their heads.

"You don't mind staying over on a weekend night?" Steve asked to make sure he'd heard her right.

"Not at all. Once he's used to me and I get his routine down, then I won't mind."

Jack bolted off the couch and quickly walked toward Erin. He reached down, touched her cheek, and pulled his hand away. The light coming in through the blinds caught his attention. He followed a sunbeam toward the window and stood rocking back and forth, watching the outside world.

Donna shot Steve a look that told him to intercept.

"He's fine." Steve went back to questioning Erin. "Let's continue. First thing, I guess, do you have a criminal record?"

"My gosh, no." Erin blushed. "I've never had a run-in with the law."

"Donna is a police officer." Steve nodded toward his wife. "Can you provide a certificate of conduct?"

"Yes, there's one stapled to the back of my resumé."

Donna flipped to the last page. "Here it is." She passed it to Steve. "We have to ask that question because Jack is very vulnerable."

"I understand."

"Erin, you completed the early childhood development diploma course?" Donna asked.

"Yes. Now, that was a few years ago. But I do renew my first aid and CPR courses every couple of years. I also did the Applied Behavioural Analysis course to be able to work with people with autism."

"I'm glad you brought up the first aid and CPR courses," Steve put in, "because Jack doesn't always chew up his food properly. So, he could have a choking episode. You have to watch him closely when he eats. He also has epilepsy, so you have to know what to do in case he has a seizure. Of course, I'll never be far away."

"I did see that in the job description from the agency." Erin's shoulders visibly relaxed, and she adjusted herself in the chair. "George also had epilepsy and the same chewing problem. I'm used to that now."

A deep breath escaped Donna. She wanted to hire Erin right on the spot, but she knew she had to let Steve finish the questions they had agreed to ask.

"You obviously have your driver's licence." Steve looked toward Jack, who was still rocking as he looked out the window. "We would like you to use our car for continuity. Jack doesn't take well to change. He likes to go for a drive at one o'clock every afternoon, and he drinks one Pepsi on that drive. Are you okay with that?"

"Yes, absolutely. I know how important it is to keep him on his schedule."

As if he knew they were talking about him, Jack turned around and stood in front of Erin. He picked up her hand, kissed the back of it, then went back to the window.

She smiled sweetly at him. "He's a lovely young man. You've done an amazing job with him."

Donna and Steve exchanged glances.

"Steve does most of the caregiving." Donna reached over and took his hand. "Jack would not be as well taken care of if he didn't."

"Families in your situation have to make incredible sacrifices." Erin easily recognized the look of hurt on their faces. "The family I worked with did the same thing. Except the mother stayed home."

Donna knew Erin hadn't meant to insult her, but she still flinched at the statement. "Your references are all from families you worked with?"

"Yes, you can call all of them."

"Jack is very active. He's in constant motion." Steve watched Donna from the corner of his eye. He could feel her hurt. "You have to be in great shape to keep up with him."

"Oh, I know," Erin agreed. "George would run a marathon every day."

"You have to be patient, also. Jack can be very persistent when he wants something." Donna looked at her son, who was now holding the stuffed giraffe up to his face and repeatedly rocking with a jerking motion. "You have to be very calm with him. We don't yell, and we certainly don't hit him. But sometimes he is relentless when he wants to get the day over with."

"Aren't we all?" Erin assured her.

"Jack doesn't know what social boundaries are," Steve continued. "He may give you a hug. Or grab your hand. Or give you a kiss. He doesn't mean anything by it. Are you okay with that?"

"My God, who wouldn't be okay with a hug?" Erin looked at Jack lovingly. "I'm familiar with these repetitive behaviours. I know it's how he calms his anxiety. I believe it's how he communicates his mental and emotional state with us."

A feeling of relief came over Steve. He felt himself relax for the first time in years. "I think you get it. The most important thing is to keep him on his routine. We don't want anyone changing it."

"That's understandable," Erin agreed. "What about food preparation? If you set out a menu for the week, I can prepare his meals. Just let me know what he likes and what he doesn't."

"You cook?" Steve raised his brows questioningly.

"Yes, absolutely. I'll also do his laundry and a bit of housework, too, if you want. I'm here all day, anyway."

Steve and Donna glanced at each other, eyebrows raised.

"That's marvellous," Donna exclaimed. "This is all new to us. We haven't had a caregiver before."

"You've been doing this all by yourself?" Erin spoke with empathy in her voice. "You poor things. You must be exhausted."

A lump was forming in Donna's throat, and she coughed to make it go away. "We have cameras set up all over the house. Are you okay with working knowing you're being recorded?"

"I prefer it, really. It's good for you to know what I'm doing. I would do the same thing in your position."

Donna looked at Steve. "Do you have any other questions? I think I'm done."

Jack sat between his parents and curled up in his father's arms.

"He does this when he's tired." Steve stroked his hair as he rocked him. "You're okay with giving him his medications, are you?"

"Yes, that's no problem."

"We want someone who is a team member with us. Not someone who is an employee. We've never let anyone into our home like this, so it's new to us. I know there'll be an adjustment period. I'm not used to having someone around the house." Steve continued to stroke Jack's head until he closed his eyes.

"We'll work together. Eventually you will get used to me and trust me."

Donna felt the lump in her throat again. "Do you have any questions for us?"

"The agency has given me all the employment information. It's the same as when I worked for George's family. I guess . . . just let me know if I'm hired and when you want me to start."

Steve moved as if to say something, but Donna cut him off. "We'll be making our decision today, and I'll call the agency."

Erin stood up and straightened out her floral top. "Thank you for interviewing me, and I do hope you consider me." She gave Jack a small wave goodbye. "You've got a grand boy there."

Donna walked her to the door. "We really appreciate you coming today."

"Thanks for having me." Erin waved as she headed back to her car.

Donna stood in the doorway to the living room, watching Jack sleeping in his father's arms. She threw her arms in the air and began a happy dance. "What did you think?"

Steve sounded exhausted. "Hire her. She's Mary Poppins, for God's sake."

"I'll call the agency now and get her to start tomorrow if she can." Donna fist-pumped the air. "I can't believe it. We're finally getting some help."

Steve hugged his son tighter as he smiled at his wife. "Hey, Donna. Want to go out on a date with me this Friday night?"

Her voice quivered as a single tear rolled down her face.

"Yes. Yes, I would love to go on a date with you."

23

Insp. Myra sat in his office flipping through the Williamses' yearbook. The pages had yellowed and gave off a sweet, musty smell. He scanned each page of black-and-white school photos, time capsules of high school kids with late 1980s mullets, teased hair, acid-washed jean jackets, and oversized tops with shoulder pads. He studied the scribblings and autographs on the inside cover. Lots of friends signed off with *Love you*, *Stay in touch*, and *Here's to the future.*

One stood out to him: *Barbara, whenever you think of me, remember, I know your secret. For love is as strong as death, jealousy is fierce as the grave. XOXOXOXO Your secret admirer.*

It was the same quote that had been written on the note next to Mortimer's body. A detail only the killer would know.

It gave Myra the creeps. It seemed so innocent yet so threatening at the same time. It was like that feeling of being threatened yet making yourself a fool if you spoke up. He had dealt with many cases of innocent victims complaining about "secret admirers" throughout his career. Each encounter usually started off with that nervous, hopeful, excited feeling, or it was just downright cringe-inducing "Oh dear God, how can I let him/her down easy" kind of feelings.

He recalled what a past supervisor once told him: A stalker feels creepy. But an admirer feels like something you want. Yet Myra knew few did. His thoughts were interrupted when he heard Cst. Whiffen opening the door to their offices. He closed the yearbook and headed out to greet her.

"You're just in time." He waved the book in the air. "Have a look at this."

Whiffen threw her purse under the desk and slipped off her winter coat. "What is it?" She flipped through the pages. "Oh, please tell me your high school picture is here. I'm going to need to see that 'stache in the 1980s."

"Very funny. I was very cool in high school," Myra retorted. "And so was my 'stache."

Whiffen let out a loud laugh. "You were probably born with it. Hate to tell you, but nobody was cool in the '80s."

"And when did you graduate?" he asked, a little insulted.

"2005."

Myra let out a sigh. "Let's move on."

"What is this, anyway?" she asked, thumbing through the pages.

"It's Barbara and Bucky Williams's high school yearbook." Myra went to the whiteboard and wrote *Yearbook* under Mortimer's name. "I interviewed Bucky yesterday."

Myra explained in detail everything Bucky Williams had said to him while Whiffen settled at her desk.

"So, is he off our suspect list?"

"Not yet," Myra admitted. "Look at the page with the fold in it."

Whiffen did as instructed and found Barbara and Bucky's photos. "Wow, they are almost identical twins."

"Yeah, Bucky says the twin bond was always strong with them."

"But why are we looking at their yearbook photos?"

"Look at who else was in their class." Myra walked over and pointed at the page.

"Oh my God." Whiffen looked at him, wide-eyed. "They're all here."

"Exactly." Myra took the cap off a marker and began to make a new list on the board.

"Barbara had a secret boyfriend." He wrote *Boyfriend* at the top of the list. "But who was it?" He put the first black dot below the word. "In her class were Tom Miller, James Fitzgerald, and Art Pardy."

Whiffen scanned the photos of each man. "What are the chances of that happening?"

"Which one was the boyfriend?" Myra stood back and looked at the names. "We need to find out. They all denied knowing Mortimer before joining the Masons. But why?"

Whiffen closed the book. "This makes all three suspects. That makes six, including Doreen Williams, Flora Pardy, and Bucky."

"Someone signed the book as her secret admirer." Myra picked up the yearbook and pointed out the quote to Whiffen. "It's the same quote from the note found next to the body."

Whiffen re-examined the entry. "That's our killer. We could get handwriting samples, but I don't know if that would do us any good, considering their handwriting may have changed over the past forty years."

Myra tugged at his moustache as he paced in front of the whiteboard. "Bucky described the ex-boyfriend as a stalker who was threatening Morty."

"Oh, God." Whiffen rolled her eyes. "I hate the 'if I can't have you nobody will' kind of stalker."

"There is a thin line between stalker and admirer." Myra picked up the yearbook and looked at the quote again. "Just curious. What's your definition of both?"

"A secret admirer is someone who'll like a picture you posted yesterday, but a stalker is someone who'll like a picture you posted a couple of years ago."

Myra gave a low chuckle. "That about sums it up."

"One is *not* harmful, but the other is." Whiffen looked at the quote again.

Myra wrote *Computer Search* on the whiteboard. "We need to get Morty's computer to see if he was getting any threats. Let's see if he was receiving any correspondence that was offensive or unwelcomed. We need to know if he refused or blocked anyone."

"I wonder if Doreen would tell us if he was receiving anything that made him feel afraid for his safety."

"Bucky said this guy wanted something from Morty." Myra put a big question mark on the list. "What was it? He said it wasn't money but *power*." Myra stood back and looked at the board. "How could Morty give this guy power?"

Whiffen pulled out her chair and sat down. "Stalkers try to manipulate and frighten their targets into compliance with their obsessive fantasy. Was the guy just stringing Morty along to keep control of him with ridiculous requests?"

Myra pointed the marker at her and wrote *Stalker* down on the list. "Good point. But which one is it?"

Whiffen clicked her tongue. "Time to bring them in. Well, this is getting more and more intriguing."

Myra waved the yearbook. "I think it's time we organized a high school reunion."

24

Art Pardy looked around the lobby of the Royal Newfoundland Constabulary's headquarters as if he didn't know where he was or why he was there. He watched someone opening the glass front door and considered taking a step toward it. He stopped when he heard his name.

"Mr. Pardy, thanks for coming in." Insp. Myra extended his hand toward him.

He shook the officer's hand with a grunt.

"Let's go in through here." Myra led him in through the secure door to a short hallway and into a private room.

The small room was neatly decorated with a brown leather couch, a matching chair, and a coordinated wooden coffee table. A department-store painting hung on one beige wall. The other three were bare.

"Have a seat." Myra pointed at the couch as he closed the door and sat in the chair.

Art looked around, as though surprised at his surroundings, then sat. "I thought your interrogation room was going to be a little starker than this."

Myra smiled. "You're not being interrogated. I just have some follow-up questions I want to ask you."

Art's gaunt face was stony. "Do I need a lawyer?"

"I don't know." Myra undid the button on his blazer and sat back, crossing his legs. "Do you?"

Art ran his rough hands over his knees. "I don't think so."

"If you change your mind at any point, let me know." Myra watched him for a few seconds before continuing. "Why didn't Flora come with you today? I asked both of you to be here."

Art closed his heavy-lidded eyes and drew in a deep breath before opening them again. "Inspector, you're not a stupid man, and neither am I. You wouldn't ask us to come in here unless you did your homework. You know why Flora is not here."

"I'm trying to figure out how you got caught up in this."

"I ask myself the same question every goddamn day." His voice was husky and low. "You know about our son, Michael?"

"I do."

Art tilted his head back against the couch. "He was our only child. He was our whole world. He had just started university when he took a fentanyl overdose." He looked at Myra, his face filled with pain. "He lived for almost eight days. It's still like a dream to me."

"I'm sorry for your loss." Myra couldn't help but think of his own daughters.

"Flora found him on the floor in his bedroom. He was foaming at the mouth. His lips were blue. He was having a seizure. We didn't even know he had been doing drugs. He was a good kid." Art blinked continuously. "We had a good life. A house. A business. A future. A family. Now all we are is broken."

"You lost it all?"

"We both dealt with it in our own way." Art's forehead was a map of lines. "I went into a deep depression and couldn't get out of bed. Flora had a breakdown. She's still not stable. Then she started gambling online to keep her mind busy. It seemed harmless at first."

"But it got out of control?"

"It wasn't all her fault. My business went under. There was no money coming in, but lots going out. Before we knew it, we lost everything."

"Where did Morty—or should I say Barbara Williams—come into it?"

Art looked up and grinned. "You know, then."

"Yes, I know."

"I went to high school with Barb and Bucky. I knew her more than him. Barb and I were on student council together." He snickered. "We were going to change the world back then."

"She was a friend, then?"

"Yes, but we lost contact after high school. I reached out to her after I heard about the death of her parents. I went to the funeral, but I don't think she even knew I was there."

"Do you remember who else from your class was at the funeral?"

Art looked at the ceiling and thought for a moment. "A lot of the girls she used to hang around with, and the guys Bucky hung out with. I couldn't tell you offhand. I mean, that was decades ago."

"I understand. When did you make contact again?"

"After Michael died." His shoulders sank each time he said his son's name. "I got a call out of the blue about a year ago from a Mortimer Williams. I didn't know who that was. I didn't know anything about his life at that point. I barely knew what was happening in my own."

"But you're both Masons."

"Yes, but in different lodges. There are twenty-eight lodges in the province. Some have roots in the English constitution and some in the Scottish. We don't see each other that often. I'm with an English lodge. He's with a Scottish lodge. At that point I hadn't been active in the Masons for a few years."

"Were you shocked to hear from him?"

"I don't know if shocked is the right word—maybe surprised. But we had been through such tragedies that nothing fazed us."

"What did Mortimer want?"

"He asked me to meet him for a coffee, which I did. Once I saw him, I knew who it was. He looked more like Bucky. He explained what was going on in his life."

"How were you with that information?"

"Oh, I didn't care. Look, once you lose a child, nothing matters to you anymore."

"What did he want?"

"Morty said he knew about Michael's death, and someone had told him we had hit hard times. He wanted to help us."

"And did he?"

"I didn't know what to say. I thanked him but said no. We talked for a long time. You see, Morty was one of the kindest people you'd ever meet. Always had been. He had the ability to sense other people's pain. I guess he knew what pain felt like."

"I've heard a lot of people describe him as a very nice person."

"Look, if Morty knew you were hungry, he'd give you half his lunch, if not the whole thing. I guess when you've had that much pain in your life . . ." Art's voice trailed off.

"Did Morty help you?"

"Yes. He owned the house next door to his, and he rented it out to us. He charged us a hundred dollars a month."

"A hundred dollars a month?" Myra let out a low whistle as he thought of the big, spacious kitchen and well-manicured backyard.

"I know. It's ridiculous. I wouldn't take it for free, and that's the most he would take. Morty also paid off our credit card debt and Flora's gambling debts. He paid for both of us to get counselling, and because of that, we're in a much better place. He helped us get back on our feet."

"Why would he do all that for you?"

"He was just a nice guy."

Myra leaned forward. "Art, somebody was blackmailing Morty."

"Do you know who?"

"Well, that's what I'm trying to find out."

"You don't think it was me or Flora, do you?"

"Why would Morty pay off all your debt and let you live in a mansion for a hundred dollars a month?"

"I told you. He just wanted to help us. Poor Flora is still not herself. You met her. Her mind is gone. She's constantly doing crazy things. She's on all kinds of prescription drugs."

Myra tapped his fingers on the arm of the chair as he studied Art's face. "Did he owe you anything? A favour, maybe? Had he promised you anything?"

Art glanced around the room before coming back to Myra. "No."

Myra knew he was lying. "Tell me about Doreen."

Art's face tightened up. "We're not friends."

"Did she know about Morty helping you?"

"Not at first, but she figured it out."

"Was she angry?"

"She's always angry." Art screwed up the corner of his mouth. "Morty told us that he asked his lawyer to state in his will that he forgave all the money we owed him and left us the house."

"And did he?"

"Doreen told us he couldn't because the houses were hers. This was before he died." Art became silent and broody for a moment before continuing. "Flora went over the night the window was shot in to ask her. Doreen told her she expected us not only to pay her back in full, but she was raising our rent to what it should be, twenty-five hundred dollars a month. She gave us thirty days' notice."

"Do you know who shot out the window?"

"No, but I tell you I certainly could have."

Myra had a gut feeling that there was something not being said, but he knew it wasn't going to be said today.

"Art, did you kill Morty?"

Art's eyes widened. His hand flung to his heart. "Me? Oh my God, after everything I just told you? No. No, I didn't kill Morty."

"Do you know who did?"

"Doreen is the only one who's going to benefit from Morty's death. Ask her." He leaned in closer. "I also don't trust Tom Miller or James Fitzgerald. They wanted to keep the Masonic Temple because they believed there's some treasure in it. It's all hogwash to me. But they kept asking Morty to meet them there to search for some hidden staircase."

"Really?"

"Yeah. Miller in particular."

"Okay. Thanks for that." Myra noticed the sheen of sweat on Art's top lip. "Where were you the night he died?"

"Flora and I were home watching TV. Flora was having some lady problems, so we stayed home."

"You didn't go out at all?"

"No. If you're looking for his killer, talk to Doreen. But I also wonder about Miller and Fitzgerald."

"I'll talk to all of them." Myra leaned back in the chair. "Did you date Barbara in high school?"

Art's face reddened. "No, we were just friends."

"Do you know who she dated?"

"I don't recall her dating anyone, to tell you the truth."

"Do you know how long Morty and Doreen have been married?" Myra leaned on the arms of the chair and hoisted himself up.

Art stood and followed him to the door. "You don't know?"

"Know what?" Myra opened the door and let Art out into the hallway.

Art stopped and let out a laugh. "They've never been married."

25

Cst. Whiffen stopped what she was doing when Insp. Myra walked into the office. "What did Art Pardy have to say?"

"Everything we already knew." Myra picked up the black marker on the ledge of the whiteboard. He wrote down brief details as he spoke. "Art gave me some details on what happened after their son died. He says Morty paid off their debt and rented them that house for only a hundred dollars a month."

"What a deal." Whiffen folded her arms and leaned back in her chair.

"Why would Morty do that? A hundred bucks a month! Was Art the one blackmailing Morty?" Myra wrote *Blackmail* under Art's name. "I know he was lying to me."

"That's a lot of money to give away to an old high school chum," Whiffen noted, "unless he owed Art in some way."

"What do you mean?" Myra turned to face her.

"Like a favour. Maybe Art did something in return for that money."

"That's what I'm thinking, too." Myra continued making notes on the board. "But what? Art told me Doreen and Morty were not legally married."

"Really?" Whiffen let out a small laugh. "But you said she showed you a framed picture on her mantel of their wedding day."

"I know. I took a picture of it with my phone." He scratched at the five o'clock shadow forming around his jaws. "But lots of people live together without getting legally married and still refer to themselves as husband and wife. They'd been together for thirty years. She certainly would be entitled to all the benefits of a married person."

Whiffen filled Myra in on her efforts. "The warrant was finally approved to get the Williamses' bank statements. I emailed Doreen's lawyer earlier. I'm waiting for them to be sent to me. If Doreen had just handed them over, it could have saved us a lot of time. The real holdup, though, is Morty and Doreen had separate bank accounts."

"Really? She seems to be blocking this investigation at every turn." Myra rested his hands on the back of the nearest chair. "According to Art, Morty told him that when he died, his will would forgive all debt and he was leaving the house to him and Flora. Flora met with Doreen about that the night her window was shot out. Doreen told her that wasn't going to happen and jacked up their rent."

"Oh, that's a kick in the teeth." Whiffen screwed up her face. "The bigger question is this. Was Morty expecting to die? And if so, why? Did he know something?"

"It certainly seems like it, doesn't it?" Myra stood back and looked at the jumble of information on the board. "Did he really change his will?"

"I'll find out from his lawyer." Whiffen added it to her list of things to do.

Myra took out his notebook. "I need you to do an interview. Bucky called. Apparently, the witness who contacted Morty about their parents' death was his elderly aunt, Shirley Williams. She claims to have had a conversation with Bucky's mother the day of their deaths. Here's her info."

Myra placed the notebook in front of Whiffen, allowing her to write down the contact information.

"I'll call her as soon as I finish with the bank statements."

"Take your time. It's not a race. I'm going to pop in on James Fitzgerald this afternoon and see what this treasure hunt thing is about. That could be the missing piece of the puzzle."

Whiffen relaxed a little. "Okay. Sorry, I'm so used to watching the clock and worrying about being on time to get home to Jack."

"What do you mean?" Myra laid the marker back on the ledge.

She smiled. "I forgot to tell you. Now that Jack is an adult, we are able to get a care worker, paid for by government."

Myra's face lit up. "That's fantastic. Congratulations."

"Thanks. What a difference it makes." Whiffen picked up her phone, opened the texts, and held it up. "Steve has texted me three times today. The first time, he was getting groceries and having a panic attack wondering how Jack was doing. The second time, he picked up a coffee at a drive-through and sat in the parking lot drinking it. The third time, he was sitting in the driveway watching Jack interact with the care worker through the front window."

Myra was pleased. "He doesn't know what to do with himself."

"He's never had this freedom before." Whiffen suddenly felt choked up. "We're just so tired."

"Maria is getting the girls used to daycare for when she goes back to work, and she says it's like being let out of jail. She texted two hours ago to tell me the coffee at the drive-through is too hot." He let out a chuckle. "Not that she doesn't love being with the girls, but she misses her life. And that's okay, too. As parents we make choices every day and wonder if they're the right ones. It's okay to have a career and have children. You can love your career and still love your kids."

"You can't have it all, though, can you?" Whiffen sighed.

"You can, just not at the same time. Donna, I know this is diffi-cult for you. Let me know how I can help. Really, I'm here for you."

Whiffen lowered her head and bit her lip. The silence was bro-ken by a ping from her phone. "That's Morty's bank records." She turned to her computer without making eye contact with Myra. "Don't you have to pay Fitzgerald a surprise visit?"

"I do." Myra grabbed his coat off the rack and struggled to get his arms into the sleeves. When he got out to the car, he opened his phone, reread Maria's text, and realized he had not answered her.

He typed: You're just not used to hot coffee anymore LOL. Thank you for all you do with the girls. I love you.

26

The door to James Fitzgerald's office was ajar. The room was lit, and Insp. Myra could hear someone inside. He knocked loudly on the door, causing it to open slightly.

"Good Lord." Fitzgerald opened the door, his hand on his heart. "You frightened the life out of me."

"Sorry about that." Myra just grinned.

"Inspector." Fitzgerald looked up at the tall police officer. "Why didn't you tell me you were coming?"

"Am I interrupting?" Myra looked over Fitzgerald's head into the office. "Are you in a meeting?"

"No." Fitzgerald glanced at the map of the city, which was still stretched out over the table. "No. Not at all. Come in."

He opened the door wider, allowing Myra room to get by him. Myra quickly scanned the room and took note of the map.

"What's this?" He bent over the table, his eye instantly drawn to a series of red circles around some buildings.

"I told you about the Ecclesiastic Circle." Fitzgerald pointed out the Basilica. "This is it."

Myra walked over to the door and closed it. Fitzgerald quickly turned around to face him.

"What's going on?" He started to move backward.

"We need to have a chat." Myra pulled out a chair, sat down, and pointed at Fitzgerald's office chair. "Take a seat."

The colour drained from the historian's face as he did what he was told. "What's this about?"

"You told me you met Mortimer Williams through the Masons."

"Yes. That's right." Fitzgerald was holding his breath.

"But that's not true, is it?" Myra rested his arm on the map.

Fitzgerald sat with a straight back. "Yes, it is. We met through the Masons."

"You were in his class in high school."

"No, I wasn't," an indignant Fitzgerald answered.

Myra took a folded, photocopied sheet of paper out of the inside pocket of his blazer and straightened it out in front of him. "Take a look."

Fitzgerald snatched the paper from him and looked it over.

"My God, that's a page from my yearbook." He looked up at Myra. "But what's that got to do with Morty?"

Myra pointed to the small photo of Barbara Williams. "That's Morty."

Fitzgerald looked back and forth from the photo to Myra. "No." His mouth formed a circle. "That can't be."

Myra leaned back and took a good look at the historian. He wasn't sure if Fitzgerald was pulling his leg.

"Come on, you didn't know Mortimer Williams was Barbara Williams?"

Fitzgerald picked up his glasses, put them on, and took a closer look, his mouth still hanging open.

"God, no." He looked up. "That explains a lot."

"Like what?"

"Like why he kept his distance from me. He didn't want me to know."

"Did you hang around with Barbara in high school?"

"No, she was one of the sporty, more popular kids." Fitzgerald kept his eyes on the paper.

"That wasn't your group?"

Fitzgerald tilted his head toward Myra. "Now, Inspector, do I look like I was in with the popular kids?"

"You weren't friends?"

"Not friends, but we weren't enemies, either. I was into history, and she was into sports."

"Did you date her?" Myra watched for his reaction.

Fitzgerald let out a loud laugh. He held up the photo of him at seventeen, with thick glasses and short hair.

"Seriously? No."

"Do you know who she dated?"

"No, and I wouldn't have noticed that, really. We didn't run in the same circles."

"Why did you join the Masons?"

"History is not only my job but also my hobby. I've worked and studied all over the world to obtain my credentials." Fitzgerald looked at the yearbook page again and handed it back to Myra. "A little over six years ago, I found historical documents in the Basilica's archives that stated, around 1835, a very important item was moved by ship to St. John's from Ireland. The ship was from Portugal. Newfoundland had a very tight relationship with Portugal and Ireland for many years."

"What was it?" Myra tucked the yearbook page back into his blazer's pocket.

"Don't laugh. The Ark of the Covenant." Fitzgerald grinned awkwardly. "It's believed by scholars that the Ark is closely guarded in Aksum at the Church of St. Mary of Zio. But this document said the prophet Jeremiah took the Ark from Aksum to protect it. He brought the Ark to Ireland. I contacted my counterpart in Dublin and found out that a few Irish manuscripts hinted at the prophet being there in the sixth century."

Myra raised an eyebrow but continued to listen with interest. Fitzgerald carried on.

"The Irish refer to Jeremiah as Ollamh Fodhla. They believe the Ark is buried on the Hill of Tara, an ancient ceremonial and burial site near Skryne in County Meath. The Irish documents say, before he died, Jeremiah sent the Ark somewhere where it would never be found . . . in the New World."

Myra slapped his knee. "Oh, come on. Not you, too?"

"Why? Who else mentioned that?"

"Forget about it." Myra waved the question aside. "Go on."

Fitzgerald regarded him suspiciously. "Those who possess this mythical relic could rule the world. It's what Hitler was searching for."

"You want to rule the world?" Myra leaned on the arm of the chair, peering at the historian intently.

"No, I want to tour the world. I want to be the one who finds the Ark," Fitzgerald explained. "Do you know what a discovery like this could do for us? To be the location of the greatest discovery of the century?"

"It would certainly help your career."

"Well, yes, that too, of course."

"What makes you think it's in St. John's?"

Fitzgerald stood up and leaned over the map. "Let me explain. This is the Ecclesiastic Circle." He ran his finger over a small section of the map. "Do you know where Campbell Avenue is?"

"Yes." Myra stood and looked closely at the map.

"It was named after Admiral John Campbell, Governor of Newfoundland. In 1784, Campbell issued an order that said: 'Pursuant to the King's instructions to me, you are to allow all persons inhabiting this Island to have full liberty of conscience and the free exercise of all such modes of religious worship as are not prohibited by law, provided they be contented with a quiet and peaceable enjoyment of the same, and not giving offence or scandal to Government.'"

Myra shrugged. "Why is that significant?"

"Because he was giving everyone the right to practise their own religion as long as they maintained the peace." Fitzgerald looked at him like he should have known this. "Where else in the world does this happen? Countries are still going to war over religion."

"I guess so. But what's this got to do with anything?"

"I believe he was setting in motion a plan to move treasure."

The corners of Myra's mouth twisted up in a forced smile. "Are you for real?"

"Let me show you." Fitzgerald pointed to the map. "St. Thomas' Anglican Church was built in 1836. The architect was Patrick Keough, a Catholic Irishman. Why did the Anglicans hire a Catholic?" He didn't wait for an answer. His fingers trailed across Military Road and down Church Hill. "The Anglican Cathedral was built in 1850 by Sir Gilbert Scott. And here, the Basilica was built in 1855 by John Philpot Jones." He moved his finger along to Buchanan Street. "This is the George Street United Church, a Methodist church built in 1873 by Elijah Hoole."

Myra tried to keep track of the years in his head.

"This part is important." Fitzgerald stood up straight to face Myra. "On July 8, 1892, the Great Fire wiped out most of St. John's. At that time, the Masonic Temple, which was the first Masonic Temple in North America, was on Long's Hill, where the Kirk is now. It burned to the ground, and the Masons rebuilt on Cathedral Street in 1894. Where it stands today. It was designed by the English architect James Wills, Sr."

"Okay," Myra said.

Fitzgerald's fingers slid over to Queen's Road. "The Congregational Church was built in 1895. It's now a condo building, but the leading light of the harbour that was put on its spire in 1902 still shines."

The historian's excitement was infectious. "I forgot it was once a church," Myra said.

Fitzgerald pointed at a dot on Queen's Road. "St. Andrew's Presbyterian Church, which is known as the Kirk because it's a Scottish church, was built in 1896 by James Wills, Sr., the same guy who built the Masonic Temple."

Myra leaned in. "Interesting."

"The last one." Fitzgerald pointed to another dot on Queen's Road. "Gower Street United Church, built by Elijah Hoole, who I already told you about, built the George Street United Church."

"That's a lot of history and architects." Myra stretched his back. "But what does it all mean?"

"These churches are built in a circle by Masons. Where else have you ever seen so many religions build churches next to each other and live in harmony for so many years?"

"I don't know offhand."

"If you take the Masonic symbol of a dot within a circle and put it over the map, it fits perfectly." Fitzgerald took out a sheet of tracing paper and laid it over the map.

Myra grinned. "This is really why you joined the Masons, isn't it?"

"I needed information that I could only get by joining and moving up through the ranks."

"But St. Thomas' and George Street United are not in the circle," Myra pointed out.

"No, but look at this. The lines on either side of the circle represent St. John the Evangelist and St. John the Baptist. The two Masonic patron saints. That's where those churches fall."

Myra scrunched up his face. "I think you're pulling at straws there, James. Just speaking as an investigator."

"Hear me out," Fitzgerald protested. "For years we thought the treasure was buried under the Masonic Temple. There are rumours that the cornerstone of the building had the map that can tell exactly where it is. There's also the matter of a hidden staircase in the basement that leads to tunnels under all these churches and down to Government House on Military Road. The tunnels were built so Masons could move freely from place to place without being seen. But the map shows there is a second tunnel from the Masonic Temple that leads to a concrete room the same size as the Chamber of Reflection."

"Now that you mention it, I *have* heard about the tunnels, but they have never been found. I've never heard about a hidden staircase."

"The Temple caretaker says it was there, but now it's gone. There's a wall there now, but I don't know who put it there or why."

"Maybe the new owners just walled it off for space. Where is the map?"

"The cornerstone was opened before the building was sold and its contents removed. Only the Grand Masters have access to it. It's the Masons' greatest secret here. They protect it at all costs."

"Did you ask Morty if you could see it?"

"I did." Fitzgerald's shoulders fell. "He straight up refused."

"That's why you dislike him."

"The map could prove those tunnels exist."

Myra looked closely at the tracing paper. "Where does the dot fall now, using the Masonic symbol?"

"The dot falls on top of the Sergeants' Memorial in Veteran's Square."

Myra smirked in disbelief. "Really? So, every Remembrance Day I've been marching on top of the Ark of the Covenant?"

"The Cross on the memorial came from Edinburgh, Scotland." Fitzgerald pointed at the map. "The first Masonic Temple was built where the Scottish church, the Kirk, is now built. The Masons have two lodges here: the English lodge and the Scottish lodge."

"You should have your own show," Myra said with a grin.

"I believe there's treasure under that memorial." Fitzgerald slammed his hand down on the table. "I absolutely believe it."

"I think you need another hobby."

"Look, I know it's hard to believe, but I think it's worth pursuing. You should also know about the mirror, too." Fitzgerald gave him a sideways glance.

"What mirror?"

"In the basement of the Temple, outside the women's washroom, there's a huge mirror. People say they see the dead in it."

"Oh, come on. There are no ghosts in the twenty-first century." Myra stood back from the table and looked around. "Morty didn't believe you, did he?"

Fitzgerald rubbed his palms together and thought a moment before answering. "No, he didn't."

"What did he think?"

"At first, he laughed. He thought it was all a crock of crap."

"Did he change his mind?"

"No. Why do you ask?"

"Because you said 'at first,' like he had changed his mind."

"No. No, he didn't change his mind."

"Okay, but you needed him to put his support behind this as the current Grand Master. His support would have given you more support inside the Masons, and outside, with politicians. I would imagine the Masons still have a lot of politicians on their roll call."

Fitzgerald nodded sadly. "He wouldn't do it. He didn't want the Masons involved."

"You were angry about it?"

"I was." Fitzgerald picked up the tracing paper and examined it. "I put years of work into this. It's my whole life. I can't let it go that easily."

"Did you argue with Morty about it?"

"Oh, yes. We had some very angry words."

"But he didn't change his mind."

"No." Fitzgerald sighed. "He wouldn't budge, even though I had a past Master who believed me."

"That's why you hated him," Myra suggested. "But did you kill him over it?"

Fitzgerald laughed. "No. I'm crazy, but not that crazy. All I needed was a letter." He threw the tracing paper down. "A simple letter saying it was possible, but he wouldn't do it."

"Because it was possible but not probable," Myra answered. "There's no treasure, James. It's just not true."

"You don't know that. We have been researching this for years. There are too many coincidences."

"Where were you the night he died?"

"I left work around five and went home. I have two schnauzers, and I walk them every day after work. I didn't know when the storm was going to start getting bad, so I walked them right away. Then we stayed home for the rest of the night."

"When you were talking about your treasure hunt, you said 'we' several times," Myra stated. "Who is 'we'?"

"I have a silent partner, if you will." Fitzgerald brooded as he rolled up his map.

"I need the name." Myra's voice was hoarse and a little louder than he intended. "Who is this past Master?"

"We went to school together, also. He's the one who sponsored me into the Masons." He stopped rolling the map and looked at Myra. "I just remembered something."

"What's that?"

"He dated Barbara in high school." Fitzgerald resumed rolling up the map.

Myra's patience was wearing thin. "Well, who is it?"

"Tom Miller."

27

Insp. Myra slowly drove over a gravel road riddled with potholes and parked behind some large tombstones.

"Ever notice that humans are the only living creatures who bury their dead and mark the spot with monuments?"

"Your mind is a scary place," Cst. Whiffen observed.

"Just saying. When animals die, they lie down on the ground and decompose to fertilize the earth. Lot to be said for that."

Whiffen gave him a reproachful look. "When my sister's parrot died, she held a funeral complete with a burial that cost over three thousand dollars. My mother made me send flowers and a card."

Myra gave her a sideways glance to confirm she was serious. The vibration of his phone gave him an excuse to look away. "Simon says he can meet us in an hour. Let's stick around for a while and see what happens."

Whiffen shook her head. "A hearse is coming."

A black, chauffeur-driven hearse carrying the body of Mortimer Williams pulled into the graveyard, followed by a black limousine carrying his wife, and a long line of cars driven by friends and family.

Myra and Whiffen sat in an unmarked police car hidden near-by. He turned off the engine, and a morning mist began to cover the windshield.

Myra adjusted an earpiece. "I'm not sure where Ident hid the mic, but it's close by. I can hear them. Can you hear them?"

"Ten-four." Whiffen gave him a thumbs-up.

Six pallbearers shivered in the winter sun as they unloaded the shiny grey coffin. One wore a simple black suit. Five were dressed in black suits, black hat, white gloves, and plain white Masonic aprons. Each wore a black crepe upon the left arm above the elbow and a sprig of evergreen on the left breast. Dozens of other Masons followed the casket to its final resting place.

Whiffen turned her telescopic lens toward the gravesite and began taking pictures. "Can you see who the pallbearers are?" she asked.

"I can, and that's a little surprising." Myra watched as Bucky Williams, Art Pardy, Tom Miller, James Fitzgerald, and two other Masons carried Mortimer Williams to the grave, followed by Doreen Williams, who was letting out loud bursts of sobs and dabbing her eyes with a tissue. Flora Pardy held Doreen up as she manoeuvred through the snow-covered graveyard. "All the usual suspects are here."

"The funeral director said Morty's will was very specific in what he wanted."

Myra scratched the morning growth on his chin. "It's like he knew who his killer would be, and he wanted that person to suffer."

An officer of the Masons, wearing the same regalia as the pall-bearers and a heavily jewelled collar around his neck, opened the Holy Bible at the twelfth chapter of Ecclesiastes. Another Mason held a black umbrella over his head as he read from the Good Book. The pallbearers carefully laid the coffin on the brass bars above the six-foot hole that would be Mortimer's final resting place.

"Friends and brethren," he began, "from time immemorial, it has been the custom among the Fraternity of Free and Accepted Masons to accompany a Brother's remains to the place of interment, there to deposit him with the usual formalities. In conformity to this usage, we have assembled in the character of Masons to offer a tribute of affection to the memory of our Brother, Mortimer Williams, thereby demonstrating the sincerity of our esteem for him and our steady attachment to the principles of our Order."

Doreen's sobs had quieted down, allowing the ceremony to continue. Flora stood next to her, holding her hand.

"Give me a tissue," Doreen whispered hoarsely.

Flora pulled a crumpled tissue out of her coat pocket and checked it before handing it to Doreen. "Here."

"Bucky hasn't taken his eyes off me all morning," Doreen whispered harshly in Flora's ear. "He'd better keep his distance if he knows what's good for him."

Flora glanced at Bucky and noted his intense stare. "He's very hurt, Doreen. It must be harder on a twin. I bet it feels like losing half of yourself."

"*I bet it feels like losing half of yourself,*" Doreen said mockingly. "Whose side are you on?"

"There are no sides," Flora answered apologetically. "You both lost somebody you loved. Can't you just put your differences aside for today?"

"Oh, shut up," Doreen whispered, then let out another loud sob for the crowd.

The officiating Masonic brother continued the service. "The lambskin, or white apron, is an emblem of innocence, and the badge of a Mason, and is a mark of distinction when worthily worn. This emblem I now deposit in the grave of our deceased Brother."

He deposited Mortimer's apron into the grave and continued.

"By it we are reminded of the universal dominion of death.

The arm of friendship cannot interpose to prevent his coming; the wealth of the world cannot purchase our release; nor will the innocence of youth, or the charms of beauty, propitiate his purpose. This scene reminds us of our mortality and that, sooner or later, these frail bodies must return to their parent dust."

Bucky navigated his way through the crowd to get closer to Doreen. He was stopped by Tom Miller.

"It's not the time or place, Bucky."

"Get out of my way, Tom." Bucky tried to duck and weave his way past him.

"No good will come of it."

"I'm going to have my say."

"Not here. Not now."

Bucky spoke through clenched teeth. "She fucking killed my whole family. You all know it." His voice rose over the crowd, and heads turned in his direction.

"Lower your voice," Miller warned.

Art Pardy moved next to Bucky. "People heard you."

"Good. That's why I said it," said Bucky, his voice carrying over the crowd.

Art grabbed Bucky by the arm and dragged him away from the grave. "You had all day to confront her. Why here?"

"What are you afraid of, Art?" Bucky stood solidly before him. "She got you by the balls, too?"

"Stop it," Art growled. "We'll sort this all out later."

"She fuckin' got you by the balls, too." Bucky lifted both hands and pushed Art, sending him backward into a snowbank.

The officiating Masonic brother missed what was happening at the back of the crowd and focused on the ceremony.

"The evergreen, which once marked the temporary resting place of the illustrious dead, is an emblem of our faith in the immortality of the soul. By this we are reminded that we have an immortal part within us that shall survive the grave, and which shall never, never die. By it we are admonished in the habiliments of death and deposited in the silent tomb, yet, through our belief in the mercy of God, we may confidently hope that our souls will bloom in eternal spring. This, too, I deposit in the grave. Alas, my Brother!"

Each Mason dropped his sprig of evergreen into the grave and followed with the exclamation, "Alas, my Brother!"

Art got to his feet and brushed the snow off his black suit. He stood in front of Bucky and pushed a finger into his chest. "Watch your mouth."

James Fitzgerald pushed his way in between the two men. "What's wrong with you? It's a goddamn funeral. Stop it."

"What's your role in this, James?" Bucky pushed him, sending him sliding on a patch of ice.

Fitzgerald wavered and caught himself on Miller's arm. "Jesus, Bucky. Watch it. It's your brother's funeral."

"I know that." Bucky waved his arms around. "What I don't know is which one of you helped her kill him."

Fitzgerald tried to put his hand over Bucky's mouth. Bucky smacked him in the face, sending him over a headstone and landing on his back. Fitzgerald struggled to get up off a grave in the foot-high snow. Those gathered were now more interested in what was happening behind them than in front. The officiating Masonic brother, oblivious to the scuffle beyond the crowd, continued.

"Unto the grave we consign the body of our deceased Brother Mortimer Williams. Earth to earth." He sprinkled a handful of earth on the coffin. "Ashes to ashes, there to remain till the trumpet shall sound on the resurrection morn. We can cheerfully leave him in the hands of a Being who doeth all things well."

Art grabbed one of Bucky's arms, and Miller grabbed the other. "We're taking you home."

"I'm not leaving my brother's side." Bucky dug his boots into the snow and leaned backward against their tugging.

Art stopped. "Bucky, I'll let you go, but you better keep your mouth shut till this is over."

Bucky freed himself from their hold. He shook off the snow, straightened his tie, and turned to face them.

"As soon as he's buried, I'm coming for every one of you." He pointed in each of their faces. "Do you hear me? You're not getting away with this."

Miller, Fitzgerald, and Pardy lowered their heads and walked back to the gravesite to hear the officiating Masonic Brother finish the final payer.

"That we may be received into Thine everlasting kingdom and there join in union with our friend and enjoy that uninterrupted and unceasing felicity which is allotted to the souls of just men made perfect. Amen."

All Masons responded with, "So mote it be."

Myra and Whiffen watched the exchange between Bucky and the rest with great interest.

"What do you think?" Whiffen asked.

Myra watched Doreen leave the graveyard, still holding the tissue to her nose.

"I think the Oscar for Best Actress goes to Doreen Williams."

28

"Well, that was interesting." Myra used a back road through the graveyard to drive away.

"Bucky's on the warpath," Whiffen observed. "We could use that to our advantage."

Myra pulled out into traffic. "He's hell-bent on Doreen being the killer, but he's convinced someone helped her."

"I'm not ready to point a finger at either of them yet. I need more information," Whiffen said, picking up her phone. She scrolled through her email as he drove.

"Maybe Simon can help us make up our mind." Myra saw her face change. "Everything all right?"

She quickly looked up at him, then back at her screen. "Yeah, everything's great. Jack's caregiver started working fully without Steve this week. I'm just checking on the video."

"How is Steve handling it?"

"He texted me an hour ago. He's gone to get groceries. He's so used to being on a time limit when he leaves the house."

"I'm happy this is working out for you." Myra pulled into the parking lot of the Health Sciences Complex. "We should only be about an hour here. Why don't you meet him for lunch?"

"Lunch." She looked up from the phone. "That never even occurred to me. Would you mind? I won't be more than an hour."

Myra nodded. "Take your time and enjoy your lunch."

The medical examiner's office carried the same disinfectant smell as the morgue. The medical assistant seated at the front desk didn't seem to notice it. She looked up at Myra and Whiffen.

"Can I help you?"

"We're here to see Simon." Myra showed his badge. "Insp. Myra and Cst. Whiffen."

The assistant looked at the appointment calendar on her screen. "Oh yes, he's waiting for you in his office." She pointed to the left. "Down that hall, through the double doors. First door on your left."

"Thanks." Myra led the way down the cold, sterile hallway. He stopped before the office door and leaned into Whiffen. "He likes to entertain with crazy stories. You'll get used to it."

"Oh, I know." Whiffen reached for the doorknob. "I've lived through one of his autopsies."

"Morning, mate," Simon called out from his desk. "Come in and close the door behind you."

Simon's office was a mess of organized confusion. His grey metal desk and filing cabinet were covered in files and medical books. An anatomy chart was pinned to one wall, and a framed picture of Queen Elizabeth II hung on the opposite wall. Simon pulled his glasses out of the breast pocket of his blazer and put them on, balancing them on the tip of his nose as he scrolled through his computer screen.

"Sit down. Sit down." He pointed to the two chairs in front of his desk. "I've got quite a brilliant presentation for you."

Myra and Whiffen took their seats.

"But do you have a cause of death yet?" Myra asked.

"Well." Simon looked up from the computer. He tapped his index finger on his lips excitedly as he considered his answer. "I'm a little gobsmacked by the whole thing, really."

Myra leaned toward Whiffen and lowered his voice. "He's a Brit. You'll get used to his words."

Whiffen hid her smile behind her hand and nodded in agreement.

"And what has you so gobsmacked?" Myra asked.

"Well, the whole case got me buzzing. The poor bloke had a rough go of it, for sure. Someone really wanted him dead."

"What do you mean?"

Simon turned the screen to enable the police officers to see his report. "Let's start with his head." He opened a photo of Mortimer Williams's cold body on the morgue table with his skullcap flipped open. Both officers grimaced at the sight. Simon used his pen as a pointer. "There was blunt force trauma to the back of his head."

"There was a small wooden table seized from the site that had the victim's blood and hair on it. We believed it could have been the murder weapon." Myra kept his eyes on the gruesome photo.

"Then that would be it." Simon opened another photo that showed the back of Mortimer's clean-shaven head. "See the swelling here, and the cut?" He used his pen to show the injury, then opened another photo. "See the slight bruising under his eyes?"

Both officers leaned in.

"These injuries are fairly common and are usually caused by blunt force trauma, or shaking of the brain, which can happen in car accidents or shaken baby syndrome," Simon explained. "It seems Mr. Williams's injury was very severe. I would classify it as a diffuse axonal injury. He was hit very hard. It would have dazed him, but if he received medical attention, he may have lived."

"If the killer hit him with the table, did he intend to kill him that night, or did it happen in the heat of the moment?" Whiffen inclined her head, looking at Myra. "Whoever made him go to the Masonic Temple that night didn't bring a weapon."

"They wanted something he couldn't give them." Myra was back to tugging at his moustache. "But what?"

"Well, with this injury he certainly wouldn't have been able to lay himself out in his Masonic uniform in that concrete room," Simon continued. "He would have had difficulty with walking, loss of consciousness, slurred speech, or a number of other things."

Myra made a clicking noise with his tongue. "The way he was laid out seemed like a sign of respect for his position in the Masons. Maybe even a sign of remorse."

"Are there any defensive wounds on him?" Whiffen asked. "I wonder if he was fighting with someone, or was he surprised from behind?"

"There's some bruising around both forearms like he had been grabbed forcibly. That leads me to believe he was in a fight," Simon added. "But there's more." He handed Myra a report. "That's the results of his stomach content and blood analysis."

"Thank you for not showing us the picture." Myra read through the report. "What am I looking at?"

"His stomach showed the delightful fish and chips he shared with his brother, followed by a soda. He also had a very bad stomach ulcer." Simon leaned back in his chair and steepled his fingers. "I checked his medical file. He had been prescribed pantoprazole for the ulcer. During the autopsy I found a small, empty decorative pill case in the inside pocket of his blazer. Not one the pharmacist gives you, but a fancy one that grand people use. I did a swab test on it before Cst. Whiffen took it into evidence."

"Have you got the results back yet?" Myra asked.

"Yes." He handed Myra a second report. "There are traces of pantoprazole in the pill case, but also traces of antimicrobials, which are commonly used for urinary tract infections. The pills look very similar. I checked the victim's blood and found antimicrobials."

"Okay." Myra waved his hand in a circular motion to tell him to go on.

"Antimicrobials contain sulphites," Simon explained. "According to Mr. Williams's medical chart, he is severely allergic to sulphites. He goes into anaphylactic shock if he digests it. It's highlighted in red on his chart."

"Then why did he take pills with sulphur in them?" Myra read over the report again. "His doctor would know the difference."

"His doctor didn't prescribe them." Simon slowly shook his head. "I called his doctor, and she told me he didn't have a urinary tract infection and that she didn't prescribe that drug. All the same, the dose was low. It would have caused a reaction, but I can't say for sure if it would have sent him into full anaphylactic shock."

Myra and Whiffen exchanged excited glances.

"We'll get a warrant for Doreen's medical chart," Myra offered.

Whiffen eagerly studied the report in Myra's hands. "Would Doreen switch her pills for Mortimer's ulcer pills, knowing he was allergic?"

"One more thing," Simon added. "His bloodwork shows he took the antimicrobials about a half-hour after he ate. He would have been in considerable pain."

Myra's eyes widened. "Doreen knew he was meeting Bucky for supper. She had to know."

"But why did he go to the Masonic Temple and not home if he was in pain?" Whiffen asked. "Especially considering that a snowstorm was hitting the city at that point."

"He had to be meeting someone about something that was important to him," Myra concluded.

The medical examiner took off his glasses and began to clean them in his shirt. "The injury to the back of his head, in my opinion, was the cause of death. If he was in the throes of anaphylactic shock while that was happening, it would have hindered his ability to defend himself. But there's one more thing."

"What do you mean?" Myra asked. "I know that look on your face, Simon. There's a story coming."

"Remember the footprints found on either side of his body?"

"Yes. There were footprints found all over the chamber, but those two looked like someone stood over him, and they didn't match the responding officer's boots."

"I found slight bruising on his cheeks." Simon opened a photo on his screen. "One on the right cheek and four on the left. As if someone grabbed his face."

Simon brought up a picture of Mortimer's body lying in the Chamber of Reflection and the footprints on either side of him in the dust.

"That would explain the positioning of the footprints," Myra added.

"Yes, it would." Simon opened the picture of Mortimer's blue, puffy face.

Myra tried to reason it out. "But why?"

Simon put his glasses back on the edge of his nose, then looked over them. "Somebody could have tried to revive him after he was injured and grabbed his face to try to shake him awake."

Whiffen was dumbfounded. "Jesus. Talk about a hundred ways to die."

"You see," Simon went on, pushing his glasses up the bridge of his nose, "I think either someone may have tried to revive him, or the killer wanted to make sure he was dead."

Myra rubbed his hands over his knees. "Or did someone else find him and try to revive him?"

"If someone tried to revive him, could it be the person who called it in as a break and enter?" Whiffen leaned forward on the chair, resting her elbows on her thighs. "Could that be who laid him out so neatly? It's very weird."

"It's not the weirdest way to die, though," Simon added excitedly. "Have you ever heard of Burking?"

They both answered no. Myra gave Whiffen a warning side glance as Simon settled back in his chair.

"William Burke was a merchant in Edinburgh, Scotland, in the early 1800s. In 1827, he hooked up with William Hare, who ran a beggars hotel in the village of Tanners Close. One day, a resident of the hotel died, and Burke arranged to sell the body to a doctor who needed corpses for his dissection demonstrations. They delivered the body and received seven pounds and ten shillings. The men struck an arrangement whereby Burke and Hare would deliver the doctor more bodies for eight pounds in summer, and ten in winter."

Simon let out a hearty laugh.

"Apparently grave robbing was more difficult when the ground was cold. At first they robbed graves to get the money, but the local populace refused to die fast enough for the greedy men. They began kidnapping and killing people who were not likely to be missed. Burke sat on his victims, blocking their mouths and noses until they suffocated."

Myra waited for Simon to get to the point.

"Eventually the police caught up with them. Hare cut a deal and testified against Burke. Burke was convicted and experienced asphyxia himself when he was hanged in 1829, an event attended by as many as forty thousand people."

Myra rolled his eyes. "Where do you come up with this stuff?"

"I'm fascinated by death. I read whatever I can get my hands on." Simon clapped his hands together. "You never know, Officers, one day that information may come in handy for you."

Myra pressed down on the arms of the chair and stood. "Yes, if I come across grave robbers, I'll get in touch."

"We still don't know who killed Williams or why." Whiffen gathered up the files from Simon.

"The killer is always the one who is not getting what they desperately want—the one who has to have what they can't have," Myra stated flatly.

29

Doreen Williams and her lawyer sat at a black metal table inside the interview room at Royal Newfoundland Constabulary Headquarters. Her lawyer tapped Doreen on the forearm and nodded toward the small camera mounted on the ceiling. She moved closer to Doreen's ear while covering her mouth with her hand and whispered while her client's head bobbed up and down.

Insp. Myra and Constable Whiffen watched the video monitor in the room next door. Whiffen looked up at him. "Are you surprised she showed up with a lawyer?"

"No, I expected it." Myra flipped through a white file folder as he spoke.

"She knows a lot more than she's letting on."

"Doreen Williams is not stupid," Myra observed. "If Bucky is right, she has gotten away with murder for decades."

"It would be amazing if we could prove that."

Myra agreed. "Bucky provided a lot of information in his statement. Thankfully, he was able to shake the family tree and find out who Morty's secret witness was."

"I made contact yesterday, and I'm meeting up with her this afternoon."

Myra put his hands on his hips and stretched his spine backward. The sound of cracking made Whiffen grimace.

"For the love of God, man, see a chiropractor."

"No time for that." Myra exhaled heavily. "I gotta go to work." He tucked the file folder under his arm.

"I'm going over Bucky's statement one more time before I head out. Good luck with it." Whiffen hurried down the hallway and out of sight.

The door to the interview room swung open, sending a gust of stale air and the faint smell of musk. The two women stopped whispering and looked up.

Myra extended his hand. "Mrs. Williams, thanks for coming in."

Doreen stood, shook his hand, and sat back down. "This is my lawyer, Raylene McKay."

McKay reached a manicured hand across the table and exchanged a firm handshake. "Nice to meet you."

"You, too." Myra pulled out the black metal chair across from them and laid the file folder and a notebook on the table.

"I have a right to have my lawyer present," Doreen stated emphatically.

"Yes, you do," Myra agreed and folded his hands on the table. "I just have a few questions for you."

McKay opened a blue, leather-bound legal pad, fountain pen at the ready to take notes. She tucked a strand of long red hair behind her ear and nodded at her client to proceed.

"Let's get on with it." Doreen spoke as if she had somewhere better to be, her time too valuable to be spent discussing her husband's murder.

Myra looked up at the camera in the corner of the room recording their meeting. "For the record, I would like to state that, before this interview, you identified the coat and bag found on the bar at the Masonic Temple as that of Mortimer Williams, your husband."

"Yes, I did." Doreen wiped the back of her hand across her eyes. "It's the bag he carried his Masonic apron and other items in."

"You've received the results of Mortimer's autopsy?"

"Yes, I have." She answered with a wry twist of her mouth. "What I don't understand is why I'm here and not Bucky Williams."

"You're here of your own free will to answer some questions that may help me with the investigation. Do you think you're here for another purpose?"

McKay touched Doreen's arm and shook her head. Doreen acknowledged her lawyer's prompt and looked back at Myra.

"I don't need to answer that."

"You don't have to answer anything, but that's not going to help me solve your husband's murder."

Doreen folded her arms and leaned back in the chair. "I want to be honest with you. I'll answer whatever I can."

"I want you to be honest, too. When I first spoke to you, the day after Mortimer died, you told me he was having supper with someone. Is that right?"

Doreen looked up toward the ceiling, as though it might contain answers, then back at Myra. "Yeah. He went out to supper that night. It was the last time I saw him."

"Who did he go out to supper with?"

"Um . . ." She looked back at the ceiling. "Someone he worked with."

"You told me at that time he was meeting someone he was involved with in charity work."

"Uh, no, wait, I meant charity work." Doreen gestured with both hands. "I have so much going on right now."

Myra leaned across the table. "Morty had supper with Bucky that night. But you knew that, didn't you?"

Doreen rocked backward. McKay whispered something in her ear, shielding her mouth from Myra with her hand.

"I knew he was meeting Bucky. We fought about it."

"Why?"

"Bucky is bad news." She viciously poked a finger onto the table. "Morty was clear of him. He didn't want Bucky back in his life, but Bucky just wouldn't let it go."

Myra stared at her. "Let what go?"

"He wanted money. That's all he ever wanted . . . money."

"Why did you lie to me about it?"

"I didn't think it was important." Doreen blinked excessively as she spoke.

"You didn't think it was important? He was the last person who saw your husband before he was murdered."

Doreen ran her hand over her short grey hair. "I wasn't thinking straight."

"Morty was going to leave you, wasn't he?"

"No," she replied, her voice rising.

"His lawyer had filed the papers." Myra tapped his index finger on the file. "You had separate bank accounts. He gave you an allowance every month. You had no idea he sold the coffee shops and cleaned out the bank account."

McKay leaned closer to Doreen, whispering at a fast rate. Doreen pulled away, straightening her jacket.

"That's not true," she answered defensively. A sudden sadness came over her face. "Yes, we were going through a hard time, but we were in counselling. I can prove it. We were together for thirty-seven years. Morty was the love of my life." Her lip quivered as she spoke. "He was the only one who ever loved me. We had a good marriage. I would never hurt him."

Myra looked into her eyes with a piercing stare. "Doreen. You and Morty were never married."

"Marriage is a state of mind. We didn't need that piece of paper." Doreen wiped away a stray tear from the corner of her eye. "You don't understand. Morty was my only family. My parents threw me out when I was a teenager. Morty accepted me. I was safe with him. I loved him."

A calm came over Myra as he listened to her. It was the same way he spoke about Maria. He allowed her a moment to collect herself before continuing the interview, but Doreen continued without prompting.

"When he transitioned, I supported him. I even thought life would be easier for us. But he had to go get involved with that boys club. Prove he was a real man."

"Are you referring to the Masons?"

"Yes, the goddamn Masons. That's all he cared about. He was obsessed with being accepted by them."

Myra opened the file folder and slid a document out. "Morty sold the coffee shops to a bigger chain. Your name was never on the business."

Doreen pulled the document closer and tried to read it while wiping a bead of sweat off her forehead. "Is that true?"

The lawyer pulled the document close to her. "Was your name on the business?"

"No." Doreen looked shaken. "He handled all the business affairs. I just assumed I'd inherit everything."

"We can fight any challenge otherwise in court," McKay warned.

Myra's ears perked up. "Why would you be thinking about inheriting anything?"

"Um, wait. Actually, that's not what I meant. You're twisting my words."

"Morty had made up with Bucky, and he gave his brother back his rightful inheritance and a lot more." Myra pushed another document across the table. "He gave a large amount to an elderly aunt and the rest to charity."

Doreen's mouth hung open. She rolled her tongue around her lips, trying to moisten them. McKay looked over her shoulder, reading through the bank report.

"That bastard," Doreen said, glaring at Myra. "That goddamn bastard. Why would he do this?" She clutched her chest as she crumpled over, a flood of panic in her face. "I would have died for him."

Myra sat up with his back straight. "But would you kill him? Or for him?"

Her pale lips moved. McKay pulled her closer, feverishly whispering into her ear. Doreen shook her head, then looked at the police officer.

"No, I did not." The blood had left her face.

"Then who did?" Myra asked sedately.

"How the fuck do I know?" She took another look at the documents in front of her and sent them flying across the table. "Everyone thinks I had the most to gain. But really I have the most to lose. I loved Morty."

Myra slapped his hand down, catching the documents before they hit the floor. "Who shot out your window?"

"I don't know." Doreen slid her hands under the table and rubbed her knees.

"You must have some idea," Myra encouraged her.

"I don't know," she yelled at him. "I think it was Bucky. Who else would do that?"

"Was anyone threatening Morty? Blackmailing him?" Myra tucked the documents back into the folder.

"I don't know if it was blackmail or not, but somebody was harassing him." Doreen fidgeted in her chair.

"In what way? Did they want money?"

"No, not like that. They wanted a letter or something to do with him being the Masonic Grand Master, and he wouldn't give it to them. They threatened to out him as a transgendered male. He would have had to step down. Morty knew he would be voted out. It would destroy everything he had worked for."

Myra considered her answer. He kept hearing James Fitzgerald in his head talking about the Ecclesiastic Circle. "What kind of letter?"

"I'm trying to be truthful with you, but it was all Masonic business, and he couldn't discuss that with me. Secrecy is part of their vow."

"They're not a secret society. They're a society with secrets," Myra said, quoting Tom Miller.

She threw her hands in the air. "I hate that friggin' statement. He said it all the time. It makes me crazy."

"Do you know who Morty dated in high school?"

Doreen looked at him vaguely. "High school? I didn't meet him until university."

"Did he mention someone from high school coming back into his life?"

"Morty surrounded himself with the losers he hung out with in high school. He considered them family." Doreen rubbed at her temples. "They didn't want him then, but once they found out he had money, they all came running. One of them doesn't even know he was Barbara in high school. That's how focused they were on the money." She huffed a laugh.

"What do you mean?"

"None of those losers liked Morty in high school. Not one of them stayed in touch with him after school ended."

"You think they were using him?"

"Fuck, yes," Doreen spat. "Everyone is your best friend when you're paying off their debt."

"Like Art and Flora Pardy?"

"Two leeches right there. Pay off this. Pay my rent. Pay my car. Pay my insurance. It was never-ending."

"Did Morty leave them the house they're living in?"

"No, he didn't." Her face reddened. "I can show you the mortgage papers. The house we live in, and the one next door, are in my name. He couldn't have changed that without my permission. Morty made me sign a pre-nup years ago when he was starting his business. I thought it was just a joke. He put the property in my name in case the business went under. I showed Flora the mortgage papers. His name is not even on the houses."

"Are you sure?"

"Yes, I'm sure. They're my houses."

"Can I have a copy of your mortgage papers, his will, the pre-nup, and Morty's computer?"

"Absolutely."

"When did you show Flora the papers?"

Doreen bit the inside of her cheek as she looked around the room. "It was two days before Morty died. She told me they wanted to sell the house and buy something smaller. I told her she was mad. That she was only renting." She laughed. "Flora was convinced Morty said the house was theirs after he died, anyway, so she thought why not turn it over it to them now?"

"What did you do?"

"I showed her the mortgage file. You should have seen the look on her face."

Myra's left eyebrow lifted. "Flora must have been shocked."

"Shocked?" Doreen's face broke out in a crooked smile. "She about fainted. She was angrier than a wet cat. I had to ask her to leave."

"Interesting." Myra tapped his fingers on the table. "Did you talk to Morty?"

"When Morty got home I went up one side of him and down the other." Doreen folded her arms. "He swore that he never said that. He told me she had asked him several times if they could rent to own. He swore she got it in her head and wouldn't let it go. She gets crazy like that sometimes."

"Did he talk to Flora?"

"He went over that night and told her in no uncertain terms that he was not leaving them the house. He said Flora threatened to sue. Morty wasn't one for conflict. He was suffering like a dog that day from his ulcer. He was taking his stomach pills like candy. So, he walked out and came back to our house."

"What else did he say?"

"Morty said she was nuts." Doreen looked at her lawyer for permission to keep going, and McKay nodded her head. "The night my windows were shot out, she came over saying Morty sent her an email before he died, promising her the house. She showed it to me, but that's not what it said. It said: 'I'll think about it.' Like I said, Morty didn't like conflict. It hurt his stomach."

"What about Art?"

"He doesn't seem to get involved with her craziness. I think he just lets her go off instead of dealing with her."

"Did she really think Morty would just give her the house?"

"I know, right? That's not the best of it. A few days later, this guy showed up on my doorstep looking for Flora and Art. I told him they lived next door. He said he knocked on the door, but they wouldn't answer. He was very distraught. I asked what he wanted, and he said he gave them a twenty-thousand-dollar deposit because he bought the house from them privately. He had found my name on the house by doing the title search. Then he found me in the phone book and realized I lived next door. Well, I lost it. I went over, mad like the dog."

McKay spoke up. "I have a statement from the gentleman explaining the whole situation. I'll email it to you. He went to the police and made a formal complaint."

"Please do. Thank you for that information."

"That's why she was in such a panic to get the house turned over to her," Doreen put in.

"What about Tom Miller and James Fitzgerald?" Myra asked.

"Morty gave Fitzgerald money to fix windows in the church, but I don't think Miller got anything. Not that I know of."

"Doreen, let's talk about the autopsy. What did you make of it?"

"I don't know." She tried to hide her distress. "I don't understand it. Someone hit his head and gave him a pill with sulphur in it. How is this possible?"

Myra moved on. "Have you ever had a urinary tract infection?"

"What?" Doreen looked at him with disgust. "What the Jesus does that have to do with Morty's death?"

"The medication found in Mortimer's blood was used for a urinary tract infection. I think someone switched his ulcer medication with it, someone who knew he took the medication after everything he ate and also knew he was allergic to sulphur."

Doreen rolled her eyes. "Well, I have not had a urinary tract infection. Go ask my pharmacist."

McKay leaned in and whispered into Doreen's ear again. Doreen shook her head. "I've got nothing to hide." She looked at Myra. "It wasn't me.

"Who has access to Morty's pillbox?" Myra asked.

Doreen shook her head and grinned. "I don't know. Someone is setting me up."

"My client will not be answering any more questions, Inspector." McKay closed her expensive leather folder and pursed her lips. "This interview is over."

Doreen batted her away. "No, I want to straighten this out."

"Let's go back to the night Morty died." Myra clasped his hands together on the metal table. "So, Morty was getting dressed up to go out. He wore his expense suit. Too expensive for meeting his brother at a fish-and-chip shop. But he also took his Mason Grand Master uniform. Why was that?"

"I don't know. We were having a heated argument before he left." Doreen scanned the room, deep in thought. "Oh, wait," she exclaimed. "He had to get his photo taken for their newsletter. That's why he was dressed up."

Myra scribbled a note. "You've never mentioned that before."

"Inspector, I had a huge fight with my husband, who went out to meet the brother who tried to break us up. He went missing in a snowstorm, and then you showed up on my doorstep to tell me he had been murdered. Forgive me if I forgot about a damn photo."

"Did you know he was going to the Masonic Temple for that photo?"

"No, he didn't say, and I never asked."

Myra shook his head. "Was there anyone in the house with you that day or night?"

"No." Doreen bit her lip. "Actually, yes there was. Flora was there. She's always under my feet. I forgot about it."

"Flora?" Myra made a note. "Why was she there?"

"She had a migraine. Flora is the biggest hypochondriac you'll ever meet. She was looking for some extra-strength pain relievers. As usual, she couldn't afford to buy any because of her goddamn gambling problem."

Myra looked up. "You know about the gambling problem?"

"Yes. Constantly in debt. It started after their son died. I guess she was trying to fill a hole."

"Did you give her the painkillers?"

"I was busy with something in the kitchen, so I told her to go on upstairs and get it herself. It's not like she didn't know where I kept my medications."

"And did she?"

"Yes, she got it and left. She's always looking for a pill for her arse or an elbow."

"Doreen, is there anything you would like to add to this interview?"

She looked around the room, shifting in her seat. "Yeah, Morty's Masonic ring," she exclaimed. "It's missing. He was wearing it when he left the house, but it was not in his personal effects when they were returned to me. His name is engraved on the inside."

"I'll make note of that. Just one more thing." Myra stood and pushed the chair in. "Just a professional courtesy, really."

"What's that?" Doreen stood and tucked her hands into her pants pockets.

"I have a court order to exhume the bodies. It will be done tomorrow." He watched her face go white again.

"I just buried him yesterday! The autopsy has already been done. What else are you looking for?"

"Not Mortimer." He opened the door. "His parents."

30

Cst. Whiffen drove slowly down New Cove Road, looking for Tunis Court. The sun reflected off the snow, blinding her, and she lowered the visor. The snow was melting under the heat of the morning sun on the pavement, causing a buildup of slush and water at every curb. The quiet street was lined with equally spaced rows of small, converted American military houses. They were built in the 1940s to house servicemen and families working at the Fort Pepperrell base. They had been sold off to locals when the Americans left St. John's and turned the base over to the Canadians.

Whiffen checked her notebook to confirm the house number and parked in front of a small, pink bungalow. The old storm door was locked from the inside, so Whiffen tapped on the glass.

Shirley Williams struggled to undo the lock. "Yes?" Her head shook with old age as she looked at the stranger at her door.

"Mrs. Williams, I'm Cst. Donna Whiffen from the Royal Newfoundland Constabulary. I spoke to you on the phone."

"Oh yes, my child." Her voice had a grandmotherly, welcoming tone. "Come in out of the cold. I just boiled the kettle. Leave your boots on, love, in case you have to run."

Whiffen followed her into the tiny foyer and into the living room beyond.

"Sit down and I'll get the tea." Mrs. Williams shuffled back into a galley kitchen and returned with a plastic tray loaded down with a floral teapot, two cups and saucers, sugar and milk, and a plateful of cookies. The old woman held a newspaper tucked under her arm. She laid the tray down and slid the newspaper under Whiffen's boots.

"Have some tea, now, and a biscuit. It'll take the cold out of your bones." She poured the hot tea into a porcelain cup and laid it in front of Whiffen.

"Thank you." Whiffen poured milk and sugar into the cup and sat back on the autumnal-coloured floral couch. Everything about this room and Mrs. Williams felt like her favourite nan's house.

Mrs. Williams held up the fancy plate in front of Whiffen. "Take a biscuit. They're good with tea. I made them yesterday."

Whiffen knew that saying no would offend the lady. "Thank you." She slipped a chocolate chip cookie from the plate and bit into it. She let out a long *mmm* sound. "Oh my God, these are delicious."

"Dunk it in your tea, if you want," Mrs. Williams told her. "It tastes better that way."

Whiffen smiled at the elderly lady. "My nan used to say that."

Mrs. Williams sat in the matching chair across from her with an uneasy look on her face. Her white hair was short and thin. It still held the curls from rollers. Her kind eyes shone with affection, and her thin skin was mapped with lines of aging.

"Do you live alone?" Whiffen finished her cookie and looked at the full plate in front of her, wondering if she should take another and maybe a few for the road.

"Yes, all by myself." Mrs. Williams's thin lips turned up into a smile. "I'm eighty-five and I've lived in this house since 1970. Poor

Gary died in 2019. We raised a family in this house." She looked up at the framed photos hung around the room. "We had two daughters and a son and six grandchildren."

Whiffen looked around and then got straight to the point of her visit. "Mrs. Williams, you're the sister-in-law of Kate and Joseph Williams?"

"Yes. My husband, Gary, and Joe were brothers."

"Were you close to Kate and Joe?"

"Oh, yes. Kate and I were very close, like sisters, really." The smile left her face. "I did what I could to help Bucky and Barbara after they died."

"Bucky told us you spoke to Mortimer Williams before he died and gave him some information."

The elderly lady nodded. "He visited me a while ago and had some questions about the day his parents died."

"What were they?"

"I had no idea my information was of value, really. The police didn't speak to us when it happened." She looked off in the distance and sighed. "Looking back on it, I think Morty was trying to come to terms with the past."

"How so?"

"He explained his transition to me. I didn't understand it, really, but I didn't have a problem with it." A flush of red hit her cheeks. "Every now and then I still called him Barbara, but I didn't mean anything by it."

"Okay, that's understandable." Whiffen gave her an encouraging smile. "What was the information you gave Morty?"

"Well, like I said, he came to talk with me." She joined her hands over her lap. "It seemed more like a confession, really. He talked about the death of his parents and asked what I thought of it."

"What did you tell him?"

"I remember that day like it was yesterday. Kate and I talked every day on the phone." Mrs. Williams glanced toward the black phone hung on the kitchen wall. "She phoned that morning. She told me she had bought a dress at Ayres for a wedding that they were going to."

"She was making plans for the future?"

"Oh yes, they both were. She told me she had bought a new shirt and tie for Joe to wear. Then she told me the oddest thing. She said she and Joe were going to Bennett's Pond."

"Now, this was in April, and I asked her why they were going there. Well, Mortimer was Barbara then. She told me Barbara and Doreen asked them to meet there for lunch. Kate told me she thought Barbara was going to tell her they were moving away because they had talked about going to Vancouver."

"Who asked them to go to Bennett's Pond, Doreen or Barbara?"

"Kate said Doreen phoned her. She asked to speak to Barbara, but Doreen told her she wasn't at home because she was picking up some things for the picnic."

"Was this normal for them to go on a picnic?"

"God, no!" Mrs. Williams exclaimed. "Joe and Kate never went on a picnic in their lives, and they certainly wouldn't do it in April. That was a very rainy and foggy month in 1992. I remember telling Kate to dress up warm because it was cold enough that day to skin you."

"So, it was odd for them to do that?"

"It's just not a Newfoundland thing to do that time of year. Like I said, that day was very cold."

"How did Kate feel about Doreen?"

"She didn't like Doreen, see." Mrs. Williams lowered her voice. "Kate thought Doreen was very pushy and bossy. She was very forward, if you know what I mean."

"And Kate didn't like that?"

"No, not at all. Barbara was easily led. You know, she was extremely smart, but not very street-smart. She didn't leave the house until she met Doreen."

"What did you think of Doreen?"

"I only met her the once." Mrs. Williams eased herself back in her chair. "I could easily see why Kate didn't like her. She just had an air about her that struck me wrong."

"I see. Did Kate say anything else?"

"Let me see. Where was I?" She looked to the ceiling for help. "Oh yes, I was saying that Doreen asked to meet them at Bennett's Pond for a picnic lunch. Joe didn't want to go, but Kate said they had to be nice to Doreen because they didn't want to lose their daughter, so they went."

"The police investigation showed that they fell asleep in their car with the engine running and the windows up."

"I didn't believe that. Not for a second."

"Why?"

"It just wouldn't happen. Joe would know better."

"The report also says two empty wine bottles were found in a paper bag in the back seat."

"Let me stop you right there." Mrs. Williams pointed a shaking finger at the officer. "Joe and Kate did not drink. Joe would have a little drink of something at Christmas. Kate never touched a drop. She didn't even take the wine at church because it would make her chest break out in big red splotches."

"She had an allergy to it?"

"Kate had a lot of issues with her stomach. She was very picky over what she ate and drank. Now, today she would probably be diagnosed with food allergies."

"Okay. The mechanic's report says their vehicle had a defective exhaust system, and the cause of death was ruled as carbon monoxide poisoning."

"That car was only four years old. Bucky had fixed the exhaust system himself, and he is a good mechanic. There's no way there was anything wrong with that car. Joe took great pride in it. He vacuumed it out every Saturday and washed it. He would know if there was a problem."

"What do you make of the two bottles of wine and the sandwiches found in the back of the car?"

"Nonsense. Like I said, they didn't drink."

"You know that for sure?"

"Yes. We played cards all the time, and Kate only drank tea."

"Were you surprised when Bucky was left out of the will?"

"Oh, my God, yes." Mrs. Williams clapped her thin hands together. "Gary was the executor of their will, so we knew what was in it. We did our wills up together. We knew the estate was to be divided equally. How the will got changed, I don't know. But it was not what Joe and Kate wanted, I can tell you that. Then we found out Gary was not the executor anymore, that Doreen was."

"Doreen?"

"Yes, Doreen. We were shocked to our core."

"What else did Morty ask you about?"

"He asked me about that day. I told him his mother said Doreen called her about the picnic and said he—as Barbara—was out picking up supplies."

"Did he agree with that?"

"No. He was outraged. He said it wasn't true and told me he wasn't picking up supplies. He always suspected Doreen was involved. They had a shared bank account at that time, and he checked her credit card and found the charge for the liquor store, and he kept the statement. I hadn't talked to him for years after the funeral because he moved away and didn't keep in touch."

"How did the will get changed?"

"He told me he suspected Doreen impersonated Kate and

changed the will over the phone. We used the same lawyer, and back then you mostly dealt with the secretary for minor things like that, so it wasn't too hard to do. Morty said he didn't know about it until after the funeral. He said Doreen had convinced him that Bucky planned the murder and planted the evidence to frame her."

"What do you think?"

"That was a bold-faced lie." Mrs. Williams pursed her lips tightly. "Bucky was at the garage all that day. I know that for a fact because Gary had to get the alternator on our car fixed, and he loved to tinker with things. He stayed at the garage and helped Bucky. Joe was supposed to meet him there."

"What do you think happened?"

"Kate told me that, a few days before, she and Barbara had a big fight about Doreen. They were coming to terms with her lifestyle, but they felt Doreen was too controlling, and they even suspected she was physically hurting Barbara. I think Doreen knew Joe and Kate were trying to break them up and decided to do something about it."

"You think Doreen killed Kate and Joe?"

Mrs. Williams's eyes glistened. "Yes, I do, and she got away with it for too long. She has destroyed a whole family, and I think she also had something to do with Morty's death. Why hasn't she been charged?"

"We have reopened the investigation into Kate and Joe's death. Anything you give me will help with that."

"Morty had her credit card statement, and I gave him proof."

"You did?" Whiffen's ears perked up.

"Yes. They went to the picnic at 10:00 a.m. Then, Joe was going to drop Kate off here at noon, because we had a hair appointment at one o'clock. We always went together. Joe and Gary had a moose licence, and they were supposed to leave that weekend to go hunting. Joe was supposed to pick Gary up at Bucky's garage to gather up their hunting gear while we were at the hairdressers."

"What happened when he didn't show up?"

"There were no cellphones back then, so I called their house and got no answer. I called Bucky's garage and spoke to Gary. He hadn't heard from Joe, either. We didn't know what to do. We waited until five o'clock, and Gary called the police. He was told they had to be missing for twenty-four hours before they were considered missing. Then, the police notified Bucky around eight that night that their bodies had been found."

"You said you gave Bucky proof."

"Yes. Kate and I went to the same beauty salon for years. Their deaths were all over the media. It's all anyone talked about. Weeks later, I finally got up the strength to get my hair done. My beautician went on about how she suspected it had been murder. She gave me her appointment book with our names and times clearly written in it. She used to read a lot of those true-crime magazines, and she was convinced the police would want it."

"Is the beautician still alive?"

"No, she died a few years ago. I go to a different girl now." Mrs. Williams put her hands to her face. "Why would Kate and Joe drink two bottles of wine at ten in the morning and fall asleep? It doesn't make sense. They both had plans."

"What did Morty say?"

"He said he was going to talk to Bucky and they would go to the police together. I told him I would give a statement, too."

"I'll arrange for you to come in to headquarters to do that. It's the first I'm hearing about the appointment book, and we haven't found Doreen's credit card statement. Bucky doesn't have it."

"Oh. I forgot." Mrs. Williams went into the kitchen and came back with a manila envelope and a paper towel. "Here you go." She gave the envelope to Whiffen and wrapped a half-dozen cookies in the paper towel.

"What's this?"

"Morty gave me this for safekeeping. It's the credit card statement, the appointment book, and a letter from him in a sealed envelope. Mortimer was doing his own investigation into his parents' death. He didn't feel comfortable having it at home."

Whiffen opened the envelope and looked inside. "Thank you for this, Mrs. Williams. I can't believe you have all this."

"Put these in your pocket, child, for later."

She handed the wrapped cookies to Whiffen. Whiffen gratefully took them.

"Mrs. Williams, this is too kind of you."

"There's no one here to eat them, so take a few with you." She paused as if remembering something important. "One last thing." Her face took on a slightly obstinate look. "Mortimer told me he was scared. Someone was blackmailing him and threatened his life. He suspected Doreen was feeding this person information. He said he didn't feel safe."

"Who was it?"

Mrs. Williams seemed a little hesitant. She lowered her voice. "There was a guy who wanted a letter from Morty so he could dig up some treasure. It was crazy, if you ask me."

"Do you know his name?"

"Yes. I know him from my church. It's James Fitzgerald."

31

The office seemed to close in around them. Insp. Myra sat on the corner of a desk, staring at the whiteboard now covered in details and pictures. Cst. Whiffen shuffled through files of information, searching for information. Sgt. Morgan thumbed through the original crime folder in his hand.

"Who killed Mortimer Williams?" Whiffen sounded more impatient than she intended.

"We're missing something," Myra said absentmindedly.

"If Doreen didn't kill Morty, then who did?" Whiffen pressed.

"I think with Shirley Williams's statement and the documents Morty gave her, we have enough evidence to consider charging Doreen Williams with murder," Morgan offered.

"I agree," said Whiffen, "but I don't think she killed Morty. I think she really loved him."

"There's a thin line between love and hate," Morgan said with a grimace.

Whiffen lifted her shoulder in a half-shrug. "The poor guy must have been tortured before he died. He was threatened with losing everything he worked for. He was drugged and beaten. Someone really wanted him dead. How can a sane person do all that?"

"The truth of the matter is sane people commit evil acts all the time." Myra stood up and looked at the whiteboard. "Morty sold his businesses and gave all the money away. Why? Did he know he was going to die? What was he afraid of?"

"Maybe he was sick of the leeches in his life bleeding him dry. Or maybe he planned to leave Doreen and start over new." Morgan closed the file and handed it to Whiffen. "I've updated my notes and put them in the file. I'll let you take over from here."

Whiffen took the file and added it to her tidy stack. "I can't imagine what that must have been like for him. The threat of losing everything hanging over your head."

"Psychological fear is the worst form of torture." Myra plucked a photo of Mortimer Williams off the board and examined it. "It paralyzes people."

A shiver ran down Whiffen's spine. "What do you mean?"

"People who inflict psychological pain spend months getting close to their victims." Myra stuck the photo back on the board. "It's the fear of knowing that you can be taken at any time. It cripples a victim. I believe it's why battered women stay with abusive husbands."

"What's your theory?" Whiffen asked.

"I don't have one yet." Myra turned to face her. "The objective of psychological warfare is not to kill people. The primary objective is to control someone. To force them to accept their belief system."

"Then why did Mortimer have to die?" Morgan asked.

"I don't know. Everyone on our suspect list needed Morty alive to continue their comfy lives." Myra turned back to the board and looked at the photos of Tom Miller and James Fitzgerald. "These guys are chasing power with their treasure hunt."

Morgan nodded. "What do you make of that?"

"The Ark of the Covenant?"

Whiffen took out the files on both men and put them aside. "Would they kill to find it?"

"Hitler did," Myra answered with a grimace. "He believed he could win the war and rule the world if he had it."

"I didn't once think I would be involved with a case that involved Hitler." Whiffen blew out a long breath.

"Let's go through what we have." Myra sat on the corner of the desk again. "Doreen's lawyer sent over the mortgage papers and the pre-nuptial agreement. I'm waiting on Morty's lawyer to send over his will. Doreen's lawyer said Morty promised to leave her one million dollars, and they are holding him to it."

Morgan let out a whistle. "A million bucks. People have killed for less."

"I guess Flora is not paying off her gambling debts," Whiffen noted. "Flora and Art Pardy get nothing. Morty's death left them homeless."

"Flora is also a retired nurse and had access to Doreen and Morty's medicine cabinet," Myra reminded them. "I checked with our Financial Crime Section, and they do have a complaint from a guy who gave them twenty grand as a down payment on their house."

"If she believed she was in the will, would she kill to get the house? If she believed she wasn't in the will, would she kill out of anger knowing what a predicament they were now in?" Morgan asked. "It goes to her motive."

"Doreen told me Morty's Masonic ring is missing." Myra pointed to the note on the whiteboard. "Why would someone want his ring?"

Morgan shrugged. "Is it worth anything?"

"It was gold, but it only cost about six hundred dollars," Myra answered.

"Once again, I've seen people kill for less." Morgan whistled again.

"But what's the resale value of it, really?" Whiffen jumped in. "Who would want to buy a used Masonic ring with our victim's name engraved on it?"

"This is true." Myra went back to the board and put a question mark next to the details about the ring. "We need to know who asked Morty to meet at the Temple for a photo. That's who our killer is going to be."

Whiffen opened a file and ran her finger down through the information. "Forensics went through Morty's computer, but someone had tried to wipe it clean."

"Wiped clean?" Myra cocked his head to the side. "By who?"

"Don't know, but it was done at one in the afternoon of the day he died."

"Would Morty have wiped his own computer? Or could it be someone else?"

"Forensics were able to recover some of it. They didn't find anything of value yet. There were emails from both Fitzgerald and Miller demanding he write a letter to support their theory that there's treasure buried under the Sergeants' Memorial. A few referred to the hidden staircase at the Masonic Temple that leads to underground tunnels. Mortimer didn't believe them and told them in no uncertain terms that he would not support it. But there wasn't anything threatening in the emails. They're still combing through them."

"The killer had to know about the stained glass window with the spelling mistake." Myra pointed to a photo of the note found near the victim's chest. "There's only one suspect who knows that: James Fitzgerald. But he did give a tour of the Basilica's windows to other Masons, including Tom Miller and Mortimer. He showed them the window with the spelling mistake."

"*Tota Pulchra* means 'You are completely beautiful.' Meaning the Virgin Mary is completely beautiful.' Whiffen referred to the notes Myra had made after his interview with Fitzgerald. "But our victim had *Iota pulchra* written on a note next to his body, meaning 'you're ugly.' So, our killer thinks Mortimer Williams was ugly. Why? Was it because he was a transgendered man? Or was it because he wouldn't do what the killer wanted? Then we have the Song of Solomon. What's that about?"

"What do we know?" Myra went back to the whiteboard. "Who is not getting what they want? Doreen gets the house and a million dollars. Flora and Art Pardy are not getting anything. Bucky got his inheritance and a lot more from Morty. Fitzgerald and Miller are not getting their letter to dig up the memorial looking for treasure."

Whiffen stood and stretched. "But even with the letter from Morty as the Grand Master, the province would never agree to dig up the Sergeants' Memorial. The letter would have been useless. The veterans would never agree to it."

"What if Fitzgerald and Miller really believed there was a hidden staircase and tunnel that led to a room under the memorial?" Morgan asked. "Would they kill for the map that proves it?"

"I don't think they really wanted the letter." Myra took a closer look at the pictures of the crime scene. "Masons use all kinds of symbols and codes. I think 'letter' was code for the map."

"Would Morty really know where that was?" asked Whiffen.

"As Grand Master, that information would have been passed down to him, and he would protect it with his life. But Miller is a past Master. He would have been given the same information. Why would he need it from Morty?" Myra pointed at a picture of the Masonic Temple. "I think Fitzgerald believes everything about this treasure, but I think Miller is going along for fun. We need to go back and tear that basement apart. If there's a staircase, we need to find it."

Whiffen clapped her hands. "I'm all for that. I love treasure hunting."

"I'm not missing it, either," Morgan agreed.

Myra shoved his hands in his pockets. "I think it's about time I sat down with Tom Miller. I've been saving him for last." He looked at Whiffen. "Please do the paperwork for the warrant to search the basement. While we're waiting, I'll go visit Miller."

"You didn't answer my question," Whiffen reminded him. "Who killed Mortimer Williams?"

"Ah." Myra cocked his head to one side. "In a murder investigation you never ask *who* killed the victim. You ask *why* they killed the victim. The why is always more interesting than the who."

32

Tom Miller's rusted and dented black pickup truck was parked outside his small, blue bungalow. A light snow covered the driveway and walkway, telling Myra that no one had entered or left in the last few hours. The house was located about a ten-minute drive from downtown St. John's in the town of Logy Bay. A quiet blanketed the street as the working class of the neighbourhood were still at their jobs.

The front door opened as Myra approached, and Tom Miller stood in the doorway with his hand outstretched. "No problem finding the place?" An uncomfortable grin spread across his sallow face.

"Not at all." Myra took his hand and shook it. "Thanks for taking the time to meet with me. I'm still doing research on the Masons. This morning I asked myself why I'm wasting my time using Google when I have access to a Grand Master."

"Google?" Miller screwed his face up in disgust. "Nothing but garbage about the Masons on that. And the title is *Past* Master."

Myra repeated it. "Past Master. Nice ring to it."

"We don't use it every day." Miller led Myra into the kitchen. "I have coffee on, but I bet you'd like something a little stronger. I have a nice bottle of rum here." He pointed at the small, black glass bottle on the counter and slid it toward Myra.

Myra picked it up and read the label. "Nice, but I'm working." He laid it back down. "Thanks, anyway."

"Can I get you a coffee, then?"

"Sure." Myra pulled out a chair and sat at the table. "You're not working today?"

"I am." Miller looked over his shoulder as he poured the coffee. "I'm a chartered accountant. I have my own firm, so I can work from home when I want to."

"That's right. You're an accountant and a part-time photographer." Myra looked around the small, yellow, immaculately kept kitchen. The cabinets were a bright white, not a smudge or stain on them. The marble countertop was empty with the exception of the expensive stainless-steel coffee maker and rum bottle. The fridge, of polished stainless steel, was unadorned. Not a picture or sign of a family anywhere.

Miller laid the two coffees down and then returned with a white glass tray that held sugar and creamer. "Help yourself." He laid a spoon next to Myra's cup.

"I take it black." Myra blew the steam off the top of the cup. "Nice place. You can't have kids. It's too clean here."

Miller grinned. "No. No children. I never married."

"Smart man." Myra returned the smile.

Miller took the seat at the head of the table. He scratched at the greying stubble on his chin. The fluorescent lights glared down on his bald head. His glasses sat on the top of his nose, the lenses thick and grimy with fingerprint smudges. Myra watched him carefully, trying to decipher the extraordinary air of mystery around Tom Miller.

He laid the cup down. "I'm having trouble understanding your statement: *We're not a secret society. We're a society with secrets.* I don't get it. Can you explain that a little more?"

"Sure," Miller answered eagerly. "There is a difference. Masons don't hide who we are." He put his left hand in the air to show off his gold ring engraved with the Masonic symbol. "I wear this ring that tells everyone I'm a Mason."

"You wear it on your wedding finger. I noticed others wear it on the right hand."

"Yes." Miller twisted the ring around while he spoke. "Unmarried men are free to wear their ring on their wedding finger. Married men wear the ring on their third finger on the opposing hand."

"Does it matter which way the crest goes?"

"Yes. If you're a newer member, the symbol of the compass must be worn facing toward you because it shows you're taking the pledge seriously. A more advanced member, or Master, can turn their compass legs to face away from his body to show they are a symbol of his commitment to outwardly reflect the fraternity."

"It's a nice ring. Looks new."

"I keep it polished."

"Can you take it off? I'd like to get a better look." Myra held out his palm toward Miller.

Miller put his hand under the table as though protecting the ring. "We're not allowed to do that, and you won't trick me into showing you our secret handshake, either."

"I guess Freemasons aren't known for divulging details or dispelling myths." Myra drummed his fingers on the table as he always did when stressed. His eyes locked on the ring.

"The Order has shrouded itself in mystery, but in reality, it's just a fraternal organization that seeks to improve men, and thereby the society around them." Miller sat hunched over in his chair, resting his elbows on the table.

"I've always thought of Freemasonry as an elite group," Myra said.

"Look, I'm neither a publicist nor an apologist for the order." Miller laid a palm on the table. "For me, it's just a social group that does charity work. I volunteer a lot with the Shriners Keystone Kops."

Myra raised an eyebrow, wondering if it was a dig at him. "Do many men join the Masons nowadays?"

"Not a lot. Maybe a dozen a year. A lot of them lose interest when their curiosity has been satisfied about what we do and what we don't do. Most think we're searching for the Holy Grail. Once they realize the volunteer work we do, they lose interest."

"They're disappointed when they find out you don't have the Holy Grail?"

"Some are disappointed when they find out. No, we don't have the Holy Grail." Miller gave a deep laugh from deep within his belly. "I wish we did. Most of us are working-class men struggling to make a living."

"I've done some research," Myra admitted. "I find the Masons fascinating. Your Freemasons include fourteen US presidents and five British monarchs."

Miller gave a lopsided grin of embarrassment. "Once again, just old history. Tie that in with the secrets of any religion and a few tall tales, and you've got a bloody good story. But intelligent people don't take that sort of thing seriously."

"I wonder if Masons have woven mystery and suspicion into the history of Freemasons to keep people wondering about it," Myra said. "What about your initiation? What happens there?"

"When I was initiated, two mousetraps were placed on a table. I was told that one worked and one was broken." He let out a deep, relaxed breath. "I was told to touch them. I did. Both were broken. It was just an exercise for me to realize I was in good hands and there was nothing to fear."

"You said a few moments ago that you don't have the Holy

Grail, but James Fitzgerald told me you both are on a treasure hunt for the Ark of the Covenant."

A mischievous grin spread across Miller's thin lips. "You don't really believe that, do you? Seriously? The Ark of the Covenant is buried on Queens Road under the Sergeants' Memorial? Come on, Inspector." He reached over and play-punched the officer's arm.

Myra sat back in his chair, looking Miller over. There was something curious about him that he couldn't put his finger on. "Then why are you going along with Fitzgerald? He thinks it's real."

"I hope he's right." Miller fiddled with his Masonic ring. "I just go along with it for fun."

Myra softened his voice. "You go along with it for more than that. You wanted a letter from Mortimer Williams to give you permission to access the site."

"But I knew he couldn't write that letter," Miller cut in. "I was just going along with James. He's the one who is hell-bent on this treasure thing. I'm just having fun."

"That afternoon you showed us around the Masonic Temple, you unlocked the door. Where did you get the keys?"

"The new owners didn't change the locks, and a few of us still have the keys." Miller blinked at Myra as if realizing something for the first time. "I didn't break in. I always call the manager down there first to let them know I'm coming."

"Who else has keys?"

Miller thought about it and shook his head. "Well, me and Morty. It's hard to say, really. Whoever needed them at the time, I guess."

"Are you Mortimer's accountant?" Myra asked.

"Yes. Why? Is that a crime?"

"Then you know he sold the businesses?"

"Of course." Miller interrupted Myra before he could ask the next question. "I can't discuss Morty's business with you. It's client confidentiality, even after his death. I'd have to consult with my lawyer and his first."

"You had an axe to grind with Morty, didn't you?" Myra pushed the empty coffee cup to the side.

Miller picked it up along with his own and went to the dishwasher. "I don't know what you're talking about." He placed the two cups inside and closed the door.

"You told me the Masonic Temple is probably the most significant and historic building in all of North America," Myra reminded him. "You wanted to keep it, but Mortimer wanted to sell it."

"That's well-known. A lot of us wanted to keep it, and a lot of us wanted to sell it. In the end a vote was taken, and the majority voted to sell." Miller ambled back toward the chair.

"You seem a little out of sorts," Myra noted.

"My sugars are down. I haven't eaten yet." Miller rubbed his big belly.

"Do you need to get something to eat?"

"No, I'm good." He looked toward the hallway that led to the front door. "I'll eat after you leave."

A thin smile spread across Myra's lips. "You were more than Morty's accountant, weren't you? You knew him in high school."

Miller looked at Myra for a moment before saying, "Yes, I knew him."

"You dated."

Miller's jaw moved in a grinding fashion. "He was Barbara then."

"She left you."

"We were high school sweethearts. Nothing more." Miller turned his Masonic ring around his finger as he spoke.

"Someone wrote in Barbara's yearbook, 'Whenever you think of me, remember, I know your secret. Your secret admirer.' It was you, wasn't it?"

Miller looked unwell. "No, it wasn't. We were only friends. I would never have divulged her secret."

"You were in love with her. You kept harassing her after her parents died. That's why she and Doreen moved away."

"No. It wasn't me. It wasn't like that. We dated, yes, but it was only for a couple of weeks. We stayed friends and stayed in touch. I knew about his transition, and I helped him through that. I know how tough that was for him. I wouldn't out him."

"Would Doreen?"

"Doreen?" Miller spat out the name. "She took Morty away from his family and his friends."

"But Morty loved Doreen. They wanted to be together."

Miller banged a tight fist on the table, causing the sugar and milk dishes to rattle. "He was controlled by Doreen. Under some kind of spell."

"Is Morty why you joined the Masons?"

"He introduced me to it, yes."

Myra sized him up. "Did you focus on going up through the ranks faster just to prove you were the real man?"

"That's not true." Miller shifted his bulk out of his chair. "It was a coincidence."

Myra stared him down. "There's no such thing as a coincidence. Were you blackmailing him?"

Miller turned on him, furious. "No. It wasn't me!"

"Then who?" Myra shouted as his body jolted forward, shaking the table.

"I don't know." Miller ran his hand over his bald head, wiping away a bead of sweat. "Morty told me about it. But it wasn't me."

"Fitzgerald gave some Masons a tour of the Basilica," Myra informed him. "You and Morty were seen arguing on the tour. What were you arguing about?"

Miller paused as he tried to recall the incident. "He told me that he was selling the business at a loss. I told him he was crazy to do that. But he was determined."

"Morty was known to help his friends out, give them a loan or a hand up." Myra tugged at his moustache. "How did he help you?"

Miller's eyes narrowed. "He didn't. I didn't need any help."

"He hired you when he was already with another accounting firm." Myra took out his notebook and opened it to a bookmarked page. "He was with Butler's Chartered Accounting for ten years. Then he switched to you. Why?"

"We were friends. That's all."

"You were doing everything you could to keep Morty in your life," Myra stated. "You never got married. You didn't get over your first love."

"That's not true," Miller stated. "There have been plenty of girls."

Myra let out a long sigh. "You know, you talk about these Masonic beliefs that make you all good men, but Morty was the only one among you who truly lived that way."

Miller gestured toward the door with his head. "I think it's time you left."

"Tom, did you shoot out Doreen's windows?" Myra watched his face, but Miller didn't flinch. "You didn't want a letter from Morty. You've already seen that map. You know there's no treasure. You wanted him back in your life and threatened to out him to the hierarchy in the Masons if he didn't return your affections." Myra lowered his voice. "Was Morty leaving Doreen for you?"

"I want to speak to my lawyer."

"Then we're finished." Myra stood and headed toward the front door. While passing the living room, the glint of sunlight on a silver frame caught his eye. He about-faced and leaned back toward the door.

On the mantel stood a framed photo of Tom Miller and Barbara Williams smiling, arm in arm. Next to it stood another framed photo of Miller with Mortimer Williams—smiling, arm in arm.

33

"I hate this place." Whiffen followed Insp. Myra and Sgt. Morgan up the concrete stairs to the Masonic Temple.

"It's a treasure hunt," Morgan exclaimed. "It's going to be fun."

Whiffen shuddered. "I hope so. This place gives me the creeps. It's full of ghosts and weird Masonic stuff."

"I keep telling you, there are no ghosts in this century," said Myra as he reached the top landing. "If you're looking for ghosts, look over at the unmarked graves in the Anglican cemetery across the street."

Whiffen peered through the tall trees in front of the Cathedral. "Where? I don't see a cemetery."

"That field is full of unmarked graves." Myra pointed to the land spreading out in front of them. "The wooden Crosses have long been gone."

"When there's heavy rain, it's not unusual to get a call saying a body has been found in that field," Morgan added, "but it's always a hundred years old."

"You're making this up," Whiffen said with a grimace. "I'm calling bullshit on that."

"You're a researcher," said Myra. "Google it. It's a fact. That's an unmarked graveyard. There's a Haunted Hike from there every night during the summer."

"Now I know you're pulling my leg." Whiffen followed them into the foyer.

Myra took a set of keys out of his pocket and tried each in the lock on the front door. "Bingo. These are Morty's keys." He turned the key until the deadbolt retracted. "He did have a key to the building."

Four officers from the tactical response unit were on the floor organizing digging gear. Loud rap music blared out from a wireless speaker.

"Turn that down," Myra yelled. "Why do so many young officers shave their heads and grow beards?" he muttered under his breath. "They all look the same to me."

"The tac team offered to help us as part of their training." Morgan said. "It gives them some experience working in historical buildings. It also saves us from having to do the heavy lifting."

"I'm good with that." Myra looked at the officers with clear admiration. "I miss those days. But those days are also why my knees and hips are giving out."

The lead tactical officer stopped what he was doing to look up. "We already went through the basement and identified a hollow wall. There's a crowbar next to it if you want to give it a swing and relive your glory days."

"Once they take down that wall, there's going to be a lot of dust and dirt, I suspect." Morgan zipped up his jacket and searched the pockets of his jeans for a dust mask. "I'm too old to breathe in hundred-year-old dust. I'm going to hang out with these guys until they're ready to start."

"That's why I dressed for it." Whiffen looked down at her police boots, jeans, T-shirt, and police bomber jacket.

Myra's face fell as he straightened the black tie on his white shirt and shoved his hand into the front pocket of his blue jeans. His grey blazer folded back around his waist, revealing his Sig Sauer P226 handgun concealed in its shoulder holster.

"A little overdressed today?" Whiffen remarked. "You miss the old days of tactical gear and weekend warriors?"

"The good old days." He pressed his lips together in a thin line. "Policing is fun when you're young." He yawned as he watched them lay out their gear. "I don't plan on crawling through any tunnels. That's what these guys are for."

He looked down the narrow stairs to the basement and began his descent with Whiffen in tow. "Let's give that crowbar a swing." He rolled his eyes when he heard the rap music being turned back up.

"You look like you had a hard night," Whiffen said to her supervisor. "Did your babies keep you up all night?"

"Yes." He placed his hands on his lower back and cracked it when they reached the basement.

The lower level was small with a lady's washroom to the left, a huge mirror hanging on the wall next to it. A short hallway on the right led to offices. Myra looked at his haggard reflection in the mirror.

"Where's that crowbar? I need to hit something."

"What a weird-looking mirror." Whiffen ran her fingers over the glass. "It looks like you could walk right into it."

"Apparently it's a haunted mirror. If you look into it, you'll see dead people." He added spooky sound effects.

"All I see is you and me." Whiffen's phone vibrated. She pulled it out of her coat pocket and looked at the screen. "That's Steve. The lawyer was supposed to call this morning to give us the outcome of Jack's case."

She went into the women's bathroom and swung the door closed. The door failed to latch, and Myra caught part of the conversation. "Good news?" he asked when she returned.

"Yeah, finally." Whiffen tucked the phone back in her pocket. "The court has agreed to give us legal guardianship of Jack."

"Congratulations." Myra gave a rare full smile. "At least that's over."

"It cost a thousand dollars for the court to give us care of our own son."

"Not every child with special needs is lucky enough to have parents like you and Steve," Myra answered thoughtfully. "It's for their own protection."

"I know. Sometimes I just get so overwhelmed, and I don't know who or what to lash out at."

"I have big shoulders whenever you feel the need." His hands instinctively reached out to hug her, then he stopped himself.

Whiffen had impulsively moved to receive it, then pulled away. "It would be weird for cops to hug. Let's destroy this wall."

The monotonous beat of rap music filled the staircase. "I told them to turn that down." Myra looked up the narrow stairs. "You may as well talk to that wall there."

He found the crowbar leaning up against a wall leading to the offices. He ran his hand over the plaster, knocking every few inches.

"It does feel hallow," he observed.

"It doesn't really fit with the rest of the rooms, does it?" Whiffen moved from office to office. "It's right in the middle of everything." She came to a closed door and put her ear to it. "Someone is in there."

Myra knocked the crowbar along the wall. He turned to the next wall and did the same thing. "This wall is solid. Hear that?" He went back to the first wall. "This may be something."

He gave it a few taps. "See, it's hitting something. But over here," he said, moving back to the first wall and tapping the crowbar on the centre, "nothing. Completely hollow."

The office door opened. "We're just leaving." A gentleman

emerged from the office with a broad smile, followed by a lady with flowing blonde hair, who was holding a briefcase.

"We're the theatre owners." The lady extended a hand. "I'm Kathie, and this is Peter."

"You own the building?" Myra asked.

"Yes, we bought it from the Masons twenty years ago," Peter answered.

"You're okay with us tearing this wall out?" Myra knocked the crowbar off the wall.

"Yes, we signed all the necessary papers," Kathie informed him. "We hope you find those mysterious tunnels," she added excitedly.

Myra pointed to the opposite wall. "Was there ever a staircase here?"

"Not since we bought the building," Peter answered. "We've done some renovations and found some really cool things, but no staircase."

"What did you find?" Whiffen asked.

"We found a Knights Templar uniform in a wall upstairs." Kathie pointed back to her office. "Do you want to see it? It's locked in the safe."

Myra and Whiffen exchanged glances.

"Absolutely," Myra answered. "We've got to get at this wall first, while the team is here, but we'll have a look another time."

"Was there really treasure in the cornerstone?" Whiffen asked with a smirk on her face.

"The cornerstone was opened years ago." Peter folded his arms, happy to chat. "Everything in it was taken out and given to the Masons. It was part of the deal for the sale of the building."

"What was in the cornerstone?" Myra laid the crowbar down.

"There was a gold watch, a newspaper, some Masonic stuff, and a bunch of papers." Peter scratched his head as he thought back to that day. "There was a map that they were all excited about. Anyway, they have it. They wouldn't let us see anything up close."

"Who has it?" Myra asked. "Who did you give it to?"

"Ironically, Mortimer Williams. Everything was handed to him, and my understanding is he was the keeper of it. Now, how weird is that?"

Myra bit the inside of his cheek to keep himself from smiling. Whiffen turned and looked into the mirror.

"Be careful looking into that mirror," Kathie warned her.

"Why?"

"Because it's full of spirits." Kathie grinned as she slid her fingers over the glass. "People say they see ghosts in it. Others say it records everything. One guy even told me he saw a body laid out on the floor in the mirror, and when he turned around, there was nothing there."

Whiffen turned around. "This place keeps getting creepier and creepier."

"We're very excited." Peter's face lit up. "If you find that mythical tunnel to Government House, it's certainly going to boost the promotion of this building."

"We can't get started until all civilians are out of the building," Whiffen told the owners. "We have to ask you to leave now."

"Understandable." Kathie hugged the briefcase to her chest. "We just had to do the payroll. We'll get out of your hair now."

Peter followed her up the staircase and out of the building.

"All right." Myra held up the crowbar. "Let's give it a go."

The first swing dented the wall. The second left a hole and the third broke through. He hooked the crowbar into the wall and pulled off a large piece of plaster, sending dust everywhere.

"I've got to take this blazer off." Myra threw his blazer and tie on the staircase, then laid his holstered gun on top of it. He undid his top button and rolled up his sleeves. "This old plaster just crumbles." He gave it another swing.

"You mean business now." Whiffen opened the flashlight on her phone and shone it into the hole. Her heart seemed to stop for a moment. "There is a staircase inside here."

Myra picked up the crowbar and gave the wall another smack, leaving a bigger hole.

"Hold this."

Myra handed Whiffen the crowbar and stood back. He lifted his size twelve police boots and kicked the wall. His foot easily went through the old plaster. They both pulled at the crumbling remains until the wall was down to the studs.

"There's a five-foot door under the staircase." Whiffen shone the light from her phone around the dark space. "It looks like a hobbit door." She looked at the bars on her phone. "Damn, my phone is dying."

"People were a lot smaller a hundred years ago." Myra tried to squeeze his bulk between the wood frame. "I don't want to take these down in case it's a load-bearing wall."

The air inside the hidden area had a dusty stillness. He pushed himself between the frame, breaking decades of cobwebs.

"There's no opening at the top of the stairs. It could be another hatch in a floor somewhere that was floored over. Yell out and let the team know we're in and to come on."

Whiffen hurried back to the stairs. The music still blared around the foyer. "We're in," she yelled. She waited but got no response. She caught a member of the tactical team walking by. "Hey, tell your team lead we're in."

"Sure," he acknowledged before continuing on.

"I'll text Morgan," she said to herself as she walked back into the basement.

"Are they coming? Jesus, the dust and dirt in here."

"I told a team member, and I texted Morgan." Whiffen looked at her phone and tucked it back in her pocket. "I don't know if it went through because of these thick rock walls." She bounced with excitement. "Morgan's going to miss it if he doesn't come on."

"There's a lock on the door. Look at this handle. I bet it hasn't been touched for a century." Myra examined the tarnished brass handle, then ran his hands over the thick wooden door's seams. "I can feel cold air here."

"Do you want the crowbar?" Whiffen picked it up off the floor.

Myra tugged on the rusted lock, which fell apart in his hands. "Don't need it now." He carefully laid the pieces on the staircase and pulled on the brass handle. "It's stuck."

"Hang on, let me try." Whiffen easily slipped in between the framing and gave the door a tug. It opened slightly.

They exchanged excited glances.

"I loosened it up for you." Myra grabbed the handle, and they both tugged.

A loud creak was followed by a cloudburst of dust. It covered them like a sudden snowstorm. They both bent over in coughing fits. The smell of dank, stale air mixed with mould and bits of cobwebs, filling their lungs.

Whiffen stood first, her hair and clothes covered in a layer of grey dust. She began to brush herself off as she coughed the taste of dirt out of her mouth. "You all right?"

Myra let out a dry cough, his white shirt now a muddy grey. The dust swirled throughout the basement. "It went up my nose." He wiped the back of his hand across his mouth and nose, leaving a dark streak. His hair and moustache were now a twilight grey.

Whiffen shone her phone's light through the crack between the door and the frame. "Fitzgerald was telling the truth. It's a tunnel."

Myra reached up and pulled the door fully open, sending another cloud of dust into the air. "Cover your mouth. Damn, where's

Morgan with his face mask when you need him? It doesn't look safe."

They stared into the rock tunnel.

"It's only about five feet high and drilled through solid rock." Myra bent down to get a better look.

"It must have taken years of labour to dig this thing out."

"This tunnel was abandoned for a good reason," Myra remarked.

"Are we going in?"

Myra shook the cobwebs and dust out of his hair. "We're in for a penny, we're in for a pound. Let's go. But we'll stick together, and don't venture in too far alone." He crouched down to get through the door. "The tactical guys can crawl the length of it. My knees are killing me. It's very narrow, and I don't think it widens out. It's all dirt and rock."

Whiffen squatted down behind him, keeping the light shining. "It's all rock: the floor, walls, and ceiling. It's like a mine."

At twenty feet, they stopped crawling.

"It slopes down from here." Myra ran his hands over the floor. I think we must be outside the building, getting near the street. I'm not going any farther."

"Well, goddamn," Whiffen yelled. "The tunnels do exist, but only hobbits can use them. I bet they meet up with a labyrinth of tunnels under the city."

"Let's back up and let the tac guys do the rest." Myra looked back at Whiffen, sweat dripping down his face. "They can send in the remote camera. I'm finding it hard to breathe."

"Me, too." Whiffen ran her hand through her hair. "I'm soaking with sweat." She looked back over her shoulder. "I can't turn around. I'll have to back up."

"Okay. I'll follow your lead."

"Ouch," she yelled.

"You all right?"

"My knee just hit a sharp rock."

A rock let loose from the ceiling and hit Myra's hand. He picked it up and glanced back toward the faint light at the start of the tunnel.

"Donna, hurry. I think the tunnel is collapsing."

She looked back toward the opening. A cloud of dust was choking out the light.

"Oh, fuck." She shuffled backward as fast as she could.

Myra struggled to move his six-foot-four frame. The building growled and groaned above them and unleashed a mass of thick, grey dust that formed a funnel cloud and closed out all the light around them. A boulder pinned Myra to the ground. The swirling dust blocked his vision and filled his lungs.

Whiffen tried to turn around to face the opening when a rock hit her shoulder. Another fell on her hip, pinning her to the ground. The phone was knocked out of her hand as she desperately struggled to free herself.

* * * * *

Upstairs, the continuous beat of rap music filled the foyer.

Morgan was at the entrance and stopped what he was doing. He felt the floor vibrating and heard a faint rumble. "You hear something? Turn the music off!"

34

The only light in the small tunnel came from Whiffen's dying cell-phone. She shook herself to get back to her senses and struggled to get her hand free from beneath a heavy boulder to reach for it. The phone gave off a dim yellowish glow around her face. She pointed it up toward Myra. His legs were covered in large rocks. She spotted the treads of his police boots, reached up, and grabbed one by the heel, shaking it.

"Nick. Nick, answer me."

She could hear his heavy breathing and groans.

"I can hear you." He tried to look back toward her. He squinted through the gloom.

"Are you okay?"

"Never been better."

She tugged at his boot again. "Seriously. Are you okay?"

"Other than being trapped in a tunnel, lying on my chest with a huge rock on my back, and I can't breathe, I'm okay."

"At least you have your sense of humour. Which you don't have in the office, so I'm going to say, you're delirious." Whiffen tried to worm her body closer to him. "Let me see if I can move some rocks from around your legs."

"Stay where you are. The tunnel is not stable. Are you all right yourself?"

"My left arm is pinned under my body, and I can't move it. There are rocks all around my legs. But my right hand is free."

"Anything broken?"

"Just my spirit." She tried to adjust her torso to move away from a sharp rock digging into her hip.

"Can you see the opening?"

Whiffen tried to look behind her. "No, it looks like it's closed in."

"Is that the glow of your cellphone I'm seeing?"

"Yes. I only have about five per cent of my battery left. Can you reach your phone?"

"My phone is in my blazer, which is lying on the stairs outside this tunnel."

"Oh, shit! I'd better save my battery." Whiffen turned off the light function. The tunnel became still and dark.

"Try texting Morgan. I'm sure they've heard something upstairs." Myra squirmed to free his long arms from the confined space. The position he lay in made him struggle to breathe.

"I don't have any bars on my phone, but I'll try." She fumbled with the phone, holding it and texting with the same hand. She heard the swish of the text. "I think it went through. Actually, no it didn't." A red circle and exclamation point stared back at her. "The walls are too thick."

"The team will be down here any second. They had to have heard the collapse of the tunnel." Myra wheezed with each word.

Whiffen groaned as she tried to move. "I hope you know I'm calling in sick tomorrow. I'm going to need a week of massage therapy to get rid of the aches in my body."

"Don't call me," Myra panted. "I'll be in emerg, because I'm pretty sure my lungs have collapsed."

"Don't make me laugh. It hurts."

"What's so funny?"

"You. Calling in sick." Whiffen shook the heel of his boot again. "Everyone knows the great Insp. Myra doesn't use sick days. You'll be in tomorrow. Just wait and see."

He drew in a ragged breath. "We'll see. Can you snake yourself backward and try to kick at the closure with your boot? We can't be too far from the entrance."

Whiffen wriggled her body from side to side and struggled to back up, but her feet floundered. She was firmly stuck. "No, I can't reach it."

"How close are you to the opening?"

"Probably about five feet."

"Can you see if there's much rock behind you?"

She turned on her phone light and tried to writhe toward the opening of the tunnel. "A lot of rock has fallen, but we're not completely closed in. I can't move at all."

"Can you hear anything?"

"I can hear rumblings, but I don't know if it's from voices or the rocks moving."

"Let's hope it's voices, because it's not a good sign if the rocks are rumbling." Myra gulped in dirty air. "I can smell something. I think it's sewer."

Whiffen wrinkled her nose. "Ew. We're probably next to some hundred-year-old sewer system. Jesus, I hope it doesn't break."

"It seems to be getting stronger." Myra's voice faded as he fought with his body, forcing it to move and lift his heavy chest off the floor. Sweat ran down his face, and he began to lose focus.

"Myra? Myra? Stay with me." Whiffen grabbed his boot and shook it as hard as she could. "Don't you pass out on me."

Myra's breath was shallow. "I'm here."

The thought of Myra passing out felt like a bucket of ice water.

For the first time, she thought about Steven and Jack. She was glad Myra could not see her face as she became emotional.

Myra's voice was weak as he called to her. "Donna? Donna, can you hear me?"

"Yes."

"We need to keep talking." He tried to lift his body up to allow more air into his lungs. "Do you hear me? We're going to be fine. You know what Morgan is like. He's meticulous. He's outside right now pulling those rocks out with the team."

"I know." She wiped tears from her dirty face. "I was just thinking about Steve and Jack. How is Jack going to live? It's my greatest fear. How is Steve going to take care of him if I don't make it out?."

Myra's thoughts raced to Maria. About how she would be giving Clara and Doris their afternoon snack. He laid his head down on the dirt floor when he realized that at any moment she would be receiving a phone call from the RNC Communication Centre telling her that he was trapped under the Masonic Temple. Steve would be receiving the same call.

He shook himself. "Donna, don't think about anything but surviving. We are going to be okay," he gasped. "And tomorrow we will laugh about this."

"Do you know why I gave up patrol duties?" Her voice was low and weak.

"Got tired of the shifts and long hours, I suppose."

"No." Whiffen struggled to keep her voice from cracking. "Jack had a substitute teacher who wasn't familiar with him. He left the classroom and walked to the hill behind the school. He was missing for hours. At one point I thought we'd be looking for a body. Then we found him." She sucked back dirty air as thick as wool. "He was just sitting on a rock. Looking up at the sky."

"You must have been out of your mind."

"I had worked all night and was sleeping during the day. That's when I decided that I needed to work nine to five, Monday to Friday, or close enough to it. He needed a full-time supervisor, and Steve was exhausted."

"I can't tell you I know what it's like, Donna, but I can listen any time you want."

"Thank you." She shook her hand to get rid of the numbness. "I am claustrophobic. People have nightmares about being buried alive, and here we are. I've got to get out of here." She pushed the palm of her hand into the dirt and began to draw in deep, heaving breaths. "We shouldn't have looked into that damn mirror."

Myra could hear the panic in her voice and rocked his torso back and forth, shaking a boulder off his lower back. It allowed him to shift a little to his side. He took in a deep breath of sewer vapours and exhaled in what sounded like a smoker's cough.

"Donna, stay still. You're going into shock. Listen to me," he yelled. He frantically kicked at the rocks around his legs. "Here's what's going to happen. We're getting out of here. And tonight, while you're showering, your body will go into shock again. You'll begin to shake. You will urinate on yourself. You may even throw up. Your body will be freezing, even under the hot water. But the whole time it's happening, you have to tell yourself that you survived. It's just shock, and it comes at you when you least expect it."

He could hear a sound coming from her but wasn't sure if it was crying or laughing.

"Donna, are you okay?"

"Why did you have to mention pissing myself?" She went into a belly laugh that sent waves of pain into her lungs. "I just realized I'm going to be the only female in the room when we get out of this place, and I just pissed myself." She was laughing so hard, the rocks on her back were moving up and down, sending shocks of pain into her spine.

Myra knew he had to keep her laughing. "Well, you're not the

only one. And I'm pretty sure I pissed myself about five minutes ago."
He joined her in a course of laughter. "Maybe they won't notice."

"I don't care if they do." She worked to adjust her arm and ease
the pain in her shoulder. "I'm going to need a massage."

"Donna, earlier you asked me if my daughters kept me up all
night." He whimpered as he worked to free his arm. "They're actually good sleepers. It's me. I'm the one who kept me up all night."

He finally pulled his arm free and stretched it out to get the
feeling back in it. "I was up all night because I have PTSD, and
I suffer from night terrors whereby I relive all my past investigations."

The toxic air entered his lungs again, and the taste of sewage
snaked deep into the pit of his stomach, causing him to urge. "I
think it's important that we talk about things like this." The dust
and emotion made him choke on every word.

Whiffen was gobsmacked. "Thank you for telling me that."
As the smell of sewage swirled around her, she tried to take short
breaths. "I honestly thought I was the only one. I was wondering
how you got through your career unscathed."

"Everyone we work with is carrying baggage with them. Believe me." He coughed violently. His morning coffee came up, soaking his lips and moustache. "You think Morgan is not going home
and beating himself up over the Kate and Joseph Williams file?" He
tried to wipe the puke off his lips. "Today, that baggage is going to
be a little heavier for us and everyone outside that wall."

The dust and fumes overtook her, and Whiffen coughed until
she choked.

"Are you okay?"

"It's the sewer," she gasped. "I can smell it now." She laid her
head down on the cold rock. "I just need to rest for a second." The
tunnel began to fade from her vision, and her cheeks stung, flushing a crimson red.

"Donna," he yelled. "Don't close your eyes. Stay with me."

Another rumble shook the building. Newly loosened rock and dust fell around them in the blackness. Myra looked back and saw a beam of light coming from behind Whiffen. He squinted to see if it was her phone.

Sweat ran into his eyes, blinding him. The light was gone. The heaviness of the rocks on his back, pinning his chest to the ground, weakened him. His breath became shallow as everything faded to black.

* * * * *

"Hurry," Morgan shouted. "Form a chain. Pass the rocks back."

"I can see the opening," shouted a tac team member at the front of the line. "There's a tunnel." He passed back rock after rock. "I see a boot. We found them."

Morgan climbed in over the rocks past the tac members. He reached in and grabbed Whiffen's boot.

"Help me. She's pinned under the rocks." He climbed in and frantically took the stones off her legs and back as a team member gently pulled her out.

Whiffen's limp body eased out from the rubble. Morgan flipped her over and grabbed her wrist.

"I can't get a pulse," he cried.

35

James Fitzgerald paced in front of the police cars and media trucks parked at the top of Cathedral Street.

"Just tell me if they found the tunnel," he begged the police officer blocking him from the Masonic Temple.

"Look, I told you I can't give you any information." The officer looked past him, keeping an eye on all the looky-loos standing around.

"Who can I talk to?" He tried to spot someone on the street that he knew. "I'm the historian for the Ecclesiastic Circle. If they found a tunnel, it would be of the utmost historical importance. I must get in there," he demanded.

The officer let out a bored sigh. "I don't have any information for you, and I don't know anything."

The Masonic Temple was surrounded by a flurry of police cars, fire trucks, ambulances, and government vehicles. Officers formed a perimeter around the area, blocking traffic and people. Engineers, police officers, fire department officials, and city staff, all wearing protective gear and haz-mat suits, walked in and out of the building, holding clipboards and taking measurements.

"Get back over the line," the officer yelled at a newspaper pho-tographer. He stomped over to the opposite end of the protective line to deal with the reporters who were leaning on the tape, vying for a closer look. Fitzgerald seized the opportunity and made a run for it. He dodged in and out between police and firefighters and up the stairs to the Masonic Temple but was stopped at the top land-ing. A young police officer held up his hand.

"Can I see your ID?"

Fitzgerald reached into his coat pocket and pulled out a sil-ver business card holder. He handed over a formal-looking black, embossed card that brightly featured the Basilica Heritage Founda-tion's crest.

The officer scrutinized the name and information and hand-ed it back. "Go ahead." He moved to one side to let Fitzgerald pass.

The foyer of the Temple was full of emergency personnel. EMTs were caring for Insp. Myra and Cst. Whiffen. Both were strapped to stretchers in the banquet room, awaiting the signal to move.

Myra struggled to remove his oxygen mask, but his arms were strapped to his sides. His shirt and pants were hanging in shreds from his body, cut off by an EMT who was trying to attach elec-trodes to his chest, arms, and legs. He had gained consciousness once the tac team pulled him out, and Morgan kept him awake while they waited for the ambulance.

Whiffen had been pulled out first and carried to safety. She had regained consciousness for a short time, then passed out. Her hair was matted with dust, mud, and sweat. An oxygen mask clung tightly to her face. An EMT had administered an injection to keep her sedated. A thick, beige blanket was pulled up over her body, and she was secured to the stretcher.

"Let's move," the lead EMT yelled. They grabbed the head and foot of Whiffen's stretcher and began wheeling her toward the front door.

Morgan's voice carried over everyone as he yelled orders in the foyer. "Tell the front line to move the media back. I don't want anyone taking pictures of her being brought down over the stairs."

The EMTs moved past him and within minutes had her loaded in an ambulance. Lights and sirens blared.

"Bill . . . Bill," Myra tried to scream inside his mask.

Morgan looked down at his friend. "Shut up, will you? They're trying to move you."

Myra let out a barrage of muffled orders laced with profanities.

Morgan lifted the mask. "I'll let you talk for a few seconds, but you're going to listen to me. You're going to the hospital whether you like it or not."

"Unhook me," Myra ordered. "I don't need to go to the hospital." He winced with every word.

"Your ribs are broken. You need X-rays and some good drugs."

"How's Whiffen?" Myra fell back on the stretcher.

"She's doing good. They think her lung may have collapsed and a rib may be broken. But there doesn't seem to be anything more than that."

Myra craned his neck to try to see her. "It didn't look like she was moving on the stretcher."

"They gave her something to sedate her because of the pain. She'll be okay. Whiffen is a lot stronger than you think." Morgan moved back to allow the EMTs room to work. "When we took her out, she was more concerned about you than herself. Her husband is waiting for her at the hospital."

Myra gasped for air. "What's happening downstairs?"

Morgan placed the mask back over his face. "The structural engineers from the city and the fire department are here. They said there are some highly toxic gases coming from the sewer system and the tunnels are extremely unstable. That's probably why they were closed down and boarded up in the first place."

While they spoke, an EMT injected a drug into Myra's arm and mouthed *He'll be out soon* to Morgan.

"Let's move." The EMT unlocked the stretcher, and four assistants surrounded Myra to wheel him out.

"Myra," Morgan called. "Be a good patient. You're in for a hard time when you get to the hospital."

Myra tried to look back at him. "I'm not going for surgery, am I?" he murmured through the mask.

"No," Morgan chuckled. "Maria's waiting for you at the hospital, and she's fit to be tied."

The EMTs worked to manoeuvre the stretcher through the foyer doors. Fitzgerald spotted Myra and ran to his side.

"Inspector?" Fitzgerald shook his arm. "Did you find the tunnel?"

Myra's eyes were vacant. He tried to focus on the frantic face above him. His lips moved, but only garbled words came out.

"Just say yes or no." Fitzgerald hung on to the stretcher as it wheeled out.

An EMT pushed him away. "Move back."

Myra's stretcher was carried out of the building to an awaiting ambulance.

Fitzgerald grabbed the sleeve of a passing firefighter. "Did they find the tunnel?"

The firefighter kept moving. "They're filling it in now. Are you authorized to be here?"

"Yes, I'm the historian." He spotted a steady stream of firefighters going down into the basement, and Fitzgerald followed.

A city inspector with an ID lanyard around the neck of his protective white haz-mat suit was deep in conversation with a fire captain at the bottom of the stairs. The stench of rotten eggs coming up from the sewer filled the basement.

A rapid intervention crew worked around the opening to the tunnel, under the hidden staircase, preparing it for demolition.

"Excuse me," Fitzgerald interrupted. "Is the tunnel open?"

The inspector stopped talking and looked at him. "Who are you? How did you get in here?"

"I'm James Fitzgerald, the Basilica historian and the expert on the Ecclesiastic Circle." He waited for recognition, and when he received none, he continued. "I've been searching for that tunnel for years. It's a major historical find."

Fitzgerald shifted from one foot to the other as he tried to see over the firefighters, each dressed in bunker gear with breathing apparatus. The fire chief and inspector watched him in disbelief.

"Let me put it this way," Fitzgerald continued. "It's like opening the Great Pyramid at Giza and finding its treasures. You can't just send a bunch of firefighters in there. I need to go first to document the find."

The fire chief reached up under his helmet and scratched his perspiring head. "You're not going in that tunnel. It's full of toxic gases, and it's about to cave in. You shouldn't even be down here without a haz-mat suit on."

"It's condemned," added the inspector. "We're closing it in now to maintain the integrity of the building. It could bring the whole place down if we don't."

"What do you mean by closing it in?" Fitzgerald asked in astonishment. "Do you mean just boarding it up?"

"There's a cement truck parked outside right now. We're putting a hose in through this window to fill it." The captain moved back to reveal the window.

The men moved away from where they were standing. Two

firefighters, using an axe and crowbar, smashed out the glass. "Clear," they shouted to their counterparts outside.

Fitzgerald looked out through the empty hole. The red tail lights of a large cement truck were moving closer to the Temple as the crew guided it into place.

Fitzgerald turned back to the two men. "You can't do that. I have to go in. You don't understand the historical significance of this find." He shuffled around the room to see over the backs of the firefighters blocking the door to the tunnel. "Can I just see it? Can I just see the tunnel?"

A firefighter, unaware of Fitzgerald's purpose, moved to allow him closer access. Bright spotlights lit up the collapsing tunnel. Debris from the falling rock and dirt was scattered over the muddy floor. The smell of methane gushing out was overwhelming.

"I just need to go in." Fitzgerald covered his nose and mouth with his hands and tried to step over the piles of rock. "You don't have to come with me."

The captain grabbed him by the back of the coat and pulled him back. "You can't go in there. Can't you smell the methane?"

"If that tunnel collapses, this whole neighbourhood could slide down into the harbour," the inspector roared. "You don't know how far they run."

"I do. There's a map that shows where they go."

"You have a map?" The chief pulled Fitzgerald back. The haunted mirror reflected the whole operation.

"Not on me," said Fitzgerald. He rubbed his fingers through his white hair. "There's a map to the tunnels that the Masons have, but they won't let me see it."

"Is there a map or not?" the chief demanded. "A map could really help us out."

"There are rumours of a map, but they have it locked away

because it leads to some very valuable items." Fitzgerald paused before the mirror, surprised to see himself.

"Like what?" The inspector looked at his watch and gave an acknowledging wave to a nearby firefighter. The firefighter nodded and turned his back to them as he spoke into his radio.

Firefighters and police formed a line next to the gaping window and helped direct a large hose in through it, guiding it directly in through the tunnel.

"What are they doing?" Fitzgerald raised his voice to a pitch. "There are rumours the Masons have buried some significant treasure at the end of those tunnels." He clutched his chest. "Treasures like the Ark of the Covenant."

"Oh, really? The Ark of the Covenant, you say?"

The chief caught the eye of a police officer standing nearby and raised his hand to his head. He made a circular motion with his index finger. The officer nodded and came over.

"Mr. Fitzgerald needs to be escorted out of the building, please." The fire chief rubbed the deep lines in his forehead. "He's in search of the Ark of the Covenant. Can you show him to the door?"

The officer grabbed the historian by the elbow and dragged him up the stairs.

"Wait." Fitzgerald tried to break free. "You don't understand. Please believe me. Just give me an hour. One hour."

Another officer came over to assist. They picked Fitzgerald up, body and bones, and carried him up the stairs, kicking and screaming. His voice faded under the noise of the truck's backup beepers, heavy engines, and countless voices of emergency workers.

He was escorted to the sidewalk outside the Masonic Temple, where in disbelief he watched the truck pump tons of concrete into the tunnels he had spent years searching for. The smell of exhaust fumes from the concrete mixer burned his nostrils and made him dizzy. A police officer yelled at him to move out of the way.

He slowly walked to the top of Cathedral Street and turned around to view the scene of organized chaos. A light snow began to fall, settling on his winter coat and dripped down from his white hair onto his face.

A deep pain of despair overtook him. A gut-wrenching sound escaped his throat. His body trembled.

He took out his phone and pressed a number.

"It's over." He could barely say the words. "It's over."

36

Insp. Myra leaned against the kitchen counter, watching his daughters fight over who had the most cereal in their bowls. Clara picked up a handful of milk-drenched Cheerios and raised her hand to throw them at Doris. Maria sprang from the stove like a ninja and caught her hand mid-flight.

"Nick! Cripes, you can spot an expired licence plate at two hundred feet in a rainstorm, but you can't see what's going on in front of your face?" Maria shook Clara's hand over her bowl and grabbed a paper napkin to dry it.

Nick kept his head bowed over his coffee cup to hide his grin. "I see it, and I'm enjoying every second of it."

She threw the napkin in the garbage, then went to him, wrapping her arms gently around his sore ribs. "I wish you'd stay home with me for another week. I don't think you're ready to go back."

"We're so close to finishing this file." He wrapped his arms around her. A shooting pain made him flinch when he lifted his arms. "I gotta get back."

"Do you think Donna is going back?" Maria tossed her long, dark hair back as she looked up at his tired face.

"I don't know. She was pretty shaken up. I wouldn't blame her if she didn't."

"I suppose she was. She's the breadwinner in that family. If anything happened to her, can you imagine where Steve and Jack would be?"

"I think about it a lot, actually."

"Imagine poor Steve trying to live on her pension while dealing with Jack's needs. She must have been out of her mind with worry."

"She didn't show it, though." Myra rubbed Maria's back as he pushed her away and finished the last of his coffee. "She stayed focused. She didn't freak out at all. I know I was out of my mind with worry."

"I suppose you were. I wouldn't be any better off than Steve with two daughters to raise."

He jammed his hands in his front pockets. "You don't have to worry about me."

Maria rolled her eyes. "You had another dream last night. You were tossing and turning. Didn't you notice how wet the sheets were on your side of the bed?"

He slowly shook his head.

"It's time, Nick. You need to go back to the psychologist and unpack a lot of your crap. You've got to learn to let some of this baggage go."

He sighed, knowing she was right. "I'll book an appointment as soon as I get into the office."

"Nick, I admire your dedication to your work . . . that you're driven to give every family you deal with some peace and closure." She opened the fridge and took out the lunch she had packed for him. "I just wish you would give yourself the same peace and closure."

Myra put his cup in the dishwasher and took the lunch. For a moment he hesitated, lost in thought.

"There was a brief moment, when I was lying in that tunnel, I thought I was going to die in a goddamn sewer." He let out a short chuckle that sent a sharp pain to his ribs. "Certainly not going out in a blaze of glory like I had imagined. I pictured you here with the girls, and I just wanted to go home."

Maria embraced him tightly, forgetting about his ribs. They both laughed as he winced in pain.

"I'm sorry. I forgot." She put a hand to her mouth to hide her smile.

"I'm good. I'm good." He limped down the hallway toward the front door.

"Hey, Nick?"

"What?"

"You and Whiffen are a good team."

"We are. I hope she shows up this morning. I'm lucky to play on a lot of good teams."

37

Cst. Whiffen pulled her long, brown hair back over her shoulders. She leaned closer to the mirror to inspect her eyes.

Steve sat on the bed, his face filled with concern. "How are you feeling?"

"A lot better now." Donna reached up and rubbed her shoulder. "Steve, don't worry. My lung only collapsed ten per cent. The doctor said I'd be fine in a week, and I am."

"Every time you go through that door, I feel an incredible sense of guilt." He buried his hands in his hair.

She turned around to face him. "What are you talking about? We agreed that my career had better benefits. That's all."

"I should be the one doing your job, not staying home all day. The men you work with must laugh at me." Steve grabbed a fistful of his short hair and pulled till it hurt.

"The men I work with couldn't do your job." She enunciated every word.

He started to sob.

"Steve. Stop that, right now." She knelt before him and grabbed him by the forearms. "Don't do this. This is not how we deal with our problems."

"I keep thinking about you being trapped under a building while I was getting a haircut and grabbing a coffee."

Donna jerked away and stood up, her voice shaking with emotion. "Every morning I pull out of that driveway, I am filled with guilt and anxiety. I feel bad about leaving you behind. Then, when I have to leave work early, or even on time, I worry my co-workers won't respect me. I feel like I'm failing at work and at home.

Steve reached up and wrapped his arms around her waist. "Donna, you're not failing at anything."

She sniffed back a tear of frustration that tried to roll down her cheek. "I'm a bad mother. I'm a bad wife."

"Donna, don't you say that." He hugged her tighter.

"Sometimes when I'm driving to work, I think about what it must be like to have a normal life. What it would be like for us if we didn't have Jack."

He squeezed his eyes closed. "You don't think that I wonder about that, too? Donna, every parent in our shoes thinks the same thing."

"The whole time I was lying there, covered in rocks, all I could think about was Jack being put in a home. If people would be nice to him. If they would understand why he needs to keep his schedule the same. Would they remember he doesn't like peas and he doesn't want his carrots touching his potatoes?" Her chest rose and fell with rapid breaths.

"And when the time comes, we will both be there to tell them."

Steve pulled himself up off the bed and wrapped his arms around her shoulders. She buried her face in his chest, and he embraced her, kissing the top of her head.

"Donna, I wouldn't change anything." He massaged the back of her neck. "You, Jack. Nothing. I get frustrated at times. But I love my life." He pushed her away so he could see her face. "You're not a bad mother or wife, and I'm not a bad father. We're just two parents doing the best we can."

She let out a ragged breath. "We are that. We are definitely that."

"Now, get off your arse and go make some money." He swatted her backside and pulled her closer. They exchanged a tearful kiss goodbye. Donna picked up the silver badge in the black leather holder from her dresser and attached it to her belt.

"I don't know what I'd do without you, Steve."

"You'll never know." He lifted his shoulder in a half-shrug. "Because you'll never be without me."

38

Cst. Whiffen was unpacking her briefcase when Insp. Myra opened the office door. He stopped and looked at her, then smiled and closed the door behind him.

"Good morning, Whiffen." He unlocked his office door and pulled it open. "Some weather we're having. Nice to see the sun for a change."

"I was thinking the same thing myself."

Whiffen grimaced, sliding off her winter coat and hanging it up. She glanced down at herself, grateful that Steve had talked her into dressing for comfort, in jeans and a sweater.

"Simon and Morgan are on their way over," he called out from behind his desk.

"I'm just sorting out the files now," she called back.

Myra suddenly appeared in his doorway, leaning against the door casing. "You okay?" He dug his hands into the front pockets of his jeans.

Whiffen slowly slipped into her chair. "I'm okay."

"You sure?"

"I hurt like a bastard." She pointed at her chest. "It hurts when I breathe."

He opened his blazer to show his pressed white shirt. "My ribs are killing me, so don't make me laugh today."

"So, no foot chase today is what you're saying." She laughed, then regretted it as she folded her arms around her body. "I have screens of emails to go through. I'm hoping the forensics on Mortimer's computer and phone are here somewhere."

"Luckily, working in Major Crime is ninety per cent brain work and ten per cent rolling around on the ground with a criminal. Good to see you back." Myra turned and headed back to his desk.

"Good to be back, sir."

Sgt. Morgan elbowed his way through the door, holding a tray of coffee and two plastic tubs, his face red and covered in a sheen of sweat. "Good morning. I just spotted Simon parking his car. He should be here shortly." He laid the coffee and tubs on an empty desk. "Come and get it."

Morgan slipped off his heavy navy blue police parka that had been issued to him in 1995 and tossed it across a chair. He took a tissue out of the front pocket of his khaki pants and dabbed a spot of coffee on his blue polo shirt. "The wind took the tray just as I got out of the car." He continued to dab the stain.

Whiffen carefully lifted herself out of the chair and sauntered toward him. "Yay, coffee, and are those homemade muffins?"

"Yes." He flipped the top off a plastic tub. "Sharon whipped these up this morning." He handed her the other tub. "These are for Jack. Sharon phoned Steve to see how you were doing and if he needed anything. I think you were sleeping when she called. They had a chat, and he told her Jack liked chocolate chip muffins, so she made a batch for him."

Whiffen opened the tub and peeked in at twelve freshly made muffins. She snapped it closed again. "Tell her I said thank you." She picked up a coffee cup and looked into Morgan's kind eyes.

"Thank you, Bill. For everything. For getting us out of that tunnel. For weekly coffee and for muffins." She choked up on the last word before turning and limping back to her desk.

Morgan looked toward the framed photo of Jack on her desk. "Donna, I'm sorry about the other day."

She cut him off. "No worries. Forget it."

Morgan picked up his coffee and headed to a vacant chair. "The worst thing you can tell Sharon is that you love muffins, because she'll make them every week. You know, she just likes to have something to do." His voice trailed off as the office door opened.

Simon strode in, swinging his worn, overstuffed briefcase. "Glorious morning. I would fancy a cuppa right now."

Morgan lifted a paper cup out of the tray. "One cream, two sugar."

"You are an officer and a gentleman, mate." Simon raised the cup. "Cheers."

The medical examiner unbuttoned his waxed-cotton Barbour jacket, then folded his flat cap and stuffed it in his pocket. His tailored blue suit was offset by a vibrant plaid vest and crisp white Oxford shirt with a blue tie. One leg of his pants was accidentally tucked into his Wellie boots, and the other hung outside. He sat in the nearest available chair, took the plastic lid off his cup, and sipped his tea. He spotted the plastic container.

"Are there muffins? I hear you guys and gal had quite the adventure."

Morgan pushed them across the desk. "Enjoy." He took note of Simon's vest. "You look rather spiffy today."

"Court, mate." Simon bit into a large muffin, sending crumbs down over the vest. "You get me for thirty minutes, and then I have to run."

Myra joined them in the main office and took the remaining coffee. "Yeah, Simon, we did have a bit an adventure in the sewers.

Oh, Sharon's muffins!" He opened the top for a look. "Chocolate chip." He looked around the office. "She knows these are my favourite. She made these for me, didn't she?"

Morgan nodded and tried to hide a smile. "Just for you."

"I'll have one in a minute." He walked to the whiteboard, which was now covered in notes, pictures, maps, and ideas.

"How's the investigation going?" Simon asked. "I hear that the media are claiming you both have tunnel vision."

"Ha, ha." Whiffen wrapped her arms around her ribs. "Don't make us laugh."

"I will hurt you if you make another lame joke." Myra rubbed his ribs while Morgan hid another grin behind a muffin. "This week off gave me some time to step back and get some perspective." He picked up his marker and scanned the jumble of information. "I know we're missing something, but I don't know what.

"I've been notified by Mortimer's lawyer that the will reading is tomorrow afternoon at the Masonic Temple. He won't release the will to us until an hour before the reading."

"The scene of his murder?" Whiffen made a jerking motion toward him that made her flinch.

"I know." Myra gave a dismissive wave of his hand. "I'm wondering if he predicted his own death." He looked at Morgan. "Can you give us an update on the murder of Kate and Joseph Williams?"

"Simon exhumed the bodies. The blood evidence collected from their original autopsy was still documented, collected, and stored properly, so he was able to run new tests. Simon, you should explain."

"Simply put, toxicology tests are a lot more sophisticated now than they were in the 1980s." Simon sat forward and threw his paper cup into the garbage bin beside the far wall. "The results of tests on Kate and Joseph Williams show that they both had traces of sleeping pills, and obviously carbon monoxide from the muffler. There were no traces of alcohol."

"I think the sleeping pills were ground up and put in the soda," said Morgan.

"How do you think that happened?" Myra asked Morgan.

"Mrs. Williams, the sister-in-law, puts Doreen at Bennett's Pond, alone with Kate and Joseph Williams. I believe she tricked them into meeting her there under the assumption that Barbara was coming, too. She gave them the sandwiches and soda to eat while they waited for Barbara to show up. I'd say the Williamses were too polite to say no, and remember, they wanted to stay in Doreen's good books so they didn't lose their daughter."

"I believe Barbara knew nothing about it." Whiffen listened with great interest.

Morgan nodded. "That's what I suspect, too. Once they got drowsy, she helped them back in the car and turned it on. But she forgot, or didn't know, that Kate couldn't drive. I believe she punctured the hole in the exhaust when she borrowed it days before. She staged the wine bottles and picnic supplies in the back seat to make us believe they got drunk and fell asleep."

"Do we have enough to charge her all these years later?" Myra asked.

"After reviewing it with the Crown prosecutor, we feel we do have enough evidence to proceed with charges against Doreen." Morgan released a pent-up breath.

Myra lifted his chin. His lips spread thinly under his thick moustache. "Good job. In the process of trying to solve one murder, we accidentally solved two more."

Whiffen gave Morgan a thumbs-up. "At least Bucky will get some closure. I feel sorry for the poor guy. Losing his parents, and now his twin."

Myra turned back to the whiteboard. "What do we know?"

He tapped the butt of the marker on his chin. "We know Mortimer Williams's evening started off by meeting his brother, Bucky, for supper."

"Wait," Whiffen called out as she opened an email. "I have the report on Mortimer's computer and phone from forensics." She began to speed-read through it.

"What does it say?" Myra asked.

"They were able to recover most of the information on it. It's mostly work-related." She continued to read as fast as she could. "It looks like he had a Hotmail account, but he used it from two computers. Probably one he used at home and one at work. They are having trouble confirming that, though. There are a couple of emails flagged for us.

"There's an exchange between Mortimer and Miller around six the night he died. Which would have been before supper with Bucky. He asked Miller to meet him at eight thirty at the Temple to take his official Grand Master portrait. Miller agreed." She looked up from the screen. "Remember, Miller said he was a part-time photographer."

"Did Miller answer?"

"He did. He said he would. But then it gets weird."

"How could it possibly get bloody weirder?" Simon threw up his hands.

"Forensics also went through Mortimer's phone, and it doesn't jive. There's a text exchange between Mortimer and Miller around seven twenty-five, which is when he left the restaurant. Miller asked him if he wanted to cancel because of the storm. Mortimer acted like he didn't know what he was talking about. Miller told him he had permission from the manager to use the building if he wanted to go ahead with the photo. Mortimer said he didn't recall sending that email. But he said he had his Masonic stuff in the trunk of his car and would see him there."

"Why would he act like he didn't know about the portrait? I think someone is playing us here." Myra made a note of it on the whiteboard. "Did someone else send that email from the victim's account?"

"Forensics found the last text Mortimer sent." Whiffen turned her screen toward them. "Or I should say didn't send. He typed *What time?* but didn't send it."

"He was rushing to the Temple," Myra offered. "Maybe he thought he sent it. Why wouldn't he know what time the photo shoot was? He arranged it."

Whiffen pointed at an italicized paragraph. "There's also an email to Fitzgerald at six thirty saying he would give him the letter and the map. Mortimer asked him to meet at the Masonic Temple at seven thirty. He promised to show him where the tunnel was."

"Really?" Myra came around her desk to read the email. "Why did Fitzgerald hide that from us?"

"Good question. Maybe he was afraid of having the murder pinned on him." Whiffen continued reading.

"Or maybe he figured out he was being set up to have the murder pinned on him." Myra rubbed his chin. He went back to the board. "What do we know for sure?"

"Well, we now know that Mortimer, or someone acting as him, arranged to meet both Miller and Fitzgerald at the Masonic Temple the night he died." Whiffen filed the report in the folder.

"We know the bloke was allergic to sulphites, but traces were found in his blood and in the pill case he carried his ulcer medication in," Simon offered. "For the record, the pills are very similar in size and colour, but I don't think there were enough sulphites in his blood to kill him. I believe he digested only one pill. He would have needed to take another two to three pills to make it lethal. Maybe the killer didn't know that."

Myra thought about that. "The killer expected him to die after taking the pills. But he didn't, and that's why he was struck with the table. But who changed the pills? We know only Doreen and Flora had access to the pills. They both knew that if he took them, he would go into anaphylactic shock." Myra pointed to the medical information pinned to the board. "But who switched them, and was it to kill him or scare him?"

"He had quite the knob on the back of his head." Simon leaned back in his chair to get a better look at the whiteboard. "Someone hit him with the table, which means they didn't bring a weapon. That tells me the killer flew into a rage and grabbed the first thing they could find."

"Ident confirmed the blood and hair found on the table belonged to Mortimer Williams, and they found prints which we're running now." Morgan laid down his empty cup and took out his cellphone. "I just sent you their report." He looked at Whiffen.

"Don't forget the bruising around Mr. Mortimer's face," Simon reminded them. "To me, it looked like someone grabbed his face while either sitting on him or standing over him. But were they trying to revive him or make sure he was dead?" He steepled his fingers. "It's my opinion that the anaphylactic shock incapacitated him so he couldn't fight back, and the blunt force trauma to his head killed him."

Simon looked at his watch. He pulled out his cap and put it on. "I must get going. I have other autopsies to deal with, but first I must deal with the most gruesome part of my job." He opened the office door. "Going to court."

They bid their goodbyes as Simon left. The three police officers sat in silence while each pondered the investigation.

"Maybe someone found him and tried to revive him," Whiffen pointed out. "When they couldn't, they panicked and left. Then they called the police and reported a break and enter."

"Then which one killed him?" Morgan asked. "And which one tried to save him? They all blame each other."

"Whiffen, Morgan, you're both geniuses." Myra threw the marker back in the basket.

"What if everybody is telling the truth?"

39

Max Burke was a friendly sort of fellow. His natural expression, a smile, was a permanent fixture on his face. For a lawyer, he exuded a kindness that was unexpected. He walked like he was on a mission as he opened the grand doors to the banquet room in the Masonic Temple. A white tablecloth had been neatly pulled over a long table that sat eight. Burke laid down his briefcase at the head of the table. At 1:45 p.m. his assistant unlocked the front door and allowed the invitees to enter. A gust of cold wind blew in behind them as if the building had finally inhaled. They were directed into the banquet room of the Masonic Temple.

The tall, narrow windows let in brilliant blades of sunlight that lit up the dust dancing in the air. Fluorescent lights flickered overhead, unable to light the entirety of the enormous room. Concave arcs of plaster mouldings, painted white, were expertly positioned on the burgundy walls. The embellished, faded-white ceiling was elaborately divided into a grid of recessed squares. The original hardwood floor was scuffed from dragging chairs and dancing feet.

The Masonic motto, *Ordo Ab Chao*, translated to *Order from Chaos*, was engraved in a hidden corner. The building secretly held on to the dignity of its birthright, cleverly hiding its belief in the existence of a Supreme Being in plain view while clinging to the immortality of its soul.

"I don't know why I'm here." James Fitzgerald clasped his hands behind his back as he circled the foyer. He stopped to observe the dusty boot prints left behind by emergency workers. The pain in his chest returned. He couldn't bear to look down the basement stairs. He extended a hand to Mr. Burke, who politely shook it and continued dragging files out of his briefcase.

"Did he leave me something?" Fitzgerald asked, chuckling.

"Take any seat at the table," Burke deflected, and continued on with his work.

Bucky had made a futile attempt to clean himself up. His hands and nails were permanently stained with mechanic's grease. He looked around at the others, hiding his hands in the front pockets of his shabby jeans, and took a seat. He tucked his chin down in his zipped-up parka and kept his eyes on the table without saying a word.

Tom Miller was angrily whispering something to Fitzgerald in a distant corner. He carried his winter coat across his arm. The armpits and back of his blue shirt showed sweat stains, his bald head glistening under the lights.

Art and Flora Pardy walked in together, holding hands. Flora made a beeline to the lawyer. "You must be Mr. Burke." She held onto the tailored sleeve of his black blazer. "Does this mean we are in the will?"

Burke pointed to the empty chairs. "Ma'am, please take a seat, and I'll begin shortly."

"But we're getting the house, right?" She tugged at his sleeve again. He promptly pulled it from her grasp.

Burke looked over her head at the next person who was joining them. "Please take a seat." He gestured to the table.

Art took Flora by the arm and nudged her toward a chair.

Doreen took her time walking into the room. She stopped short when she spotted Bucky with his chin tucked down in his coat. Miller was pulling out a chair next to Art when he noticed the scowl on Doreen's face. He sniffed, looking away.

Doreen nodded to Fitzgerald. "I wasn't expecting to see you here tonight."

"It's a bit of a shock to me," he admitted. "I have no idea why I'm in the will. I certainly wasn't expecting it."

"Well, I'm surprised and angry about all of you being here." She clapped her hands together and rubbed them as she spoke. "I am his wife, and only family." She sent an angry look toward Bucky. "I'm the only one who should be in the will."

Burke looked up from his briefcase, checked his expensive gold watch, and called, "Everyone sit down, please. It's time for the reading of the will."

Those still standing took the available seats.

"Why is there an empty chair?" Flora asked.

"They don't set tables for seven, idiot," Doreen snapped.

Burke squinted in Doreen's direction. He took a pair of glasses from the inside pocket of his suit, flipped them open, and put them on.

"Good afternoon, everyone." A warm smile spread across his face. "My name is Max Burke, and I am Mortimer Williams's attorney." He took a white file folder out of his briefcase. "I am also the executor of his estate. Mr. Williams rewrote his will four weeks before his death, as he was making major changes in his life."

He tapped the folder on the table before opening it.

"I will be reading Mortimer's last will and testament. This document expresses Mortimer's wishes as to how his property is to be distributed after his death. I will manage the property until its final distribution."

"What do you mean by *manage*?" Doreen put air-quotes around her last word.

"We'll get into that as we go." Burke opened the folder and cleared his throat. "Let's begin." He looked around the table.

"To my wife, Doreen." Burke looked up over his glasses at her. "I leave the sum of one million dollars. Mr. Williams had noted that you already owned two houses."

Doreen slowly nodded while chewing the inside of her cheek but said nothing. Flora shot her a worried look.

"He wrote a personal note to his brother, Bucky," the lawyer continued. "It says: I leave a perfectly preserved baseball card collection." Burke locked eyes with him as he read, "I would never destroy something we both built." The lawyer cleared his throat again. "Bucky, you are my brother. My twin. Half of me. My greatest regret is cutting you out of my life. I want you to know that I thought of you all those years. I hope you can forgive me."

Bucky pushed his hands farther into his pockets. His shoulders shook as he ducked his chin deeper inside his parka. Doreen glared at him from across the table.

The lawyer moved on. "James Fitzgerald. I leave two hundred thousand dollars to the Basilica of St. John the Baptist for the restoration of the Immaculate Conception window. James, we did not always get along, but I always admired your determination and devotion to history and the Masons."

"Oh, my goodness." Fitzgerald's hands flew to his face. "Two hundred thousand dollars." He looked around the table. "I was not expecting that. My goodness, what a nice man he was."

"To Art and Flora Pardy." Flora and Art adjusted themselves in their chairs. "I leave the sum of five hundred thousand dollars." The lawyer looked up at them. "Art and Flora, as I explained, the houses were not mine to leave you, but I hope you take this money and buy a house of your own."

Flora dabbed a tissue to her eyes. Art joined his hands together in prayer and bowed his head, repeating, "Thank you."

Burke looked back at the document. "To Tom Miller. Tom, you loved me in high school, and I couldn't return that. But throughout my life, my struggles, we stayed good friends.

"I leave you one hundred thousand dollars and my Masonic ring." Miller fought to control a sob.

Burke closed the file and put it back in his case. He pointed at the empty chair. "Now, as you can see, there is an empty chair."

They all looked toward the chair as if expecting Mortimer to manifest into it.

"This chair is for a special guest who will join us after I explain the conditions of the will."

"What conditions?" Art asked.

Burke took off his glasses and put them back in his blazer pocket. "If someone is convicted, and I am not talking about just being *charged* of the murder of Mortimer Williams, but if one of you are *convicted* of his murder," he paused, "and you are a beneficiary of his estate, then you become disentitled from any inheritance from him to which you would otherwise be entitled under this will. This not only includes the murder of Mortimer Williams, but also his parents, Kate and Joseph Williams. Your inheritance will then be shared among everyone else."

Burke paused as he looked around the table.

"You see, Mortimer feared he would be murdered because of the changes he was making in his life and because of the greed of those around him."

Bucky's head shot up from his parka, and he met Doreen's glare. Everyone else sat up straight, looking around at each other.

"Also, the administrator or executor of this will," Burke continued, clearing his throat again, "who is me, will refuse to distribute any inheritance until the final result of the trial is known and any appeals are exhausted. Otherwise, I would be personally liable for wrongful distribution if a conviction was entered and not overturned in a final appeal."

"What does that mean?" Doreen asked, perturbed.

"Basically, if you killed Mortimer or his parents you get nothing. If you didn't, you could get it all."

40

James Fitzgerald leaned forward. "Do I have to wait for my money until these guys are cleared?"

"What do you mean by *these guys*?" Miller jumped up, looking around defensively. "I didn't kill Morty."

Doreen pushed herself back from the table. "This is ridiculous," she shouted at the lawyer. "He's just playing with us."

The lawyer waved at them. "Please, everyone needs to sit down."

They all took their places, grumbling to themselves and those around them.

Burke pointed at the empty chair. "I told you that there was a special guest."

The two doors to the large room opened, bringing much-needed light into the room. The group turned around to see Insp. Myra flanked by Cst. Whiffen and Sgt. Morgan.

Morgan closed the doors and stood sentry in front of them. Whiffen followed Myra, who was carrying a leather briefcase.

Burke nodded at Myra and Whiffen. "The floor is yours." He stood behind the officers, holding his briefcase.

Myra took Burke's place at the head of the table.

"Mr. Burke has just read Mortimer Williams's will." He looked at the lawyer and back at the table. "And he explained the conditions."

The group sat in stunned silence. Each was concerned with losing their unexpected windfall, and one of them would be convicted of murder. They nodded in understanding as they eyed Myra nervously from their seats.

"Mortimer Williams rewrote his will four weeks ago because he feared for his life." Myra's baritone voice echoed around the room. "And with good cause. He knew what his enemy was capable of."

Art rubbed Flora's back as she bent over in a wheeze. When she recovered, he put his finger to his lips and made a shushing sound.

Myra undid the button of his black wool blazer. "Greed will make you do things you would never normally consider. Greed will drive you to rob your mother's grave."

Each looked around the table with a suspicious eye.

"Morty was the only one among you who truly lived by the Masonic beliefs. He was by all accounts a good man."

They sat listening with their eyes cast down. Not one of them looked toward the large police officer at the head of the table.

"The beliefs of Freemasonry can be boiled down to three simple concepts. One: brotherly love. Which is love for each other and for all mankind. This was at the core of Mortimer's soul. His will is proof of his love and respect for everyone in this room."

Bucky let out a sob that surrendered his grief to the room.

Myra looked around the table. "Two: charity for others and mutual aid for fellow Masons." He looked toward Fitzgerald and Miller. "Mortimer devoted his life to charity and helping others. But it was never enough, was it?"

Fitzgerald's mouth fell open as he looked around the table. "Why are you looking at me?"

Miller shot him a steely glance that shut him up.

"And the third is truth: the search for answers to the universal questions of morality, and the salvation of the soul, that only a man's individual faith and his relationship with God can provide."

Myra leaned over the table and looked at Doreen. "Mortimer spent his life trying to find the answers to questions. The truth." He sat back and continued. "The night Mortimer died, he met Bucky for supper at six thirty."

Myra nodded toward Bucky, whose head popped out of his coat, waiting for the accusations.

"It wasn't your first meeting, was it, Bucky?"

Bucky slowly looked around the table and stopped at Doreen. "We had agreed to let bygones be bygones. We buried the past."

"He had given you the inheritance that you should have received when your parents died," Myra stated.

The colour drained from Doreen's face. Bucky seemed to enjoy every minute of it.

"Yes, he did." The legs of his chair scraped across the old wooden floor as he leaned toward Doreen. "That's not all he gave me."

"We will get back to that." Myra held up a hand. "Let's establish a timeline first."

Myra tugged at his moustache while turning his gaze on James Fitzgerald. "*Tota Pulchra*, not *Iota pulchra*. Only you would know what that meant."

Fitzgerald frantically looked around at the accusatory stares.

"That's not true." He slammed his hand on the table. "I told you several people knew."

"But no one who desperately wanted a letter and a map from Mortimer." Myra turned back to Whiffen, who handed him a thick file. He opened it and looked back at Fitzgerald.

"Morty sent you an email asking you to meet him at the Masonic Temple at seven thirty because he was going to give you the letter and the map. He also told you he would show you where the tunnel was."

Fitzgerald's mouth went dry. He shivered but stayed quiet.

"When I interviewed you at your office, I suggested to you that Morty didn't believe the tunnel existed. You answered with *at first* he didn't. I questioned you on it, and you backtracked. When we searched his computer, we found the email he sent you asking for the meeting here and offering to give you what you wanted."

Myra slipped a photocopy of a map out of the file and unfolded it. "Morty refused to let you see the original, not because he didn't like you, but because you weren't of the right Masonic degree to have that information. You told me Mortimer didn't like you, but really, he was keeping you away to protect his secret. He knew you didn't recognize him as Barbara from high school."

A sheen of sweat spread across Fitzgerald's round face. His cheeks flushed red. "I was shocked when you told me. I really didn't know he was the former Barbara, but when it came to that information I needed, I tried to tell him I am a historian. A respected academic. That should have trumped a bunch of secret handshakes."

Myra slid the photocopied map to him. "Morty didn't let you see it for another reason."

Fitzgerald dragged the map toward him and tried to read the tiny type around the 1784-era streets of St. John's.

"He was protecting your reputation." Myra went back to the file in his hand. "The tunnel doesn't lead to any treasure—it leads to the sewer. That's why it was boarded up. But as long as no one knew that, including you, you could keep the whole fantasy alive. Maybe even attract new members to the organization or gain more interest in the Ecclesiastic Circle."

Fitzgerald looked up from the map. "Is this really it?"

Myra gave a half-shrug. "The Masons gave me a photocopy."

The historian stared at the map in disbelief. "That can't be. I have other documents that prove I'm right."

"Let's go back to the night Mortimer died." Myra tapped his hand on the table, and Fitzgerald looked at him. "Tell me what happened."

Fitzgerald let out a defeated sigh. "I was surprised to receive his email. Especially so late in the evening with a storm looming. I found him upstairs in the lodge room. He was getting ready for a photo shoot with Tom Miller." He gave Miller a sideways glance before continuing. "He seemed surprised to see me. I asked him if we could hurry, because I wanted to get home and walk my dogs before it got too stormy."

Fitzgerald looked around the table before continuing.

"He didn't know what I was talking about. I thought he was fooling around with me. I showed him the email that he sent, and he denied it. I became really frustrated with him, and we began to argue about it."

Fitzgerald looked at the map again. "He offered to give me the money to have the Immaculate Conception window fixed instead of giving me the map." He hung his head in shame. "He picked up a sheet of paper off the floor and offered to write an agreement on it. He asked me to write it out while he continued to get ready for the picture."

"Did you?" Myra asked.

"I wrote *iota pulchra* on it and threw it at him. I was just so angry. I felt like a fool for falling for this, and I didn't understand why he would do it."

"Did he take any pills while you were arguing?"

Fitzgerald ran his fingers over his short white hair. "Pills? I think he did. I thought they were breath mints or something. They were in a fancy pillbox like old ladies use. He started freaking out and ran away from me. I said the hell with that and left."

"What you didn't know was he was about to go into anaphylactic shock because someone replaced his stomach pills with pills that had sulphur in them. He had left his coat on the bar downstairs, and his EpiPen was in the pocket. He was suffocating."

Fitzgerald became fidgety. "I didn't know that. How could I have known? He was alive when I left," he protested as he looked around at the accusatory faces at the table. "I wouldn't have left him there if I knew that. How was I to know that?"

"Why didn't you tell me?" Myra asked.

"I was afraid. I swear he was alive when I left. I thought Tom murdered him. I knew he was there after me. I also knew, as a past Grand Master, he would have seen the real map, even though he told me he didn't. When Morty was murdered, I thought Tom did it to get him out of the way. It just proved to me that the treasure really did exist. I thought Tom wanted the treasure for himself and that I was going to be next. I didn't know what to do."

"Me?" Tom Miller's mouth dropped. "Are you serious? Why would I do it? It wasn't me." He pleaded his case to the questioning looks around the table.

Myra turned his attention to Tom Miller. "You dated Mortimer in high school. Before he transitioned. You didn't get over the relationship, which is why you still have a photo of both of you on your mantelpiece."

Miller closed his eyes. He rubbed his hands over his face but said nothing.

"Morty sent you an email, also. He asked you to meet him at eight thirty to take his photo. You texted him at six asking if he still wanted to go ahead with it, due to the storm coming. He seemed confused and didn't know what you were talking about. He agreed to meet you, anyway."

Miller sat back and looked around at the ancient walls of the Masonic Temple. "I didn't know what he was getting on with. He wanted me to take his photo, and then he didn't. I didn't care, either way."

Myra shook his head slowly. "You never did believe in any hidden treasure, did you?"

"You didn't believe it?" Fitzgerald yelled. "They found the tunnels. It does exist."

Miller didn't look at him.

"Tell me what happened when you got here." Myra folded his arms and waited.

"I dragged my photography gear in here. At that point it was starting to snow. I was pissed because I wanted to wait till the weather was better."

"Did you have a relationship with Morty that was closer than friendship?" Myra asked.

"We were friends, that's all." Miller lifted his hands up. "Barbara was my first love, but Morty was my best friend. That's it."

"Where was Morty when you arrived here?"

"I spotted his coat on the bar, and I heard a sound upstairs. I called out to him, but I didn't get an answer, so I went up."

Myra motioned for him to continue.

"When I got up there, I couldn't find him. I looked around, but he wasn't there."

"Did you go to the Chamber of Reflection?"

"No. Why would I?" Miller returned the question. "I wouldn't expect him to be there. I suspected that's where you found him when I showed you around that day and spotted the blue rubber glove on the floor."

"You're saying you didn't see a thing?"

Miller hid his face behind his hand and sank in his chair. "I didn't see a thing. I waited for about twenty minutes, then I went home. I knew he had been there because his coat was still on the bar. I figured something happened and he left in a hurry. His car wasn't parked in front of the building, either."

"Did you try to contact him?"

"No, I was too angry. I was going to call him the next day, and then, of course, I got the news that his body had been found." He glanced at Fitzgerald and then lowered his eyes. "Then I was afraid that I would get the blame, so I stayed quiet. I didn't know he was meeting Fitzgerald earlier."

Myra looked at them both. "Great friends you are."

Miller flushed. "Maybe we should have said something, but we were afraid of Doreen. We both believed she killed him, and we knew you'd figure that out without us."

The two men kept their heads lowered, eyes averted. Myra took a moment and continued. "Did either of you smell candles burning while you were here?"

Both men shook their heads.

"Then that means Mortimer's killer was still here, hiding."

Miller and Fitzgerald exchanged glances.

"Doreen was here?" Fitzgerald blurted out.

"Don't be so quick to judge." Myra half-smiled. "You see, Morty didn't email either of you. The killer did. You were being set up to take the fall. The killer was counting on your personal greed."

"What do mean by *our greed*?" Miller asked.

"Greed is one of the seven deadly sins," Myra informed them. "Fitzgerald, you wanted fame, and Miller, you wanted his money."

"I didn't need his money," Miller jumped in.

"Your accounting business was failing. That's why Morty switched from his long-time accountant to you." Myra stood up straight to his six-foot-four height and cast a long shadow over the table.

"I hit a rough spot, that's all. I lost a few big clients. I wasn't going under, and Morty offered me his business to help out, but I didn't take any money from him. I worked for it," Miller pleaded.

Myra locked his eyes on Flora and Art.

"Mr. and Mrs. Pardy. You met with Mortimer a few days before his death and asked him to give you the house. He tried to explain to you that the house wasn't his to give, but you wouldn't listen. Arguing with you was causing his ulcer to flare up, and you watched him take pills out of his pillbox and eat them like candy."

"My fucking house," Doreen exploded.

Flora and Art jolted back in their chairs.

"It's my house," Flora screamed back at her.

Myra put his hand up to stop the exchange. "Doreen confirmed that the houses were hers. You were both angry and scared. Then Doreen found out why. She discovered your secret."

Everyone at the table looked toward the Pardys as Flora buried her face in her hands. Art pulled her to his chest, his shaking arms protecting her from the looks coming their way.

Myra continued. "You had the audacity to try to sell your house, even though you didn't own it. You did it in a private sale and took a twenty-thousand-dollar deposit that you couldn't pay back. When the buyer found out you didn't own the house, he went to the police. He knew he was being scammed and eventually took the law into his own hands.

"But why did you think you could get away with that? It took me a while to figure that one out. I'll explain that in a moment."

He looked at Doreen. "The buyer showed up at your doorstep once he did a title search. I have his statement. You knew Mortimer had left them the money to buy a house in his will and they would be able to give the man back his money. But you kept that from them."

"You bitch." Art tried to stand, moving the table abruptly.

Flora grabbed his arm and pulled him down, staring with open hatred at Doreen. "You're so hateful. You enjoy causing pain."

"The guy you owed the money to was the man who shot your windows out, because he had been watching you and Flora. He thought you were in cahoots." Myra held up a handwritten statement. "He made a full confession, but you knew that, didn't you, Doreen? You just wanted us to believe it was Bucky."

Doreen turned her face away.

Myra leaned over the table as he looked at Flora. "You were so angry after your conversation with Mortimer that you had an idea." The fluorescent lights shone down over Myra's face, deepening the dark blue circles under his eyes.

Flora held her hands to her ears as if to stop Myra from talking.

"You went over to his house and asked Doreen for medication for a migraine. You acted confused like you always pretend to. She told you to go to the upstairs bathroom and get what you needed, like she had offered in the past."

Myra tapped his finger on the table. "You knew Mortimer was allergic to sulphur. You're a nurse, and you recognized the pills he was taking for his ulcer."

"That's not true," cried Flora.

"When I interviewed you and Art about the windows being shot out, you revealed you weren't feeling well the night he died, so you both stayed home." He took out a small black leather notebook from his inside blazer pocket and flipped through the pages. "You said you had 'women problems.'

"We obtained a warrant for your medical records and found out you were treated for a urinary tract infection and your doctor prescribed antimicrobials, which contain sulphur. You specifically told the doctor you wanted those pills."

Flora held on to the edge of the table and looked at Sgt. Morgan standing guard at the exit door. "That doesn't mean anything," she cried.

"You put your pills in Mortimer's pillbox."

The group gasped as if the air had gone out of the room. All heads turned toward the Pardys.

"You have no proof," Art yelled, and stood up, knocking over his chair. It hit the floor with a bang that reverberated around the room.

"Give me your Masonic ring, Art." Myra held out his hand.

"No." Art hid his hand behind his back.

"It's not your ring, is it? Morty had his name engraved on the inside of his ring." Myra pounded on the table. Everyone jumped. "What business were you in before your son died, Art?"

Art wrapped his arms around his body and refused to answer.

"You were a computer programmer, and you created the website for Morty's business. You had all his passwords. You had access to everything.

"You had no problem accessing his email. You knew about Miller dating Barbara in high school because you were there. You knew about Fitzgerald's obsession with the treasure, because it's all he ever talked about. Mortimer refused to meet with you again, so you lured him here for a photo, pretending to be Miller. You had the keys because you were a senior warden when the building was sold. You called the theatre manager, pretending to be Miller. Then you lured Miller and Fitzgerald to the Temple. You planned to frame them."

"I'm not staying for this." Art grabbed Flora by the arm and pulled her to her feet. He made his way to the door, only to come face to face with Sgt. Morgan.

Morgan pointed toward the table. "Sit back down."

Art backed up, pulling Flora behind him. Whiffen picked up his chair and positioned it next to Flora's. She stood by until they sat down.

"You arranged to have Fitzgerald and Miller show up at the Masonic Temple that night because you had planned to kill Mortimer and you needed them to take the blame. After they left, you had what you wanted . . . their fingerprints on everything, and an email trail.

"Then you made a mistake. See, I thought it was Miller who wrote the cryptic phrase in Barbara's notebook because they had dated. But it wasn't him. It was you."

Myra jabbed his index finger on the table. "You were the stalker who wrote *For love is as strong as death, jealousy is fierce as the grave* in Barbara's yearbook, with the implied threat of knowing her secret. That's why Morty let you live in the house. You were the person who was blackmailing him."

"That's not true." Art looked up at Myra, then at Flora. "It wasn't me. Miller dated her."

"For a few weeks," Miller yelled at him. "We were just friends. I'm not a stalker."

"Here's the thing about stalkers." Myra moved closer to Art Pardy and bent down until they were almost nose to nose. "They always think they're smarter than their prey. You purposely argued with Morty about the house when he got here, and you presented yourself to him. You wanted his ulcer to flare up and cause him to take a pill. You knew Flora had switched them earlier that day."

"That's not true," Art protested.

"You had access to his email. You read the emails between Morty and his lawyer. You knew he was leaving you five hundred thousand dollars. You needed him to die, so you set it up for him take the pill, but there wasn't enough sulphur in it. He wasn't going into full anaphylactic shock.

"Maybe he got away and you had to think quickly. You hit him with the nearest thing, which was a small table. Your prints are all over everything. Then, just to play with your Masonic brothers and cast doubt amongst them, you mimicked the death of Hiram Abiff, laying Morty out in the Chamber of Reflection with his own Masonic tools laid next to him. The Chamber of Reflection: the place that all Masons go to confess their sins. How ironic. Once you laid him out, you realized he was still breathing, so you grabbed his face and smothered him. As a last indignity, you stole his ring as a trophy."

Art sat shaking and mumbling, his head in his hands.

Myra moved closer to him. "You were hiding when Fitzgerald and Miller were here. You watched Fitzgerald write that note, and you couldn't resist. You wrote down the same quote you left in Morty's yearbook. Then you lit the candles, left, and called the police."

"Art, no." Flora grabbed his arm. "This is all a big lie. Tell him. It's not true. You only went out for a few hours that night." She looked to Myra. "Art just wanted to scare him, not kill him. He wouldn't do that."

"Shut up, Flora." Art pushed her away. "Shut up."

The room went silent.

Doreen seized the opportunity to jump in. She jerked her head in the direction of the Pardys. "She killed him. They both did." She clapped her hands together, impressed with the officer's clever investigation. "And you all thought it was me."

Bucky's eyes shot daggers across the table. She childishly stuck out her tongue. Within seconds, Bucky's agile frame flew across the table to thrust a claw-like hand toward Doreen's throat.

Morgan and Whiffen rushed toward him, grabbing him by the waist and coat. They dragged him back and forced him to his chair. Morgan returned to the door, while Whiffen stood over Bucky with her two hands firmly holding his shoulders.

Flora clung on to Art to get away from the commotion, and Miller pushed himself to a safe distance. Doreen, taking advantage of Bucky's outburst, jumped up screaming.

"He's trying to kill me," she screeched at Myra. "You just saw him do it." She turned on Bucky, who was being restrained by Whiffen. "I didn't kill my husband."

"Doreen, that's the first time you told the truth," Myra said as he straightened out the files that had been upset on the table. "What virtue has joined together, death shall not separate," he quoted eloquently. "That's the motto of the Scottish Rite Freemasons. You see, I do believe you loved Morty."

Doreen looked up at him, doe-eyed and sharp-tongued. "I did love him, and I didn't kill him."

"No, you didn't," Myra agreed. Then he looked her straight in the eye. "But you did kill his parents so you could control him."

Doreen turned a shocked face to Bucky, then back to Myra. "Not this again."

Sgt. Morgan left his post and joined Myra at the top of the table. He was pleased to deliver the news to her. "We retested the blood samples belonging to Kate and Joseph Williams and found traces of the sleeping pills you ground up and put in their soda."

"That's not possible." She tried to push herself away from the table, but Myra grabbed the back of her chair.

"Before Mortimer died," Myra informed her, "he put together a file containing enough information to charge you with the murder of his parents. He gave it to a family member for safekeeping. Turns out the person is a credible witness against you. We can prove you tampered with their car and caused their deaths.

"We are also charging you with fraud for changing the Williamses' will and collecting the insurance money."

"I want my lawyer." Doreen pushed Myra's hand off the chair and stood up.

Myra spread his large hand across her shoulder and sat her back down. "You're not going anywhere."

Bucky let out a piercing, blood-curdling, scream. The whole room stood still. "Look at me." He beat both of his fists on the table. "Look. At. Me."

The room seemed to dim as everyone sat in stunned silence.

Bucky released an animalistic scream that came from the pit of his gut. He wrapped his arms around his body and rocked violently. Drool fell from the corners of his gaping mouth.

"Look at me," he cried out to Doreen. His breath caught in his raw throat. "Look at me." His broken voice faded in the dusty air. "You took everything." A wave of emotion overtook him, sending his body into forceful tremors. "I have nothing."

Bucky tried to stand, but his knees gave out and he fell across the table. "You all killed him."

Cst. Whiffen gently helped him back into his chair.

"Why?" Bucky cried. "Why did they kill my family? My life has been ruined. I have nothing left. Why did they take everything from me?" He collapsed in Whiffen's arms.

Myra looked around the table and considered the years of senseless tragedies that had become Bucky's life. The years of suspicion for killing his own parents. The incredible losses that could never be replaced.

He shook his head. "Greed, Bucky. Plain old greed."

41

The waitress's eyes were brighter than the Christmas lights that dangled all around the restaurant. She handed out menus and danced to the Christmas music on her way back to the kitchen. Parents struggled to get kids out of snowsuits and boots and into fancy shoes and Christmas clothes. The smell of gingerbread cookies piled high on plates around the room mesmerized the children and sent them to the brink of uncontrollable tantrums. Exhausted parents gave in and passed the cookies around the room.

The glass door opened, and a gust of cold wind brought in Simon, who was dragging a black garbage bag. He shook the snow off his flat cap and stomped his gaiters. "Is it ever going to stop? What a bloody mess on the roads today."

He laid the bag next to his feet and stood next to Cst. Whiffen. "I play Father Christmas every year," he whispered in her ear. "It gives me a chance to finally surround myself with people who are happy to be alive."

Insp. Myra pointed toward the two little girls fighting over cookies on the opposite side of the room. "They're mine." His voice was barely audible over the clatter of dishes. "Both mine."

Whiffen laughed at the sight of Maria tearing the two of them apart and giving them a tongue-lashing. "They're adorable."

Myra shook his head. "Maria should work for the United Nations. She's an expert at peace negotiations."

Simon picked up the black garbage bag. "Time to put on my Santa suit." He swung it over his shoulders. "Point me to the nearest loo, and so you know, I'm not coming out until it's time for presents."

They watched him stroll down to the bathroom and close the door behind him.

Sgt. Morgan balanced boxes of cupcakes in both arms, looking for an empty space to lay them. Maria rushed to his rescue and cleared a space on a table.

"Sharon's coming behind me with another couple of dozen." Morgan shook the snow out of his hair. "Nothing makes her happier than baking for kids at Christmas."

"That's so sweet." Maria hugged him. "There she is. I'll go thank her." She hurried off across the room.

Morgan lowered his voice and leaned in toward Myra and Whiffen. "This is just an hour, right?"

Myra smiled broadly. "Three hours."

"Santa's coming soon," Maria yelled over the commotion. "Is everybody being good?"

Clara and Doris jumped excitedly. "We are," they screamed in unison.

Maria looked across the room and spotted Myra. She shook her head and mouthed, *Relax*. Myra's shoulders dropped. He smiled as wide as he could until she looked away, then went back to his normal, expressionless face.

Whiffen spotted Steve's car pulling into the parking lot. She wiped off the condensation on the window and waved excitedly at him.

"Donna," Maria said, making her way across the room, "I know Steve couldn't bring Jack because of his sensory issues, but I don't want you to think Santa forgot him."

She pulled out a ten-inch-by-two-inch box from behind her back and gave it to Whiffen. "It's just something small."

Whiffen looked at Myra and Morgan, who instantly looked at their boots. She ran her finger over the beautifully wrapped gift and tried to say thank you. With each attempt, her lips quivered and tears formed in the corner of her eyes.

"Open it. Go on," Maria encouraged her. "Everyone in the unit went in on it."

Whiffen tore the paper off and uncovered a small square blue box. She carefully lifted the top off and picked up a thick, black leather bracelet with a silver charm attached to the centre. On the front was engraved: JACK. On the back was his address, followed by: *Mother is RNC.*

"It's in case he gets lost again." Maria reached out and pulled her into a tight embrace. "Maybe this summer we can have our family day in a place where he can go, like a park."

Overcome with gratitude, Whiffen found herself hugging Maria tightly. For the first time in years, she could feel a life preserver being thrown to her.

"You have no idea how much this means to me." She gave a final hug and let Maria go. She turned away and wiped the back of her hand across her eyes.

Maria dabbed the corner of her eye with a tissue. "Donna, we're all drowning at times. It's not just you."

Steve arrived just in time to see Donna looking vulnerable. He crept up behind her and put his arm around her shoulders. "Are you my date for this afternoon?" He softly kissed her on the cheek.

"Look." Her hand shook as she handed him the bracelet. "It's a Christmas gift from the unit to Jack."

Steve picked it up and ran his finger over the engraving. "It's beautiful. I can't believe you guys did this. Thank you." An untold pain lined his eyes.

"Now, stop that," Maria demanded. "This is a party, and I worked too hard for anyone to be sad. Now help me clear a path for Santa."

The excited squeals of children filled the room as Santa came around the corner.

"Ho, ho, ho," he yelled cheerily with a hint of a thick British accent.

Some children surrounded him, some clung to his legs, while others ran off screaming in horror.

"Everyone, sit down. Santa has presents for everyone." Maria tried to reason with an army of children hopped up on cookies and cupcakes. "Remember, Santa's watching."

Myra stood at the back of the room with his arms folded. Simon winked under his red velvet hat with the thick, white fur trim.

"Is that your dad over there?" Santa asked as he plopped Doris on one knee and Clara on the other. "Is he getting you a pony for Christmas?"

Myra shook his head with such vigour that his eyes hurt.

"You're not Santa," Doris declared and pulled at the beard, much to Clara's fright, sending her into a tsunami of tears.

"Here we go." Myra made a move toward them. Whiffen grabbed him by the arm.

"Let it go." She twirled the bracelet between her fingers. "You're going to laugh about this someday. And you don't know how lucky you are to be able to do that."

42

The waitress's face, which glowed with youth before the Christmas party, was now tired and weary. She limply waved a fresh pot of coffee in front of them. Whiffen adjusted herself in the booth and rubbed a hand over her tired eyes.

"They're all gone home, finally." She pushed her empty mug toward the waitress. "I'd love one, thanks."

"And you?"

"Yes, please." Insp. Myra tried to adjust his spine in the rigid seat while the waitress poured.

"Thanks for staying. I figured, why go back to the office? Let's just debrief here and go home for Christmas." Myra tried his best to smile. He waited until the waitress was out of sight before asking, "How are you?"

"My ribs still hurt, depending on which way I sit." Whiffen stretched until her spine cracked. "I'm only taking over-the-counter pain pills for it now. The doctor told me to try yoga, so I'm going to give that a go when things calm down."

She looked across the table at Myra's deeply carved face. It was battered by years of traumatic cases. Yet when he smiled, his eyes managed to sparkle with kindness and a hint of who he once was.

"How about you?"

"I've got too many injuries to talk about." He rubbed his fingers over his red, scarred knuckles. "But I think that tunnel enflamed them all."

"Do you ever think about that day?"

Myra looked off as he considered her question. "I think about all the things I should have done differently."

"I keep having this dream that I can't breathe, and I wake up screaming."

He stared at the swirls in his coffee. "I have that dream while I'm awake. Donna, this is not an easy job. I understand your family situation, and I wouldn't blame you if you wanted to transfer to another unit."

Donna raised her chin and took in a slow breath. "I'm not going to lie. I've thought about it. But I don't want to be sent to a unit where I'm filing papers in the basement. That's not what I joined for. I love what I do. I just need to adjust my life to do it. I need to keep that balance between work and home."

Myra nodded as he considered her answer. "We all need to do that. As a manager, I should be leading by example, but if you ask my wife, she'll tell you I don't know what a home-work life balance is."

"But you look like you do." Whiffen fidgeted with the cup and moved it around in circles on the table. "You always seem to know what you're doing."

"Donna, let me save you years of therapy. Everybody questions themselves. You did a great job on this file, and I'm lucky to have you in this unit. I want you to stay, and I'm willing to accommodate your family life to make that happen."

Her cheeks flushed, and she hid her face behind her hand. She bit her lips together and looked up at him. "Then I guess that means you're stuck with me."

Their conversation was cut short when Sgt. Bill Morgan slid in next to Myra.

"It's beginning to look a lot like Christmas," he sang merrily.

"Where did the year go?" Myra asked. "It seems like September was yesterday."

"That was one, two, three murders ago." Morgan counted on his fingers.

"I lost track," Myra said wryly.

"Keeps us in a job." Morgan nudged him with an elbow.

Simon joined them, now back in his normal clothes, with red blotches over his face and neck. "That bloody fake beard must be full of fleas. It itches like hell." He scratched at his cheek. "I think I'll grow one myself for next year."

The waitress returned with a fresh pot of coffee and a small silver pot of tea.

"Oh, I've been dreaming about a cuppa tea ever since one of your kids kicked my privates after they discovered the beard was fake." Simon ran his fingers through his knotted hair. "And this is why I don't have children."

"Coffee here, please." Morgan pushed a cup across the table and bent his head to hide his laughter.

"I've been following the media coverage, but I'm anxious to hear what you decided to do with the lot of them and why." Simon looked around the table. "It's not easy, is it?"

"Murder is never easy," Myra answered. "People think it's a TV show where it's solved in sixty minutes. But it's much more complicated than that. These are real people. Real lives."

Whiffen shivered. She wrapped her arms around herself and rubbed over the goosebumps on her skin.

"This case is different from the rest. Mortimer Williams was a nice guy. He didn't have a greedy bone in his body, yet greed is what killed him. Funny thing is, I think he would have given each of them what they wanted if they had just been reasonable with him."

Myra nodded in agreement. "They all played a role in his death, and it seems like he himself knew it was inevitable."

Simon raised an eyebrow. "What about Flora and Art?"

"It comes down to intent," Whiffen added. "Did she intend to kill him or scare him? Her lawyer will use her well-established craziness to argue she was a victim, too."

"They all wanted to kill him at different times." Myra finished his coffee and pushed the cup aside.

Simon pursed his lips as he listened. "Intent." He rolled the word around with his stiff upper lip. "Funny word, isn't it? Does anyone really intend to kill?"

"We debated over Flora but settled on her being charged with involuntary manslaughter, because I don't believe we can convince the court that her intent was to kill Mortimer," Myra stated. "Art, we all agreed on him. He was charged with first-degree murder because he planned Morty's death. I believe he had been planning it for a long time."

Whiffen chimed in. "Who needs enemies when you have friends like that? I feel bad for poor Bucky. He lived under the suspicion of killing his parents for most of his life. Then he lost touch with his twin. They finally reunited, but then Morty was killed."

Myra considered her statement. "When evil touches you, it changes you, but it doesn't own you. Bucky's life hasn't been an easy one, that's for sure, but he's a survivor."

"What about James Fitzgerald?" Simon asked. "Pity that he got involved with this."

"He got what he wanted. He wanted to be famous for finding lost treasure, and now he is. His name and picture are all over the media. People will be lined up to do the tours of his Ecclesiastic Circle all summer."

"You don't think this will affect his professional standing?" Morgan questioned.

"I think it will enhance it," said Myra. "Make him more mysterious. If an investigation affected your professional standing, we wouldn't have any politicians."

Whiffen smirked. She had a twinkle of mischief in her eyes. "His Ecclesiastic Circle theory is already trending online. I'm sure there will be Masons and Knights Templar from all over the world, planning their trips to St. John's, searching for the Ark of the Covenant."

"Just between us . . ." Simon leaned over the table and spoke in a hoarse whisper. "There are over thirty Knights Templar already in St. John's."

Myra twirled his moustache as he studied Simon's face. "No there aren't. Who are they?"

"Businessmen, military, police, common joes." The corner of Simon's mouth twitched. "If I give you more than that, I'd have to kill you."

Myra waved him away. "You're pulling my leg. I never know when to take you seriously."

"And what about Tom Miller?" Simon asked.

"I kind of feel bad for him," Whiffen admitted.

"The irony is," Myra added, "Miller was probably the only one who wanted Mortimer to live. I think he did love him."

"What about this whole treasure map thing?" Simon asked. "Is there any truth to that?"

"I think Miller was getting a kick out of leading Fitzgerald on a wild goose chase. Miller knew what was on the map. He knew there was no treasure." Myra laughed. "He was a past Grand Master, but it was an excuse to be around Morty."

Simon grinned. "That's only if the Masons gave you the right map. Masons don't give up their secrets easily. Did the greedy lot get their inheritance?"

"Fitzgerald has already hired an expert to fix the window, Miller got his cheque, Bucky got his baseball cards back." Myra listed them off. "But Art and Flora, and Doreen's money will be held. If they are found innocent, they get the money. If they are found guilty, Bucky gets everything.

"On the bright side, we charged Doreen with two counts of first-degree murder for the deaths of Kate and Joseph Williams."

Myra cocked his head to the side and adjusted the kink in his neck.

"Could that have been Mortimer's plan all along?" Whiffen wondered out loud. "I mean, he rewrote his will weeks before he died. Did he suspect someone was going to kill him? Did he want to make sure his parents' murderer was brought to justice?"

"It's funny what murder victims do before they die," said Myra.

"It's like they get a sixth sense. Suddenly they feel like they need to get their affairs in order. You'd be surprised how often that happens. Most victims know their murderer. Very few people are killed by strangers." Morgan kneaded his hands together in an effort to rub away his arthritis.

"So true," agreed Simon. "My autopsy table and I have seen first-hand what people who love each other *do* to each other."

"What about all this Masonic nonsense?" Whiffen asked. "This whole idea that they are not a secret society but a society with secrets." She looked around the table for answers. "A simple search on Google can tell you all the secrets you want to know about them."

"It's all smoke and mirrors." Simon removed a piece of lint from his sleeve. "The whole idea of Masonic secrecy is just the wrapping that gets men interested in being part of something bigger than themselves."

The four sat in silence for a few moments.

"During this investigation, I stumbled on one Masonic tenet that I do believe in." Insp. Myra looked to each of his fellow workers. "All that is essential for the triumph of evil is that good men—and women," he said, looking toward Cst. Whiffen, "do nothing."

Epilogue

A silent snow fell around the Sergeants' Memorial in Veteran's Square along Queen's Road and Cathedral Street in downtown St. John's. A city council crew stood scratching their heads around a water main break at the intersection, backing up traffic. It was all much to the dismay of busy shoppers, with their last-minute Christmas gifts, anxious to start their holidays.

A bronze statue of a peacekeeper about to release a dove into the cold winter air stood silent, watching. The Canadian flag proudly flying behind it. Both hoped for the peace that only Christmas brings. A hundred feet away, the Sergeants' Memorial stood protected by a short black iron fence. At its base lay a half-dozen weathered wreaths that had lain there since Remembrance Day. A large slab of Newfoundland granite in the middle bore a plaque with faded letters stating it had been donated by the Royal Newfoundland Regiment. On top stood a large Celtic Cross sourced from Edinburgh, Scotland, at the end of the First World War.

The foreman shook his head as he watched a river of water turn into ice as it flowed down toward Gower Street.

"Ever since they found the tunnel that collapsed, we've had nothing but problems in this area."

"They say those tunnels all run under this area," a worker informed him. "There was some historian on the news saying they never should have filled that in. He thinks there's some kind of treasure buried here."

The foreman pulled his coat tighter. "We had no choice. I was here that night. The whole area could have caved in. We would have lost all those churches." He waved his gloved hand around in the frosty air.

"I suppose." The worker leaned against his shovel. "Not much down there now but five-hundred-year-old sewage, and that's the last thing we need to deal with in this weather."

A police car was parked next to the Anglican Cathedral, and a lone constable, covered in snow, stood outside and did her best to direct angry motorists through one by one.

"Here comes the backhoe now." The foreman signalled for the driver to come through. "Let's get this fixed and filled in so we can be home for Christmas Eve supper."

The beep of tractors and trucks intermingled with the roar of cars slowly splashing through the intersection. Above it all, the sound of Christmas carols floated in the air from nearby stores.

Nobody noticed the bronze peacekeeper slightly tilting to the left and the Celtic Cross slightly tilting to the right.

One hundred and seventy years of settled gravel and dirt shifted minutely as a lost tunnel gave way beneath them. It came down hard on top of a concrete chamber. Small cracks ran through the surface but stayed sealed, ready to protect the contents for all eternity.

The peacekeeper stood on the front line, closely guarding the true meaning of this clandestine operation.

The Scottish Celtic Cross, laden down with snow, stretched out its four arms, representative of the four elements: fire, earth, air, and water.

Which are also Masonic symbols.

acknowledgements

I make Newfoundland and Labrador a main character in all my books. I want my readers to be able to see, hear, taste, smell, and touch everything good about this amazing province and our colourful history.

When I do my research, there is never a shortage of people who step up to help me with details and facts that make my readers wonder: Is this real or fiction?

I would like to thank the many experts who helped on this book.

Masonic Past Grand Master Todd Miller, who gave me a tour of the Masonic Temple and filled me in on its historic past. Todd is a wealth of knowledge about the Masons, and although he refused to divulge any secrets (especially the handshake), he did ensure I had the right information to write this book. Throughout these pages I gave tidbits of Newfoundland and Labrador's history and how it intertwines with the Masonic history. *This is all real.*

Thank you to Peter Halley and Kathie Hicks at Spirit of Newfoundland, whose home is the Masonic Temple. They let me spend hours searching for information in this historic building. This building is the first Masonic Temple in North America. There is a mirror in the basement through which people have seen ghosts, and there is a hidden staircase that we have not found yet. The Chamber of Reflection is located on the second floor. It's real.

Thank you to John Fitzgerald, the executive director of the Basilica Heritage Foundation. John is just an incredible resource for historical accuracy and information. You will be shocked to find out that the Immaculate Conception stained glass window in the choir loft does indeed have a spelling mistake. During the summer, John gives tours of the Ecclesiastic Circle. Yes, that's real, too. Be sure to do one! He is also an accomplished organist, and hopefully you'll have the pleasure of hearing him play someday. Be sure to do his tour when you are in St. John's.

Thank you to my friend Denise Whiffen, who became my inspiration for Cst. Donna Whiffen. Denise and her husband, RCMP Sgt. Oliver Whiffen, have an autistic son, Jackson. While writing this novel, they shared with me their struggles, fears, and realities of raising an adult with autism. I thank them for giving me such a personal look at their life. It is a reminder that police officers are real people with problems, issues, children with disabilities, and families just like us all. Be kind.

Thank you to my lawyer, Bradford Wicks, for his free legal advice. You saved me hours of research. It is kind of you to not notify the police when you receive emails from me titled, "Can you still inherit money from someone you murdered?" I appreciate that.

Police officers are always my main source of information in all my books. I always write from their perspective. If a police officer does not believe my fictional investigation, then I know it won't work. There are a few police veterans who I always go to for information. Retired RNC Sgt. Robert Morgan is the inspiration behind Sgt. Bill Morgan. The real Sgt. Morgan spent years in the RNC Identification Unit and is the reason why my autopsy chapters are so real. Thank you, Bob, for always being an accurate source for me.

My Insp. Nicholas Myra character is inspired by my husband, Retired RNC Sgt. Robert Escott. Throughout our life together, I have been inspired by his compassion, dedication, and have been left in awe by his sense of right and wrong. He has always been a cop's cop, and he drops whatever he is doing when an officer contacts him for help or advice. He is now president of the RNC Veterans Association and continues to support his force.

What is fact and what is fiction? Well, that's up to you to find out. The tunnels under the city are rumoured to be real, but no one has found them yet. The Ecclesiastic Circle and Masonic Temple are available for tours. The Masons are still very active and mysterious. They are also looking for members.

Thank you to Arts NL, who supported me during the writing of this novel. I acknowledge the support of Arts NL, which last year invested $3.2 million to foster and promote the creation and enjoyment of the arts for the benefit of all Newfoundlanders and Labradorians.

Thank you to my publisher, Flanker Press, for the myriad supports required to transform a manuscript into the book you have before you.

And finally, thanks to all my readers of the "Operation" series of books.

Helen

Helen C. Escott is an award-winning, bestselling Canadian author. Her crime thriller *Operation Vanished* was awarded a Silver Medal for Best Regional Fiction at the 24th annual Independent Publisher Book Awards. *Operation Vanished* is a mind-bending, sophisticated psychological crime thriller that will keep you guessing who the real killer is.

In *Operation Wormwood: The Reckoning*, Escott's main character, Sgt. Nick Myra, is back with a vengeance, and he is looking for blood. This roller coaster of a crime thriller is the explosive follow-up to the bestselling crime thriller *Operation Wormwood*, a finalist for the 2019 Arthur Ellis Awards for Best First Crime Novel.

In addition to her fiction work, Escott is the author of *In Search of Adventure: 70 Years of the Royal Canadian Mounted Police in Newfoundland and Labrador*, culminating from two years of research and interviewing veterans to create this comprehensive collection of personal stories and history of the province.

(continued)

Her hysterically funny blog, *I Am Funny Like That*, was turned into a bestselling memoir. It is a collection of humorous stories about raising children, keeping a marriage together, working, cleaning, and life in general.

Escott is also a playwright who wrote and created the brilliant musical comedy *If It's Not One Thing, It's Your Mother*.

She is a retired civilian member of the RCMP and was the communications lead on high-profile events, including the RCMP's NL response to the 9/11 terrorist attacks. Helen wrote and implemented the Atlantic Region Communication Strategies to combat organized crime and outlaw biker gangs, created a media relations course, and taught it in several provinces as well as at the Canadian Police College in Ottawa. She also served as a communications strategist at the 2010 Vancouver Olympics.

Before joining the RCMP, Escott worked in the media for ten years. In 2017, she was presented with the CLB Governor and Commandant's Medallion in recognition of her achievements of excellence in volunteering and fundraising work, including creating the idea and concept for the Spirit of Newfoundland dinner theatre show *Where Once They Stood*.

In 2019 she was presented with the Governor General's Sovereign's Medal for Volunteers.

OPERATION
MASONIC

Visit Flanker Press at:

www.flankerpress.com

https://www.facebook.com/flankerpress

https://twitter.com/FlankerPress

https://www.instagram.com/flanker_press

http://www.youtube.com
/user/FlankerPress